PILGRIM'S PROGRESS

ORIGINAL EDITION
STUDY GUIDE

From This World to That Which Is to Come

by
John Bunyan
Annotated by Shawn P. Robinson

BrainSwell Publishing
Ingersoll, Ontario

Dedication and Thanks

To Juanita, who is such an encouragement to me as I follow this path of writing for God's glory.
To my family who still manages to get excited about new books I write.
To John Bunyan for a book that has captivated my heart since I was a small boy.
And to all of you! I hope you are blessed and encouraged by the notes and questions and more alongside this classic Christian allegory, Pilgrim's Progress!

Table of Contents

Bunyan's Apology[1] for his Book

When at the first I took my pen in hand
Thus for to write, I did not understand
That I at all should make a little book
In such a mode; nay, I had undertook
To make another; which, when almost done,
Before I was aware, I this begun.
And thus it was: I, writing of the way
And race of saints, in this our gospel day,
Fell suddenly into an allegory
About their journey, and the way to glory,
In more than twenty things which I set down.
This done, I twenty more had in my crown;
And they again began to multiply,
Like sparks that from the coals of fire do fly.
Nay, then, thought I, if that you breed so fast,
I'll put you by yourselves, lest you at last
Should prove ad infinitum, and eat out
The book that I already am about.
Well, so I did; but yet I did not think
To shew to all the world my pen and ink
In such a mode; I only thought to make
I knew not what; nor did I undertake

---

[1] The word *Apology* in this sense carries with it the meaning of *argument* or "reason".

Thereby to please my neighbour: no, not I;
I did it my own self to gratify.
Neither did I but vacant seasons spend
In this my scribble; nor did I intend
But to divert myself in doing this
From worser thoughts which make me do amiss.
Thus, I set pen to paper with delight,
And quickly had my thoughts in black and white.
For, having now my method by the end,
Still as I pulled, it came; and so I penned
It down: until it came at last to be,
For length and breadth, the bigness which you see.
Well, when I had thus put mine ends together,
I shewed them others, that I might see whether
They would condemn them, or them justify:
And some said, Let them live; some, Let them die;
Some said, JOHN, print it; others said, Not so;
Some said, It might do good; others said, No.
Now was I in a strait, and did not see
Which was the best thing to be done by me:
At last I thought, Since you are thus divided,
I print it will, and so the case decided.
For, thought I, some, I see, would have it done,
Though others in that channel do not run:
To prove, then, who advised for the best,
Thus I thought fit to put it to the test.
I further thought, if now I did deny
Those that would have it, thus to gratify.
I did not know but hinder them I might
Of that which would to them be great delight.
For those which were not for its coming forth,
I said to them, Offend you I am loth,
Yet, since your brethren pleased with it be,
Forbear to judge till you do further see.
If that thou wilt not read, let it alone;
Some love the meat, some love to pick the bone.
Yea, that I might them better palliate,
I did too with them thus expostulate:--
May I not write in such a style as this?
In such a method, too, and yet not miss
My end--thy good? Why may it not be done?
Dark clouds bring waters, when the bright bring none.

Yea, dark or bright, if they their silver drops
Cause to descend, the earth, by yielding crops,
Gives praise to both, and carpeth not at either,
But treasures up the fruit they yield together;
Yea, so commixes both, that in her fruit
None can distinguish this from that: they suit
Her well when hungry; but, if she be full,
She spews out both, and makes their blessings null.
You see the ways the fisherman doth take
To catch the fish; what engines doth he make?
Behold how he engageth all his wits;
Also his snares, lines, angles, hooks, and nets;
Yet fish there be, that neither hook, nor line,
Nor snare, nor net, nor engine can make thine:
They must be groped for, and be tickled too,
Or they will not be catch'd, whate'er you do.
How does the fowler seek to catch his game
By divers means! all which one cannot name:
His guns, his nets, his lime-twigs, light, and bell:
He creeps, he goes, he stands; yea, who can tell
Of all his postures? Yet there's none of these
Will make him master of what fowls he please.
Yea, he must pipe and whistle to catch this,
Yet, if he does so, that bird he will miss.
If that a pearl may in a toad's head dwell,
And may be found too in an oyster-shell;
If things that promise nothing do contain
What better is than gold; who will disdain,
That have an inkling of it, there to look,
That they may find it? Now, my little book,
(Though void of all these paintings that may make
It with this or the other man to take)
Is not without those things that do excel
What do in brave but empty notions dwell.
Well, yet I am not fully satisfied,
That this your book will stand, when soundly tried.'
Why, what's the matter? 'It is dark.' What though?
'But it is feigned.' What of that? I trow?
Some men, by feigned words, as dark as mine,
Make truth to spangle and its rays to shine.
'But they want solidness.' Speak, man, thy mind.
'They drown the weak; metaphors make us blind.'

Solidity, indeed, becomes the pen
Of him that writeth things divine to men;
But must I needs want solidness, because
By metaphors I speak? Were not God's laws,
His gospel laws, in olden times held forth
By types, shadows, and metaphors? Yet loth
Will any sober man be to find fault
With them, lest he be found for to assault
The highest wisdom. No, he rather stoops,
And seeks to find out what by pins and loops,
By calves and sheep, by heifers and by rams,
By birds and herbs, and by the blood of lambs,
God speaketh to him; and happy is he
That finds the light and grace that in them be.
Be not too forward, therefore, to conclude
That I want solidness--that I am rude;
All things solid in show not solid be;
All things in parables despise not we;
Lest things most hurtful lightly we receive,
And things that good are, of our souls bereave.
My dark and cloudy words, they do but hold
The truth, as cabinets enclose the gold.
The prophets used much by metaphors
To set forth truth; yea, who so considers Christ,
his apostles too, shall plainly see,
That truths to this day in such mantles be.
Am I afraid to say, that holy writ,
Which for its style and phrase puts down all wit,
Is everywhere so full of all these things--
Dark figures, allegories? Yet there springs
From that same book that lustre, and those rays
Of light, that turn our darkest nights to days.
Come, let my carper to his life now look,
And find there darker lines than in my book
He findeth any; yea, and let him know,
That in his best things there are worse lines too.
May we but stand before impartial men,
To his poor one I dare adventure ten,
That they will take my meaning in these lines
Far better than his lies in silver shrines.
Come, truth, although in swaddling clouts, I find,
Informs the judgement, rectifies the mind;

Pleases the understanding, makes the will
Submit; the memory too it doth fill
With what doth our imaginations please;
Likewise it tends our troubles to appease.
Sound words, I know, Timothy is to use,
And old wives' fables he is to refuse;
But yet grave Paul him nowhere did forbid
The use of parables; in which lay hid
That gold, those pearls, and precious stones that were
Worth digging for, and that with greatest care.
Let me add one word more. O man of God,
Art thou offended? Dost thou wish I had
Put forth my matter in another dress?
Or, that I had in things been more express?
Three things let me propound; then I submit
To those that are my betters, as is fit.
1. I find not that I am denied the use
Of this my method, so I no abuse
Put on the words, things, readers; or be rude
In handling figure or similitude,
In application; but, all that I may,
Seek the advance of truth this or that way
Denied, did I say? Nay, I have leave
(Example too, and that from them that have
God better pleased, by their words or ways,
Than any man that breatheth now-a-days)
Thus to express my mind, thus to declare
Things unto thee that excellentest are.
2. I find that men (as high as trees) will write
Dialogue-wise; yet no man doth them slight
For writing so: indeed, if they abuse
Truth, cursed be they, and the craft they use
To that intent; but yet let truth be free
To make her sallies upon thee and me,
Which way it pleases God; for who knows how,
Better than he that taught us first to plough,
To guide our mind and pens for his design?
And he makes base things usher in divine.
3. I find that holy writ in many places
Hath semblance with this method, where the cases
Do call for one thing, to set forth another;
Use it I may, then, and yet nothing smother

*Truth's golden beams: nay, by this method may
Make it cast forth its rays as light as day.
And now before I do put up my pen,
I'll shew the profit of my book, and then
Commit both thee and it unto that Hand
That pulls the strong down, and makes weak ones stand.
This book it chalketh out before thine eyes
The man that seeks the everlasting prize;
It shews you whence he comes, whither he goes;
What he leaves undone, also what he does;
It also shows you how he runs and runs,
Till he unto the gate of glory comes.
It shows, too, who set out for life amain,
As if the lasting crown they would obtain;
Here also you may see the reason why
They lose their labour, and like fools do die.
This book will make a traveller of thee,
If by its counsel thou wilt ruled be;
It will direct thee to the Holy Land,
If thou wilt its directions understand:
Yea, it will make the slothful active be;
The blind also delightful things to see.
Art thou for something rare and profitable?
Wouldest thou see a truth within a fable?
Art thou forgetful? Wouldest thou remember
From New-Year's day to the last of December?
Then read my fancies; they will stick like burs,
And may be, to the helpless, comforters.
This book is writ in such a dialect
As may the minds of listless men affect:
It seems a novelty, and yet contains
Nothing but sound and honest gospel strains.
Wouldst thou divert thyself from melancholy?
Wouldst thou be pleasant, yet be far from folly?
Wouldst thou read riddles, and their explanation?
Or else be drowned in thy contemplation?
Dost thou love picking meat? Or wouldst thou see
A man in the clouds, and hear him speak to thee?
Wouldst thou be in a dream, and yet not sleep?
Or wouldst thou in a moment laugh and weep?
Wouldest thou lose thyself and catch no harm,
And find thyself again without a charm?*

Wouldst read thyself, and read thou knowest not what,
And yet know whether thou art blest or not,
By reading the same lines? Oh, then come hither,
And lay my book, thy head, and heart together.

John Bunyan

Shawn P. Robinson's Apology for This Book

I'm so glad to share this book with you, and I am glad to share this brief apology with you.[1]

Pilgrim's Progress has always been a favourite of mine. Even as a child, this book fascinated me. Over the years, I have read it countless times, and despite how often I've read it, I continue to learn and grow each time!

This book has, of course, not only fascinated *me*, but it's inspired and encouraged countless pilgrims over the course of the last 340 and years! I hope you find that God speaks to you from these pages, calling you to walk more faithfully along this path leading to the Celestial City!

As you dive into this Annotated Study guide, I want to point out some details concerning the approach I took to the layout of this book.

This study guide is based on a study I did with my church years ago when I was still pastoring, so the questions you see are based on those questions. I have added new questions and tweaked some of the old, but the goal is to encourage deep reflection on the matters addressed in this wonderful allegory. As such, in the back of the book, there are additional helps to guide readers through some of the more challenging questions as well as to address some of the difficult topics contained within these pages.

---

[1] The word *Apology* in this sense carries with it the meaning of *argument* or *reason* as in, "This is Shawn Robinson's reasoned argument for writing this book." I kept this language (rather than use the word "Introduction") because Bunyan gives an *Apology* for his book.

To assist readers in using this original version, I've taken the following approach:

1. Historically, or at least in the versions I have read, there are countless Scripture references inserted in the text. I have, throughout the book, taken these and put them into footnotes, rather than in a bracket included in the text. Since there were often multiple Scripture references within a single paragraph, I have typically grouped those references together into one footnote, attached to the end of the paragraph. In addition to this, a few more references have been added based on my own observations and from the feedback of one of my beta readers.[2]

2. I have broken the book into fifteen chapters. Most of these breaks come at appropriate times based on the flow of the story. This allows for those moving through this book to spread it out over a weekly study covering approximately four months.

3. I have added footnotes with definitions for many of the words which a contemporary reader might find unusual. Words such as *trow*, *cogitations*, *runigate*, and *Sirrah* have footnotes attached to the word. In addition to this, there are some extra footnotes defining familiar words that have changed meaning in the 340 years since this book was written as well as clarifying some of the complicated concepts that are easily missed or misunderstood throughout these pages.

4. This Annotated version as well as the *Rewalked* edition[3] are designed to be used side by side. If these books are used in a group setting, both versions can be used together as the chapter breaks and the questions line up, allowing everyone to read their preferred version.

Please understand that the purpose of this book is to, in Bunyan's words, *make a traveller of thee* and *make the slothful active be; the blind also delightful things to see.*

So, my friends, take this book and let it inspire you to be a traveller on the path to the Celestial City!

Shawn P. Robinson

---

[2] Thanks to Rev. Matthew Richards for his help in this area and to all my beta readers—you're awesome!

[3] The *Rewalked* edition is a rewrite in a modern narrative style that seeks to remain true to the details of the allegory while adjusting the flow to make it easier for a contemporary reader to work through the story.

Using This Study Guide

I'm excited you're ready to dive into Pilgrim's Progress, and I truly hope this Study Guide will be a wonderful blessing for you! I want to give a few pointers for how you can get the most out of the helps offered in this guide.

So here we go!

1. The questions at the end of each chapter are designed to encourage and challenge. Take your time with them, and don't be afraid to struggle through some of the more difficult topics.

2. Discuss what you're learning with others. As believers, we grow best in community with those who know and love Christ. Take advantage of that!

3. If you're doing this in a group study, both the *Rewalked* Edition and the Annotated Original Edition can be used together as the chapters and questions line up. So feel free to use the edition you prefer!

4. At the back of the book, there is a section offering extra thoughts and answers to some of the difficult questions and topics throughout Pilgrim's Progress. Feel free to use this section as a resource to work through some of the more challenging questions and to spark additional conversations.

*Remember above all else, this book is, in the words of John Bunyan,
written to make a traveller of thee. Let the words and ideas and
teachings encourage you to walk this path more faithfully in God's grace.*

My fellow pilgrim, you are deeply loved by Jesus.

1. The Beginning

In the Similitude of a Dream

As I walked through the wilderness of this world, I lighted on a certain place where was a Den, and I laid me down in that place to sleep: and, as I slept, I dreamed a dream. I dreamed, and behold, I saw a man clothed with rags, standing in a certain place, with his face from his own house, a book in his hand, and a great burden upon his back.[1] I looked, and saw him open the book, and read therein; and, as he read, he wept, and trembled; and, not being able longer to contain, he brake out with a lamentable cry, saying, "What shall I do?"[2]

In this plight, therefore, he went home and refrained himself as long as he could, that his wife and children should not perceive his distress; but he could not be silent long, because that his trouble increased. Wherefore at length he brake his mind to his wife and children; and thus he began to talk to them:

"O my dear wife, said he, and you the children of my bowels, I, your dear friend, am in myself undone by reason of a burden that lieth hard upon me; moreover, I am for certain informed that this our city will be burned with fire from heaven; in which fearful overthrow, both myself, with thee my wife, and you my sweet babes, shall miserably come to ruin, except (the which yet I see not) some way of escape can be found, whereby we may be delivered."

At this his relations were sore amazed; not for that they believed that what he had said to them was true, but because they thought that some

---

[1] Isa. 64:6; Luke 14:33; Ps. 38:4; Hab. 2:2; Acts 16:30,31.
[2] Acts 2:37.

frenzy distemper had got into his head; therefore, it drawing towards night, and they hoping that sleep might settle his brains, with all haste they got him to bed. But the night was as troublesome to him as the day; wherefore, instead of sleeping, he spent it in sighs and tears. So, when the morning was come, they would know how he did. He told them, "Worse and worse": he also set to talking to them again; but they began to be hardened. They also thought to drive away his distemper by harsh and surly carriages to him; sometimes they would deride, sometimes they would chide, and sometimes they would quite neglect him. Wherefore he began to retire himself to his chamber, to pray for and pity them, and also to condole his own misery; he would also walk solitarily in the fields, sometimes reading, and sometimes praying: and thus for some days he spent his time.

Now, I saw, upon a time, when he was walking in the fields, that he was, as he was wont, reading in his book, and greatly distressed in his mind; and, as he read, he burst out, as he had done before, crying, "What shall I do to be saved?"

I saw also that he looked this way and that way, as if he would run; yet he stood still, because, as I perceived, he could not tell which way to go. I looked then, and saw a man named Evangelist coming to him and asked, "Wherefore dost thou cry?"[3]

He answered, "Sir, I perceive by the book in my hand, that I am condemned to die, and after that to come to judgement; and I find that I am not willing to do the first, nor able to do the second.[4]

Then said Evangelist, "Why not willing to die, since this life is attended with so many evils?"

The man answered, "Because I fear that this burden is upon my back will sink me lower than the grave, and I shall fall into Tophet.[5] And, Sir, if I be not fit to go to prison, I am not fit, I am sure, to go to judgement, and from thence to execution; and the thoughts of these things make me cry."

Then said Evangelist, "If this be thy condition, why standest thou still?"

He answered, "Because I know not whither to go."

---

[3] Job 33:23.
[4] Heb. 9:27; Job 16:21; Eze. 22:14.
[5] Isa. 30:33.

Then he gave him a parchment roll, and there was written within, Flee from the wrath to come.[6]

The man therefore read it, and looking upon Evangelist very carefully, said, "Whither must I fly?"

Then said Evangelist, pointing with his finger over a very wide field, "Do you see yonder wicket[7]-gate?"[8]

The man said, "No."

Then said the other, "Do you see yonder shining light?"[9]

He said, "I think I do."

Then said Evangelist, "Keep that light in your eye, and go up directly thereto: so shalt thou see the gate; at which, when thou knockest, it shall be told thee what thou shalt do."

So I saw in my dream that the man began to run.

Now, he had not run far from his own door, but his wife and children, perceiving it, began to cry after him to return; but the man put his fingers in his ears, and ran on, crying, "Life! life! eternal life!"[10] So he looked not behind him, but fled towards the middle of the plain.[11]

The neighbours also came out to see him run;[12] and, as he ran, some mocked, others threatened, and some cried after him to return; and, among those that did so, there were two that resolved to fetch him back by force. The name of the one was Obstinate and the name of the other Pliable. Now, by this time, the man was got a good distance from them; but, however, they were resolved to pursue him, which they did, and in a little time they overtook him.

Then said the man, "Neighbours, wherefore are ye come?"

They said, "To persuade you to go back with us."

But he said, "That can by no means be; you dwell, said he, in the City of Destruction, the place also where I was born: I see it to be so; and, dying there, sooner or later, you will sink lower than the grave, into a place

---

[6] Matt. 3.7.
[7] A wicket is a small door or gate. So... this is a "small gate-gate." ☺
[8] Matt. 7:13,14.
[9] Ps. 119:105; 2 Pet. 1:19.
[10] Luke 14:26.
[11] Gen. 19:17.
[12] Jer. 20:10.

that burns with fire and brimstone: be content, good neighbours, and go along with me."

OBSTINATE: What! said Obstinate, and leave our friends and our comforts behind us?

CHRISTIAN:[13] Yes, said Christian, for that was his name, because that ALL which you shall forsake is not worthy to be compared with a little of that which I am seeking to enjoy; and, if you will go along with me, and hold it, you shall fare as I myself; for there, where I go, is enough and to spare. Come away, and prove my words.[14]

OBSTINATE: What are the things you seek, since you leave all the world to find them?

CHRISTIAN: I seek an inheritance incorruptible, undefiled, and that fadeth not away, and it is laid up in heaven, and safe there, to be bestowed, at the time appointed, on them that diligently seek it. Read it so, if you will, in my book.[15]

OBSTINATE: Tush! said Obstinate, away with your book; will you go back with us or no?

CHRISTIAN: No, not I, said the other, because I have laid my hand to the plough.[16]

OBSTINATE: Come, then, neighbour Pliable, let us turn again, and go home without him; there is a company of these crazy-headed coxcombs, that, when they take a fancy by the end, are wiser in their own eyes than seven men that can render a reason.[17]

PLIABLE: Then said Pliable, Don't revile; if what the good Christian says is true, the things he looks after are better than ours: my heart inclines to go with my neighbour.

OBSTINATE: What! More fools still! Be ruled by me, and go back; who knows whither such a brain-sick fellow will lead you? Go back, go back, and be wise.

CHRISTIAN: Nay, but do thou come with thy neighbour, Pliable; there are such things to be had which I spoke of, and many more glorious besides. If you believe not me, read here in this book; and for the truth of

____

[13] Notice this is the first moment when our character is called Christian.
[14] 2 Cor. 4:18; Luke 15:17.
[15] 1 Pet. 1:4; Heb. 11:16.
[16] Luke 9:62.
[17] Prov. 26:16.

what is expressed therein, behold, all is confirmed by the blood of Him that made it.[18]

PLIABLE: Well, neighbour Obstinate, said Pliable, I begin to come to a point; I intend to go along with this good man, and to cast in my lot with him: but, my good companion, do you know the way to this desired place?

CHRISTIAN: I am directed by a man, whose name is Evangelist, to speed me to a little gate that is before us, where we shall receive instructions about the way.

PLIABLE: Come, then, good neighbour, let us be going. Then they went both together.

OBSTINATE: And I will go back to my place, said Obstinate; I will be no companion of such misled, fantastical fellows.

Now, I saw in my dream, that when Obstinate was gone back, Christian and Pliable went talking over the plain; and thus they began their discourse.

CHRISTIAN: Come, neighbour Pliable, how do you do? I am glad you are persuaded to go along with me. Had even Obstinate himself but felt what I have felt of the powers and terrors of what is yet unseen, he would not thus lightly have given us the back.

PLIABLE: Come, neighbour Christian, since there are none but us two here, tell me now further what the things are, and how to be enjoyed, whither we are going.

CHRISTIAN: I can better conceive of them with my mind, than speak of them with my tongue. God's things unspeakable: but yet, since you are desirous to know, I will read of them in my book.

PLIABLE: And do you think that the words of your book are certainly true?

CHRISTIAN: Yes, verily; for it was made by Him that cannot lie.[19]

PLIABLE: Well said; what things are they?

CHRISTIAN: There is an endless kingdom to be inhabited, and everlasting life to be given us, that we may inhabit that kingdom for ever.[20]

---

[18] Heb. 9:17-22; 13:20.
[19] Titus 1:2.
[20] Isa. 45:17; John 10:28, 29.

PLIABLE: Well said; and what else?

CHRISTIAN: There are crowns and glory to be given us, and garments that will make us shine like the sun in the firmament of heaven.[21]

PLIABLE: This is very pleasant; and what else?

CHRISTIAN: There shall be no more crying, nor sorrow: for He that is owner of the place will wipe all tears from our eyes.[22]

PLIABLE: And what company shall we have there?

CHRISTIAN: There we shall be with seraphims and cherubims, creatures that will dazzle your eyes to look on them. There also you shall meet with thousands and ten thousands that have gone before us to that place; none of them are hurtful, but loving and holy; every one walking in the sight of God, and standing in his presence with acceptance for ever. In a word, there we shall see the elders with their golden crowns, there we shall see the holy virgins with their golden harps, there we shall see men that by the world were cut in pieces, burnt in flames, eaten of beasts, drowned in the seas, for the love that they bare to the Lord of the place, all well, and clothed with immortality as with a garment.[23]

PLIABLE: The hearing of this is enough to ravish one's heart. But are these things to be enjoyed? How shall we get to be sharers thereof?

CHRISTIAN: The Lord, the Governor of the country, hath recorded that in this book; the substance of which is, If we be truly willing to have it, he will bestow it upon us freely.

PLIABLE: Well, my good companion, glad am I to hear of these things: come on, let us mend our pace.

CHRISTIAN: I cannot go so fast as I would, by reason of this burden that is on my back.

Now I saw in my dream, that just as they had ended this talk they drew near to a very miry slough, that was in the midst of the plain; and they, being heedless, did both fall suddenly into the bog. The name of the slough was Despond. Here, therefore, they wallowed for a time, being grievously bedaubed with the dirt; and Christian, because of the burden that was on his back, began to sink in the mire.

---

[21] 2 Tim. 4:8; Rev. 3:4; Matt. 13:43.
[22] Isa. 25.6-8; Rev. 7:17, 21:4.
[23] Isa. 6:2; 1 Thess. 4:16,17; Rev. 5:11; Rev. 4:4; Rev. 14:1-5; John 12:25; 2 Cor. 5:4.

PLIABLE: Then said Pliable; Ah! neighbour Christian, where are you now?

CHRISTIAN: Truly, said Christian, I do not know.

PLIABLE: At this Pliable began to be offended, and angrily said to his fellow, Is this the happiness you have told me all this while of? If we have such ill speed at our first setting out, what may we expect betwixt[24] this and our journey's end? May I get out again with my life, you shall possess the brave country alone for me. And, with that, he gave a desperate struggle or two, and got out of the mire on that side of the slough which was next to his own house: so away he went, and Christian saw him no more.

Wherefore Christian was left to tumble in the Slough of Despond alone: but still he endeavoured to struggle to that side of the slough that was still further from his own house, and next to the wicket-gate; the which he did, but could not get out, because of the burden that was upon his back: but I beheld in my dream, that a man came to him, whose name was Help, and asked him what he did there.

CHRISTIAN: Sir, said Christian, I was bid go this way by a man called Evangelist, who directed me also to yonder gate, that I might escape the wrath to come; and as I was going thither[25] I fell in here.

HELP: But why did not you look for the steps?

CHRISTIAN: Fear followed me so hard, that I fled the next way, and fell in.

HELP: Then said he, Give me thy hand: so he gave him his hand, and he drew him out, and set him upon sound ground, and bid him go on his way.[26]

---

[24] *Betwixt* is another word for *between.*
[25] The word *thither* appears a fair amount in the book. Rather than assume it is a lispy pronunciation of the word scissors, I will define it now. Thither means *to or toward that place.* So, "as I was going to that place, I fell in here."
[26] Ps. 40:2.

WHAT WE COVERED IN WEEK ONE

The City of Destruction
The Slough of Despond
Help's explanation of the Slough

In Matthew 13:1-9, 18-23, Jesus tells a story about a man who goes out into his field. While there, he sows seed, and the way Jesus tells it, it sounds like he just throws it wildly, and it ends up going everywhere!

Of course, if you know the story, you know that some seed lands on good soil, and it takes root, growing into a healthy plant and giving a great harvest.

Some, sadly, falls on the path, and it cannot take root. A bird comes and steals it.

This parable is a picture of the Word of God, the Bible, the message of the gospel in our lives, and we learn what it does or can do in our hearts. For some, it takes root. We believe it, we trust it, and God does great things in our lives, producing a great harvest.

In others, the Word of God lands, yet does not take root. In fact, nothing happens with it because it's stolen away. It's simply gone.

But there are also seeds which fall on two other types of soil, neither of which are good. In one, the seed lands on rocky soil, and it takes root, shooting up quickly. Since it doesn't have a deep root, because the soil is all rocky, the plant looks good, and it gives the impression that it's a healthy plant. However, as soon as the sun comes out, the plant withers.

It is a plant which cannot handle the day's heat. Does that sound like anyone in our story?

In today's story, we read about the beginning of Christian's journey. He is a man who has a heavy burden on his back, and he desperately desires to be rid of it!

The burden, of course, comes to him as he reads God's Word, and we see illustrated for us how in our reading of Scripture, the Holy Spirit brings us to know our sin problem.

For Christian, the Word of God has landed in his heart, and his heart is good soil. The seed often needs to be in the soil for a time to germinate before we see the new plant break the surface, and Christian's time of waiting to see where to grow is a difficult time for him.

But God rarely leaves us alone for long in our faith, that is, if we can only see those he's sent and welcome them into our own lives. And on Christian's journey, God brings forward a man named Evangelist.

So, here is Christian, weighed down under this burden, and Evangelist shows up. Evangelist is the exact person who Christian needs at this point in his journey, and this new arrival explains where Christian needs to go, and the next thing you know, Christian is running towards the path and followed by two others: Obstinate and Pliable. They are two interesting people. They say opposites attract, and these two friends are certainly opposites.

Obstinate is a stubborn man, and Pliable is an easily led man. The two show up intending to stop Christian from seeking the cross, but when faced with refusal, one sticks with Christian (Pliable), the other returns. This is not a surprise since Obstinate is stubborn, and Pliable is easily led!

And once our stubborn friend is gone, we find Christian sharing with Pliable all about the hope he has in Jesus.

But then tragedy strikes.

Imagine that… the timing of this experience. They fall into the Slough of Despond right while they are speaking of hope. And it's no surprise to see the effect it has on Pliable.

Pliable wants the good stuff, and he's easily attracted—easily fooled one way or another—but his faith and trust in God is not genuine. He easily runs to a faith without difficulty but runs away once life gets hard.

While Christian carries on. Through the difficulties. Through the challenges. Through the trials.

Pliable is a man living on rocky soil.

How about you? When trials come… when you fall into a major difficulty in life… are you more like our friend Christian, or more like our friend Pliable?

Lord, I am often like Pliable, but I thank you for your grace. Work in me a heart that loves and trusts you as I travel this road to your Holy City.
Amen

1. In the first part of this story, we read of Christian's struggle with fear over the coming judgement. Such a struggle cost him his relationship with his family and his ability to sleep. In the Christian faith, we would call this conviction. Do you ever find that when you are under conviction, you try to push away the thoughts rather than face the issue?[27]

2. We find in Scripture that conviction for sin is the work of the Holy Spirit—it is God's work in our lives.[28] Have you ever seen someone else under heavy conviction for sin and tried to console them rather than encourage them to listen to the Spirit's leading on this matter? Have you tried to ease their burden?

3. When we see someone we know who is under conviction for sin, what would be a proper way to respond? Should we ease their conviction, or is that fighting against the Spirit's work? Should we pour more conviction on, or is that trying to do God's work for him? Is there a way we can let God's Spirit work and yet not add to the burden our friend carries for their sin? If so, what might that look like?

---

[27] These questions are, ideally, best worked through *both* personally and as a group. If you are doing this study alone, I encourage you to find someone else you know and trust with whom you can talk about some of the questions raised in this book.
[28] John 16:8.

4. Consider the part in our story when Christian's family sees him flee and calls for him to turn back. Now, we might lean towards the idea of turning back out of compassion for family, but remember that this is an allegory of the Christian walk towards eternity with Christ. In terms of the allegory, what do you think the calling out from loved ones to return means? What does it illustrate?

5. Why do you think Pliable doesn't have a burden?

6. What do you think about the journey so far? How does it relate to your own experience?

7. The journey ahead for Christian will get much more difficult, and your own journey in the days/weeks/years ahead might get more difficult as well. Do you think you are up for it? Do you believe you can endure the hard times? Consider John 15:20 and John 16:33. Consider also how the end of John 16:33 should affect your attitude towards difficulties.

8. Would it have been better for Christian not to read the Bible, and then not to have the burden?[29] Have you ever wished not to know? How does Colossians 3:1-2 and Romans 8:18 help us work through this frustration with difficulty here on earth?

9. Notice how Christian runs toward the wicket gate. What does his running symbolize and what would that look like in your life today? Try to address this for you personally rather than generalizing for everyone else.

10. In Bunyan's words, he hopes his story *will make a traveller of thee*. How do you see yourself travelling this road to the Celestial City differently because of this week's reading? What change in heart, attitude, theology, or lifestyle do you believe God is calling you to as you seek to be the traveller he desires you be?

---

[29] Hopefully we will give a quick, "No way!" answer, but consider this for a moment: have you ever wished not to know about salvation? What is it that drives you to that desire?

2. The Gate

Then I stepped to him that plucked him out,[1] and said, "Sir, wherefore, since over this place is the way from the City of Destruction to yonder gate, is it that this plat is not mended, that poor travellers might go thither with more security?"

And he said unto me, "This miry slough is such a place as cannot be mended; it is the descent whither the scum and filth that attends conviction for sin doth continually run, and therefore it is called the Slough of Despond; for still, as the sinner is awakened about his lost condition, there ariseth in his soul many fears, and doubts, and discouraging apprehensions, which all of them get together, and settle in this place. And this is the reason of the badness of this ground.

"It is not the pleasure of the King that this place should remain so bad.[2] His labourers also have, by the direction of His Majesty's surveyors, been for above these sixteen hundred years employed about this patch of ground, if perhaps it might have been mended: yea, and to my knowledge, said he, here have been swallowed up at least twenty thousand cart-loads, yea, millions of wholesome instructions, that have at all seasons been brought from all places of the King's dominions, and they that can tell, say they are the best materials to make good ground of the place; if so be, it might have been mended, but it is the Slough of Despond still, and so will be when they have done what they can.

---

[1] There is a shift here in the narrative. It is difficult to see right away, but Christian has already moved on. This discussion over the next few paragraphs follows the Dreamer in his conversation with Help and then in observing Pliable's experience as he returns to the City of Destruction.

[2] Isa. 35:3, 4.

"True, there are, by the direction of the Law-giver, certain good and substantial steps, placed even through the very midst of this slough; but at such time as this place doth much spew out its filth, as it doth against change of weather, these steps are hardly seen; or, if they be, men, through the dizziness of their heads, step beside, and then they are bemired to purpose, notwithstanding the steps be there; but the ground is good when they are once got in at the gate.[3]"

Now, I saw in my dream, that by this time Pliable was got home to his house again, so that his neighbours came to visit him; and some of them called him wise man for coming back, and some called him fool for hazarding himself with Christian: others again did mock at his cowardliness; saying, "Surely, since you began to venture, I would not have been so base to have given out for a few difficulties." So Pliable sat sneaking among them. But at last he got more confidence, and then they all turned their tales, and began to deride poor Christian behind his back. And thus much concerning Pliable.

Now, as Christian was walking solitarily by himself, he espied one afar off, come crossing over the field to meet him; and their hap was to meet just as they were crossing the way of each other. The gentleman's name that met him was Mr. Worldly Wiseman, he dwelt in the town of Carnal Policy, a very great town, and also hard by from whence Christian came. This man, then, meeting with Christian, and having some inkling of him—for Christian's setting forth from the City of Destruction was much noised abroad, not only in the town where he dwelt, but also it began to be the town talk in some other places—Mr. Worldly Wiseman, therefore, having some guess of him, by beholding his laborious going, by observing his sighs and groans, and the like, began thus to enter into some talk with Christian.

WORLDLY WISEMAN: How now, good fellow, whither away after this burdened manner?

CHRISTIAN: A burdened manner, indeed, as ever, I think, poor creature had! And whereas you ask me, Whither away? I tell you, Sir, I am going to yonder wicket-gate before me; for there, as I am informed, I shall be put into a way to be rid of my heavy burden.

WORLDLY WISEMAN: Hast thou a wife and children?

---

[3] 1 Sam. 12:23.

CHRISTIAN: Yes; but I am so laden with this burden that I cannot take that pleasure in them as formerly; methinks I am as if I had none.[4]

WORLDLY WISEMAN: Wilt thou hearken unto me if I give thee counsel?

CHRISTIAN: If it be good, I will; for I stand in need of good counsel.

WORLDLY WISEMAN: I would advise thee, then, that thou with all speed get thyself rid of thy burden; for thou wilt never be settled in thy mind till then; nor canst thou enjoy the benefits of the blessing which God hath bestowed upon thee till then.

CHRISTIAN: That is that which I seek for, even to be rid of this heavy burden; but get it off myself, I cannot; nor is there any man in our country that can take it off my shoulders; therefore am I going this way, as I told you, that I may be rid of my burden.

WORLDLY WISEMAN: Who bid thee go this way to be rid of thy burden?

CHRISTIAN: A man that appeared to me to be a very great and honourable person; his name, as I remember, is Evangelist.

WORLDLY WISEMAN: I beshrew him for his counsel! there is not a more dangerous and troublesome way in the world than is that unto which he hath directed thee; and that thou shalt find, if thou wilt be ruled by his counsel. Thou hast met with something, as I perceive, already; for I see the dirt of the Slough of Despond is upon thee; but that slough is the beginning of the sorrows that do attend those that go on in that way. Hear me, I am older than thou; thou art like to meet with, in the way which thou goest, wearisomeness, painfulness, hunger, perils, nakedness, sword, lions, dragons, darkness, and, in a word, death, and what not! These things are certainly true, having been confirmed by many testimonies. And why should a man so carelessly cast away himself, by giving heed to a stranger?

CHRISTIAN: Why, Sir, this burden upon my back is more terrible to me than all these things which you have mentioned; nay, methinks I care not what I meet with in the way, if so be I can also meet with deliverance from my burden.

WORLDLY WISEMAN: How camest thou by the burden at first?

CHRISTIAN: By reading this book in my hand.

---

[4] 1 Cor 7:29.

WORLDLY WISEMAN: I thought so; and it is happened unto thee as to other weak men, who, meddling with things too high for them, do suddenly fall into thy distractions; which distractions do not only unman men, as thine, I perceive, have done thee, but they run them upon desperate ventures to obtain they know not what.

CHRISTIAN: I know what I would obtain; it is ease for my heavy burden.

WORLDLY WISEMAN: But why wilt thou seek for ease this way, seeing so many dangers attend it? Especially since, hadst thou but patience to hear me, I could direct thee to the obtaining of what thou desirest, without the dangers that thou in this way wilt run thyself into; yea, and the remedy is at hand. Besides, I will add, that instead of those dangers, thou shalt meet with much safety, friendship, and content.

CHRISTIAN: Pray, Sir, open this secret to me.

WORLDLY WISEMAN: Why, in yonder village—the village is named Morality—there dwells a gentleman whose name is Legality, a very judicious man, and a man of very good name, that has skill to help men off with such burdens as thine are from their shoulders: yea, to my knowledge, he hath done a great deal of good this way; ay, and besides, he hath skill to cure those that are somewhat crazed in their wits with their burdens. To him, as I said, thou mayest go, and be helped presently. His house is not quite a mile from this place, and if he should not be at home himself, he hath a pretty young man to his son, whose name is Civility, that can do it (to speak on) as well as the old gentleman himself; there, I say, thou mayest be eased of thy burden; and if thou art not minded to go back to thy former habitation, as, indeed, I would not wish thee, thou mayest send for thy wife and children to thee to this village, where there are houses now stand empty, one of which thou mayest have at reasonable rates; provision is there also cheap and good; and that which will make thy life the more happy is, to be sure, there thou shalt live by honest neighbours, in credit and good fashion.

Now was Christian somewhat at a stand; but presently he concluded, "If this be true, which this gentleman hath said, my wisest course is to take his advice;" and with that he thus further spoke.

CHRISTIAN: Sir, which is my way to this honest man's house?

WORLDLY WISEMAN: Do you see yonder hill?

CHRISTIAN: Yes, very well.

WORLDLY WISEMAN: By that hill you must go, and the first house you come at is his.

So Christian turned out of his way to go to Mr. Legality's house for help; but, behold, when he was got now hard by the hill, it seemed so high, and also that side of it that was next the wayside did hang so much over, that Christian was afraid to venture further, lest the hill should fall on his head; wherefore there he stood still and wotted[5] not what to do. Also his burden now seemed heavier to him than while he was in his way. There came also flashes of fire out of the hill, that made Christian afraid that he should be burned. Here, therefore, he sweat and did quake for fear.[6]

When Christians unto carnal men give ear,
Out of their way they go, and pay for 't dear;
For Master Worldly Wiseman can but shew
A saint the way to bondage and to woe.

And now he began to be sorry that he had taken Mr. Worldly Wiseman's counsel. And with that he saw Evangelist coming to meet him; at the sight also of whom he began to blush for shame. So, Evangelist drew nearer and nearer; and coming up to him, he looked upon him with a severe and dreadful countenance, and thus began to reason with Christian.

EVANGELIST: What dost thou here, Christian? said he: at which words Christian knew not what to answer; wherefore at present he stood speechless before him. Then said Evangelist further, Art not thou the man that I found crying without the walls of the City of Destruction?

CHRISTIAN: Yes, dear Sir, I am the man.

EVANGELIST: Did not I direct thee the way to the little wicket-gate?

CHRISTIAN: Yes, dear Sir, said Christian.

EVANGELIST: How is it, then, that thou art so quickly turned aside? For thou art now out of the way.

CHRISTIAN: I met with a gentleman so soon as I had got over the Slough of Despond, who persuaded me that I might, in the village before me, find a man that would take off my burden.

EVANGELIST: What was he?

---

[5] *Wotted* is the simple past tense and past participle of *wot*. Does that help? Not for me, yet that was more or less the definition I found for this word! Crazy! Anyway, *wot* means *to know*, so this section means that Christian didn't know what to do.

[6] Ex. 19:16, 18; Heb. 12:21.

CHRISTIAN: He looked like a gentleman, and talked much to me, and got me at last to yield; so I came hither; but when I beheld this hill, and how it hangs over the way, I suddenly made a stand lest it should fall on my head.

EVANGELIST: What said that gentleman to you?

CHRISTIAN: Why, he asked me whither I was going, and I told him.

EVANGELIST: And what said he then?

CHRISTIAN: He asked me if I had a family? And I told him. But, said I, I am so loaden with the burden that is on my back, that I cannot take pleasure in them as formerly.

EVANGELIST: And what said he then?

CHRISTIAN: He bid me with speed get rid of my burden; and I told him that it was ease that I sought. And said I, I am therefore going to yonder gate, to receive further direction how I may get to the place of deliverance. So he said that he would shew me a better way, and short, not so attended with difficulties as the way, Sir, that you set me in; which way, said he, will direct you to a gentleman's house that hath skill to take off these burdens, so I believed him, and turned out of that way into this, if haply I might be soon eased of my burden. But when I came to this place, and beheld things as they are, I stopped for fear (as I said) of danger: but I now know not what to do.

EVANGELIST: Then, said Evangelist, stand still a little, that I may show thee the words of God. So, he stood trembling. Then said Evangelist, "See that ye refuse not him that speaketh. For if they escaped not who refused him that spake on earth, much more shall not we escape, if we turn away from him that speaketh from heaven."[7] He said, moreover, "Now the just shall live by faith: but if any man draw back, my soul shall have no pleasure in him."[8] He also did thus apply them: Thou art the man that art running into this misery; thou hast begun to reject the counsel of the Most High, and to draw back thy foot from the way of peace, even almost to the hazarding of thy perdition.

Then Christian fell down at his feet as dead, crying, "Woe is me, for I am undone!"

---

[7] Heb. 12:25.
[8] Heb. 10:38.

At the sight of which Evangelist caught him by the right hand, saying, "All manner of sin and blasphemies shall be forgiven unto men."[9] "Be not faithless, but believing."[10] Then did Christian again a little revive, and stood up trembling, as at first, before Evangelist.

Then Evangelist proceeded, saying, "Give more earnest heed to the things that I shall tell thee of. I will now show thee who it was that deluded thee, and who it was also to whom he sent thee. The man that met thee is one Worldly Wiseman, and rightly is he so called; partly, because he savoureth only the doctrine of this world (therefore he always goes to the town of Morality to church): and partly because he loveth that doctrine best, for it saveth him best from the cross. And because he is of this carnal temper, therefore he seeketh to pervert my ways, though right. Now there are three things in this man's counsel, that thou must utterly abhor.[11]

1. His turning thee out of the way.

2. His labouring to render the cross odious to thee. And,

3. His setting thy feet in that way that leadeth unto the administration of death.

"First, thou must abhor his turning thee out of the way; and thine own consenting thereunto: because this is to reject the counsel of God for the sake of the counsel of a Worldly Wiseman. The Lord says, "Strive to enter in at the strait gate,"[12] the gate to which I sent thee; for "strait is the gate that leadeth unto life, and few there be that find it."[13] From this little wicket-gate, and from the way thereto, hath this wicked man turned thee, to the bringing of thee almost to destruction; hate, therefore, his turning thee out of the way, and abhor thyself for hearkening to him.

"Secondly, thou must abhor his labouring to render the cross odious unto thee; for thou art to prefer it 'before the treasures in Egypt.'[14] Besides the King of glory hath told thee, that he that 'will save his life shall lose it.'[15] And, 'He that cometh after me, and hateth not his father, and mother, and wife, and children, and brethren, and sisters, yea, and his own life also, he cannot be my disciple.'[16] I say, therefore, for man to labour to

---

9 Matt. 12:31; Mark 3:28.
10 John 20:27.
11 1 John 4:5; Gal 6:12.
12 Luke 13:24.
13 Matt. 7:14.
14 Heb. 11:25, 26.
15 Mark 8:35; John 12:25; Matt. 10:39.
16 Luke 14:26.

persuade thee, that that shall be thy death, without which, THE TRUTH hath said, thou canst not have eternal life; this doctrine thou must abhor.

"Thirdly, thou must hate his setting of thy feet in the way that leadeth to the ministration of death. And for this thou must consider to whom he sent thee, and also how unable that person was to deliver thee from thy burden.

"He to whom thou wast sent for ease, being by name Legality, is the son of the bond-woman which now is, and is in bondage with her children;[17] and is, in a mystery, this Mount Sinai, which thou hast feared will fall on thy head. Now, if she, with her children, are in bondage, how canst thou expect by them to be made free? This Legality, therefore, is not able to set thee free from thy burden. No man was as yet ever rid of his burden by him; no, nor ever is like to be: ye cannot be justified by the works of the law; for by the deeds of the law no man living can be rid of his burden: therefore, Mr. Worldly Wiseman is an alien, and Mr. Legality is a cheat; and for his son Civility, notwithstanding his simpering looks, he is but a hypocrite and cannot help thee. Believe me, there is nothing in all this noise, that thou hast heard of these sottish men, but a design to beguile thee of thy salvation, by turning thee from the way in which I had set thee."

After this, Evangelist called aloud to the heavens for confirmation of what he had said: and with that there came words and fire out of the mountain under which poor Christian stood, that made the hair of his flesh stand up. The words were thus pronounced: "As many as are of the works of the law are under the curse; for it is written, Cursed is every one that continueth not in all things which are written in the book of the law to do them."[18]

Now Christian looked for nothing but death and began to cry out lamentably; even cursing the time in which he met with Mr. Worldly Wiseman; still calling himself a thousand fools for hearkening to his counsel; he also was greatly ashamed to think that this gentleman's arguments, flowing only from the flesh, should have the prevalency with him as to cause him to forsake the right way. This done, he applied himself again to Evangelist in words and sense as follow:

CHRISTIAN: Sir, what think you? Is there hope? May I now go back and go up to the wicket-gate? Shall I not be abandoned for this, and sent back from thence ashamed? I am sorry I have hearkened to this man's counsel. But may my sin be forgiven?

---

[17] Gal 4:21-27.
[18] Gal. 3:10.

EVANGELIST: Then said Evangelist to him, Thy sin is very great, for by it thou hast committed two evils: thou hast forsaken the way that is good, to tread in forbidden paths; yet will the man at the gate receive thee, for he has goodwill for men; only, said he, take heed that thou turn not aside again, "lest thou perish from the way, when his wrath is kindled but a little."[19] Then did Christian address himself to go back; and Evangelist, after he had kissed him, gave him one smile, and bid him God-speed. So, he went on with haste, neither spake he to any man by the way; nor, if any asked him, would he vouchsafe them an answer. He went like one that was all the while treading on forbidden ground, and could by no means think himself safe, till again he was got into the way which he left, to follow Mr. Worldly Wiseman's counsel. So, in process of time, Christian got up to the gate. Now, over the gate there was written, "Knock, and it shall be opened unto you."[20]

He that will enter in must first without
Stand knocking at the Gate, nor need he doubt
That is A KNOCKER but to enter in;
For God can love him, and forgive his sin.

---

[19] Ps. 2:12.
[20] Matt 7:8.

WHAT WE COVERED IN WEEK TWO

The Village of Morality
Meeting Evangelist (again)
Arrival at the Wicket Gate

In this week's chapter, we met a man by the name of Worldly Wiseman.

That name should give you a bit of an idea of who this guy is and what he's like. He's ultimately concerned about two things: 1) how did Christian get himself into such terrible shape, and 2) what is he doing with his burden on his back.

Worldly Wiseman is not concerned for Christian's eternal state because Worldly Wiseman has made his home entirely here on earth. He is wise… only in the ways of the world. His concern is with worldly things and *nothing* to do with the eternal.

He describes the life our friend is heading towards—that is, the life of following Jesus—and he uses the following phrase to describe the path ahead: "there is not a more dangerous and troublesome way in the world than is that unto which [Evangelist] hath directed thee."

It's an interesting statement. Consider for a moment what the assumption is lying underneath such a statement. Often it's the assumptions behind our beliefs that are the dangers, the threats, the traps into which we fall.

And for Worldly Wiseman, the assumption he clings to seems to be that the comfort of this life is what's truly important.

Pause for a moment and think about that. What difference will it make in your life if you believe that what is primarily important is your comfort, as opposed to a belief that what is primarily important is your eternal salvation?

You'll notice this man seems to see no benefit in reading God's Word. It's the thing that he describes as being too high for us, and we should be concerned with what's "important" to us. The things of God are "beyond" us, in Worldly Wiseman's opinion.

Not only does Worldly Wiseman miss the point by focusing on temporary things which have no eternal value, but—and here's the real problem—Christian listens to him!

What's offered to Christian is nothing more than a form of good living, a life with some rules and some more morality, but no true salvation.

Later, when Evangelist finds us again, Christian worries that perhaps he's strayed too far, and perhaps Evangelist's response is both painful and beautiful.

He declares that Christian's sin is very great as he has forsaken the good way and has walked on forbidden paths. But then he uses this word: *Yet.*

Remember that word: Yet! "*Yet* will the man at the gate receive thee!"

When we look at our lives before Christ, we should certainly see the terrible weight of our sin and wickedness (if we do not, we need some time to reflect upon sin and forgiveness). *Yet* the Lord still received us.

Yet that is true for us. *Yet* that is true for others as well.

Jesus is the eternal and beautiful and loving *Yet!*

I have, in my years as a pastor, met many men like Worldly Wiseman. They sat in my pews. They listened to the Word of God—often for many, many years. In fact, most of them had been members of a church for longer than I'd been alive. They sat on boards. They perhaps led in the church, taught Bible studies, and more. Yet when it came to a point of actual sacrifice, any point of actual difficulty in following Christ, any point in the faith which might hinder their safety, security, comfort, or way of life, they *invariably* offered their worldly advice. What they brought forward typically came sounding of great wisdom, almost *consistently* presented from the standpoint of age and maturity.

It often came like this: "Well, one thing I've found over time is that these things come and go, and they sound good, but..." or "You might say that because you're young, but I've learned that..."

Rarely did these men ever speak of sacrifice, obedience to Christ, or a love for Christ that might cost us anything—*anything at all.* They wished for stability, comfort, and ease.

I remember one such man, not on an issue of salvation, but of walking this "dangerous and troublesome way." He was someone who could just as easily talk about grace and love and the gospel of Christ as he could rage against anyone who didn't do what he wanted. He could speak of following the Lord, yet also break confidence without a hint of regret. At one point, my wife and I were going through the final stages of an adoption for our youngest son and running up against some serious challenges. He came to me one day and encouraged me simply to give up on the adoption. His view was that since it was difficult, it was perhaps God's way of saying it's not the thing to do. He didn't directly tell me to give it up. No, he counselled me to consider that since we were running up against difficulty, maybe the Lord wasn't in it.

Of course, in hindsight, when I look at my son, my gift from the Lord, a young man the Lord directed me to—my SON!—I shudder as I ask myself, "What if I had listened to Worldly Wiseman?"[21]

Does God ever call us to the difficult path? Does God ever call us to suffer? Does God ever call us to struggle, paying a high price for the pearl of great value?[22]

Do you know people who view the world like Worldly Wiseman?

Are you someone who views the world like Worldly Wiseman?

Lord, let me be a servant of Christ who follows you, never one to follow the advice of Worldly Wiseman. Protect me and lead me to walk your path till the day I see your face!
Amen

---

[21] I still feel a revulsion, a horror, if you will, at the thought of this question. As I write this, my son is in the other room. I hear him on his computer. I might not have him—dare I say I *wouldn't* have him—if I'd listened to Worldly Wiseman and his temporal advice. I would also have disobeyed God's leading as I'm confident God led us to our son. He might have been born half-way around the world, but he is ours! If I had listened to Worldly Wiseman... oh, what a nightmare of a thought!

[22] Matt. 13:45-46.

TALKING POINTS

1. Why do you think that millions of good instructions (presumably encouragements and teachings of God's grace and goodness) could not fill the Slough of Despond? Is there something which could? Is it a bad thing that the Slough is there? Could it be a good thing that true teaching cannot fill the Slough?

2. Our story mentions Pliable again and that his neighbours mocked him. What do you think of the three different responses he received when he returned to the City of Destruction?[23] What do we learn from this?

3. The story also mentioned in the part about Pliable's return that people eventually mocked Christian, though he had already left. Why do you think this mocking happens? Go deep with this question—no simple answers. Don't be afraid to struggle with it!

---

[23] Some called him wise for returning; some called him a fool for taking the risk with Christian; and still others called him a coward for giving up when he faced some difficulties.

4. Isn't it interesting that Worldly Wiseman comes from the town of Carnal Policy, and it was near the town Christian came from, named The City of Destruction? Think on that one for a little bit. What is the relationship between Carnal Policy and The City of Destruction? They are neighbours, after all!

5. Worldly Wiseman told Christian he should listen to him because he was older than Christian. Why do you think such a reason is given?

6. Why do you think Christian was so easily deceived at this point? Sure, he falls away again later in his journey, but at this point, he is so quickly led away. What does this mean for us and what does this mean for those who are in the process of coming to know Jesus Christ? And how should this affect the way we approach new believers and people who are clearly on their way to coming to know Christ?

7. Worldly Wiseman sends Christian to the village of Morality to see a man named Legalist. It has been said that the difference between Christianity and all the other religions of the world is simply this: grace. The opposite of grace is, of course, legalism—righteousness found through morality.[24] The way of morality is a common path. Though we might disagree with others on what all is moral, most people in this world are trying to follow a certain set of moral values for their lives. Worldly Wiseman is actually sending Christian down the path that comes naturally and easily to all of us. So, for us right now, we need to ask, "Why, when grace is so wonderful and so freeing, do we run to the man named Legality in the village of Morality?" What is the attraction? Why might we consider it a natural and "easy" option? Why does morality often pull us in easier than does grace?

8. Notice when Worldly Wiseman gives directions to Christian, he asks if Christian sees yonder hill. Christian's response is very helpful: "Yes, very well." Compare that response with what Christian could see of the Wicket Gate when Evangelist pointed him in that direction. Why do you think Christian could see one clearly and the other he had to just focus on the "light"?

---

[24] Perhaps a good way to think of *legalism* is to see it in terms of law. Legalism is following laws and rules hoping that by holding to those laws and rules, you will be good enough, deemed righteous before God. Grace, however, is relying on Jesus to be our hope and relying on Jesus to be our goodness, rather than trying to be good enough on our own. For sure, we are called to act with goodness and kindness (to follow a *law* of grace), but those actions *never* make us good, they come *after* a work of grace in our lives. For salvation and acceptance by God, we can only stand on Jesus's goodness. Nothing else. That is grace!

9. Look back at the paragraph describing Christian's approach to the hill where Mr. Legality lived. What insights does this paragraph share with us about pursuing legalistic morality?

10. In Bunyan's words, he hopes his story *will make a traveller of thee*. How do you see yourself travelling this road to the Celestial City differently because of this week's reading? What change in heart, attitude, theology, or lifestyle do you believe God is calling you to as you seek to be the traveller he desires you be?

3. The Interpreter

He knocked, therefore, more than once or twice, saying—
"May I now enter here?
Will he within open to sorry me,
though I have been an undeserving rebel?
Then shall I not fail to sing his lasting praise on high.

At last there came a grave person to the gate named Good-will who asked who was there? And whence he came? And what he would have?

CHRISTIAN: Here is a poor burdened sinner. I come from the City of Destruction, but am going to Mount Zion, that I may be delivered from the wrath to come. I would therefore, Sir, since I am informed that by this gate is the way thither, know if you are willing to let me in?

GOOD-WILL: I am willing with all my heart, said he; and with that he opened the gate.

So when Christian was stepping in, the other gave him a pull. Then said Christian, "What means that?"

The other told him, "A little distance from this gate, there is erected a strong castle, of which Beelzebub is the captain; from thence, both he and them that are with him shoot arrows at those that come up to this gate, if haply they may die before they can enter in."

Then said Christian, "I rejoice and tremble."

So when he was got in, the man of the gate asked him who directed him thither?

CHRISTIAN: Evangelist bid me come hither, and knock, (as I did); and he said that you, Sir, would tell me what I must do.

GOOD-WILL: An open door is set before thee, and no man can shut it.[1]

CHRISTIAN: Now I begin to reap the benefits of my hazards.

GOOD-WILL: But how is it that you came alone?

CHRISTIAN: Because none of my neighbours saw their danger, as I saw mine.

GOOD-WILL: Did any of them know of your coming?

CHRISTIAN: Yes; my wife and children saw me at the first, and called after me to turn again; also, some of my neighbours stood crying and calling after me to return; but I put my fingers in my ears, and so came on my way.

GOOD-WILL: But did none of them follow you, to persuade you to go back?

CHRISTIAN: Yes, both Obstinate and Pliable; but when they saw that they could not prevail, Obstinate went railing back, but Pliable came with me a little way.

GOOD-WILL: But why did he not come through?

CHRISTIAN: We, indeed, came both together, until we came at the Slough of Despond, into the which we also suddenly fell. And then was my neighbour, Pliable, discouraged, and would not venture further. Wherefore, getting out again on that side next to his own house, he told me I should possess the brave country alone for him; so he went his way, and I came mine—he after Obstinate, and I to this gate.

GOOD-WILL: Then said Good-will, Alas, poor man! is the celestial glory of so small esteem with him, that he counteth it not worth running the hazards of a few difficulties to obtain it?

CHRISTIAN: Truly, said Christian, I have said the truth of Pliable, and if I should also say all the truth of myself, it will appear there is no betterment betwixt him and myself. It is true, he went back to his own house, but I also turned aside to go in the way of death, being persuaded thereto by the carnal arguments of one Mr. Worldly Wiseman.

---

[1] Rev. 3:8.

GOOD-WILL: Oh, did he light upon you? What! he would have had you a sought for ease at the hands of Mr. Legality. They are, both of them, a very cheat. But did you take his counsel?

CHRISTIAN: Yes, as far as I durst; I went to find out Mr. Legality, until I thought that the mountain that stands by his house would have fallen upon my head; wherefore there I was forced to stop.

GOOD-WILL: That mountain has been the death of many, and will be the death of many more; it is well you escaped being by it dashed in pieces.

CHRISTIAN: Why, truly, I do not know what had become of me there, had not Evangelist happily met me again, as I was musing in the midst of my dumps; but it was God's mercy that he came to me again, for else I had never come hither. But now I am come, such a one as I am, more fit, indeed, for death, by that mountain, than thus to stand talking with my lord; but, oh, what a favour is this to me, that yet I am admitted entrance here!

GOOD-WILL: We make no objections against any, notwithstanding all that they have done before they came hither. They are in no wise cast out;[2] and therefore, good Christian, come a little way with me, and I will teach thee about the way thou must go. Look before thee; dost thou see this narrow way? THAT is the way thou must go; it was cast up by the patriarchs, prophets, Christ, and his apostles; and it is as straight as a rule can make it. This is the way thou must go.

CHRISTIAN: But, said Christian, are there no turnings or windings by which a stranger may lose his way?

GOOD-WILL: Yes, there are many ways butt down upon this, and they are crooked and wide. But thus thou mayest distinguish the right from the wrong, the right only being straight and narrow.[3]

Then I saw in my dream that Christian asked him further if he could not help him off with his burden that was upon his back; for as yet he had not got rid thereof, nor could he by any means get it off without help.

He told him, "As to thy burden, be content to bear it, until thou comest to the place of deliverance; for there it will fall from thy back of itself."

Then Christian began to gird up his loins, and to address himself to his journey. So, the other told him that by that he was gone some distance

---

[2] John 6:37.
[3] Matt 7:14.

from the gate, he would come at the house of the Interpreter, at whose door he should knock, and he would show him excellent things. Then Christian took his leave of his friend, and he again bid him God-speed.

Then he went on till he came to the house of the Interpreter, where he knocked over and over; at last one came to the door, and asked who was there.

CHRISTIAN: Sir, here is a traveller, who was bid by an acquaintance of the good-man of this house to call here for my profit; I would therefore speak with the master of the house. So he called for the master of the house, who, after a little time, came to Christian, and asked him what he would have.

CHRISTIAN: Sir, said Christian, I am a man that am come from the City of Destruction, and am going to the Mount Zion; and I was told by the man that stands at the gate, at the head of this way, that if I called here, you would show me excellent things, such as would be a help to me in my journey.

INTERPRETER: Then said the Interpreter, Come in; I will show that which will be profitable to thee.

The First Excellent Thing[4]

So, he commanded his man to light the candle, and bid Christian follow him: so, he had him into a private room, and bid his man open a door; the which when he had done, Christian saw the picture of a very grave person hang up against the wall; and this was the fashion of it. It had eyes lifted up to heaven, the best of books in his hand, the law of truth was written upon his lips, the world was behind his back. It stood as if it pleaded with men, and a crown of gold did hang over his head.

CHRISTIAN: Then said Christian, What meaneth this?

INTERPRETER: The man whose picture this is, is one of a thousand; he can beget children, travail in birth with children, and nurse them himself when they are born. And whereas thou seest him with his eyes lift up to heaven, the best of books in his hand, and the law of truth writ on his lips, it is to show thee that his work is to know and unfold dark things to sinners; even as also thou seest him stand as if he pleaded with men: and

---

[4] These titles were not in the original Pilgrim's Progress, but have been added here, based on Good-Will's description of them, in the hopes of easing us through the reading of these signs and interpretations.

whereas thou seest the world as cast behind him, and that a crown hangs over his head, that is to show thee that slighting and despising the things that are present, for the love that he hath to his Master's service, he is sure in the world that comes next to have glory for his reward. Now, said the Interpreter, I have showed thee this picture first, because the man whose picture this is, is the only man whom the Lord of the place whither thou art going, hath authorised to be thy guide in all difficult places thou mayest meet with in the way; wherefore, take good heed to what I have shewed thee, and bear well in thy mind what thou hast seen, lest in thy journey thou meet with some that pretend to lead thee right, but their way goes down to death.[5]

The Second Excellent Thing

Then he took him by the hand, and led him into a very large parlour that was full of dust, because never swept; the which after he had reviewed a little while, the Interpreter called for a man to sweep. Now, when he began to sweep, the dust began so abundantly to fly about, that Christian had almost therewith been choked. Then said the Interpreter to a damsel that stood by, "Bring hither the water, and sprinkle the room;" the which, when she had done, it was swept and cleansed with pleasure.

CHRISTIAN: Then said Christian, What means this?

INTERPRETER: The Interpreter answered, This parlour is the heart of a man that was never sanctified by the sweet grace of the gospel; the dust is his original sin and inward corruptions, that have defiled the whole man. He that began to sweep at first, is the Law; but she that brought water, and did sprinkle it, is the Gospel. Now, whereas thou sawest, that so soon as the first began to sweep, the dust did so fly about that the room by him could not be cleansed, but that thou wast almost choked therewith; this is to shew thee, that the law, instead of cleansing the heart (by its working) from sin, doth revive, put strength into, and increase it in the soul, even as it doth discover and forbid it, for it doth not give power to subdue.[6]

Again, as thou sawest the damsel sprinkle the room with water, upon which it was cleansed with pleasure; this is to show thee, that when the gospel comes in the sweet and precious influences thereof to the heart, then, I say, even as thou sawest the damsel lay the dust by sprinkling the

---

[5] 1 Cor. 4:15; Gal. 4:19.
[6] Rom. 5:20; Rom. 7:6; 1 Cor. 15:56.

floor with water, so is sin vanquished and subdued, and the soul made clean through the faith of it, and consequently fit for the King of glory to inhabit.[7]

The Third Excellent Thing

I saw, moreover, in my dream, that the Interpreter took him by the hand, and had him into a little room, where sat two little children, each one in his chair. The name of the eldest was Passion, and the name of the other Patience. Passion seemed to be much discontented; but Patience was very quiet. Then Christian asked, "What is the reason of the discontent of Passion?" The Interpreter answered, "The Governor of them would have him stay for his best things till the beginning of the next year; but he will have all now: but Patience is willing to wait."

Then I saw that one came to Passion, and brought him a bag of treasure, and poured it down at his feet, the which he took up and rejoiced therein, and withal laughed Patience to scorn. But I beheld but a while, and he had lavished all away, and had nothing left him but rags.

CHRISTIAN: Then said Christian to the Interpreter, Expound this matter more fully to me.

INTERPRETER: So he said, These two lads are figures: Passion, of the men of this world; and Patience, of the men of that which is to come; for as here thou seest, Passion will have all now this year, that is to say, in this world; so are the men of this world, they must have all their good things now, they cannot stay till next year, that is until the next world, for their portion of good. That proverb, "A bird in the hand is worth two in the bush," is of more authority with them than are all the Divine testimonies of the good of the world to come. But as thou sawest that he had quickly lavished all away, and had presently left him nothing but rags; so will it be with all such men at the end of this world.

CHRISTIAN: Then said Christian, Now I see that Patience has the best wisdom, and that upon many accounts. First, because he stays for the best things. Second, and also because he will have the glory of his, when the other has nothing but rags.

INTERPRETER: Nay, you may add another, to wit, the glory of the next world will never wear out; but these are suddenly gone. Therefore, Passion had not so much reason to laugh at Patience, because he had his good things first, as Patience will have to laugh at Passion, because he had

---

[7] John 15:3, 13; Acts 15:9; Rom. 16:25, 26; Eph. 5:26.

his best things last; for first must give place to last, because last must have his time to come; but last gives place to nothing; for there is not another to succeed. He, therefore, that hath his portion first, must needs have a time to spend it; but he that hath his portion last, must have it lastingly; therefore it is said of Dives,[8] "Thou in thy life-time receivedst thy good things, and likewise Lazarus evil things; but now he is comforted, and thou art tormented."[9]

CHRISTIAN: Then I perceive it is not best to covet things that are now, but to wait for things to come.

INTERPRETER: You say the truth: "For the things which are seen are temporal; but the things which are not seen are eternal."[10] But though this be so, yet since things present and our fleshly appetite are such near neighbours one to another; and again, because things to come, and carnal sense, are such strangers one to another; therefore it is, that the first of these so suddenly fall into amity, and that distance is so continued between the second.

The Fourth Excellent Thing

Then I saw in my dream that the Interpreter took Christian by the hand, and led him into a place where was a fire burning against a wall, and one standing by it, always casting much water upon it, to quench it; yet did the fire burn higher and hotter.

Then said Christian, "What means this?"

The Interpreter answered, "This fire is the work of grace that is wrought in the heart; he that casts water upon it, to extinguish and put it out, is the Devil; but in that thou seest the fire notwithstanding burn higher and hotter, thou shalt also see the reason of that." So, he had him about to the backside of the wall, where he saw a man with a vessel of oil in his hand, of the which he did also continually cast, but secretly, into the fire.

Then said Christian, "What means this?"

The Interpreter answered, "This is Christ, who continually, with the oil of his grace, maintains the work already begun in the heart: by the means of which, notwithstanding what the devil can do, the souls of his

---

[8] *Dives* is an old word (from the Latin Vulgate) to refer to the rich man in the parable of Lazarus and the Rich Man.
[9] Luke 16:25.
[10] 2 Cor. 4:18.

people prove gracious still. And in that thou sawest that the man stood behind the wall to maintain the fire, that is to teach thee that it is hard for the tempted to see how this work of grace is maintained in the soul."[11]

The Fifth Excellent Thing

I saw also, that the Interpreter took him again by the hand, and led him into a pleasant place, where was builded a stately palace, beautiful to behold; at the sight of which Christian was greatly delighted. He saw also, upon the top thereof, certain persons walking, who were clothed all in gold.

Then said Christian, "May we go in thither?"

Then the Interpreter took him, and led him up towards the door of the palace; and behold, at the door stood a great company of men, as desirous to go in; but durst[12] not. There also sat a man at a little distance from the door, at a table-side, with a book and his inkhorn before him, to take the name of him that should enter therein; he saw also, that in the doorway stood many men in armour to keep it, being resolved to do the men that would enter what hurt and mischief they could. Now was Christian somewhat in amaze. At last, when every man started back for fear of the armed men, Christian saw a man of a very stout countenance come up to the man that sat there to write, saying, "Set down my name, Sir:" the which when he had done, he saw the man draw his sword, and put a helmet upon his head, and rush toward the door upon the armed men, who laid upon him with deadly force; but the man, not at all discouraged, fell to cutting and hacking most fiercely. So, after he had received and given many wounds to those that attempted to keep him out, he cut his way through them all, and pressed forward into the palace, at which there was a pleasant voice heard from those that were within, even of those that walked upon the top of the palace, saying—"Come in, come in; Eternal glory thou shalt win."[13]

So, he went in, and was clothed with such garments as they. Then Christian smiled and said; I think verily I know the meaning of this.

"Now," said Christian, "let me go hence."

"Nay, stay," said the Interpreter, "till I have shewed thee a little more, and after that thou shalt go on thy way."

---

[11] 2 Cor. 12:9.
[12] *Durst* is an archaic form of the word *dare* as in, "I double dog durst you!"
[13] Acts 14:22.

So, he took him by the hand again, and led him into a very dark room, where there sat a man in an iron cage.

Now the man, to look on, seemed very sad; he sat with his eyes looking down to the ground, his hands folded together, and he sighed as if he would break his heart. Then said Christian, "What means this?" At which the Interpreter bid him talk with the man.

Then said Christian to the man, "What art thou?"

The man answered, "I am what I was not once."

CHRISTIAN: What wast thou once?

MAN: The man said, I was once a fair and flourishing professor, both in mine own eyes, and also in the eyes of others; I once was, as I thought, fair for the Celestial City, and had then even joy at the thoughts that I should get thither.[14]

CHRISTIAN: Well, but what art thou now?

MAN: I am now a man of despair, and am shut up in it, as in this iron cage. I cannot get out. Oh, now I cannot!

CHRISTIAN: But how camest thou in this condition?

MAN: I left off to watch and be sober. I laid the reins, upon the neck of my lusts; I sinned against the light of the Word and the goodness of God; I have grieved the Spirit, and he is gone; I tempted the devil, and he is come to me; I have provoked God to anger, and he has left me: I have so hardened my heart, that I cannot repent.

Then said Christian to the Interpreter, "But is there no hope for such a man as this?"

"Ask him," said the Interpreter.

"Nay," said Christian, "pray, Sir, do you."

INTERPRETER: Then said the Interpreter, Is there no hope, but you must be kept in the iron cage of despair?

MAN: No, none at all.

INTERPRETER: Why, the Son of the Blessed is very pitiful.

---

14 Luke 8:13.

MAN: I have crucified him to myself afresh; I have despised his person; I have despised his righteousness; I have "counted his blood an unholy thing;" I have "done despite to the Spirit of grace." Therefore, I have shut myself out of all the promises, and there now remains to me nothing but threatenings, dreadful threatenings, fearful threatenings, of certain judgement and fiery indignation, which shall devour me as an adversary.[15]

INTERPRETER: For what did you bring yourself into this condition?

MAN: For the lusts, pleasures, and profits of this world; in the enjoyment of which I did then promise myself much delight; but now every one of those things also bite me, and gnaw me like a burning worm.

INTERPRETER: But canst thou not now repent and turn?

MAN: God hath denied me repentance. His Word gives me no encouragement to believe; yea, himself hath shut me up in this iron cage; nor can all the men in the world let me out. O eternity, eternity! how shall I grapple with the misery that I must meet with in eternity!

INTERPRETER: Then said the Interpreter to Christian, Let this man's misery be remembered by thee, and be an everlasting caution to thee.

CHRISTIAN: Well, said Christian, this is fearful! God help me to watch and be sober, and to pray that I may shun the cause of this man's misery! Sir, is it not time for me to go on my way now?

INTERPRETER: Tarry till I shall show thee one thing more, and then thou shalt go on thy way.

The Seventh Excellent Thing

So, he took Christian by the hand again, and led him into a chamber, where there was one rising out of bed; and as he put on his raiment, he shook and trembled.

Then said Christian, "Why doth this man thus tremble?"

The Interpreter then bid him tell to Christian the reason of his so doing. So he began and said, "This night, as I was in my sleep, I dreamed, and behold the heavens grew exceeding black; also it thundered and lightened in most fearful wise, that it put me into an agony; so I looked up

---

[15] Luke 19:14; Heb. 6:6; Heb. 10:28-29.

in my dream, and saw the clouds rack at an unusual rate, upon which I heard a great sound of a trumpet, and saw also a man sit upon a cloud, attended with the thousands of heaven; they were all in flaming fire: also the heavens were in a burning flame.

"I heard then a voice saying, 'Arise, ye dead, and come to judgement;' and with that the rocks rent, the graves opened, and the dead that were therein came forth. Some of them were exceeding glad, and looked upward; and some sought to hide themselves under the mountains. Then I saw the man that sat upon the cloud open the book, and bid the world draw near. Yet there was, by reason of a fierce flame which issued out and came from before him, a convenient distance betwixt him and them, as betwixt the judge and the prisoners at the bar.[16]

"I heard it also proclaimed to them that attended on the man that sat on the cloud, 'Gather together the tares, the chaff, and stubble, and cast them into the burning lake.' And with that, the bottomless pit opened, just whereabout I stood; out of the mouth of which there came, in an abundant manner, smoke and coals of fire, with hideous noises. It was also said to the same persons, 'Gather my wheat into the garner.'[17] And with that I saw many catched up and carried away into the clouds, but I was left behind. I also sought to hide myself, but I could not, for the man that sat upon the cloud still kept his eye upon me; my sins also came into my mind; and my conscience did accuse me on every side. Upon this I awaked from my sleep."[18]

CHRISTIAN: But what is it that made you so afraid of this sight?

MAN: Why, I thought that the day of judgement was come, and that I was not ready for it: but this frighted me most, that the angels gathered up several, and left me behind; also the pit of hell opened her mouth just where I stood. My conscience, too, afflicted me; and, as I thought, the Judge had always his eye upon me, shewing indignation in his countenance.

Then said the Interpreter to Christian, Hast thou considered all these things?

CHRISTIAN: Yes, and they put me in hope and fear.

---

[16] 1 Cor. 15:52; 1 Thess. 4:16; Jude 14; John 5:28, 29; 2 Thess. 1:7, 8; Rev. 20:11-14; Isa. 26:21; Micah 7:16, 17; Ps. 95:1-3; Dan. 7:10; Mal. 3:2, 3; Dan. 7:9, 10.

[17] A *garner* is a *storehouse for grain*.

[18] Matt. 3:12; 13:30; Mal. 4:1; Luke 3:17; 1 Thes. 4:16,17; Rom. 3:14,15.

INTERPRETER: Well, keep all things so in thy mind that they may be as a goad in thy sides, to prick thee forward in the way thou must go. Then Christian began to gird up his loins, and to address himself to his journey. Then said the Interpreter, The Comforter be always with thee, good Christian, to guide thee in the way that leads to the City.

So, Christian went on his way, saying—

"Here I have seen things rare and profitable; Things pleasant, dreadful, things to make me stable in what I have begun to take in hand; Then let me think on them, and understand wherefore they showed me were, and let me be thankful, O good Interpreter, to thee."

WHAT WE COVERED IN WEEK THREE

The Wicket Gate/The Sheep Gate
Interpreter's House

We're finally here! We've finally arrived! We have reached the Wicket-Gate! Our journey must certainly be at an end!

Or perhaps this is just the beginning?

Through the gate, Christian meets a man by the name of Goodwill, and Christian reflects on what has happened until this point.

It's interesting that this reflection—this recap of the story—happens many times throughout the book. Perhaps this is important?

Have you ever noticed in Scripture how often God says, "Remember…"? Not just remember everything… but remember what God has done. It is difficult to move forward in trust and faith without remembering what God has done in the past, without remembering his faithfulness!

We must be a people who have a faith rooted in the past work of God if we are to be a people who hold faith in the present and future work of God!

Moving on from the gate, Goodwill points out the way, informing Christian that the path is straight—no turning to the left or right, no winding along the journey. Nothing to cause someone to lose their way. While other paths are crooked and wide, the path that leads to life is straight and often narrow!

Okay, we need to stop and be honest about something.

This is offensive.

It is offensive to suggest that there is a certain path—only *one* path—that can lead to Christ. Even aside from cultural pressures, this is *personal!* This view attacks our personal desire to carve out our own path in life, and it is only by bending the knee to Christ in submission to *his* path and in trusting *his* way that we can walk the narrow path with joy.

This truth that Christ is the only way[19] is offensive as it attacks our natural desire to be our own god who determines our own path!

Often, when you look down through history, you'll find that certain parts of the Christian faith—either the theology or the morality—will be acceptable to those who do not believe, while other parts are unacceptable. Jump forwards or backwards a generation and the formerly acceptable parts of Christianity will be deemed unacceptable while the formerly unacceptable will suddenly be acceptable. The world is fickle in this manner, but Christ remains the same. There are always aspects of the Christian faith that stand as heresy to the world but remain as truth and life to those who believe in Christ.

This matter of a narrow, straight path is not only upsetting on a personal level to those who have not bent the knee to Jesus, the Lord of the Way, but it is the current cultural heresy to those who reject Christ. It is taught that there are many roads—in fact, it's taught that all roads lead the same way. To suggest a belief is true is entirely acceptable in today's culture. To suggest that a belief is *exclusively* true… that is considered the speech of a hater.

It's worth reflecting at this point on what you personally see in the path ahead. Is it the only road to take, or is it one of many? That is the difference between someone who follows the path of Christ and someone who follows the ways of the world.

The path the world calls us to is relatively easy because it is a path that you choose based on your desires. At its root, it is a declaration that "I am god, and I will choose my way." At the root of God's path—the straight and narrow path—is a declaration that "I need God, and my only hope lies in the person of Jesus Christ."

Reflect on your own attitude towards a singular, narrow path as you walk this journey with Christian.

But there is more in this section! Next, we come to Interpreter's house, and our friend here shows us seven sights. I won't write about each of these, but consider this:

Interpreter understands that these are matters that will be helpful for Christian as he starts his journey.

First, we have a picture of what someone looks like who leads us in the way we should go.

---

[19] John 14:6.

Second, there is also a room which illustrates how the Law cannot save us, but only point out our sin.

Third, there are also the two children, Passion and Patience.

Fourth, you have the fires of grace that mysteriously burn higher and hotter even though Satan pours water on it.

Fifth, there is the gate into the palace of glory that the brave man had to fight hard to get through—forcing his way in.

Sixth, there's the man in the cage who had gone beyond the point of repentance.

And finally, there is the man who dreamed of judgement.

There is much we need to keep in mind in the Christian life, and these things we've read in this section are helpful to keep us on the straight and narrow path.

I encourage you to keep these things in mind as you seek the Lord.

Lord, I see that my heart sometimes wishes to go its own way, but your grace draws me in and shapes me, giving me the desire to follow you more faithfully. Thank you. Continue your work of grace in me as I move forward, seeking the eternity with you that I have been promised!
Amen

TALKING POINTS

1. Remember how Worldly Wiseman considered the safety and comfort in this world to be of utmost importance? Consider Good-Will's perspective regarding Pliable's return: "Alas, poor man! is the celestial glory of so small esteem with him, that he counteth it not worth running the hazards of a few difficulties to obtain it?" Consider Matthew 13:45-46. What is in your heart when it comes to this matter of comfort vs. difficulty?[20]

2. After speaking of Pliable, Christian makes this statement: "I have said the truth of Pliable, and if I should also say all the truth of myself, it will appear there is no betterment betwixt him and myself." Why is it important to evaluate not only Pliable's failing but also our own? How does that help us in our view of others? How does that help us in the path ahead?

3. At the gate, we find Beelzebub (i.e. Satan) shoots arrows at those trying to go through. Why do you think Beelzebub doesn't want people to go through that gate? Don't rush through this answer. Really think through this one.

---

[20] This matter of comfort vs. difficulty in walking the path is a HUGE theme throughout Pilgrim's Progress. Bunyan was someone who suffered for his faith, so is it any surprise that he brings this topic forward a lot? To add to this, Jesus talks a lot in the gospels about suffering for the faith. Don't be surprised in this book at continual references to struggling!

4. Why do you think Christian's burden doesn't fall off at the gate?

5. Why should Christian recap his story with Good-will? Why would we need to hear that? Do we benefit from hearing the testimony of others of their walk on the path or of ministries from around the world?[21]

6. Think of one or two difficult times in your life. Would remembering the Lord's faithfulness and work in and around your life have been helpful during that difficult time? Would it have merely been for encouragement, or would it have offered direction as well?

7. Did you understand all seven of the "Excellent Things" in the story? Did you find their meaning obvious? Or, like me, did you struggle to understand? What do you think the House of the Interpreter is all about? What does the Interpreter and his house represent?

---

[21] Acts 14:27

8. See if you can nail down a basic, one or two sentence explanation of each of the Seven Excellent Things.

First:

Second:

Third:

Fourth:

Fifth:

Sixth:

Seventh:

9. The two children are troubling and raise a tough question. Rather than ask if we are patient or driven by a passion for instant gratification, let's approach it from a different angle. Patience was content; Passion was discontent. In this life, do you find yourself content or discontent?

10. Oh, the fires of grace! When I think of the illustration of Satan trying to put out the fire and Christ keeping it going, it brings a smile to my face. Yet, why won't Christ make himself more visible when the fires of grace are being doused? Why does Jesus remain behind the wall?

11. Consider the fifth excellent thing: the palace. Christian said he did not need an interpretation of that event, but what do you think it really means? And how should that concept affect your life? Don't brush this aside with a simple answer. Think about it.

12. For the sixth excellent thing, we find a man in a cage—a very troubling image. Christian asked the man who he used to be. Consider the answer. What does his answer ultimately tell us?

13. Consider again the man in the cage. Now, Bunyan did not believe someone could lose their salvation, so what do you think is really going on here? Is something missing from the man's understanding? Is there something in Interpreter's statements that are easily missed? What is the man in the cage truly missing?

14. For the seventh excellent thing, we have a dream to consider. Now, depending on your view of the end times, you might interpret this to fit in with your understanding, but I don't think this is at all the point of this illustration. What should we take from this excellent thing and how should that affect our lives?

15. What do you think about Christian's desire to quickly get back onto the path? Why do you think he's drawn to the journey? What is it that causes people to be so excited to get back on the way to following Christ?

16. What do we lose if we return to the way too quickly?

17. In Bunyan's words, he hopes his story *will make a traveller of thee*. How do you see yourself travelling this road to the Celestial City differently because of this week's reading? What change in heart, attitude, theology, or lifestyle do you believe God is calling you to as you seek to be the traveller he desires you be?

49

4. A Hilled Called Difficulty

Now I saw in my dream, that the highway up which Christian was to go, was fenced on either side with a wall, and that wall was called Salvation. Up this way, therefore, did burdened Christian run, but not without great difficulty, because of the load on his back.[1]

He ran thus till he came at a place somewhat ascending, and upon that place stood a cross, and a little below, in the bottom, a sepulchre.[2] So, I saw in my dream, that just as Christian came up with the cross, his burden loosed from off his shoulders, and fell from off his back, and began to tumble, and so continued to do, till it came to the mouth of the sepulchre, where it fell in, and I saw it no more.

Then was Christian glad and lightsome, and said, with a merry heart, "He hath given me rest by his sorrow, and life by his death." Then he stood still awhile to look and wonder; for it was very surprising to him, that the sight of the cross should thus ease him of his burden. He looked therefore, and looked again, even till the springs that were in his head sent the waters down his cheeks. Now, as he stood looking and weeping, behold three Shining Ones came to him and saluted him with "Peace be unto thee." So, the first said to him, "Thy sins be forgiven thee;" the second stripped him of his rags, and clothed him with change of raiment; the third also set a mark on his forehead, and gave him a roll with a seal upon it, which he

---

[1] Isa. 26:1.
[2] The word *sepulchre* is used here to refer to the tomb.

bade him look on as he ran, and that he should give it in at the Celestial Gate. So, they went their way.[3]

Who's this? the Pilgrim. How! 'tis very true,
Old things are past away, all's become new.
Strange! he's another man, upon my word,
They be fine feathers that make a fine bird.

Then Christian gave three leaps for joy, and went on singing:
Thus far I did come laden with my sin;
Nor could aught ease the grief that I was in
Till I came hither: What a place is this!
Must here be the beginning of my bliss?
Must here the burden fall from off my back?
Must here the strings that bound it to me crack?
Blest cross! blest sepulchre! blest rather be
The Man that there was put to shame for me!

I saw then in my dream, that he went on thus, even until he came at a bottom, where he saw, a little out of the way, three men fast asleep, with fetters upon their heels. The name of the one was Simple, another Sloth, and the third Presumption.[4]

Christian then seeing them lie in this case went to them, if peradventure he might awake them, and cried, "You are like them that sleep on the top of a mast, for the Dead Sea is under you—a gulf that hath no bottom. Awake, therefore, and come away; be willing also, and I will help you off with your irons." He also told them, "If he that 'goeth about like a roaring lion' comes by, you will certainly become a prey to his teeth." With that they looked upon him, and began to reply in this sort: Simple said, "I see no danger;" Sloth said, "Yet a little more sleep;" and Presumption said, "Every fat must stand upon its own bottom; what is the answer else that I should give thee?"[5] And so they lay down to sleep again, and Christian went on his way.[6]

Yet was he troubled to think that men in that danger should so little esteem the kindness of him that so freely offered to help them, both by awakening of them, counselling of them, and proffering to help them off

---

[3] Zech. 12:10; Mark 2:5; Zech. 3:4; Eph. 1:13.
[4] *Presumption* refers to believing something unproven.
[5] It seems that the phrase, "Every fat must stand upon its own bottom" means, "Leave me alone. You take care of yourself."
[6] Prov. 23:34; 1 Pet. 5:8.

with their irons. And as he was troubled thereabout, he espied two men come tumbling over the wall on the left hand of the narrow way; and they made up apace to him. The name of the one was Formalist, and the name of the other Hypocrisy. So, as I said, they drew up unto him, who thus entered with them into discourse.

CHRISTIAN: Gentlemen, whence came you, and whither go you?

FORMALIST and HYPOCRISY: We were born in the land of Vain-glory and are going for praise to Mount Zion.

CHRISTIAN: Why came you not in at the gate which standeth at the beginning of the way? Know you not that it is written that he that cometh not in by the door, "but climbeth up some other way, the same is a thief and a robber?"[7]

FORMALIST and HYPOCRISY: They said that to go to the gate for entrance was, by all their countrymen, counted too far about; and that, therefore, their usual way was to make a short cut of it, and to climb over the wall, as they had done.

CHRISTIAN: But will it not be counted a trespass against the Lord of the city whither we are bound, thus to violate his revealed will?

FORMALIST and HYPOCRISY: They told him, that, as for that, he needed not to trouble his head thereabout; for what they did they had custom for; and could produce, if need were, testimony that would witness it for more than a thousand years.

CHRISTIAN: But, said Christian, will your practice stand a trial at law?

FORMALIST and HYPOCRISY: They told him, that custom, it being of so long a standing as above a thousand years, would, doubtless, now be admitted as a thing legal by any impartial judge; and besides, said they, if we get into the way, what's matter which way we get in? If we are in, we are in; thou art but in the way, who, as we perceive, came in at the gate; and we are also in the way, that came tumbling over the wall; wherein, now, is thy condition better than ours?

CHRISTIAN: I walk by the rule of my Master; you walk by the rude working of your fancies. You are counted thieves already, by the Lord of the Way; therefore, I doubt you will not be found true men at the end of the way. You come in by yourselves, without his direction; and shall go out by yourselves, without his mercy.

---

[7] John 10:1.

To this they made him but little answer; only they bid him look to himself. Then I saw that they went on every man in his way without much conference one with another, save that these two men told Christian, that as to laws and ordinances, they doubted not but they should as conscientiously do them as he; therefore, said they, we see not wherein thou differest from us but by the coat that is on thy back, which was, as we trow,[8] given thee by some of thy neighbours, to hide the shame of thy nakedness.

CHRISTIAN: By laws and ordinances you will not be saved, since you came not in by the door. And as for this coat that is on my back, it was given me by the Lord of the place whither I go; and that, as you say, to cover my nakedness with. And I take it as a token of his kindness to me; for I had nothing but rags before. And besides, thus I comfort myself as I go: Surely, think I, when I come to the gate of the city, the Lord thereof will know me for good since I have this coat on my back—a coat that he gave me freely in the day that he stripped me of my rags. I have, moreover, a mark in my forehead, of which, perhaps, you have taken no notice, which one of my Lord's most intimate associates fixed there in the day that my burden fell off my shoulders. I will tell you, moreover, that I had then given me a roll, sealed, to comfort me by reading as I go on the way; I was also bid to give it in at the Celestial Gate, in token of my certain going in after it; all which things, I doubt, you want,[9] and want them because you came not in at the gate.[10]

To these things they gave him no answer; only they looked upon each other and laughed. Then, I saw that they went on all, save that Christian kept before, who had no more talk but with himself, and that sometimes sighingly, and sometimes comfortably; also, he would be often reading in the roll that one of the Shining Ones gave him, by which he was refreshed.

I beheld, then, that they all went on till they came to the foot of the Hill Difficulty; at the bottom of which was a spring. There were also in the same place two other ways besides that which came straight from the gate; one turned to the left hand, and the other to the right, at the bottom of the hill; but the narrow way lay right up the hill, and the name of the going up the side of the hill is called Difficulty. Christian now went to the spring, and drank thereof, to refresh himself, and then began to go up the hill, saying—[11]

---

[8] *Trow* means *to think or believe.*
[9] This use of the word *want* doesn't mean they desire it, but they are lacking it.
[10] Gal. 2:16.
[11] Isa. 49:10.

The hill, though high, I covet to ascend,
The difficulty will not me offend;
For I perceive the way to life lies here.
Come, pluck up heart, let's neither faint nor fear;
Better, though difficult, the right way to go,
Than wrong, though easy, where the end is woe.

The other two also came to the foot of the hill; but when they saw that the hill was steep and high, and that there were two other ways to go, and supposing also that these two ways might meet again, with that up which Christian went, on the other side of the hill, therefore they were resolved to go in those ways. Now the name of one of these ways was Danger, and the name of the other Destruction. So, the one took the way which is called Danger, which led him into a great wood, and the other took directly up the way to Destruction, which led him into a wide field, full of dark mountains, where he stumbled and fell, and rose no more.

Shall they who wrong begin yet rightly end?
Shall they at all have safety for their friend?
No, no; in headstrong manner they set out,
And headlong will they fall at last no doubt."

I looked, then, after Christian, to see him go up the hill, where I perceived he fell from running to going, and from going to clambering upon his hands and his knees, because of the steepness of the place.

Now, about the midway to the top of the hill was a pleasant arbour, made by the Lord of the hill for the refreshing of weary travellers; thither, therefore, Christian got, where also he sat down to rest him. Then he pulled his roll out of his bosom and read therein to his comfort; he also now began afresh to take a review of the coat or garment that was given him as he stood by the cross. Thus, pleasing himself awhile, he at last fell into a slumber, and thence into a fast sleep, which detained him in that place until it was almost night; and in his sleep, his roll fell out of his hand.

Now, as he was sleeping, there came one to him, and awaked him, saying, "Go to the ant, thou sluggard; consider her ways and be wise."[12] And with that Christian started up, and sped him on his way, and went apace, till he came to the top of the hill.

Now, when he was got up to the top of the hill, there came two men running to meet him a man; the name of the one was Timorous, and

---

[12] Prov. 6:6.

of the other, Mistrust; to whom Christian said, "Sirs, what's the matter? You run the wrong way."

Timorous answered, that they were going to the City of Zion, and had got up that difficult place; but, said he, "The further we go, the more danger we meet with; wherefore we turned, and are going back again."

"Yes," said Mistrust, "for just before us lie a couple of lions in the way, whether sleeping or waking we know not, and we could not think, if we came within reach, but they would presently pull us in pieces."

CHRISTIAN: Then said Christian, You make me afraid, but whither shall I fly to be safe? If I go back to mine own country, that is prepared for fire and brimstone, and I shall certainly perish there. If I can get to the Celestial City, I am sure to be in safety there. I must venture. To go back is nothing but death; to go forward is fear of death, and life-everlasting beyond it. I will yet go forward.

So, Mistrust and Timorous ran down the hill, and Christian went on his way. But, thinking again of what he had heard from the men, he felt in his bosom for his roll, that he might read therein, and be comforted; but he felt, and found it not. Then was Christian in great distress and knew not what to do; for he wanted that which used to relieve him, and that which should have been his pass into the Celestial City. Here, therefore, he begun to be much perplexed, and knew not what to do. At last, he bethought himself that he had slept in the arbour that is on the side of the hill; and, falling down upon his knees, he asked God's forgiveness for that his foolish act, and then went back to look for his roll.

But all the way he went back, who can sufficiently set forth the sorrow of Christian's heart? Sometimes he sighed, sometimes he wept, and oftentimes he chid himself for being so foolish to fall asleep in that place, which was erected only for a little refreshment for his weariness. Thus, therefore, he went back, carefully looking on this side and on that, all the way as he went, if happily he might find his roll, that had been his comfort so many times in his journey.

He went thus, till he came again within sight of the arbour where he sat and slept; but that sight renewed his sorrow the more, by bringing again, even afresh, his evil of sleeping into his mind. Thus, therefore, he now went on bewailing his sinful sleep, saying, "O wretched man that I am that I should sleep in the day-time! That I should sleep in the midst of difficulty! That I should so indulge the flesh, as to use that rest for ease to my flesh, which the Lord of the hill hath erected only for the relief of the spirits of pilgrims![13]

"How many steps have I took in vain! Thus, it happened to Israel, for their sin; they were sent back again by the way of the Red Sea; and I am made to tread those steps with sorrow, which I might have trod with delight, had it not been for this sinful sleep. How far might I have been on my way by this time! I am made to tread those steps thrice over, which I needed not to have trod but once; yea, now also I am like to be benighted, for the day is almost spent. O, that I had not slept!"

Now, by this time he was come to the arbour again, where for a while he sat down and wept; but at last, as Christian would have it, looking sorrowfully down under the settle, there he espied his roll; the which he, with trembling and haste, catched up, and put it into his bosom. But who can tell how joyful this man was when he had gotten his roll again! For this roll was the assurance of his life and acceptance at the desired haven. Therefore, he laid it up in his bosom, gave thanks to God for directing his eye to the place where it lay, and with joy and tears betook himself again to his journey. But oh, how nimbly now did he go up the rest of the hill! Yet, before he got up, the sun went down upon Christian; and this made him again recall the vanity of his sleeping to his remembrance; and thus he again began to condole with himself: "O thou sinful sleep; how, for thy sake, am I like to be benighted in my journey! I must walk without the sun; darkness must cover the path of my feet; and I must hear the noise of the doleful creatures, because of my sinful sleep."[14]

Now also he remembered the story that Mistrust and Timorous told him of; how they were frighted with the sight of the lions. Then said Christian to himself again, "These beasts range in the night for their prey; and if they should meet with me in the dark, how should I shift them? How should I escape being by them torn in pieces? Thus, he went on his way. But while he was thus bewailing his unhappy miscarriage, he lift up his eyes, and behold there was a very stately palace before him, the name of which was Beautiful; and it stood just by the highway side.

So, I saw in my dream that he made haste and went forward, that if possible he might get lodging there. Now, before he had gone far, he entered into a very narrow passage, which was about a furlong off the porter's lodge; and looking very narrowly before him as he went, he espied

---

[13] Rev. 2:5; 1 Thes. 5:6-8.
[14] 1 Thes. 5:6-7.

two lions in the way. "Now," thought he, "I see the dangers that Mistrust and Timorous were driven back by."

(The lions were chained, but he saw not the chains.)

WHAT WE COVERED IN WEEK FOUR

The Cross
Formalist and Hypocrisy
Difficulty Hill

A while back, a friend introduced me to backpacking. Not just simple hiking where you step out on a path with a bottle of water and see a few birds, but where you put a 60-to-70-pound backpack on and head off on a trail for a week.

Since that time, I've had the chance to hike for hundreds of kilometres (yes, I'm Canadian). I even went to Iceland once with a friend, climbed a mountain or two and covered a whack of trails. It was awesome! Now, while those days seem to be behind me at this stage of my life, the memories are still quite special to me.

One of the crucial things with backpacking is the actual pack. Once you get your food in there, your water, cooking utensils, tent, clothing, etc., the weight jumps up quickly. Then, the moment you heft that thing onto your back and strap it on, you notice… it's not light!

Now, truthfully, the weight isn't so bad—when you walk on level ground, that is. It's tiring, but if you've trained for the hike, you're all set. It's the hills that are the problem.

I don't know how many times I've been partway up a hill or mountain and just had to grab a tree or lean on a boulder, gasping for air. Once, I remember getting to the point of such exhaustion that I would take about ten steps, stop for a break, then ten more steps, then take a break, and so on.[15]

But at the end of the day's hike, you come to a point where you reach your campsite, you un-click the little clasp at your waist, and let the pack roll off your shoulders, dropping it to the ground. Once you are free of your burden, every step feels easier. You feel you could run up the side of a mountain and once you reach the top, just keep going!

---

[15] Now, in my defence, this was not a *hill*. This was a mountain in Iceland, and it wasn't a *gentle* ascent.

I couldn't help but think of this as I read of Christian struggling with the weight on his shoulders.

We come to this point where Christian runs up the highway with great difficulty because of his burden. Not a burden he had chosen to put on his back, but a spiritual burden he could not rid himself of.

"So, I saw in my dream, that just as Christian came up with the cross, his burden loosed from off his shoulders, and fell from off his back, and began to tumble, and so continued to do, till it came to the mouth of the sepulchre, where it fell in, and I saw it no more."

I love that picture! At the point of the cross, the burden falls, and he has the freedom of one who is suddenly released from a great weight!

At the place of Christ's suffering, we find freedom! At the place of Christ's death, the weight on our shoulders is lifted!

There's an old song that tells us burdens are lifted at Calvary. Our burdens are removed at the place where Christ's payment for sin is recognized as sufficient, as being enough. Isn't it amazing that Christian's burden rolls into the tomb?

It's gone! Buried and gone!

Isn't this a beautiful picture?

Not long after, Christian resumes his journey and, following such a beautiful spiritual moment of victory, he meets two people: Formalist and Hypocrisy.

They tell us they were born in the land of Vainglory, and they're going to Mount Zion—a place they expect to receive both praise and honour.

However, they came over the wall like a thief and a robber rather than enter by the way set out by Christ.

Is this a surprise? Isn't this always the way of Formalist and Hypocrisy? They will go their way—and *only* their way. Formalist and Hypocrisy can never be bothered to go to the gate.

And to add to it, they react to the thought that Christian believes his chosen path is better than theirs'. Who's to say one way is better? Isn't it all the same? Isn't it all about finding your own meaning? Or could it be true that Christ has a definite way—a way he lays out for us and expects us to follow?

Consider this: the story of Pilgrim's Progress was written over three hundred years ago. Is it surprising that the issues Bunyan raises, the perspectives he lays out, the lies and deceptions he challenges… that they are the same ones we are dealing with in the twenty-first century? You will find this trend continues throughout the book.[16]

Satan does not have an awful lot of new stuff in his bag of tricks. He just pulls out the same lies over and over again.

And in terms of Christian, we are glad to find he parts ways with these two men. Yet, on the hill, he meets two more people, Timorous and Mistrust. One is fearful, the other will not trust the Lord of the Way. And they run from the lions ahead.

There is no hope in their hearts that the Lord of the Way will protect them.

Can I ask you to reflect on this before you dive into the talking points? Do you trust the Lord of the Way, even when you meet lions?

Lord, I confess I've struggled to trust as I stand before the lions in the way. Give me faith, the faith I need to trust you each step of the way as I walk towards my eternal home with Jesus Christ!
Amen

---

[16] The one that fascinates me the most in this regard is when Christian meets Atheist. We quickly find out that Atheist of 340 years ago is almost identical to Atheist of today.

TALKING POINTS

1. Consider the gifts[17] given to Christian by the three Shining Ones. Can you describe in one or two sentences what each one represents?

First Gift:

Second Gift:

Third Gift:

2. Did salvation come to Christian at the Wicket Gate/Sheep Gate or at the Cross? That's a big question, and if you are discussing this as a group, don't let this divide you from one another. Listen, look at Scripture, trust the Lord!

3. Why should the cross ease you of your burden? And what does it mean for the burden to disappear into the grave/sepulchre?

---

[17] The first *gift* given isn't as tangible as the second two, but it certainly is a gift!

4. You remember Presumption?[18] He's the man who basically said, "You worry about yourself. I'm just fine." Have you ever met Presumption? How far will Presumption go to hold on to his presumption?

5. Now, Formalist and Hypocrisy… did you notice they tumbled over the wall? What do you think of that? Do you remember what the wall was called?

6. Consider Formalist and Hypocrisy some more. They came from the land of Vain-glory. What do you think that means?

7. Formalist and Hypocrisy came from a place called Vain-glory and believed they were heading to a place called Mount Zion where they expected to receive more glory. What do you think is the problem with what they expect to receive?

---

[18] *Presumption* refers to believing something unproven.

8. Formalist, Hypocrisy, and their countrymen believed that the gate for salvation was too far away, and a shortcut was commonly taken instead. What could it possibly mean that the Wicket-gate which is free, simple, available, and within reach of EVERY man, woman, and child is too far?[19]

9. Formalist and Hypocrisy mention there was a custom for what they did (climbing the wall as a thief and robber) and they had plenty of testimony to that regard, even to the point of their custom standing up in trial. Why do you think this approach is the action and belief of a formalist and a hypocrite?

10. Formalist and Hypocrisy share that though they entered the path differently than Christian, they are no doubt all on the path. What do you think of Christian's boldness towards them, and what do you think of their response? What does it tell you about Formalist and Hypocrisy as people and of the root of their belief?

---

[19] Remember, this isn't a physical distance. This story is allegory, so the distance is a picture of something.

11. The Hill Difficulty forces Christian to climb a steep, difficult hill. Do you ever find that Christ leads you into difficulty? Intentionally? Why do you think that is? Do you find you do everything you can to avoid it, even at the risk of danger and destruction? Why do you think Jesus speaks of how a life of following him will be filled with difficulty?[20] What is the purpose of difficulty, suffering, loss, and pain in our lives?

12. What do you think of the pleasant arbour left there by the Lord of the hill? Why do you think the Lord put it there? What does that tell you about the Lord of the Way? What does it tell you about his view of us in times of difficulty?

13. Why does the book make it clear that Christian was wrong to fall asleep at the arbour?

14. Now for the lions… here's the thing. We will all meet lions in our Christian lives, and we have to be ready for them. Timorous and Mistrust ran the opposite way. For us, we want to keep pushing on. What difference does trusting the Lord make for you when you meet the lions? Don't just skim over this question. Discuss it. Reflect on it.

---

[20] John 16:33.

15. In Bunyan's words, he hopes his story *will make a traveller of thee*. How do you see yourself travelling this road to the Celestial City differently because of this week's reading? What change in heart, attitude, theology, or lifestyle do you believe God is calling you to as you seek to be the traveller he desires you be?

5. The House Beautiful

Then he was afraid, and thought also himself to go back after them, for he thought nothing but death was before him. But the porter at the lodge, whose name is Watchful, perceiving that Christian made a halt as if he would go back, cried unto him, saying, "Is thy strength so small?[1] Fear not the lions, for they are chained, and are placed there for trial of faith where it is, and for discovery of those that had none. Keep in the midst of the path, no hurt shall come unto thee."

Difficulty is behind, Fear is before,
Though he's got on the hill, the lions roar;
A Christian man is never long at ease,
When one fright's gone, another doth him seize.

Then I saw that he went on, trembling for fear of the lions, but taking good heed to the directions of the porter; he heard them roar, but they did him no harm. Then he clapped his hands and went on till he came and stood before the gate where the porter was. Then said Christian to the porter, "Sir, what house is this? And may I lodge here to-night?"

The porter answered, "This house was built by the Lord of the hill, and he built it for the relief and security of pilgrims." The porter also asked whence he was, and whither he was going.

CHRISTIAN: I am come from the City of Destruction and am going to Mount Zion; but because the sun is now set, I desire, if I may, to lodge here to-night.

PORTER: What is your name?

---

[1] Mark 8:34-37.

CHRISTIAN: My name is now Christian, but my name at the first was Graceless;[2] I came of the race of Japheth, whom God will persuade to dwell in the tents of Shem.[3]

PORTER: But how doth it happen that you come so late? The sun is set.

CHRISTIAN: I had been here sooner, but that, "wretched man that I am!" I slept in the arbour that stands on the hillside; nay, I had, notwithstanding that, been here much sooner, but that, in my sleep, I lost my evidence, and came without it to the brow of the hill and then feeling for it, and finding it not, I was forced with sorrow of heart, to go back to the place where I slept my sleep, where I found it, and now I am come.

PORTER: Well, I will call out one of the virgins of this place, who will, if she likes your talk, bring you into the rest of the family, according to the rules of the house. So Watchful, the porter, rang a bell, at the sound of which came out at the door of the house, a grave and beautiful damsel, named Discretion, and asked why she was called.

The porter answered, "This man is in a journey from the City of Destruction to Mount Zion, but being weary and benighted, he asked me if he might lodge here to-night; so I told him I would call for thee, who, after discourse had with him, mayest do as seemeth thee good, even according to the law of the house."

Then she asked him whence he was, and whither he was going, and he told her. She asked him also how he got into the way; and he told her. Then she asked him what he had seen and met with in the way; and he told her. And last she asked his name; so he said, "It is Christian, and I have so much the more a desire to lodge here to-night, because, by what I perceive, this place was built by the Lord of the hill for the relief and security of pilgrims.

So, she smiled, but the water stood in her eyes; and after a little pause, she said, I will call forth two or three more of the family. So she ran to the door, and called out Prudence, Piety, and Charity, who, after a little more discourse with him, had him into the family; and many of them, meeting him at the threshold of the house, said, "Come in, thou blessed of the Lord; this house was built by the Lord of the hill, on purpose to entertain such pilgrims in."

---

[2] Ooohh... how cool is that! We learn he had a different name prior to faith in Christ!

[3] Gen. 9:27.

Then he bowed his head and followed them into the house. So when he was come in and sat down, they gave him something to drink, and consented together, that until supper was ready, some of them should have some particular discourse with Christian, for the best improvement of time; and they appointed Piety, and Prudence, and Charity to discourse with him; and thus they began:

PIETY: Come, good Christian, since we have been so loving to you, to receive you in our house this night, let us, if perhaps we may better ourselves thereby, talk with you of all things that have happened to you in your pilgrimage.

CHRISTIAN: With a very good will, and I am glad that you are so well disposed.

PIETY: What moved you at first to betake yourself to a pilgrim's life?

CHRISTIAN: I was driven out of my native country by a dreadful sound that was in mine ears: to wit, that unavoidable destruction did attend me, if I abode in that place where I was.

PIETY: But how did it happen that you came out of your country this way?

CHRISTIAN: It was as God would have it; for when I was under the fears of destruction, I did not know whither to go; but by chance there came a man, even to me, as I was trembling and weeping, whose name is Evangelist, and he directed me to the wicket-gate, which else I should never have found, and so set me into the way that hath led me directly to this house.

PIETY: But did you not come by the house of the Interpreter?

CHRISTIAN: Yes, and did see such things there, the remembrance of which will stick by me as long as I live; especially three things: to wit, how Christ, in despite of Satan, maintains his work of grace in the heart; how the man had sinned himself quite out of hopes of God's mercy; and also the dream of him that thought in his sleep the day of judgement was come.

PIETY: Why, did you hear him tell his dream?

CHRISTIAN: Yes, and a dreadful one it was. I thought it made my heart ache as he was telling of it; but yet I am glad I heard it.

PIETY: Was that all that you saw at the house of the Interpreter?

CHRISTIAN: No; he took me and had me where he shewed me a stately palace, and how the people were clad in gold that were in it; and how there came a venturous man and cut his way through the armed men that stood in the door to keep him out, and how he was bid to come in, and win eternal glory. Methought those things did ravish my heart! I would have stayed at that good man's house a twelvemonth, but that I knew I had further to go.

PIETY: And what saw you else in the way?

CHRISTIAN: Saw! Why, I went but a little further, and I saw one, as I thought in my mind, hang bleeding upon the tree; and the very sight of him made my burden fall off my back, (for I groaned under a very heavy burden,) but then it fell down from off me. It was a strange thing to me, for I never saw such a thing before; yea, and while I stood looking up, for then I could not forbear looking, three Shining Ones came to me. One of them testified that my sins were forgiven me; another stripped me of my rags, and gave me this broidered coat which you see; and the third set the mark which you see in my forehead, and gave me this sealed roll. (And with that he plucked it out of his bosom.)

PIETY: But you saw more than this, did you not?

CHRISTIAN: The things that I have told you were the best; yet some other matters I saw, as, namely--I saw three men, Simple, Sloth, and Presumption, lie asleep a little out of the way, as I came, with irons upon their heels; but do you think I could awake them? I also saw Formality and Hypocrisy come tumbling over the wall, to go, as they pretended, to Zion, but they were quickly lost, even as I myself did tell them; but they would not believe. But above all, I found it hard work to get up this hill, and as hard to come by the lions' mouths, and truly if it had not been for the good man, the porter that stands at the gate, I do not know but that after all I might have gone back again; but now I thank God I am here, and I thank you for receiving of me.

Then Prudence thought good to ask him a few questions and desired his answer to them.

PRUDENCE: Do you not think sometimes of the country from whence you came?

CHRISTIAN: Yes, but with much shame and detestation: "Truly, if I had been mindful of that country from whence I came out, I might have had opportunity to have returned; but now I desire a better country, that is, an heavenly."[4]

PRUDENCE: Do you not yet bear away with you some of the things that then you were conversant withal?

CHRISTIAN: Yes, but greatly against my will; especially my inward and carnal cogitations,[5] with which all my countrymen, as well as myself, were delighted; but now all those things are my grief; and might I but choose mine own things, I would choose never to think of those things more; but when I would be doing of that which is best, that which is worst is with me.[6]

PRUDENCE: Do you not find sometimes, as if those things were vanquished, which at other times are your perplexity?

CHRISTIAN: Yes, but that is seldom; but they are to me golden hours in which such things happen to me.

PRUDENCE: Can you remember by what means you find your annoyances, at times, as if they were vanquished?

CHRISTIAN: Yes, when I think what I saw at the cross, that will do it; and when I look upon my broidered coat, that will do it; also, when I look into the roll that I carry in my bosom, that will do it; and when my thoughts wax warm about whither I am going, that will do it.

PRUDENCE: And what is it that makes you so desirous to go to Mount Zion?

CHRISTIAN: Why, there I hope to see him alive that did hang dead on the cross; and there I hope to be rid of all those things that to this day are in me an annoyance to me; there, they say, there is no death; and there I shall dwell with such company as I like best.[7] For, to tell you truth, I love him, because I was by him eased of my burden; and I am weary of my inward sickness. I would fain be where I shall die no more, and with the company that shall continually cry, "Holy, Holy, Holy!"

---

4 Heb. 11:15, 16.

5 So... how are your *cogitations*? Does that word lead you to cogitate? For those confused (such as the guy who had to look it up in order to define it here), it refers to deep thoughts and reflections. So, inward and carnal cogitations means his inner wicked and immoral thoughts. Hmm... why couldn't he just say that?

6 Rom 7:16-19.

7 Isa. 25:8; Rev. 21:4.

Then said Charity to Christian, Have you a family? Are you a married man?

CHRISTIAN: I have a wife and four small children.

CHARITY: And why did you not bring them along with you?

CHRISTIAN: Then Christian wept, and said, Oh, how willingly would I have done it! But they were all of them utterly averse to my going on pilgrimage.

CHARITY: But you should have talked to them and have endeavoured to have shown them the danger of being behind.

CHRISTIAN: So I did; and told them also of what God had shown to me of the destruction of our city; "but I seemed to them as one that mocked," and they believed me not.[8]

CHARITY: And did you pray to God that he would bless your counsel to them?

CHRISTIAN: Yes, and that with much affection: for you must think that my wife and poor children were very dear unto me.

CHARITY: But did you tell them of your own sorrow, and fear of destruction? For I suppose that destruction was visible enough to you.

CHRISTIAN: Yes, over, and over, and over. They might also see my fears in my countenance, in my tears, and also in my trembling under the apprehension of the judgement that did hang over our heads; but all was not sufficient to prevail with them to come with me.

CHARITY: But what could they say for themselves, why they came not?

CHRISTIAN: Why, my wife was afraid of losing this world, and my children were given to the foolish delights of youth: so what by one thing, and what by another, they left me to wander in this manner alone.

CHARITY: But did you not, with your vain life, damp all that you by words used by way of persuasion to bring them away with you?

CHRISTIAN: Indeed, I cannot commend my life; for I am conscious to myself of many failings therein; I know also that a man by his conversation[9] may soon overthrow what by argument or persuasion he

---

[8] Gen. 19:14.

[9] While the word *conversation* means *talking* in our context, an older meaning has to do with how you live. That is generally the meaning of this word in this book.

doth labour to fasten upon others for their good. Yet this I can say, I was very wary of giving them occasion, by any unseemly action, to make them averse to going on pilgrimage. Yea, for this very thing they would tell me I was too precise, and that I denied myself of things, for their sakes, in which they saw no evil. Nay, I think I may say, that if what they saw in me did hinder them, it was my great tenderness in sinning against God, or of doing any wrong to my neighbour.

CHARITY: Indeed, Cain hated his brother, "because his own works were evil, and his brother's righteous;" and if thy wife and children have been offended with thee for this, they thereby show themselves to be implacable to good, and "thou hast delivered thy soul from their blood."[10]

Now I saw in my dream, that thus they sat talking together until supper was ready. So, when they had made ready, they sat down to meat. Now the table was furnished "with fat things, and with wine that was well refined:" and all their talk at the table was about the Lord of the hill; as, namely, about what he had done, and wherefore he did what he did, and why he had builded that house. And by what they said, I perceived that he had been a great warrior, and had fought with and slain "him that had the Power of death," but not without great danger to himself, which made me love him the more.[11]

For, as they said, and as I believe (said Christian), he did it with the loss of much blood; but that which put glory of grace into all he did, was, that he did it out of pure love to his country. And besides, there were some of them of the household that said they had been and spoke with him since he did die on the cross; and they have attested that they had it from his own lips, that he is such a lover of poor pilgrims, that the like is not to be found from the east to the west.

They, moreover, gave an instance of what they affirmed, and that was, he had stripped himself of his glory, that he might do this for the poor; and that they heard him say and affirm, "that he would not dwell in the mountain of Zion alone." They said, moreover, that he had made many pilgrims princes, though by nature they were beggars born, and their original had been the dunghill.[12]

Thus they discoursed together till late at night; and after they had committed themselves to their Lord for protection, they betook themselves to rest: the Pilgrim they laid in a large upper chamber, whose window

---

[10] 1 John 3:12; Ezek. 3:19.
[11] Heb. 2:14, 15.
[12] 1 Sam. 2:8; Ps. 113:7

opened towards the sun-rising: the name of the chamber was Peace; where
he slept till break of day, and then he awoke and sang--

> *Where am I now? Is this the love and care*
> *Of Jesus for the men that pilgrims are?*
> *Thus to provide! that I should be forgiven!*
> *And dwell already the next door to heaven!*

So, in the morning they all got up; and, after some more discourse,
they told him that he should not depart till they had shown him the rarities
of that place. And first they had him into the study, where they showed him
records of the greatest antiquity; in which, as I remember my dream, they
showed him first the pedigree of the Lord of the hill, that he was the son
of the Ancient of Days and came by that eternal generation.[13] Here also was
more fully recorded the acts that he had done, and the names of many
hundreds that he had taken into his service; and how he had placed them
in such habitations that could neither by length of days, nor decays of
nature, be dissolved.

Then they read to him some of the worthy acts that some of his
servants had done, how they had "subdued kingdoms, wrought
righteousness, obtained promises, stopped the mouths of lions, quenched
the violence of fire, escaped the edge of the sword, out of weakness were
made strong, waxed valiant in fight, and turned to flight the armies of the
aliens."[14]

They then read again, in another part of the records of the house,
where it was shewed how willing their Lord was to receive into his favour
any, even any, though they in time past had offered great affronts to his
person and proceedings. Here also were several other histories of many
other famous things, of all which Christian had a view; as of things both
ancient and modern; together with prophecies and predictions of things
that have their certain accomplishment, both to the dread and amazement
of enemies, and the comfort and solace of pilgrims.

The next day they took him and had him into the armoury, where
they showed him all manner of furniture, which their Lord had provided
for pilgrims, as sword, shield, helmet, breastplate, ALL-PRAYER, and
shoes that would not wear out. And there was here enough of this to

---

[13] This appears to be a clear reference to an old theological description of how
Christ is related to the Father in His Sonship—that Christ is eternally
generated of the Father.

[14] Heb 11:33, 34.

harness out as many men for the service of their Lord as there be stars in the heaven for multitude.

They also showed him some of the engines with which some of his servants had done wonderful things. They shewed him Moses' rod; the hammer and nail with which Jael slew Sisera; the pitchers, trumpets, and lamps too, with which Gideon put to flight the armies of Midian. Then they showed him the ox's goad wherewith Shamgar slew six hundred men. They showed him also the jaw-bone with which Samson did such mighty feats. They showed him, moreover, the sling and stone with which David slew Goliath of Gath; and the sword, also, with which their Lord will kill the Man of Sin, in the day that he shall rise up to the prey. They showed him, besides, many excellent things, with which Christian was much delighted. This done, they went to their rest again.

Then I saw in my dream, that on the morrow he got up to go forward; but they desired him to stay till the next day also; and then, said they, we will, if the day be clear, show you the Delectable Mountains, which, they said, would yet further add to his comfort, because they were nearer the desired haven than the place where at present he was; so he consented and stayed. When the morning was up, they had him to the top of the house, and bid him look south; so he did: and behold, at a great distance, he saw a most pleasant mountainous country, beautified with woods, vineyards, fruits of all sorts, flowers also, with springs and fountains, very delectable to behold.[15] Then he asked the name of the country. They said it was Immanuel's Land; and it is as common, said they, as this hill is, to and for all the pilgrims. And when thou comest there from thence, said they, thou mayest see to the gate of the Celestial City, as the shepherds that live there will make appear.

Now he bethought himself of setting forward, and they were willing he should. But first, said they, let us go again into the armoury. So they did; and when they came there, they harnessed him from head to foot with what was of proof, lest, perhaps, he should meet with assaults in the way. He being, therefore, thus accoutred, walketh out with his friends to the gate, and there he asked the porter if he saw any pilgrims pass by. Then the porter answered, "Yes."

CHRISTIAN: Pray, did you know him? said he.

PORTER: I asked him his name, and he told me it was Faithful.

---

[15] Isa. 33:16, 17.

CHRISTIAN: Oh, said Christian, I know him; he is my townsman, my near neighbour; he comes from the place where I was born. How far do you think he may be before?

PORTER: He is got by this time below the hill.

CHRISTIAN: Well, said Christian, good Porter, the Lord be with thee, and add to all thy blessings much increase, for the kindness that thou hast showed to me.

Then he began to go forward; but Discretion, Piety, Charity, and Prudence would accompany him down to the foot of the hill. So, they went on together, reiterating their former discourses, till they came to go down the hill. Then said Christian, "As it was difficult coming up, so, so far as I can see, it is dangerous going down."

"Yes," said Prudence, "so it is, for it is a hard matter for a man to go down into the Valley of Humiliation, as thou art now, and to catch no slip by the way; therefore," said they, "are we come out to accompany thee down the hill."

So he began to go down, but very warily; yet he caught a slip or two.

Then I saw in my dream that these good companions, when Christian was gone to the bottom of the hill, gave him a loaf of bread, a bottle of wine, and a cluster of raisins; and then he went on his way.

WHAT WE COVERED IN WEEK FIVE

House Beautiful/Palace Beautiful

And so… the lions were real after all!

Two of them, one on either side of the road!

What would you do if you came across two lions in your path?

Perhaps lions are common in your area of the world, but for me, they are not. To come across a couple lions on the street… well… I would be surprised, to say the least. Disturbed? Yes. Curious? Oh, you bet. But all this would be irrelevant, as I would be running away as fast as I can.

It is times such as this, when you come face to face with lions in the path ahead, that you hope to walk the road of life with someone else. Someone who is a slow runner.

But in the spiritual journey, lions are rarely something to run from. In Christian's case, the lions had been placed there to test his faith and discover those who had none.

In this section of the journey, we met Timorous and Mistrust—two men without faith.

God tells us that without faith, it is impossible to please him. Does that not leave us thinking that faith is a crucial part of our Christian experience? If you read the Bible from cover to cover, it is difficult to miss the fact that God desires that we be men and women of faith.

In fact, we learn in this section of the journey that our main character, who is now named Christian, used to be named Graceless. Do you recognize that if you know Christ as your Lord and Saviour, you also are now named Christian, and no longer named Graceless?

That's the difference between one who is truly on this path and one who is not. The one *not* on the path does not know God's grace—at least not well. But those who are truly on the path come to know by faith the God who gives us grace! Isn't that beautiful?

Christ did not come merely to improve our lives, our incomes, our health, our society… but to transform us entirely! He came to change everything about us, even to the point of giving us a new name, a new identity!

And so Christian, a changed man, enters the house and meets four young women: Discretion, Piety, Prudence, and Charity. Though we don't always use words like prudence and piety in everyday life, these are four important qualities in a believer's heart.

The first three have to do with a holy life, while the last one has to do with a kind and gracious love toward one another.

Now, notice this interesting point: these four women, these four qualities, did not show up during Worldly Wiseman's time in the story, but they wait until this point.

That's important!

When Christian met Worldly Wiseman, that wicked man spoke of morality and making right choices—all good things in themselves, of course. But he spoke about our actions as being good enough. These four women, however, cannot exist in a time of simple morality. At least not properly.

Worldly Wiseman was about doing what was good enough, but none of those things lead to salvation—only destruction. Those good actions can actually keep you from the gate!

But these four qualities at this point in our story flow not from moral choice, but rather from your salvation. They flow from the work of Christ in your life—an act of transformation by the Holy Spirit. Once you are on that path, the Holy Spirit begins to develop these qualities in your life in a deep and spiritual manner. And that's a good thing!

That's why these four women show up at this point in the story!

But we need to also recognize Christian's hope of eternity. He speaks about one day seeing his Saviour who hung dead on the cross. He believes at the point of seeing his living Saviour, he will be rid of all those things that are sinful and wicked, as Christ will cleanse him of it all.

This is one of the beautiful truths of the faith: Christ has begun a good work in us and will continue that work, bringing it to completion on that day when we stand before him.[16] We will not be perfected—made completely mature as we were meant to be—until we see him face to face.[17]

---

16 Phil. 1:6.
17 1 John 3:2.

And it is in that place that we will no longer face death, suffering, difficulty, or pain. There we will be with those who love him as we love him! There we will cry out, "Holy, Holy, Holy!"

As we walk this path, we long to be free of sin and every weakness we face, and to be free of this will be a gift from the one who loves us!

Lord, thank you for the hope we have in you, the promise of eternal life.
All the grace, kindness, and goodness we experience here is but a taste
of what is to come when we reach that beautiful city!
Amen.

TALKING POINTS

1. Has there been a time in your life when you have faced *lions* on the path? A time when danger or threat or loss lay ahead, yet you had no option but to move ahead in faith, trusting that the Lord of the Way would take care of you, despite what your eyes could see? Share a little about this with someone.

2. The Lions were placed there to see if the travellers had faith. So… um… well… here's the awkward question. Did Fearful and Timorous have faith? The answer is obvious, but I'm really just setting you up for the next question. Were Fearful and Timorous saved? Were they Christians?

3. For further reflection, what happens when you meet lions along the narrow path, but they aren't sleeping, nor are they tied up?[18] How should you react in a manner that honours the Lord of the Way?

---

[18] Sometimes in life the threat is real, there are no safety nets (as in ropes tying up the metaphorical lions), and yet Christ still leads us to that place where the danger is imminent. NOTE: This does not mean we should seek danger to *prove* our faith, but Christ will often put us in difficult spots to test our faith.

4. Before you go on to the rest of the questions, answer this one as it will help to shape your understanding. What is the house? What does it represent in the Christian life?

5. Christian was named Graceless before his conversion. This is, of course, the first we learn of this in the story. Take a moment and consider the difference between those two names: Christian and Graceless.

6. Why do you think Discretion has tears in her eyes after hearing Christian's request to enter the house? You might want to go back and reread that section.

7. When Christian speaks of the carnal thoughts and desires entering his heart, does that encourage or discourage you? Why?

8. Why do you think the women in the house grilled Christian so much about who he was, where he came from, and what he had experienced?

9. Christian says, "It was as God would have it; for when I was under the fears of destruction, I did not know whither to go; but by chance there came a man… whose name is Evangelist, and he directed me to the wicket-gate, which else I should never have found…" Now, the way of salvation is easy, free, and fully available, yet, Christian (or formerly Graceless) would never have found it without Evangelist. It is good to reflect on the truth that even though Christ proclaims himself in so many ways, he has ordained us to share the gospel with others. Take some time to discuss why this might be.

10. Notice how Christian speaks with the women about his ongoing struggles with sin. It's a little confusing as the language is archaic, but he speaks of his "inward and carnal cogitations."[19] If you are a believer, saved by Jesus Christ, do you still struggle with sin? The answer is obvious. But here is an important question: is it encouraging to recognize that Christian also struggles? Does it not encourage you to know that you are not alone? Satan often tries to convince us we are the only one… but in Christ, we all stand together. So, knowing we all struggle with sin, how can we help one another in this area?

---

[19] *Cogitations* means *your inner deep thoughts*.

11. Christian mentions three things that help him stand against the temptations of sin. First, the coat he wears. Second, the scroll he reads. Third, thoughts of where he is going.

What does the coat symbolize, and why would that help him stand against sin?

What does the scroll symbolize, and why would that help him stand against sin?

Why would thinking of the Celestial City help Christian resist temptation to sin?

12. The next day, in the house provided by the Lord of the Hill, they look at histories, records, and biographies of Christ and his followers. Why do you think this is important? Why do you think there is such an emphasis in Scripture on remembering—not just to remember important details, but remembering what the Lord has done? Why is this so important to God?

13. Now, Christian ends up armoured at this point in the story. Why do you think the armour came now and not right at the beginning? Is this because Christ does not want a Christian to wear the armour of God[20] when you first believe, or is there another reason it might come later? Is there a reason it shows up here at the House Beautiful?

14. The Valley of Humiliation? He's going down into the Valley of Humiliation? Are you insane? We don't want to go there! Why would these lovely ladies lead him to such a horrible place? They seemed so sweet… so kind… But seriously, why would Jesus create a path that leads through the Valley of Humiliation?

15. In Bunyan's words, he hopes his story *will make a traveller of thee.* How do you see yourself travelling this road to the Celestial City differently because of this week's reading? What change in heart, attitude, theology, or lifestyle do you believe God is calling you to as you seek to be the traveller he desires you be?

---

[20] Eph. 6:10-18.

6. The Valleys

But now, in this Valley of Humiliation, poor Christian was hard put to it; for he had gone but a little way, before he espied a foul fiend coming over the field to meet him; his name is Apollyon. Then did Christian begin to be afraid, and to cast in his mind whether to go back or to stand his ground. But he considered again that he had no armour for his back; and therefore thought that to turn the back to him might give him the greater advantage with ease to pierce him with his darts.

Therefore, he resolved to venture and stand his ground; for, thought he, had I no more in mine eye than the saving of my life, it would be the best way to stand.

So he went on, and Apollyon met him. Now the monster was hideous to behold; he was clothed with scales, like a fish (and they are his pride), he had wings like a dragon, feet like a bear, and out of his belly came fire and smoke, and his mouth was as the mouth of a lion. When he was come up to Christian, he beheld him with a disdainful countenance, and thus began to question with him.

APOLLYON: Whence come you? and whither are you bound?

CHRISTIAN: I am come from the City of Destruction, which is the place of all evil, and am going to the City of Zion.

APOLLYON: By this I perceive thou art one of my subjects, for all that country is mine, and I am the prince and god of it. How is it, then, that thou hast run away from thy king? Were it not that I hope thou mayest do me more service, I would strike thee now, at one blow, to the ground.

CHRISTIAN: I was born, indeed, in your dominions, but your service was hard, and your wages such as a man could not live on, "for the wages of sin is death;"[1] therefore, when I was come to years, I did, as other considerate persons do, look out, if, perhaps, I might mend myself.

APOLLYON: There is no prince that will thus lightly lose his subjects, neither will I as yet lose thee; but since thou complainest of thy service and wages, be content to go back: what our country will afford, I do here promise to give thee.

CHRISTIAN: But I have let myself to another, even to the King of princes; and how can I, with fairness, go back with thee?

APOLLYON: Thou hast done in this, according to the proverb, "Changed a bad for a worse;" but it is ordinary for those that have professed themselves his servants, after a while to give him the slip, and return again to me. Do thou so too, and all shall be well.

CHRISTIAN: I have given him my faith, and sworn my allegiance to him; how, then, can I go back from this, and not be hanged as a traitor?

APOLLYON: Thou didst the same to me, and yet I am willing to pass by all, if now thou wilt yet turn again and go back.

CHRISTIAN: What I promised thee was in my nonage;[2] and, besides, I count the Prince under whose banner now I stand is able to absolve me; yea, and to pardon also what I did as to my compliance with thee; and besides, O thou destroying Apollyon! to speak truth, I like his service, his wages, his servants, his government, his company, and country, better than thine; and, therefore, leave off to persuade me further; I am his servant, and I will follow him.

APOLLYON: Consider, again, when thou art in cool blood, what thou art like to meet with in the way that thou goest. Thou knowest that, for the most part, his servants come to an ill end, because they are transgressors against me and my ways. How many of them have been put to shameful deaths! And, besides, thou countest his service better than mine, whereas he never came yet from the place where he is to deliver any that served him out of their hands; but as for me, how many times, as all the world very well knows, have I delivered, either by power, or fraud, those that have faithfully served me, from him and his, though taken by them; and so I will deliver thee.

---

[1] Rom 6:23.
[2] *Nonage* means *immaturity.*

CHRISTIAN: His forbearing at present to deliver them is on purpose to try their love, whether they will cleave to him to the end; and as for the ill end thou sayest they come to, that is most glorious in their account; for, for present deliverance, they do not much expect it, for they stay for their glory, and then they shall have it when their Prince comes in his and the glory of the angels.

APOLLYON: Thou hast already been unfaithful in thy service to him; and how dost thou think to receive wages of him?

CHRISTIAN: Wherein, O Apollyon! Have I been unfaithful to him?

APOLLYON: Thou didst faint at first setting out, when thou wast almost choked in the Gulf of Despond; thou didst attempt wrong ways to be rid of thy burden, whereas thou shouldst have stayed till thy Prince had taken it off; thou didst sinfully sleep and lose thy choice thing; thou wast, also, almost persuaded to go back at the sight of the lions; and when thou talkest of thy journey, and of what thou hast heard and seen, thou art inwardly desirous of vain-glory in all that thou sayest or doest.

CHRISTIAN: All this is true, and much more which thou hast left out; but the Prince whom I serve and honour is merciful, and ready to forgive; but, besides, these infirmities possessed me in thy country, for there I sucked them in; and I have groaned under them, been sorry for them, and have obtained pardon of my Prince.

APOLLYON: Then Apollyon broke out into a grievous rage, saying, I am an enemy to this Prince; I hate his person, his laws, and people; I am come out on purpose to withstand thee.

CHRISTIAN: Apollyon, beware what you do; for I am in the King's highway, the way of holiness. Therefore, take heed to yourself.

APOLLYON: Then Apollyon straddled quite over the whole breadth of the way, and said, I am void of fear in this matter: prepare thyself to die; for I swear by my infernal den, that thou shalt go no further; here will I spill thy soul.

And with that he threw a flaming dart at his breast; but Christian had a shield in his hand, with which he caught it, and so prevented the danger of that.

Then did Christian draw, for he saw it was time to bestir him; and Apollyon as fast made at him, throwing darts as thick as hail; by the which, notwithstanding all that Christian could do to avoid it, Apollyon wounded him in his head, his hand, and foot. This made Christian give a little back.

Apollyon, therefore, followed his work amain,[3] and Christian again took courage, and resisted as manfully as he could. This sore combat lasted for above half a day, even till Christian was almost quite spent; for you must know that Christian, by reason of his wounds, must needs grow weaker and weaker.

Then Apollyon, espying his opportunity, began to gather up close to Christian, and wrestling with him, gave him a dreadful fall; and with that Christian's sword flew out of his hand. Then said Apollyon, I am sure of thee now. And with that he had almost pressed him to death, so that Christian began to despair of life; but as God would have it, while Apollyon was fetching of his last blow, thereby to make a full end of this good man, Christian nimbly stretched out his hand for his sword, and caught it, saying, "Rejoice not against me, O mine enemy; when I fall I shall arise;"[4]

And with that gave him a deadly thrust, which made him give back, as one that had received his mortal wound. Christian perceiving that, made at him again, saying, "Nay, in all these things we are more than conquerors through him that loved us." And with that, Apollyon spread forth his dragon's wings, and sped him away, that Christian for a season saw him no more.[5]

In this combat no man can imagine, unless he had seen and heard as I did, what yelling and hideous roaring Apollyon made all the time of the fight. He spake like a dragon; and, on the other side, what sighs and groans burst from Christian's heart. I never saw him all the while give so much as one pleasant look, till he perceived he had wounded Apollyon with his two-edged sword; then, indeed, he did smile, and look upward; but it was the dreadfullest sight that ever I saw.

A more unequal match can hardly be,
Christian must fight an Angel; but you see,
The valiant man by handling Sword and Shield,
Doth make him, tho' a Dragon, quit the field.

So, when the battle was over, Christian said, "I will here give thanks to him that delivered me out of the mouth of the lion, to him that did help me against Apollyon." And so he did, saying—

---

[3] *Amain* means *with all his strength.*
[4] Micah 7:8.
[5] Rom. 8:37; James 4:7

Then there came to him a hand, with some of the leaves of the tree of life, the which Christian took, and applied to the wounds that he had received in the battle and was healed immediately. He also sat down in that place to eat bread, and to drink of the bottle that was given him a little before; so, being refreshed, he addressed himself to his journey, with his sword drawn in his hand; for he said, I know not but some other enemy may be at hand. But he met with no other affront from Apollyon quite through this valley.

Now, at the end of this valley was another, called the Valley of the Shadow of Death, and Christian must needs go through it, because the way to the Celestial City lay through the midst of it. Now, this valley is a very solitary place. The prophet Jeremiah thus describes it: "A wilderness, a land of deserts and of pits, a land of drought, and of the shadow of death, a land that no man" (but a Christian) "passed through, and where no man dwelt."[7]

Now here Christian was worse put to it than in his fight with Apollyon, as by the sequel you shall see.

I saw then in my dream, that when Christian was got to the borders of the Shadow of Death, there met him two men, children of them that brought up an evil report of the good land,[8] making haste to go back; to whom Christian spake as follows:

CHRISTIAN: Whither are you going?

MEN: They said, Back! Back! And we would have you to do so too, if either life or peace is prized by you.

CHRISTIAN: Why, what's the matter? said Christian.

MEN: Matter! said they; we were going that way as you are going, and went as far as we durst; and indeed, we were almost past coming back;

---

[6] *Dint* means *a blow or strike from a weapon.*
[7] Jer. 2:6.
[8] Num. 13.

for had we gone a little further, we had not been here to bring the news to thee.

CHRISTIAN: But what have you met with? said Christian.

MEN: Why, we were almost in the Valley of the Shadow of Death; but that, by good hap, we looked before us, and saw the danger before we came to it.[9]

CHRISTIAN: But what have you seen? said Christian.

MEN: Seen! Why, the Valley itself, which is as dark as pitch; we also saw there the hobgoblins, satyrs, and dragons of the pit; we heard also in that Valley a continual howling and yelling, as of a people under unutterable misery, who there sat bound in affliction and irons; and over that Valley hangs the discouraging clouds of confusion. Death also doth always spread his wings over it. In a word, it is every whit dreadful, being utterly without order.[10]

CHRISTIAN: Then, said Christian, I perceive not yet, by what you have said, but that this is my way to the desired haven.[11]

MEN: Be it thy way; we will not choose it for ours. So, they parted, and Christian went on his way, but still with his sword drawn in his hand, for fear lest he should be assaulted.

I saw then in my dream, so far as this valley reached, there was on the right hand a very deep ditch; that ditch is it into which the blind have led the blind in all ages, and have both there miserably perished.[12] Again, behold, on the left hand, there was a very dangerous quag, into which, if even a good man falls, he can find no bottom for his foot to stand on. Into that quag King David once did fall, and had no doubt therein been smothered, had not HE that is able plucked him out.

The pathway was here also exceeding narrow, and therefore good Christian was the more put to it; for when he sought, in the dark, to shun the ditch on the one hand, he was ready to tip over into the mire on the other; also when he sought to escape the mire, without great carefulness he would be ready to fall into the ditch. Thus he went on, and I heard him here sigh bitterly; for, besides the dangers mentioned above, the pathway was here so dark, and ofttimes, when he lift up his foot to set forward, he knew not where or upon what he should set it next.

---

[9] Ps. 44:19; 107:10.
[10] Job 3:5; 10:22.
[11] Jer. 2:6.
[12] Ps. 69:14,15.

About the midst of this valley, I perceived the mouth of hell to be, and it stood also hard by the wayside.

Now, thought Christian, what shall I do? And ever and anon[13] the flame and smoke would come out in such abundance, with sparks and hideous noises, (things that cared not for Christian's sword, as did Apollyon before), that he was forced to put up his sword, and betake himself to another weapon called All-prayer.[14]

So he cried in my hearing, "O Lord, I beseech thee, deliver my soul!"[15]

Thus he went on a great while, yet still the flames would be reaching towards him. Also he heard doleful voices, and rushings to and fro, so that sometimes he thought he should be torn in pieces, or trodden down like mire in the streets. This frightful sight was seen, and these dreadful noises were heard by him for several miles together; and, coming to a place where he thought he heard a company of fiends coming forward to meet him, he stopped, and began to muse what he had best to do.

Sometimes he had half a thought to go back; then again he thought he might be half way through the valley; he remembered also how he had already vanquished many a danger, and that the danger of going back might be much more than for to go forward; so he resolved to go on. Yet the fiends seemed to come nearer and nearer; but when they were come even almost at him, he cried out with a most vehement voice, "I will walk in the strength of the Lord God!" so they gave back and came no further.

One thing I would not let slip. I took notice that now poor Christian was so confounded, that he did not know his own voice; and thus I perceived it. Just when he was come over against the mouth of the burning pit, one of the wicked ones got behind him, and stepped up softly to him, and whisperingly suggested many grievous blasphemies to him, which he verily thought had proceeded from his own mind. This put Christian more to it than anything that he met with before, even to think that he should now blaspheme him that he loved so much before; yet, if he could have

---

[13] *Ever and anon* is an old phrase which means *now and then*.
[14] Eph. 6:18.
[15] Ps. 116:4.

helped it, he would not have done it; but he had not the discretion either to stop his ears, or to know from whence these blasphemies came.

When Christian had travelled in this disconsolate condition some considerable time, he thought he heard the voice of a man, as going before him, saying, "Though I walk through the valley of the shadow of death, I will fear no evil, for thou art with me."[16]

Then he was glad, and that for these reasons:

First, because he gathered from thence, that some who feared God were in this valley as well as himself.

Secondly, for that he perceived God was with them, though in that dark and dismal state; and why not, thought he, with me? Though, by reason of the impediment that attends this place, I cannot perceive it.[17]

Thirdly, for that he hoped, could he overtake them, to have company by and by. So he went on, and called to him that was before; but he knew not what to answer; for that he also thought to be alone. And by and by the day broke; then said Christian, He hath turned "the shadow of death into the morning."[18]

Now morning being come, he looked back, not out of desire to return, but to see, by the light of the day, what hazards he had gone through in the dark. So he saw more perfectly the ditch that was on the one hand, and the mire that was on the other; also how narrow the way was which led betwixt them both; also now he saw the hobgoblins, and satyrs, and dragons of the pit, but all afar off (for after break of day, they came not nigh), yet they were discovered to him, according to that which is written, "He discovereth deep things out of darkness, and bringeth out to light the shadow of death."[19]

Now was Christian much affected with his deliverance from all the dangers of his solitary way; which dangers, though he feared them more before, yet he saw them more clearly now, because the light of the day made them conspicuous to him. And about this time the sun was rising, and this was another mercy to Christian; for you must note, that though the first part of the Valley of the Shadow of Death was dangerous, yet this second part which he was yet to go, was, if possible, far more dangerous; for from the place where he now stood, even to the end of the valley, the way was

---

[16] Ps. 23:4.
[17] Job 9:11.
[18] Amos 5:8.
[19] Job 12:22.

all along set so full of snares, traps, gins,[20] and nets here, and so full of pits, pitfalls, deep holes, and shelvings down there, that, had it now been dark, as it was when he came the first part of the way, had he had a thousand souls, they had in reason been cast away; but, as I said just now, the sun was rising. Then said he, "His candle shineth upon my head, and by his light I walk through darkness."[21]

In this light, therefore, he came to the end of the valley. Now I saw in my dream, that at the end of this valley lay blood, bones, ashes, and mangled bodies of men, even of pilgrims that had gone this way formerly; and while I was musing what should be the reason, I espied a little before me a cave, where two giants, Pope and Pagan, dwelt in old time; by whose power and tyranny the men whose bones, blood, and ashes lay there were cruelly put to death. But by this place Christian went without much danger, whereat I somewhat wondered; but I have learnt since, that Pagan has been dead many a day; and as for the other, though he be yet alive, he is, by reason of age, and also of the many shrewd brushes that he met with in his younger days, grown so crazy and stiff in his joints, that he can now do little more than sit in his cave's mouth, grinning at pilgrims as they go by, and biting his nails because he cannot come at them.

So, I saw that Christian went on his way; yet, at the sight of the Old Man that sat in the mouth of the cave, he could not tell what to think, especially because he spake to him, though he could not go after him, saying, "You will never mend till more of you be burned."

But he held his peace, and set a good face on it, and so went by and catched no hurt. Then sang Christian:

> *O world of wonders! (I can say no less),*
> *That I should be preserved in that distress*
> *That I have met with here! O blessed be*
> *That hand that from it hath deliver'd me!*
> *Dangers in darkness, devils, hell, and sin*
> *Did compass me, while I this vale was in:*
> *Yea, snares, and pits, and traps, and nets, did lie*
> *My path about, that worthless, silly I*
> *Might have been catch'd, entangled, and cast down;*
> *But since I live, let JESUS wear the crown.*

---

[20] Maybe everyone else already knows this, but I had to really search to find out what this word means. A *gin* is a kind of *trap*. So... snares, traps, gins, and nets means, traps, traps, traps, and traps.
[21] Job 29:3.

WHAT WE COVERED IN WEEK SIX

Meeting Apollyon
Valley of the Shadow of Death
Conversation about Pope and Pagan

Isn't it interesting, in one sense, that took it so long in our story for Christian to face Apollyon? But then again, it's also interesting to see that he met him so soon on his journey.

In our last section, we started out talking about lions. The lions felt overwhelming, yet in light of meeting Apollyon, the lions suddenly feel small and unimportant.

Now, first off… who is this Apollyon guy? Let's just get right down to it. In many ways, he represents Satan. In that sense, Christian comes face to face with Satan himself.[22]

Satan says a lot of stuff to Christian. Some of it feels pretty intense, but we must remember that Satan is the father of lies, and everything he says is a lie.[23] This is important to keep in mind, because right away, Satan declares Christian belongs to him.

That's a powerful statement, is it not?

Think about it for a moment. For those who have entered through the wicket gate, we now belong to the Lord of the Way. So, when Satan declares that Christian still belongs to him, what is he actually saying? Is he telling us he's not willing to let Christian go? Is he telling us he does not accept or recognize or respect the new identity in Christ? Or is he just lying… deceiving?

I think it's also very telling that Christian does not merely happen upon Satan, as though Satan was just as surprised as Christian. Consider this approach:

Satan steps out from behind a tree, checking his texts on his phone. Something catches his eye, and he glances up. "Oh, excuse me, I didn't see you there." He

---

[22] Apollyon is also thought to represent the worldly forces and influences. For more on this topic, see the *Answers and Extra Thoughts* section at the back of the book.
[23] John 8:44.

examines the man before him for a moment before adding, "Hey... wait... I know you... you're that Christian guy!"

Christian comes to a halt, shifting on his feet and offering an awkward shrug. With a sheepish smile, he replies, "Oh, riiiiight. You're... um... oh... uh... Satan? Yeah, that's right... you're Satan! Hey, fancy meeting you here! Ha ha. What a small world!"

"I know what you mean," Satan says with a laugh. "I was just out grabbing a coffee and... wait a minute! What are you doing here? Aren't you supposed to be back in the City of Destruction?"

It's not quite like that, is it?

No, Satan is coming to meet Christian, and it's intentional. I think it's important to know this truth: Satan pursues us and wants us! He wants us under his control!

Now, pay attention to how Satan approaches Christian.

First, he declares his ownership over Christian, attempting to pressure Christian to return and laying guilt upon him for leaving.

Second, he threatens but offers mercy.

Third, he tempts Christian by offering him good things.

Fourth, he tells Christian it's common for people to run back to Satan after turning to Jesus. Now... this is interesting! Part of the pressure we face is the pressure of the crowd. What are other people doing? What are other people saying? We often want to go with the flow, to make sure we never stand apart. Often, even those who declare themselves to be rebels or declare they are going their own way are often the first to do exactly what the crowd is doing—they just pretend they're going their own way.

I think it's helpful to always watch our hearts when it comes to what the masses around us are doing.

Fifth, Satan accuses Christian of his sin. Now, consider that Satan is the Father of Lies.[24] Satan is also our accuser.[25] When he accuses us, he doesn't have to make up anything, because all of us have enough sin in our past for him to accuse us accurately. But... he's a liar, right? So, is the Liar telling the truth?

---

[24] Jn. 8:44.
[25] Rev. 12:10.

Not at all. Because, and remember this simple truth always, ***Satan is always a liar!***

When he accuses us, he's speaking words of truth deceptively. Don't we call that lying? He's telling us what we've done, but the message to us is not just what we have *done*, but who we *are*! Satan is declaring us to be sinners. And that is NOT what we are. The work of Christ cleanses us through the cross. So, Satan is lying about us, declaring our sin to be who we are, calling us sinners when Jesus has declared us saints!

And that, my friend, is the lie.

The lie is that you are not worthy of Christ because of your sin. While there is a lot of truth in that, the greater truth is that Christ overcomes our sin and declares us worthy. And what Jesus declares… is true! Because just as Satan's language is always lies, Jesus's language is always truth!

The sixth approach in terms of Satan's pressure and manipulation comes when Satan tries to discourage Christian from the path because of its difficulties, then solves the problem for him by providing comfort. Satan promises to be Christian's deliverer!

Ultimately, Satan is doing all he can to drive Christian back to the City of Destruction!

Yet, here is an amazing truth.

We are not worthy of Christ's love and acceptance on our own, but Jesus does not give us his love and acceptance based on our worthiness, but because he is worthy! He gives because he is good! He gives because he is greater than our sin! He gives because he is loving!

Isn't that far more precious than our own attempts at earning Christ's love?

Christian responds to all of Satan's lies with a declaration that he now serves One who is merciful and ready to forgive. And for us, remember when the accusations come, you serve the Prince who is merciful and ready to forgive!

Finally, Christian engages in battle with Apollyon. And while I won't get into a discussion of it here, I encourage you to read through it again. Pay close attention to how the battle goes.

And finally, we enter the Valley of the Shadow of Death.[26] A time when Christian can't see what's going on. He can't see what's ahead or behind.

And what is required of Christian during this time?

Trust. And faith.

Do you see a bit of a theme developing? Without faith, it is impossible to please him![27]

Yet he hears a voice of a fellow traveller, and Christian speaks out of his trust in the Lord, recognizing that if God was with the other person along the way, he is certainly also with Christian!

Sometimes we go through valleys, and we must remember that the Lord is with us even there, whether or not we perceive it.

Lord, I thank you that you are the God of truth, and you truly love me as your own. And Lord, I thank you that you are with me, even in the dark valleys, when I see nothing but danger on every side! You will lead me home to the place where I will see your face!
Amen

---

[26] Ps. 23.
[27] Heb. 11:6.

TALKING POINTS

1. Consider Apollyon's conversation with Christian. The temptation to fall back into the old ways often includes pressure. It then presents itself as reasonable, declares obvious "claims," and even offers to solve all problems you might face, all the while ignoring the truth that Apollyon's path leads to death! Have you felt these pressures? What is a wise way to respond?[28]

2. Apollyon declares it's normal for people to leave the faith. First, this puts pressure on Christian to return to the City of Destruction. Second, it makes it easier to do so since it's a "normal" path apparently taken. And third, and this part is perhaps the most insidious, there is an assumption here that suggests what Christian has with Jesus is *worse* than what he could have if he returned. This is the assumption that is often brought to us. It's an assumption that the Christian life is missing some or all of what you could have in this life. What is the truth in all these deceptive pressures?

---

[28] Consider Psa. 73.

3. Pay attention to this statement: "Thou didst the same to me (referring to Christian leaving Apollyon), and yet I am willing to pass by all, if now thou wilt yet turn again and go back." Do you notice Apollyon is pretending to be just like Jesus here?[29] Is this not cause for reflection on how we are often pulled into sin? How does Satan *offer* the good things of Jesus? Of course, we must remember Satan is the father of lies,[30] so when Satan speaks of grace, what is the lie? When Satan speaks of holiness, what is the lie? When Satan speaks of you and your sin, what is the lie?

4. Apollyon speaks about how Jesus never saves those of his followers who suffer from their difficulties or death. Now, that's certainly not true (again, Satan is the father of lies), but often Jesus doesn't deliver us in the moment. Consider this: are you able to continue in your walk with Christ if you are about to suffer and die for Jesus? What if he does not rescue you from it? How should we understand this? What perspective is necessary for working through this? How does 1 Peter 4:17 speak into this matter?

---

[29] 2 Cor. 11:14.
[30] John 8:44.

5. Oh no! Apollyon accuses Christian of his unfaithfulness to Christ! That's one that Satan can get all of us on, right? And Christian has no argument to stand on, other than the mercy of God! Consider for a moment the accusations which Satan can bring against you. They appear true, right? But how do we see the lies behind these accusations considering John 8:44? And what part does Christ's mercy play in it all?

6. Notice that when the battle is about to begin, Apollyon straddles the road. Get that? The road! Christian can't leave the road, which means he can't proceed without facing Apollyon. On top of that, how big is this guy? Perhaps it's helpful for us to recognize the impossibility of defeating Satan on our own. So, what can we do? How does Ephesians 6:10-20 speak into this matter?

7. Did you notice Apollyon comes to a point where he believes he's conquered Christian? What made Apollyon think that he'd won? Why would this make him think he had beaten Christian?

8. Did Christian have to endure that fight with Apollyon? Could he not simply have gone through his life without the battle? And can you make it through your entire Christian life without fighting Satan?

9. In his battle with Apollyon, what happened that caused Christian to almost lose? And when he had almost lost, what was it that made him win? Those are simple questions, but let's take it a step further. What does this tell us about our own battles with Satan?

10. Did you notice that Apollyon never called Christian by his name? Why do you think that is?

11. We have not had any deep questions yet about the matter of humility (it *is* the Valley of Humiliation, after all), but I want to drop a quick one as we will speak of humility more later in the book. Considering John Bunyan's allegory, there was no avoiding this time of humbling without leaving the path. That's worth considering! Why do you think God leads us to times of humility?

12. Notice what Christian says to the two men running from the Valley of the Shadow of Death. How do you think that perspective is helpful and necessary for us as Christians?

13. After Christian meets the two fleeing men, we read he continues to hold his sword in his hand "lest he should be assaulted." It's the second time this matter of holding the drawn sword is mentioned after his fight with Apollyon. Why do you think this is important?

14. Soon, Christian's sword is of no use, and he switches to another weapon. Why do you think the new weapon, All-Prayer, was of use in this new area?

15. Part way through the Valley of the Shadow of Death, a demon steps up behind Christian, whispering wicked things in his mind, but Christian thinks it's actually his own thoughts. We should be encouraged to know that this is a wicked one doing this (not ourselves), but perhaps the more important truth is that Jesus is gracious. Amidst our struggles and discouragement and fears and more, though we might think our sin is too great for us to continue on, believing the lies of the wicked ones, Jesus is gracious to you, to me, to us. This is good news. There is no question for this part. Please, just reflect on Jesus's wonderful grace!

16. Here is another matter upon which to reflect. Christian hears the words of a man who travels before him quoting Psalm 23. Isn't it interesting to notice that just a short while before, David, the writer of that Psalm, was mentioned as having fallen into the mire, only to be rescued by God? Our first mention of David is of his terrible failing, yet here, the words of David, a man who went through this same valley, are the words of encouragement to move on through the valley. David is both the sinner and the righteous encourager. Do we fully grasp the wonder of God's grace?

17. In Bunyan's words, he hopes his story *will make a traveller of thee.* How do you see yourself travelling this road to the Celestial City differently because of this week's reading? What change in heart, attitude, theology, or lifestyle do you believe God is calling you to as you seek to be the traveller he desires you be?

7. A Faithful Companion

ow, as Christian went on his way, he came to a little ascent, which was cast up on purpose that pilgrims might see before them. Up there, therefore, Christian went, and looking forward, he saw Faithful before him, upon his journey. Then said Christian aloud, "Ho! ho! So-ho! stay, and I will be your companion!" At that, Faithful looked behind him; to whom Christian cried again, "Stay, stay, till I come up to you!"

But Faithful answered, "No, I am upon my life, and the avenger of blood is behind me."

At this, Christian was somewhat moved, and putting to all his strength, he quickly got up with Faithful, and did also overrun him; so the last was first. Then did Christian vain-gloriously smile, because he had gotten the start of his brother; but not taking good heed to his feet, he suddenly stumbled and fell, and could not rise again until Faithful came up to help him.

Then I saw in my dream they went very lovingly on together, and had sweet discourse of all things that had happened to them in their pilgrimage; and thus Christian began:

CHRISTIAN: My honoured and well-beloved brother, Faithful, I am glad that I have overtaken you; and that God has so tempered our spirits that we can walk as companions in this so pleasant a path.

FAITHFUL: I had thought, dear friend, to have had your company quite from our town; but you did get the start of me, wherefore I was forced to come thus much of the way alone.

CHRISTIAN: How long did you stay in the City of Destruction before you set out after me on your pilgrimage?

FAITHFUL: Till I could stay no longer; for there was great talk presently after you were gone out that our city would, in short time, with fire from heaven, be burned down to the ground.

CHRISTIAN: What! did your neighbours talk so?

FAITHFUL: Yes, it was for a while in everybody's mouth.

CHRISTIAN: What! And did no more of them but you come out to escape the danger?

FAITHFUL: Though there was, as I said, a great talk thereabout, yet I do not think they did firmly believe it. For in the heat of the discourse, I heard some of them deridingly speak of you and of your desperate journey (for so they called this your pilgrimage), but I did believe, and do still, that the end of our city will be with fire and brimstone from above; and therefore I have made my escape.

CHRISTIAN: Did you hear no talk of neighbour Pliable?

FAITHFUL: Yes, Christian, I heard that he followed you till he came at the Slough of Despond, where, as some said, he fell in; but he would not be known to have so done; but I am sure he was soundly bedabbled with that kind of dirt.

CHRISTIAN: And what said the neighbours to him?

FAITHFUL: He hath, since his going back, been had greatly in derision, and that among all sorts of people; some do mock and despise him; and scarce will any set him on work. He is now seven times worse than if he had never gone out of the city.

CHRISTIAN: But why should they be so set against him, since they also despise the way that he forsook?

FAITHFUL: Oh, they say, hang him, he is a turncoat! He was not true to his profession. I think God has stirred up even his enemies to hiss at him, and make him a proverb, because he hath forsaken the way.[1]

CHRISTIAN: Had you no talk with him before you came out?

FAITHFUL: I met him once in the streets, but he leered away on the other side, as one ashamed of what he had done; so I spake not to him.

CHRISTIAN: Well, at my first setting out, I had hopes of that man; but now I fear he will perish in the overthrow of the city; for it is happened

---

[1] Jer. 29:18, 19.

to him according to the true proverb, "The dog is turned to his own vomit again; and the sow that was washed, to her wallowing in the mire."[2]

FAITHFUL: These are my fears of him too; but who can hinder that which will be?

CHRISTIAN: Well, neighbour Faithful, said Christian, let us leave him, and talk of things that more immediately concern ourselves. Tell me now, what you have met with in the way as you came; for I know you have met with some things, or else it may be writ for a wonder.

FAITHFUL: I escaped the Slough that I perceived you fell into, and got up to the gate without that danger; only I met with one whose name was Wanton, who had like to have done me a mischief.

CHRISTIAN: It was well you escaped her net. Joseph was hard put to it by her, and he escaped her as you did; but it had like to have cost him his life.[3] But what did she do to you?

FAITHFUL: You cannot think, but that you know something, what a flattering tongue she had; she lay at me hard to turn aside with her, promising me all manner of content.

CHRISTIAN: Nay, she did not promise you the content of a good conscience.

FAITHFUL: You know what I mean; all carnal and fleshly content.

CHRISTIAN: Thank God you have escaped her: "The abhorred of the Lord shall fall into her ditch."[4]

FAITHFUL: Nay, I know not whether I did wholly escape her or no.

CHRISTIAN: Why, I trow,[5] you did not consent to her desires?

FAITHFUL: No, not to defile myself; for I remembered an old writing that I had seen, which said, "Her steps take hold on hell." So I shut mine eyes, because I would not be bewitched with her looks. Then she railed on me, and I went my way.[6]

CHRISTIAN: Did you meet with no other assault as you came?

---

[2] 2 Pet. 2:22.
[3] Gen. 39:11-13.
[4] Prov. 22:14.
[5] *Trow* means *think or believe.*
[6] Prov. 5:5; Job 31:1.

FAITHFUL: When I came to the foot of the hill called Difficulty, I met with a very aged man, who asked me what I was, and whither bound. I told him that I am a pilgrim, going to the Celestial City. Then said the old man, Thou lookest like an honest fellow; wilt thou be content to dwell with me for the wages that I shall give thee? Then I asked him his name, and where he dwelt. He said his name was Adam the First, and that he dwelt in the town of Deceit. I asked him then what was his work, and what the wages he would give. He told me that his work was many delights; and his wages that I should be his heir at last.[7] I further asked him what house he kept, and what other servants he had. So, he told me that his house was maintained with all the dainties in the world; and that his servants were those of his own begetting. Then I asked if he had any children. He said that he had but three daughters: The Lust of the Flesh, The Lust of the Eyes, and The Pride of Life, and that I should marry them all if I would.[8] Then I asked how long time he would have me live with him? And he told me, As long as he lived himself.

CHRISTIAN: Well, and what conclusion came the old man and you to at last?

FAITHFUL: Why, at first, I found myself somewhat inclinable to go with the man, for I thought he spake very fair; but looking in his forehead, as I talked with him, I saw there written, "Put off the old man with his deeds."[9]

CHRISTIAN: And how then?

FAITHFUL: Then it came burning hot into my mind, whatever he said, and however he flattered, when he got me home to his house, he would sell me for a slave. So, I bid him forbear to talk, for I would not come near the door of his house. Then he reviled me, and told me that he would send such a one after me, that should make my way bitter to my soul. So, I turned to go away from him; but just as I turned myself to go thence, I felt him take hold of my flesh, and give me such a deadly twitch back, that I thought he had pulled part of me after himself. This made me cry, "O wretched man!"[10] So I went on my way up the hill.

---

[7] The concept of an *heir at last* is when a lord has no heirs to leave his estate to, so instead, he (or the law) gives the inheritance to someone else.
[8] 1 John 2:16.
[9] Eph. 4:22.
[10] Rom. 7:24.

Now when I had got about half-way up, I looked behind, and saw one coming after me, swift as the wind; so, he overtook me just about the place where the settle stands.

CHRISTIAN: Just there, said Christian, did I sit down to rest me; but being overcome with sleep, I there lost this roll out of my bosom.

FAITHFUL: But, good brother, hear me out. So soon as the man overtook me, he was but a word and a blow,[11] for down he knocked me, and laid me for dead. But when I was a little come to myself again, I asked him wherefore he served me so. He said, because of my secret inclining to Adam the First; and with that he struck me another deadly blow on the breast, and beat me down backward; so I lay at his foot as dead as before. So, when I came to myself again, I cried him mercy; but he said, I know not how to show mercy; and with that he knocked me down again. He had doubtless made an end of me, but that one came by, and bid him forbear.

CHRISTIAN: Who was that that bid him forbear?

FAITHFUL: I did not know him at first, but as he went by, I perceived the holes in his hands and in his side; then I concluded that he was our Lord. So, I went up the hill.

CHRISTIAN: That man that overtook you was Moses. He spareth none, neither knoweth he how to show mercy to those that transgress his law.

FAITHFUL: I know it very well; it was not the first time that he has met with me. It was he that came to me when I dwelt securely at home, and that told me he would burn my house over my head if I stayed there.

CHRISTIAN: But did you not see the house that stood there on the top of the hill, on the side of which Moses met you?

FAITHFUL: Yes, and the lions too, before I came at it: but for the lions, I think they were asleep, for it was about noon; and because I had so much of the day before me, I passed by the porter, and came down the hill.

CHRISTIAN: He told me, indeed, that he saw you go by, but I wish you had called at the house, for they would have showed you so many rarities that you would scarce have forgot them to the day of your death. But pray tell me, did you meet nobody in the Valley of Humility?

---

[11] This idiom (*he was but a word and a blow*) seems to mean exactly what it says. It speaks of someone who says a word (maybe an insult or verbal attack) before he lets loose with violence.

FAITHFUL: Yes, I met with one Discontent, who would willingly have persuaded me to go back again with him; his reason was, for that the valley was altogether without honour. He told me, moreover, that there to go was the way to disobey all my friends, as Pride, Arrogancy, Self-conceit, Worldly-glory, with others, who he knew, as he said, would be very much offended, if I made such a fool of myself as to wade through this valley.

CHRISTIAN: Well, and how did you answer him?

FAITHFUL: I told him, that although all these that he named might claim kindred of me, and that rightly, for indeed they were my relations according to the flesh; yet since I became a pilgrim, they have disowned me, as I also have rejected them; and therefore, they were to me now no more than if they had never been of my lineage.

I told him, moreover, that as to this valley, he had quite misrepresented the thing; for before honour is humility, and a haughty spirit before a fall. Therefore, said I, I had rather go through this valley to the honour that was so accounted by the wisest, than choose that which he esteemed most worthy our affections.

CHRISTIAN: Met you with nothing else in that valley?

FAITHFUL: Yes, I met with Shame; but of all the men that I met with in my pilgrimage, he, I think, bears the wrong name. The others would be said nay, after a little argumentation, and somewhat else; but this bold-faced Shame would never have done.

CHRISTIAN: Why, what did he say to you?

FAITHFUL: What! Why, he objected against religion itself. He said it was a pitiful, low, sneaking business for a man to mind religion. He said that a tender conscience was an unmanly thing; and that for a man to watch over his words and ways, so as to tie up himself from that hectoring liberty that the brave spirits of the times accustom themselves unto, would make him the ridicule of the times. He objected also, that but few of the mighty, rich, or wise, were ever of my opinion; nor any of them neither,[12] before they were persuaded to be fools, and to be of a voluntary fondness, to venture the loss of all, for nobody knows what. He, moreover, objected the base and low estate and condition of those that were chiefly the pilgrims of the times in which they lived: also their ignorance and want of understanding in all natural science. Yea, he did hold me to it at that rate also, about a great many more things than here I relate; as, that it was a shame to sit whining and mourning under a sermon, and a shame to come

---

[12] 1 Cor. 1:26, 3:18; Phil. 3:7,8; John 7:48.

sighing and groaning home: that it was a shame to ask my neighbour forgiveness for petty faults, or to make restitution where I have taken from any. He said, also, that religion made a man grow strange to the great, because of a few vices, which he called by finer names; and made him own and respect the base, because of the same religious fraternity. And is not this, said he, a shame?

CHRISTIAN: And what did you say to him?

FAITHFUL: Say! I could not tell what to say at the first. Yea, he put me so to it, that my blood came up in my face; even this Shame fetched it up and had almost beat me quite off. But at last, I began to consider, that "that which is highly esteemed among men, is had in abomination with God."[13] And I thought again, this Shame tells me what men are; but it tells me nothing what God or the Word of God is. And I thought, moreover, that at the day of doom, we shall not be doomed to death or life according to the hectoring spirits of the world, but according to the wisdom and law of the Highest. Therefore, thought I, what God says is best, indeed is best, though all the men in the world are against it. Seeing, then, that God prefers his religion; seeing God prefers a tender conscience; seeing they that make themselves fools for the kingdom of heaven are wisest; and that the poor man that loveth Christ is richer than the greatest man in the world that hates him; Shame, depart, thou art an enemy to my salvation! Shall I entertain thee against my sovereign Lord? How then shall I look him in the face at his coming? Should I now be ashamed of his ways and servants, how can I expect the blessing?[14] But, indeed, this Shame was a bold villain; I could scarce shake him out of my company; yea, he would be haunting of me, and continually whispering me in the ear, with some one or other of the infirmities that attend religion; but at last I told him it was but in vain to attempt further in this business; for those things that he disdained, in those did I see most glory; and so at last I got past this importunate[15] one. And when I had shaken him off, then I began to sing—

> *The trials that those men do meet withal,*
> *That are obedient to the heavenly call,*
> *Are manifold, and suited to the flesh,*
> *And come, and come, and come again afresh;*
> *That now, or sometime else, we by them may*
> *Be taken, overcome, and cast away.*

---

[13] Luke 16:15.
[14] Mark 8:38.
[15] *Importune* here refers to Shame's tendency to urgently push or even beg Faithful to give in to his pressure.

CHRISTIAN: I am glad, my brother, that thou didst withstand this villain so bravely; for of all, as thou sayest, I think he has the wrong name; for he is so bold as to follow us in the streets, and to attempt to put us to shame before all men: that is, to make us ashamed of that which is good; but if he was not himself audacious, he would never attempt to do as he does. But let us still resist him; for notwithstanding all his bravadoes, he promoteth the fool and none else. "The wise shall inherit glory, said Solomon, but shame shall be the promotion of fools."[16]

FAITHFUL: I think we must cry to Him for help against Shame, who would have us to be valiant for the truth upon the earth.

CHRISTIAN: You say true; but did you meet nobody else in that valley?

FAITHFUL: No, not I; for I had sunshine all the rest of the way through that, and also through the Valley of the Shadow of Death.

CHRISTIAN: It was well for you. I am sure it fared far otherwise with me; I had for a long season, as soon almost as I entered into that valley, a dreadful combat with that foul fiend Apollyon; yea, I thought verily he would have killed me, especially when he got me down and crushed me under him, as if he would have crushed me to pieces; for as he threw me, my sword flew out of my hand; nay, he told me he was sure of me: but I cried to God, and he heard me, and delivered me out of all my troubles. Then I entered into the Valley of the Shadow of Death and had no light for almost half the way through it. I thought I should have been killed there, over and over; but at last day broke, and the sun rose, and I went through that which was behind with far more ease and quiet.

---

[16] Prov. 3:35.

WHAT WE COVERED IN WEEK SEVEN

Meeting Faithful
Telling of their stories

Week Seven! We're nearly halfway through our journey!

I hope reading this book and working through the reflections has been a powerful time of growth for you!

This week, Christian meets his first travelling companion: a man named Faithful. Remember that the names tell us a lot about the character, and Faithful proves true to his name!

But, we can't miss something important here. Remember that Christian had just finished travelling through the Valley of the Shadow of Death and the Valley of Humiliation. Ahead, he sees a man and calls out to him, but Faithful won't stop—he doesn't want to turn around. He's fleeing the Avenger of Blood!

What an interesting phrase! It refers to the Old Testament concept of one who avenges a family member who has been killed. Under Moses's Law, if you killed someone, the next of kin had the right to kill you. Your only hope was to run to a City of Refuge—to flee from the Avenger of Blood.[17]

This is interesting because it points out two things. First, Faithful is only interested in moving forward in his faith. He will not turn back from following the way Christ has laid out for him, no matter what!

And second, it shows us he recognizes the guilt his sin places upon him. Behind him is nothing but death, but ahead is life. Ahead is his refuge, his place of safety. Ahead is Jesus!

Do we recognize that our only hope for life is in Jesus? Do we recognize that our only chance to live is with Christ?

---

[17] Num. 35 & Deut. 19.

So Faithful doesn't come back for Christian, he calls Christian to come forward to join him. This is the way of the Christian life. We should always push forward and call others to catch up![18]

For me, I tend to want to see Christian, our main character, as the mature one, and the others he meets along the way as immature, but Faithful is just the opposite. He is farther along in his faith than Christian, and this will come out clearly in time.

A mature Christian will always call those along the journey to catch up—to join them along the way. To come along and run at their pace. It's called discipleship. It's what Barnabas did with Paul, and then Paul did with Timothy.

In time, we will see Christian being the mentor for someone else, someone younger in the faith than he, but, on this day, we are not far enough along on our journey. Instead, the Lord of the Way knows Christian needs a brother to help him along.

And what a message it sends to us when we see what Christian does! He gathers up his strength and runs with all his might, even passing by Faithful. For those of you who have called other Christians to a deeper level in their faith, have you seen them surpass you? Have you felt the joy of knowing they've grown more than you were capable of yourself at that time? What a gift!

However, Christian's success led him to arrogance, resulting in a fall, putting him back in need of Faithful's help.

In the end, we recognize a truth about this. Christian needs Faithful, but ultimately, Faithful needs Christian as well. And we learn we were never meant to walk this road alone. Christians who try to be independent of all others play a dangerous game. They will struggle and often not even know the danger they are in.

Be wary of walking the Way of Christ alone!

---

[18] NOTE: It's possible this statement can be interpreted to mean that we are not called to humble ourselves or to meet people where they are at. This is not true, nor is it what I'm suggesting here. Humility is necessary for a proper discipleship relationship. I don't think this allegory has anything to do with not humbling ourselves as humility is certainly the way of Christ! Instead, we should never abandon what we have learned and gained in our love and relationship for Jesus in favour of discipleship. To do so is counterproductive. Your love for Christ is the very thing you must share with those you disciple. Don't give it up!

Lord, I thank you for those you have placed in my life to stretch me, challenge me, push me closer to you. You have done this out of your grace and kindness as you lead me closer to the eternity I have with you!
Amen

TALKING POINTS

1. Have you ever met someone who is more spiritually mature than you are, then found in time you surpassed them?[19] If so, did that leave you feeling arrogant, filled with pride?

2. Do you think it's a good thing that Christian ran to catch up? Why or why not?

3. Notice something here about distance down the path (a picture, of sorts, of spiritual maturity). Faithful set out on the path *after* Christian, but in this chapter, he is now *ahead* of him on the path. This is often the way it is with us as spiritual maturity is not merely a matter of time spent as a believer. In your own experience, what makes a difference in someone's spiritual growth and maturity?[20]

---

[19] I recognize it is difficult to gauge spiritual maturity, and perhaps in many circumstances, impossible. The point here is not to *rate* ourselves or others, but more a matter of evaluating our own pride/humility.

[20] It will be easy to try to keep this on the surface here by only focusing on the good decisions you have made rather than, in humility, recognizing the poor choices. Be honest here. Own both the good choices and the bad choices.

4. Christian is at a point in his journey where he needs a brother to help him along, to strengthen him, to offer encouragement, to challenge him, and to help him grow. Is this a bad thing? Is it a sign of weakness? Is it something to avoid?

5. Spend some time thinking about what areas of your life someone like Faithful could speak into. Make a list. See this as a positive thing, and then ask yourself who in your life can be a Faithful to you.

6. Once you've finished that list, ask yourself how you could be a Faithful to someone else. In what areas could you really bless and encourage another? What part does humility (within you) play in this relationship?[21] Is there someone you know who needs a Faithful?

---

[21] Don't skip by this question of humility. You cannot be a proper Faithful to someone if you cannot find deep humility within yourself. Arrogance destroys. It has always destroyed. In the words of the Rev. Matthew Richards, "Humility is the foundation of unity."

7. Why would someone choose to walk the road of faith alone? What does that look like in real life? Is it possible to attend a church regularly, be active, be involved, even attend a small group, and yet be walking alone? We are not called to independence as believers, but *inter*dependence, but what does that look like in our hearts, actions, attitudes, and choices?[22]

8. Christian falls. He stumbles. He feels pride that leads to his fall. What does pride look like in your everyday life? How does it reveal itself in your conversations, interactions, attitudes, and more? How do you overcome pride, so a fall isn't necessary?

9. Throughout our story, our pilgrims often tell the story of their experiences along the path. From a narrative perspective, this fills in the gaps in our story, but from the standpoint of this allegory, it points out something wonderful about the Christian life. What is the benefit of this retelling of our stories (testimonies, biographies, etc.)?

---

[22] This is where it is easy to point the finger at others accusing them of not stepping into *your* life, but Pilgrim's Progress is not about finding fault with others. This book is about *our own* journey on the way to the Celestial City!

10. Notice as Faithful tells his story, he speaks of the forbidden woman named Wanton. This is a picture of sexual sin, and Faithful came into some powerful temptation in this area of his life. Now, while he says that he did not give into her temptation, he also says, "Nay, I know not whether I did wholly escape her or no." What do you think that means? And what does that mean for your life?

11. Now, remember, the book is allegory. This part about the woman named Wanton points directly to sexual sin, but since the story is allegory, what do you think it points to beyond the physical act? What else could be going on here?

12. After they finish their discussion of the temptress named Wanton, Christian asks if Faithful faced any other assaults along the way. Now… why do you think Christian would throw the idea of sexual temptation into the category of "assault" or attack?

13. What do you think of this whole matter of Faithful's experiences with the old man (Adam the First) and with Moses?

14. Now, Faithful's interaction with Moses is challenging. Faithful speaks of how Moses beat him on the path. That's all the law can do, because Moses doesn't know how to show mercy![23] Are you relying on the Law, rules, or morals at any point in your life to declare yourself righteous? Is there any part of your own efforts that you believe makes you a good person?

15. In Galatians 3:24, we read of how Moses's Law is a guardian or teacher to bring us to Christ. We also read in Romans that the Law is not evil.[24] As Christians, we tend to slide to the extremes. On one extreme, we believe we can follow laws and rules and be seen as good in God's eyes (legalism), and on the other extreme, we believe we can do whatever we want (licentiousness), assuming grace makes it all okay. In the centre is where we find true grace—a life lived trusting the Lord to cleanse us (faith in Christ's work), while living a grace-empowered life intended to glorify God (putting off the old self). Talk with others about these two extremes and how to turn away from them towards true grace.

16. What place does Moses's Law have in leading us to Christ? What place does it have in our lives once we know Christ? Remember, the Law is not evil!

---

[23] This is not to suggest that the law is bad. The Law functions as a signpost to point us to Jesus Christ, and the law is good. It is merely unable to save in any way whatsoever.
[24] Rom. 7:7.

17. Consider for a moment that Faithful walked by the house on top of the hill because he felt he could make better use of the day in moving along the way. If that house is a picture of church membership, is this allegory suggesting that not everyone needs the church?

18. Discontent pressured Faithful to avoid humiliation as he would disappoint his friends. First, what would be lost, what part of you would be offended, what area of your heart would be challenged if you were to be humbled before the Lord? Don't go all "holy" with this and respond with, "No, I never question the humbling of the Lord!" It's time to be honest. What would it cost you personally if God humbled you right now?

19. I have found in life that when I have come to a point where I have needed to humble myself, often those who react the most negatively to a choice of humility are other Christians. In fact, fellow believers have even demanded that I stand up for myself rather than humble myself. For sure, there are times to stand up for yourself, but it raises a serious question: What does it mean when we can go through life without *ever* seeing a need to humble ourselves?

20. To make this more personal, is there an area of your life right now where you need to humble yourself?

21. Faithful turned both Wanton and the First Adam away, but did you notice when he tried to get away, both Wanton and the First Adam grew angry with him? Why do you think both responded that way to Faithful?

22. Have you met with Discontent in your Christian walk? Have you found yourself disappointed with what you've faced, received, or experienced as a believer? Why do you think that was? How did you get out of your discontentment? If you are still meeting with Discontent right now, how can you leave him behind?

23. Pay attention to how Faithful pushed back against Shame (before he actually pushed him away). Reread that part and see what shifted in Faithful's perspective. Now, what about you? Where is your focus?

24. Why do you think Shame held on so long with Faithful? Do you find that in your own life?

25. Christian and Faithful's experiences are very different. This is true of all of us. Why do you think some Christians have a more difficult path to walk than others?

26. In Bunyan's words, he hopes his story *will make a traveller of thee*. How do you see yourself travelling this road to the Celestial City differently because of this week's reading? What change in heart, attitude, theology, or lifestyle do you believe God is calling you to as you seek to be the traveller he desires you be?

8. A Talkative Companion

Moreover, I saw in my dream, that as they went on, Faithful, as he chanced to look on one side, saw a man whose name is Talkative, walking at a distance beside them; for in this place there was room enough for them all to walk. He was a tall man, and something more comely[1] at a distance than at hand.

To this man Faithful addressed himself in this manner:

FAITHFUL: Friend, whither away? Are you going to the heavenly country?

TALKATIVE: I am going to the same place.

FAITHFUL: That is well; then I hope we may have your good company.

TALKATIVE: With a very good will, will I be your companion.

FAITHFUL: Come on, then, and let us go together, and let us spend our time in discoursing of things that are profitable.

TALKATIVE: To talk of things that are good, to me is very acceptable, with you or with any other; and I am glad that I have met with those that incline to so good a work; for, to speak the truth, there are but few that care thus to spend their time (as they are in their travels), but choose much rather to be speaking of things to no profit; and this hath been a trouble for me.

FAITHFUL: That is indeed a thing to be lamented; for what things so worthy of the use of the tongue and mouth of men on earth as are the things of the God of heaven?

---

[1] *Comely* means *attractive*.

TALKATIVE: I like you wonderful well, for your sayings are full of conviction; and I will add, what thing is so pleasant, and what so profitable, as to talk of the things of God? What things so pleasant (that is, if a man hath any delight in things that are wonderful)? For instance, if a man doth delight to talk of the history or the mystery of things; or if a man doth love to talk of miracles, wonders, or signs, where shall he find things recorded so delightful, and so sweetly penned, as in the Holy Scripture?

FAITHFUL: That is true; but to be profited by such things in our talk should be that which we design.

TALKATIVE: That is it that I said; for to talk of such things is most profitable; for by so doing, a man may get knowledge of many things; as of the vanity of earthly things, and the benefit of things above. Thus, in general, but more particularly by this, a man may learn the necessity of the new birth, the insufficiency of our works, the need of Christ's righteousness, etc. Besides, by this a man may learn, by talk, what it is to repent, to believe, to pray, to suffer, or the like; by this also a man may learn what are the great promises and consolations of the gospel, to his own comfort. Further, by this a man may learn to refute false opinions, to vindicate the truth, and also to instruct the ignorant.

FAITHFUL: All this is true, and glad am I to hear these things from you.

TALKATIVE: Alas! The want of this is the cause why so few understand the need of faith, and the necessity of a work of grace in their soul, in order to eternal life; but ignorantly live in the works of the law, by which a man can by no means obtain the kingdom of heaven.

FAITHFUL: But, by your leave, heavenly knowledge of these is the gift of God; no man attaineth to them by human industry, or only by the talk of them.

TALKATIVE: All this I know very well; for a man can receive nothing, except it be given him from Heaven; all is of grace, not of works. I could give you a hundred scriptures for the confirmation of this.

FAITHFUL: Well, then, said Faithful, what is that one thing that we shall at this time found our discourse upon?

TALKATIVE: What you will. I will talk of things heavenly, or things earthly; things moral, or things evangelical; things sacred, or things profane; things past, or things to come; things foreign, or things at home; things more essential, or things circumstantial; provided that all be done to our profit.

FAITHFUL: Now did Faithful begin to wonder; and stepping to Christian, (for he walked all this while by himself), he said to him, (but softly), What a brave companion have we got! Surely this man will make a very excellent pilgrim.

CHRISTIAN: At this Christian modestly smiled, and said, This man, with whom you are so taken, will beguile, with that tongue of his, twenty of them that know him not.

FAITHFUL: Do you know him, then?

CHRISTIAN: Know him! Yes, better than he knows himself.

FAITHFUL: Pray, what is he?

CHRISTIAN: His name is Talkative; he dwelleth in our town. I wonder that you should be a stranger to him, only I consider that our town is large.

FAITHFUL: Whose son is he? And whereabout does he dwell?

CHRISTIAN: He is the son of one Say-well; he dwelt in Prating Row; and is known of all that are acquainted with him, by the name of Talkative in Prating Row; and notwithstanding his fine tongue, he is but a sorry fellow.

FAITHFUL: Well, he seems to be a very pretty man.

CHRISTIAN: That is, to them who have not thorough acquaintance with him; for he is best abroad; near home, he is ugly enough. Your saying that he is a pretty man brings to my mind what I have observed in the work of the painter, whose pictures show best at a distance, but, very near, more unpleasing.

FAITHFUL: But I am ready to think you do but jest, because you smiled.

CHRISTIAN: God forbid that I should jest (although I smiled) in this matter, or that I should accuse any falsely! I will give you a further discovery of him. This man is for any company, and for any talk; as he talketh now with you, so will he talk when he is on the ale-bench; and the more drink he hath in his crown, the more of these things he hath in his mouth; religion hath no place in his heart, or house, or conversation;[2] all he hath lieth in his tongue, and his religion is, to make a noise therewith.

FAITHFUL: Say you so! Then am I in this man greatly deceived.

---

[2] Remember, the word *conversation* in older English often has to do with the way you live, not a matter of what you talk about.

CHRISTIAN: Deceived! You may be sure of it; remember the proverb, "They say and do not." But the kingdom of God is not in word, but in Power. He talketh of prayer, of repentance, of faith, and of the new birth; but he knows but only to talk of them. I have been in his family and have observed him both at home and abroad; and I know what I say of him is the truth. His house is as empty of religion as the white of an egg is of savour. There is there neither prayer nor sign of repentance for sin; yea, the brute in his kind serves God far better than he. He is the very stain, reproach, and shame of religion to all that know him; it can hardly have a good word in all that end of the town where he dwells, through him. Thus say the common people that know him, "A saint abroad, and a devil at home." His poor family finds it so; he is such a churl, such a railer[3] at and so unreasonable with his servants, that they neither know how to do for or speak to him. Men that have any dealings with him say it is better to deal with a Turk[4] than with him; for fairer dealing they shall have at their hands. This Talkative (if it be possible) will go beyond them, defraud, beguile, and overreach them. Besides, he brings up his sons to follow his steps; and if he findeth in any of them a foolish timorousness (for so he calls the first appearance of a tender conscience), he calls them fools and blockheads, and by no means will employ them in much, or speak to their commendations before others. For my part, I am of opinion, that he has, by his wicked life, caused many to stumble and fall; and will be, if God prevent not, the ruin of many more.[5]

FAITHFUL: Well, my brother, I am bound to believe you; not only because you say you know him, but also because, like a Christian, you make your reports of men. For I cannot think that you speak these things of ill-will, but because it is even so as you say.

CHRISTIAN: Had I known him no more than you, I might perhaps have thought of him, as, at the first, you did; yea, had he received this report at their hands only that are enemies to religion, I should have thought it had been a slander,--a lot that often falls from bad men's mouths upon good men's names and professions; but all these things, yea, and a

---

[3] To call someone a *churl* is to say they are rude and unpleasant, and the word *railer* refers to one who intensely complains against someone.

[4] This phrase right here is a difficult one. In the Rewalked Edition, I have used the word "violent" as a way to make sense of this. Around the time of the writing of Pilgrim's Progress, the Ottoman Empire (the "Turks") were engaging in a series of conflicts in eastern Europe (resulting in the Ottoman Empire's control over Western Ukraine) and this result came after centuries of many conflicts and conquests. Because of so many wars, I suspect the word "violent" might be a proper understanding of this reference.

[5] Matt. 23:3; 1 Cor 4:20; Rom. 2:24, 25.

great many more as bad, of my own knowledge, I can prove him guilty of. Besides, good men are ashamed of him; they can neither call him brother, nor friend; the very naming of him among them makes them blush, if they know him.

FAITHFUL: Well, I see that saying and doing are two things, and hereafter I shall better observe this distinction.

CHRISTIAN: They are two things, indeed, and are as diverse as are the soul and the body; for as the body without the soul is but a dead carcass, so saying, if it be alone, is but a dead carcass also. The soul of religion is the practical part: "Pure religion and undefiled, before God and the Father, is this, To visit the fatherless and widows in their affliction, and to keep himself unspotted from the world." This Talkative is not aware of; he thinks that hearing and saying will make a good Christian, and thus he deceiveth his own soul. Hearing is but as the sowing of the seed; talking is not sufficient to prove that fruit is indeed in the heart and life; and let us assure ourselves, that at the day of doom men shall be judged according to their fruits. It will not be said then, "Did you believe?" but, "Were you doers, or talkers only?" And accordingly shall they be judged. The end of the world is compared to our harvest; and you know men at harvest regard nothing but fruit. Not that anything can be accepted that is not of faith, but I speak this to show you how insignificant the profession of Talkative will be at that day.[6]

FAITHFUL: This brings to my mind that of Moses, by which he describeth the beast that is clean.[7] He is such a one that parteth the hoof and cheweth the cud; not that parteth the hoof only, or that cheweth the cud only. The hare cheweth the cud, but yet is unclean, because he parteth not the hoof. And this truly resembleth Talkative; he cheweth the cud, he seeketh knowledge, he cheweth upon the word; but he divideth not the hoof, he parteth not with the way of sinners; but, as the hare, he retaineth the foot of a dog or bear, and therefore he is unclean.[8]

CHRISTIAN: You have spoken, for aught I know, the true gospel sense of those texts. And I will add another thing: Paul calleth some men, yea, and those great talkers, too, sounding brass and tinkling cymbals; that is, as he expounds them in another place, things without life, giving sound.[9] Things without life, that is, without the true faith and grace of the gospel;

---

6 James 1:22-27; Matt. 13, 25.
7 Lev. 11:3-7; Deut. 14:6-8.
8 I count 14 -eth's in this paragraph. I don't know about you, but that makes it REALLY hard for me to read.
9 1 Cor. 13:1-3, 14:7

and consequently, things that shall never be placed in the kingdom of heaven among those that are the children of life; though their sound, by their talk, be as if it were the tongue or voice of an angel.

FAITHFUL: Well, I was not so fond of his company at first, but I am as sick of it now. What shall we do to be rid of him?

CHRISTIAN: Take my advice, and do as I bid you, and you shall find that he will soon be sick of your company too, except God shall touch his heart, and turn it.

FAITHFUL: What would you have me to do?

CHRISTIAN: Why, go to him, and enter into some serious discourse about the power of religion; and ask him plainly (when he has approved of it, for that he will) whether this thing be set up in his heart, house, or conversation.

FAITHFUL: Then Faithful stepped forward again, and said to Talkative, Come, what cheer? How is it now?

TALKATIVE: Thank you, well. I thought we should have had a great deal of talk by this time.

FAITHFUL: Well, if you will, we will fall to it now; and since you left it with me to state the question, let it be this: How doth the saving grace of God discover itself when it is in the heart of man?

TALKATIVE: I perceive, then, that our talk must be about the power of things. Well, it is a very good question, and I shall be willing to answer you. And take my answer in brief, thus: First, Where the grace of God is in the heart, it causeth there a great outcry against sin. Secondly--

FAITHFUL: Nay, hold, let us consider of one at once. I think you should rather say, It shows itself by inclining the soul to abhor its sin.

TALKATIVE: Why, what difference is there between crying out against, and abhorring of sin?

FAITHFUL: Oh, a great deal. A man may cry out against sin of policy, but he cannot abhor it, but by virtue of a godly antipathy against it. I have heard many cry out against sin in the pulpit, who yet can abide it well enough in the heart, house, and conversation. Joseph's mistress cried out with a loud voice, as if she had been very holy; but she would willingly, notwithstanding that, have committed uncleanness with him. Some cry out against sin even as the mother cries out against her child in her lap, when she calleth it slut and naughty girl, and then falls to hugging and kissing it.

TALKATIVE: You lie at the catch, I perceive.[10]

FAITHFUL: No, not I; I am only for setting things right. But what is the second thing whereby you would prove a discovery of a work of grace in the heart?

TALKATIVE: Great knowledge of gospel mysteries.

FAITHFUL: This sign should have been first; but first or last, it is also false; for knowledge, great knowledge, may be obtained in the mysteries of the gospel, and yet no work of grace in the soul. Yea, if a man have all knowledge, he may yet be nothing, and so consequently be no child of God. When Christ said, "Do you know all these things?" and the disciples had answered, Yes; he addeth, "Blessed are ye if ye do them." He doth not lay the blessing in the knowing of them, but in the doing of them. For there is a knowledge that is not attended with doing: He that knoweth his masters will, and doeth it not. A man may know like an angel, and yet be no Christian, therefore your sign of it is not true. Indeed, to know is a thing that pleaseth talkers and boasters, but to do is that which pleaseth God. Not that the heart can be good without knowledge; for without that, the heart is naught. There is, therefore, knowledge and knowledge. Knowledge that resteth in the bare speculation of things; and knowledge that is accompanied with the grace of faith and love; which puts a man upon doing even the will of God from the heart: the first of these will serve the talker; but without the other the true Christian is not content. "Give me understanding, and I shall keep thy law; yea, I shall observe it with my whole heart."[11]

TALKATIVE: You lie at the catch again; this is not for edification.

FAITHFUL: Well, if you please, propound another sign how this work of grace discovereth itself where it is.

TALKATIVE: Not I, for I see we shall not agree.

FAITHFUL: Well, if you will not, will you give me leave to do it?

TALKATIVE: You may use your liberty.

FAITHFUL: A work of grace in the soul discovereth itself, either to him that hath it, or to standers by.

To him that hath it thus: It gives him conviction of sin, especially of the defilement of his nature and the sin of unbelief, (for the sake of which he is sure to be damned, if he findeth not mercy at God's hand, by

---

[10] To *lie at the catch* appears to mean: *you set a trap for me!*
[11] John 13:17; 1 Cor. 13; Ps. 119:34.

faith in Jesus Christ). This sight and sense of things worketh in him sorrow and shame for sin; he findeth, moreover, revealed in him the Saviour of the world, and the absolute necessity of closing with him for life, at the which he findeth hungerings and thirstings after him; to which hungerings, the promise is made. Now, according to the strength or weakness of his faith in his Saviour, so is his joy and peace, so is his love to holiness, so are his desires to know him more, and also to serve him in this world. But though I say it discovereth itself thus unto him, yet it is but seldom that he is able to conclude that this is a work of grace; because his corruptions now, and his abused reason, make his mind to misjudge in this matter; therefore, in him that hath this work, there is required a very sound judgement before he can, with steadiness, conclude that this is a work of grace.[12]

To others, it is thus discovered:

1. By an experimental[13] confession of his faith in Christ.[14]

2. By a life answerable to that confession; to wit, a life of holiness, heart-holiness, family-holiness (if he hath a family), and by conversation-holiness in the world which, in the general, teacheth him, inwardly, to abhor his sin, and himself for that, in secret; to suppress it in his family and to promote holiness in the world; not by talk only, as a hypocrite or talkative person may do, but by a practical subjection, in faith and love, to the power of the Word.[15] And now, Sir, as to this brief description of the work of grace, and also the discovery of it, if you have aught to object, object; if not, then give me leave to propound to you a second question.

TALKATIVE: Nay, my part is not now to object, but to hear; let me, therefore, have your second question.

FAITHFUL: It is this: Do you experience this first part of this description of it? And doth your life and conversation testify the same? Or standeth your religion in word or in tongue, and not in deed and truth? Pray, if you incline to answer me in this, say no more than you know the God above will say Amen to; and also nothing but what your conscience can justify you in; for not he that commendeth himself is approved, but whom the Lord commendeth.[16] Besides, to say I am thus and thus, when my conversation, and all my neighbours, tell me I lie, is great wickedness.

---

[12] John 16:8; Rom. 7:24; John 16:9; Mark 16:16; Ps. 38:18; Jer. 31:19; Gal. 2:16; Acts 4:12; Matt. 5:6; Rev. 21:6.
[13] *Experimental* here doesn't mean *experiment* as we would understand it so much as referring to one's personal experience.
[14] Rom. 10:10; Phil. 1:27; Matt. 5:19.
[15] John 14:15; Ps. 50:23; Job 42:5-6; Eze. 20:43.
[16] 2 Cor. 10:18.

TALKATIVE: Then Talkative at first began to blush; but, recovering himself, thus he replied: You come now to experience, to conscience, and God; and to appeal to him for justification of what is spoken. This kind of discourse I did not expect; nor am I disposed to give an answer to such questions, because I count not myself bound thereto, unless you take upon you to be a catechiser, and, though you should so do, yet I may refuse to make you my judge. But, I pray, will you tell me why you ask me such questions?

FAITHFUL: Because I saw you forward to talk, and because I knew not that you had aught else but notion. Besides, to tell you all the truth, I have heard of you, that you are a man whose religion lies in talk, and that your conversation gives this your mouth-profession the lie.

They say, you are a spot among Christians; and that religion fareth the worse for your ungodly conversation; that some have already stumbled at your wicked ways, and that more are in danger of being destroyed thereby; your religion, and an alehouse, and covetousness, and uncleanness, and swearing, and lying, and vain-company keeping will stand together. The proverb is true of you which is said of a whore, to wit, that she is a shame to all women; so are you a shame to all professors.

TALKATIVE: Since you are ready to take up reports and to judge so rashly as you do, I cannot but conclude you are some peevish or melancholy man, not fit to be discoursed with; and so adieu.

CHRISTIAN: Then came up Christian, and said to his brother, I told you how it would happen: your words and his lusts could not agree; he had rather leave your company than reform his life. But he is gone, as I said; let him go, the loss is no man's but his own; he has saved us the trouble of going from him; for he continuing (as I suppose he will do) as he is, he would have been but a blot in our company. Besides, the apostle says, "From such withdraw thyself."[17]

FAITHFUL: But I am glad we had this little discourse with him; it may happen that he will think of it again: however, I have dealt plainly with him, and so am clear of his blood, if he perisheth.

CHRISTIAN: You did well to talk so plainly to him as you did; there is but little of this faithful dealing with men now-a-days, and that makes religion to stink so in the nostrils of many, as it doth; for they are these talkative fools whose religion is only in word, and are debauched and vain in their conversation, that (being so much admitted into the fellowship of the godly) do puzzle the world, blemish Christianity, and grieve the

---

[17] 1 Tim. 6:5.

sincere. I wish that all men would deal with such as you have done: then should they either be made more conformable to religion, or the company of saints would be too hot for them.

Then did Faithful say,

> *How Talkative at first lifts up his plumes!*
> *How bravely doth he speak! How he presumes*
> *To drive down all before him! But so soon*
> *As Faithful talks of heart-work, like the moon*
> *That's past the full, into the wane he goes.*
> *And so will all, but he that HEART-WORK knows.*

WHAT WE COVERED IN WEEK EIGHT

Meeting Talkative and their conversation

Oh, Talkative!

There is so much to say about him, and yet so little. He is actually an important character (although it's easy just to wander past him). In fact, if you pay attention in your Christian life, you have likely met Talkative before, and I suspect you might meet him again one day.

I love the description we read of this man: he's a tall man who looks more handsome at a distance than he does up close.

Isn't that the truth? Those who are all talk fool others into thinking there is beauty there when there is not. The challenge with "Talkatives" in our lives is it is difficult to recognize the real problem as talkative people are good at their talk!

At one point, Talkative shares that he finds nothing more profitable or pleasant than talking about the things of God. What a beautiful statement! To talk about the things of God is a form of worship and is an amazing experience! But… of course, there must be more than talk, right?

When you meet someone who is all talk, it is often easy to be fooled for a long time, but not forever. As they speak, Faithful begins to catch Talkative and challenges him.

And here's where it all falls apart. Talkative is just as his name suggests. He is not interested in anything other than talking. He speaks of prayer and of being born again, but he only knows of them in conversation—never by experience.

Talkative is fake.

And when he is called on the issue, he attacks Faithful as being judgemental and avoids the issue.

Interestingly, this is the same response you will get three hundred plus years later.

The issue for Talkatives is the words do not reach their heart and no change of life takes place.

To be clear, we are not referring to spiritual growth as if this is simply a matter of *growing* in your faith. What we are speaking about here is a life that is never transformed by the grace of God. A life that continues to just… be… talk.

And three hundred years later, if you suggest to someone who is all talk that there needs to be a life change—if you suggest that if the Son of God is present and active in their life, such presence should affect their life—you will still today be called judgemental by all Talkatives.

But… isn't it good to hear the hope in Faithful's words as he speaks of the possibility of Talkative's repentance?

There is *always* hope with a God who changes lives!

Lord, I confess I have "talked" more than I have "lived". But I thank you for your grace in welcoming me in, changing my heart, and leading me closer to you! Strengthen me, please, to live more faithfully to you as I journey this path towards the day when I will see your face!
Amen

TALKING POINTS

1. Consider Faithful's challenge to Talkative. He says that heavenly knowledge of some things is a gift of God (spiritually discerned) which no man can attain on his own. That's interesting! We see this in 1 Corinthians 2:14. Now… what kinds of things are spiritually discerned?

2. It is easy when we go through a chapter like this to focus on identifying people around us who are Talkatives, but this book is not about pointing fingers at others, but about our own spiritual journeys. I suggest that maybe it's healthier for us to ask the following question: in what areas of my life might I be Talkative?

3. Consider Talkative's question, "Why, what difference is there between crying out against, and abhorring of sin?" Isn't it interesting that this man cannot see the difference between crying out against sin (talk) and an actual hating of sin (which should lead to repentance/change of life)! What can be done about this in our own lives?

4. It's uncomfortable to discuss the topic of sincere faith and transformation of our lives. On one hand, we sometimes want to point out that no one's perfect, therefore we should just never judge. On the other hand, we wonder if there is a genuine change in our lives or if we are just… *Talkative*. Perhaps two truths can encourage us. First, God desires perfection and holiness in us, but he is the One who brings that perfection and holiness about. That is a big part of grace. Second, we remember God is at work in a genuine believer, but he often takes his time. So, it's not a matter of living a life without failure, it's a matter of whether you are growing in your love for Christ and turning away from sin. Spend some time in prayer over this matter, trusting Christ that he is at work in your life, though we all stumble along the way.

5. Christian ends up declaring that when people like Talkative are admitted into the fellowship of the godly, the world is puzzled, Christianity is disgraced, and sincere pilgrims are upset. Here is the question: How does *your* life as someone in the fellowship of the godly appear to the world?[18]

6. How should we respond to someone like Talkative? Avoid simple answers like, "Just walk away!" or "I don't think we want to judge…" Take the time to kindly and graciously work through this matter.

---

[18] Note: it is important to notice that this question is not, "Do people outside the church *like* you?" Jesus tells us in John 15:18-25 that Christians are not guaranteed a life where people *like* us. This question has to do simply with how your life appears to those who do not know Jesus as their Lord and Saviour.

7. In Bunyan's words, he hopes his story *will make a traveller of thee*. How do you see yourself travelling this road to the Celestial City differently because of this week's reading? What change in heart, attitude, theology, or lifestyle do you believe God is calling you to as you seek to be the traveller he desires you be?

NOTE: As there are fewer questions this week, this might be a good opportunity for those working through this book as a group to discuss the chapter and the interactions of the characters a bit more. Talkative is a key character and is certainly worthy of more discussion.

9. Vanity Fair

Thus they went on talking of what they had seen by the way, and so made that way easy which would otherwise, no doubt, have been tedious to them; for now they went through a wilderness.

Now, when they were got almost quite out of this wilderness, Faithful chanced to cast his eye back, and espied one coming after them, and he knew him. "Oh!" said Faithful to his brother, "who comes yonder?"

Then Christian looked, and said, "It is my good friend Evangelist."

"Ay, and my good friend too," said Faithful, "for it was he that set me in the way to the gate."

Now was Evangelist come up to them, and thus saluted them:

EVANGELIST: Peace be with you, dearly beloved; and peace be to your helpers.

CHRISTIAN: Welcome, welcome, my good Evangelist, the sight of thy countenance brings to my remembrance thy ancient kindness and unwearied labouring for my eternal good.

FAITHFUL: And a thousand times welcome, said good Faithful. Thy company, O sweet Evangelist, how desirable it is to us poor pilgrims!

EVANGELIST: Then said Evangelist, How hath it fared with you, my friends, since the time of our last parting? What have you met with, and how have you behaved yourselves?

Then Christian and Faithful told him of all things that had happened to them in the way; and how, and with what difficulty, they had arrived at that place.

EVANGELIST: Right glad am I, said Evangelist, not that you have met with trials, but that you have been victors; and for that you have, notwithstanding many weaknesses, continued in the way to this very day.

I say, right glad am I of this thing, and that for mine own sake and yours. I have sowed, and you have reaped: and the day is coming when both he that sowed and they that reaped shall rejoice together; that is, if you hold out: "for in due season ye shall reap, if ye faint not." The crown is before you, and it is an incorruptible one; so run, that you may obtain it. Some there be that set out for this crown, and, after they have gone far for it, another comes in, and takes it from them: hold fast, therefore, that you have; let no man take your crown. You are not yet out of the gun-shot of the devil; you have not resisted unto blood, striving against sin; let the kingdom be always before you, and believe steadfastly concerning things that are invisible. Let nothing that is on this side the other world get within you; and, above all, look well to your own hearts, and to the lusts thereof, "for they are deceitful above all things, and desperately wicked;" set your faces like a flint; you have all power in heaven and earth on your side.[1]

CHRISTIAN: Then Christian thanked him for his exhortation; but told him, withal, that they would have him speak further to them for their help the rest of the way, and the rather, for that they well knew that he was a prophet and could tell them of things that might happen unto them, and also how they might resist and overcome them. To which request Faithful also consented. So Evangelist began as followeth:

EVANGELIST: My sons, you have heard, in the words of the truth of the gospel, that you must, through many tribulations, enter into the kingdom of heaven. And, again, that in every city bonds and afflictions abide in you; and therefore you cannot expect that you should go long on your pilgrimage without them, in some sort or other. You have found something of the truth of these testimonies upon you already, and more will immediately follow; for now, as you see, you are almost out of this wilderness, and therefore you will soon come into a town that you will by and by see before you; and in that town you will be hardly beset with enemies, who will strain hard but they will kill you; and be you sure that one or both of you must seal the testimony which you hold with blood; but be you faithful unto death, and the King will give you a crown of life.[2]

EVANGELIST cont.: He that shall die there, although his death will be unnatural, and his pain perhaps great, he will yet have the better of his fellow; not only because he will be arrived at the Celestial City soonest,

---

[1] John 4:36; Gal. 6:9; 1 Cor. 9:24-27; Heb. 12:4; Jer. 17:9; Rev. 3:11.
[2] Acts 14:22; 20:23; Rev. 2:10.

but because he will escape many miseries that the other will meet with in the rest of his journey. But when you are come to the town, and shall find fulfilled what I have here related, then remember your friend, and quit yourselves like men,[3] and commit the keeping of your souls to your God in well-doing, as unto a faithful Creator.

Then I saw in my dream, that when they were got out of the wilderness, they presently saw a town before them, and the name of that town is Vanity; and at the town there is a fair kept, called Vanity Fair: it is kept all the year long. It beareth the name of Vanity Fair because the town where it is kept is lighter than vanity; and, also because all that is there sold, or that cometh thither, is vanity. As is the saying of the wise, "all that cometh is vanity."[4]

This fair is no new-erected business, but a thing of ancient standing; I will show you the original of it.

Almost five thousand years agone, there were pilgrims walking to the Celestial City, as these two honest persons are, and Beelzebub, Apollyon, and Legion, with their companions, perceiving by the path that the pilgrims made, that their way to the city lay through this town of Vanity, they contrived here to set up a fair; a fair wherein should be sold all sorts of vanity, and that it should last all the year long. Therefore at this fair are all such merchandise sold, as houses, lands, trades, places, honours, preferments,[5] titles, countries, kingdoms, lusts, pleasures, and delights of all sorts, as whores, bawds,[6] wives, husbands, children, masters, servants, lives, blood, bodies, souls, silver, gold, pearls, precious stones, and what not.

And, moreover, at this fair there is at all times to be seen juggling cheats, games, plays, fools, apes, knaves, and rogues,[7] and that of every kind.

Here are to be seen, too, and that for nothing, thefts, murders, adulteries, false swearers, and that of a blood-red colour.[8]

And as in other fairs of less moment, there are the several rows and streets, under their proper names, where such and such wares are vended; so here likewise you have the proper places, rows, streets, (viz. countries

---

[3] The phrase *quit yourselves like men* essentially means to be courageous and to stand strong.
[4] Eccl. 1, 2:11 & 17, 11:8; Isa. 11:17.
[5] *Preferments* can mean *a promotion.*
[6] A *bawd* is *a woman in charge of a brothel.*
[7] *Knaves* and *rogues* refer to *scoundrels and dishonest people.*
[8] The reference to a blood-red colour seems to imply that much in the fair is the result of violence, leaving all a blood-red colour.

and kingdoms), where the wares of this fair are soonest to be found. Here is the Britain Row, the French Row, the Italian Row, the Spanish Row, the German Row, where several sorts of vanities are to be sold. But, as in other fairs, some one commodity is as the chief of all the fair, so the ware of Rome and her merchandise is greatly promoted in this fair; only our English nation, with some others, have taken a dislike thereat.

Now, as I said, the way to the Celestial City lies just through this town where this lusty fair is kept; and he that will go to the city, and yet not go through this town, must needs go out of the world. The Prince of princes himself, when here, went through this town to his own country, and that upon a fair day too; yea, and as I think, it was Beelzebub, the chief lord of this fair, that invited him to buy of his vanities; yea, would have made him lord of the fair, would he but have done him reverence as he went through the town. Yea, because he was such a person of honour, Beelzebub had him from street to street, and showed him all the kingdoms of the world in a little time, that he might, if possible, allure the Blessed One to cheapen and buy some of his vanities; but he had no mind to the merchandise, and therefore left the town, without laying out so much as one farthing upon these vanities. This fair, therefore, is an ancient thing, of long standing, and a very great fair.[9]

Now these pilgrims, as I said, must needs go through this fair. Well, so they did: but, behold, even as they entered into the fair, all the people in the fair were moved, and the town itself as it were in a hubbub about them; and that for several reasons:

First, the pilgrims were clothed with such kind of raiment as was diverse from the raiment of any that traded in that fair. The people, therefore, of the fair, made a great gazing upon them. Some said they were fools, some they were bedlams, and some they are outlandish men.[10]

Secondly, and as they wondered at their apparel, so they did likewise at their speech; for few could understand what they said; they naturally spoke the language of Canaan, but they that kept the fair were the men of this world; so that, from one end of the fair to the other, they seemed barbarians each to the other.

Thirdly, But that which did not a little amuse the merchandisers was, that these pilgrims set very light by all their wares; they cared not so much as to look upon them; and if they called upon them to buy, they would put their fingers in their ears, and cry, Turn away mine eyes from

---

⁹ 1 Cor. 5:10; Matt. 4:8, Luke 4:5-7.
¹⁰ 1 Cor. 2:7-8.

beholding vanity, and look upwards, signifying that their trade and traffic was in heaven.[11]

One chanced mockingly, beholding the carriage of the men, to say unto them, "What will ye buy?"

But they, looking gravely upon him, answered, "We buy the truth."[12]

At that there was an occasion taken to despise the men the more; some mocking, some taunting, some speaking reproachfully, and some calling upon others to smite them. At last things came to a hubbub and great stir in the fair, insomuch that all order was confounded.

Now was word presently brought to the great one of the fair, who quickly came down, and deputed some of his most trusty friends to take these men into examination, about whom the fair was almost overturned. So the men were brought to examination; and they that sat upon them, asked them whence they came, whither they went, and what they did there in such an unusual garb? The men told them that they were pilgrims and strangers in the world, and that they were going to their own country, which was the heavenly Jerusalem,[13] and that they had given no occasion to the men of the town, nor yet to the merchandisers, thus to abuse them, and to let them in their journey, except it was for that, when one asked them what they would buy, they said they would buy the truth. But they that were appointed to examine them did not believe them to be any other than bedlams and mad, or else such as came to put all things into a confusion in the fair. Therefore they took them and beat them, and besmeared them with dirt, and then put them into the cage, that they might be made a spectacle to all the men of the fair.

> *Behold Vanity Fair! the Pilgrims there*
> *Are chain'd and stand beside:*
> *Even so it was our Lord pass'd here,*
> *And on Mount Calvary died.*

There, therefore, they lay for some time, and were made the objects of any man's sport, or malice, or revenge, the great one of the fair laughing still at all that befell them. But the men being patient, and not rendering railing for railing, but contrariwise, blessing, and good words for bad, and kindness for injuries done, some men in the fair that were more observing,

---

[11] Ps. 119:37; Phil. 3:19-20.
[12] Prov. 23:23.
[13] Heb. 11:13-16.

and less prejudiced than the rest, began to check and blame the baser sort for their continual abuses done by them to the men; they, therefore, in angry manner, let fly at them again, counting them as bad as the men in the cage, and telling them that they seemed confederates, and should be made partakers of their misfortunes. The other replied that, for aught they could see, the men were quiet, and sober, and intended nobody any harm; and that there were many that traded in their fair that were more worthy to be put into the cage, yea, and pillory too, than were the men they had abused.

Thus, after divers words had passed on both sides, the men behaving themselves all the while very wisely and soberly before them, they fell to some blows among themselves, and did harm one to another. Then were these two poor men brought before their examiners again, and there charged as being guilty of the late hubbub that had been in the fair. So they beat them pitifully, and hanged irons upon them, and led them in chains up and down the fair, for an example and a terror to others, lest any should speak in their behalf, or join themselves unto them. But Christian and Faithful behaved themselves yet more wisely and received the ignominy and shame that was cast upon them, with so much meekness and patience, that it won to their side, though but few in comparison of the rest, several of the men in the fair. This put the other party yet into greater rage, insomuch that they concluded the death of these two men. Wherefore they threatened, that the cage nor irons should serve their turn, but that they should die, for the abuse they had done, and for deluding the men of the fair.

Then were they remanded to the cage again, until further order should be taken with them. So they put them in, and made their feet fast in the stocks.

Here, therefore, they called again to mind what they had heard from their faithful friend Evangelist and were the more confirmed in their way and sufferings by what he told them would happen to them. They also now comforted each other, that whose lot it was to suffer, even he should have the best of it; therefore each man secretly wished that he might have that preferment: but committing themselves to the all-wise disposal of Him that ruleth all things, with much content, they abode in the condition in which they were, until they should be otherwise disposed of.

Then a convenient time being appointed, they brought them forth to their trial, in order to their condemnation. When the time was come, they were brought before their enemies and arraigned. The judge's name was Lord Hate-good. Their indictment was one and the same in substance, though somewhat varying in form, the contents whereof were this:

"That they were enemies to and disturbers of their trade; that they
had made commotions and divisions in the town, and had won a party to
their own most dangerous opinions, in contempt of the law of their prince."

Then Faithful began to answer that he had only set himself against
that which hath set itself against Him that is higher than the highest. And,
said he, as for disturbance, I make none, being myself a man of peace; the
parties that were won to us, were won by beholding our truth and
innocence, and they are only turned from the worse to the better. And as
to the king you talk of, since he is Beelzebub, the enemy of our Lord, I defy
him and all his angels.

Then proclamation was made, that they that had aught to say for
their lord the king against the prisoner at the bar, should forthwith appear
and give in their evidence. So there came in three witnesses, to wit, Envy,
Superstition, and Pickthank. They were then asked if they knew the prisoner
at the bar; and what they had to say for their lord the king against him.

Then stood forth Envy, and said to this effect: "My Lord, I have
known this man a long time, and will attest upon my oath before this
honourable bench, that he is..."

JUDGE: Hold! Give him his oath. (So they sware him.) Then he
said:

ENVY: My Lord, this man, notwithstanding his plausible name, is
one of the vilest men in our country. He neither regardeth prince nor
people, law nor custom; but doth all that he can to possess all men with
certain of his disloyal notions, which he in the general calls principles of
faith and holiness. And, in particular, I heard him once myself affirm that
Christianity and the customs of our town of Vanity were diametrically
opposite and could not be reconciled. By which saying, my Lord, he doth
at once not only condemn all our laudable doings, but us in the doing of
them.

JUDGE: Then did the Judge say to him, Hast thou any more to
say?

ENVY: My Lord, I could say much more, only I would not be
tedious to the court. Yet, if need be, when the other gentlemen have given

in their evidence, rather than anything shall be wanting that will despatch him, I will enlarge my testimony against him. So he was bid to stand by.

Then they called Superstition, and bid him look upon the prisoner. They also asked, what he could say for their lord the king against him. Then they sware him; so he began.

SUPERSTITION: My Lord, I have no great acquaintance with this man, nor do I desire to have further knowledge of him; however, this I know, that he is a very pestilent fellow, from some discourse that, the other day, I had with him in this town; for then, talking with him, I heard him say, that our religion was naught, and such by which a man could by no means please God. Which sayings of his, my Lord, your Lordship very well knows, what necessarily thence will follow, to wit, that we do still worship in vain, are yet in our sins, and finally shall be damned; and this is that which I have to say.

Then was Pickthank[14] sworn, and bid say what he knew, in behalf of their lord the king, against the prisoner at the bar.

PICKTHANK: My Lord, and you gentlemen all, This fellow I have known of a long time, and have heard him speak things that ought not to be spoke; for he hath railed on our noble prince Beelzebub, and hath spoken contemptibly of his honourable friends, whose names are the Lord Old Man, the Lord Carnal Delight, the Lord Luxurious, the Lord Desire of Vain Glory, my old Lord Lechery,[15] Sir Having Greedy, with all the rest of our nobility; and he hath said, moreover, That if all men were of his mind, if possible, there is not one of these noblemen should have any longer a being in this town. Besides, he hath not been afraid to rail on you, my Lord, who are now appointed to be his judge, calling you an ungodly villain, with many other such like vilifying terms, with which he hath bespattered most of the gentry of our town.

When this Pickthank had told his tale, the Judge directed his speech to the prisoner at the bar, saying, Thou runagate,[16] heretic, and traitor, hast thou heard what these honest gentlemen have witnessed against thee?

FAITHFUL: May I speak a few words in my own defence?

---

[14] A *pickthank* is someone who meddles in other's affairs or tells people what they want to hear in order to gain favour.
[15] *Lechery* is *extreme sexual desire or lust.*
[16] A *runagate* is a *fugitive.*

JUDGE: Sirrah! Sirrah![17] Thou deservest to live no longer, but to be slain immediately upon the place; yet, that all men may see our gentleness towards thee, let us hear what thou, vile runagate, hast to say.

FAITHFUL:

1. I say, then, in answer to what Mr. Envy hath spoken, I never said aught but this, That what rule, or laws, or customs, or people were flat against the Word of God, are diametrically opposite to Christianity. If I have said amiss in this, convince me of my error, and I am ready here before you to make my recantation.

2. As to the second, to wit, Mr. Superstition, and his charge against me, I said only this, That in the worship of God there is required a Divine faith; but there can be no Divine faith without a Divine revelation of the will of God. Therefore, whatever is thrust into the worship of God that is not agreeable to Divine revelation, cannot be done but by a human faith, which faith will not be profitable to eternal life.

3. As to what Mr. Pickthank hath said, I say (avoiding terms, as that I am said to rail, and the like) that the prince of this town, with all the rabblement, his attendants, by this gentleman named, are more fit for a being in hell, than in this town and country: and so, the Lord have mercy upon me!

Then the Judge called to the jury (who all this while stood by, to hear and observe): "Gentlemen of the jury, you see this man about whom so great an uproar hath been made in this town. You have also heard what these worthy gentlemen have witnessed against him. Also you have heard his reply and confession. It lieth now in your breasts to hang him or save his life; but yet I think meet to instruct you into our law.

"There was an Act made in the days of Pharaoh the Great, servant to our prince, that lest those of a contrary religion should multiply and grow too strong for him, their males should be thrown into the river. There was also an Act made in the days of Nebuchadnezzar the Great, another of his servants, that whosoever would not fall down and worship his golden image, should be thrown into a fiery furnace. There was also an Act made in the days of Darius, that whoso, for some time, called upon any god but him, should be cast into the lions' den. Now the substance of these laws this rebel has broken, not only in thought (which is not to be borne), but also in word and deed; which must therefore needs be intolerable.[18]

---

[17] *Sirrah* is a term kind of like *Sir* but for those of lower status than you. It's more or less here a term of disrespect.
[18] Exo. 1:22; Dan. 3:6; Dan. 6.

"For that of Pharaoh, his law was made upon a supposition, to prevent mischief, no crime being yet apparent; but here is a crime apparent. For the second and third, you see he disputeth against our religion; and for the treason he hath confessed, he deserveth to die the death."

Then went the jury out, whose names were, Mr. Blind-man, Mr. No-good, Mr. Malice, Mr. Love-lust, Mr. Live-loose, Mr. Heady, Mr. High-mind, Mr. Enmity, Mr. Liar, Mr. Cruelty, Mr. Hate-light, and Mr. Implacable; who every one gave in his private verdict against him among themselves, and afterwards unanimously concluded to bring him in guilty before the Judge.

And first, among themselves, Mr. Blind-man, the foreman, said, I see clearly that this man is a heretic. Then said Mr. No-good, Away with such a fellow from the earth. Ay, said Mr. Malice, for I hate the very looks of him. Then said Mr. Love-lust, I could never endure him. Nor I, said Mr. Live-loose, for he would always be condemning my way. Hang him, hang him, said Mr. Heady. A sorry scrub,[19] said Mr. High-mind. My heart riseth against him, said Mr. Enmity. He is a rogue, said Mr. Liar. Hanging is too good for him, said Mr. Cruelty. Let us despatch him out of the way, said Mr. Hate-light. Then said Mr. Implacable, Might I have all the world given me, I could not be reconciled to him; therefore, let us forthwith bring him in guilty of death.

And so they did; therefore he was presently condemned to be had from the place where he was, to the place from whence he came, and there to be put to the most cruel death that could be invented.

They therefore brought him out, to do with him according to their law; and, first, they scourged him, then they buffeted him, then they lanced his flesh with knives; after that, they stoned him with stones, then pricked him with their swords; and, last of all, they burned him to ashes at the stake. Thus came Faithful to his end.

Thus came Faithful to his end.

Now I saw that there stood behind the multitude a chariot and a couple of horses, waiting for Faithful, who (so soon as his adversaries had despatched him) was taken up into it, and straightway was carried up through the clouds, with sound of trumpet, the nearest way to the Celestial Gate.

---

[19] A *scrub* is a *stunted tree or shrub*. A derogatory term.

Brave FAITHFUL, bravely done in word and deed;
Judge, witnesses, and jury have, instead
Of overcoming thee, but shown their rage:
When they are dead, thou'lt live from age to age.[20]

But as for Christian, he had some respite, and was remanded back to prison. So he there remained for a space; but He that overrules all things, having the power of their rage in his own hand, so wrought it about, that Christian for that time escaped them, and went his way. And as he went, he sang, saying

Well, Faithful, thou hast faithfully profest
Unto thy Lord; with whom thou shalt be blest,
When faithless ones, with all their vain delights,
Are crying out under their hellish plights:
Sing, Faithful, sing, and let thy name survive;
For though they kill'd thee, thou art yet alive!

Now I saw in my dream, that Christian went not forth alone, for there was one whose name was Hopeful (being made so by the beholding of Christian and Faithful in their words and behaviour, in their sufferings at the fair), who joined himself unto him, and, entering into a brotherly covenant, told him that he would be his companion. Thus, one died to bear testimony to the truth, and another rises out of his ashes, to be a companion with Christian in his pilgrimage. This Hopeful also told Christian, that there were many more of the men in the fair, that would take their time and follow after.

----

[20] In the New Heaven and New Earth {footnote from one edition}.

WHAT WE COVERED IN WEEK NINE

Personally, I find Vanity Fair a difficult section to read.

I think it's the stress of it.

In most other areas of the book, when Christian undergoes challenges, he merely has to stand up against it or make the right choice. This time, along with a few other sections of the book, he loses all control.

But isn't that often the way in our journey of faith?

However, let's not get ahead of ourselves.

Just before Vanity Fair, Christian and Faithful meet up with an old friend: Evangelist. This is strange, of course, because we often think of Evangelist as someone who should appear at the beginning of our journey, but who needs him after that, right? His job is to point out the simple gospel... then he moves on to someone else, right?

Evangelist, however, functions in the journey as someone who points them to the way of salvation, but also to offer direction and comfort along on the path. He is even referred to as a prophet.

Perhaps this is a reminder that we need those in our lives who set us on the right path and can remind us of where we're going and what we are about. Perhaps the message of grace and salvation is not just a message for us at the beginning... but a message for our entire lives.

What if the message of salvation, the message of the gospel, is not just about your ticket into heaven?

What if the message of the gospel involves Jesus's ongoing work of salvation in the form of growing, shaping, changing you to be more like Christ? What if it's a matter of growing in our faith and love for Jesus and our love and compassion for others?

Do you have an *Evangelist* in your life? Are you an *Evangelist* to anyone?

It is exciting at this point to recognize that the journey which started out for Christian as a man all alone, unsure of what to do, is now a journey with friends!

I think this is an encouragement to us to recognize that Jesus never saves us into a life of solitude. He saves us into a family. A church. An assembly. A congregation of people. We join countless others who have walked this road before us.

I remember years ago reading a man's statement about his faith. He declared something along the lines of, "It's me and Jesus. That's all I need!"

While I agree with the sentiment, and I assume and hope he did not mean to say he didn't need anyone else, I think it is all too common for Christians to think this path can be walked alone without serious consequences to our faith.

As I pastor, I would often find this kind of thing. Someone, typically disillusioned by the church, would decide that they didn't need church to spend time with Jesus. Such a move reveals a profound lack of understanding of community, faith, the body of Christ, and the nature of our salvation.

We are meant to walk this path in community with others. We need to be careful of those times in our lives when we're drawn away and be wary of the words that call out, "Walk alone. You don't need anyone else." Even when it's brought forward in spiritual language such as, "Jesus is all you need. Just you and Jesus," the Christian life is meant to be lived together.

We are meant to be in a community of faith. We are adopted into a family.[21]

Before Evangelist leaves, he gives a powerful encouragement to let the kingdom always be before them and believe with certainty and consistency the things that are yet unseen.

This is, of course, a big part of how we emerge victorious through trials—we keep our eyes on the prize, trusting the Lord for what He has promised.

Now, what's interesting here is that when they enter the town of Vanity Fair, the people look at them with disdain. And when Christian and Faithful are arrested, despite their kindness and maturity, they are accused and people desire that they be put to death.

---

[21] John 1:12; Gal. 4:4-5; Eph. 1:5.

Sometimes we think that if we act with love and kindness and if we follow Jesus, everything will work out well for us—a smooth life is guaranteed! Yet, the reality is, as the people of Vanity Fair hated Jesus, others around us will often hate his followers.[22]

And when it comes to Christian and Faithful, the more they act with maturity and kindness, the angrier people get.

It is often the way for us, if we follow Christ. We can be falsely accused of just about anything.

I remember a time in my life when, as a pastor, I experienced a series of personal attacks and accusations. The number of attacks grew and grew to the point where new ones or variations of old ones came at me once or twice a week. It was a time in my ministry that was difficult to maintain a mature, respectful, and loving response to people. Very difficult.

Now, while the Lord was gracious in giving me those around who could see through the lies and accusations, the truth was I had to rely on Jesus Christ. He *was* my vindication.

Wait… no! He *will* be my vindication! When we are going through the difficult times, we look forward to a day when Christ will say, "Well done, good and faithful servant."[23] He *will* be my vindication! But that day rarely comes before the end.

And for our friends in the story, after the accusations, after the trial, we come to the beautiful, yet painful, part of the journey where we see the chariot ready to take Faithful home. And when Faithful is taken, the angels carry him to victory to the sound of trumpets!

Faithful remained faithful until the end! Well done, good and faithful servant!

Whatever we face, my brothers and sisters, my family, remember what is yet to come. Remember that God is the rewarder of those who seek him.[24]

Lord, sometimes this path you have placed me on is painfully difficult, but the hope I have in you is set on someone who can never fail! I trust that no matter what comes, you will be true to me until that day I stand before you and hear the words, "Well done, good and faithful servant."
Amen

---

22 John. 15:18.
23 Matt. 25:21.
24 Heb. 11:6.

TALKING POINTS

1. Christianity was never meant to be a lone-wolf experience. If, however, someone were to believe in an "only me and Jesus" relationship rather than a healthy faith where Jesus saves you and brings you into a community, a family of believers, discuss how that will affect your attitude toward the following aspects of the Christian life:

> Joining a church; leaving a church; your attitude toward your pastor; encouraging others; dealing with your own sin and temptations; dealing with marital challenges; giving to the church; giving to the poor; giving to Christian ministries.

2. When you take the time to consider a lone-wolf approach to Christianity in these areas, would you describe that kind of life as filled with love or with self-centeredness?

3. How might the sin of others drive you to separate from the church or even keep your distance spiritually and relationally? How might your own sin drive you away? How might your own disappointments in others and in the church drive you away?

4. What would be a healthy way to work through the issue of sin that drives us from community (either our sin or other's)?

5. When Christian and Faithful meet with Evangelist, he tells them he is glad, not that they have met with trials, but that they have been victors. Have you ever spoken with someone about the trials they've gone through and been amazed at how Jesus carried them through and how they've been victors through their trials? Have you found your heart filled with gladness for their victory? If so, why do you think that is?

6. Evangelist, speaking of tribulations, says, "and therefore you cannot expect that you should go long on your pilgrimage without them." This, of course, is spoken of in John 15:18-20 and 1 Tim. 3:12. What should a godly attitude towards persecution and tribulation be? And what should a godly attitude towards other believers who are currently enduring persecution and tribulation be?

7. When Christian and Faithful enter Vanity Fair, we read they are besmeared with dirt. What does this mean in the allegory? What would this look like in real life?

8. Why do you think there was such an extreme desire among the people of Vanity Fair to abuse Christian and Faithful? Not just arrest them... not just push them out of the city... but to *abuse* them! Why such anger?

9. Christian and Faithful stood out among the people, not fitting in because of their strange clothing. This "strange clothing" is an image of setting aside the old life and putting on a life of purity in following Christ.[25] In real life, what does it actually mean—practically—to look so out of place because of your faith? How does the difference in your life show itself?[26]

10. In Scripture, clothes often represent your identity[27] in the sense of who you were before you met Christ and who you are now. You see this in our future hope of eternity in that we will be clothed with a new body and clothed with new clothes.[28] For the people of Vanity Fair, they could immediately tell that Christian and Faithful were different. First, is that a bad thing? Second, do you feel the pressure to look and act like those who don't know Christ? Third, do you feel pressure from the church, sometimes, to look exactly like the world? What is the path here that honours God?

---

[25] Eph. 4:22-24; Gal. 3:26-27.
[26] Let me caution you. It's easy to answer here with a simple, "be nice and loving," but everyone can be nice and loving. That's not an exclusively Christian trait. The question is, what makes a Christian stand out, either in a manner that draws people to Christ, or at times, upsets them as in the case of the people of Vanity Fair?
[27] Gal. 3:26-27.
[28] 1 Cor. 5:1-5; 15:50-55; Phil. 3:21; Rev. 3:4-5; 6:9-11; 7:13-15; 19:6-8.

11. The second thing which annoyed the people of Vanity Fair was Christian and Faithful's speech. What does this look like in real life? How should a believer's actual words stand out as different? And second, does this mean something more, something deeper, something more powerful than our choice of specific words? Does this have anything to do with the focus of our speech?

12. The third thing that upset the people of Vanity Fair—and the thing that annoyed the people the most—was that Christian and Faithful were not interested in the things sold in the markets. What might this look like in your life? Remember, this is all allegory, a picture for us of the Christian experience. So, what does this look like in real life?

13. When Christians speak of reaching out in the world to share our faith, the subtle push is sometimes to fit in, to look as much like everyone around us as possible, often in action, preference, and more. However, if you are too *unchanged* by Christ, then what really are you offering? Where is the line between your Christian faith making you so out of place that everyone finds it awkward and your Christian faith making so little difference in your life that it's not even noticed?

14. At first, in Vanity Fair, Christian and Faithful managed just fine. The people laughed at them and thought they were odd, but it was manageable. What specific response moved the crowd from merely being upset to being on the verge of a riot? And why did that response make such a difference?

15. I suspect we often look at trials as something to muscle our way through, to bear up under. But what does it mean to come through victorious? Did Faithful come through his final trial victorious? Do we see the result as victory? What about in our own lives? In the lives of loved ones?

16. When Christian and Faithful face the examiners, why do you think so many of the accusations were only partly true? And why do you think the trial had very little to do with Faithful's service to Jesus, but rather focused on his disdain for sin and rebellion?

17. I'm not a big fan of poetry as I can rarely connect with it, and I can't write it to save my life! But the poem in this section is powerful:

> *Behold Vanity Fair! the Pilgrims there*
> *Are chain'd and stand beside:*
> *Even so it was our Lord pass'd here,*
> *And on Mount Calvary died.*

17. *cont.* This poem comes just after the people of Vanity Fair put our pilgrims in a cage. Take a moment and read through John 15:18-22, Philippians 3:10, and Colossians 1:24. Pause and reflect on these passages and this poem a bit. What is the purpose of Christian and Faithful's suffering? Is there good in it, or is it all evil? What should our attitude be when we face such suffering?

18. When other believers are persecuted and lies come out about them to discredit them, how can you protect yourself from believing the lies? How can you distinguish the truth from a lie?

19. In Bunyan's words, he hopes his story *will make a traveller of thee.* How do you see yourself travelling this road to the Celestial City differently because of this week's reading? What change in heart, attitude, theology, or lifestyle do you believe God is calling you to as you seek to be the traveller he desires you be?

10. Hopeful

So I saw that quickly after they were got out of the fair, they overtook one that was going before them, whose name was By-ends: so they said to him, "What countryman, Sir? And how far go you this way?" He told them that he came from the town of Fair-speech, and he was going to the Celestial City (but told them not his name).

From Fair-speech! said Christian. Is there any good that lives there?[1]

BY-ENDS: Yes, said By-ends, I hope.

CHRISTIAN: Pray, Sir, what may I call you? said Christian.

BY-ENDS: I am a stranger to you, and you to me: if you be going this way, I shall be glad of your company; if not, I must be content.

CHRISTIAN: This town of Fair-speech, said Christian, I have heard of; and, as I remember, they say it is a wealthy place.

BY-ENDS: Yes, I will assure you that it is; and I have very many rich kindred there.

CHRISTIAN: Pray, who are your kindred there? If a man may be so bold.

BY-ENDS: Almost the whole town; and in particular, my Lord Turn-about, my Lord Time-server, my Lord Fair-speech, (from whose ancestors that town first took its name), also Mr. Smooth-man, Mr. Facing-both-ways, Mr. Any-thing; and the parson of our parish, Mr. Two-tongues, was my mother's own brother by father's side; and to tell you the truth, I

---

[1] Prov. 26:25.

am become a gentleman of good quality, yet my great-grandfather was but a waterman, looking one way and rowing another, and I got most of my estate by the same occupation.

CHRISTIAN: Are you a married man?

BY-ENDS: Yes, and my wife is a very virtuous woman, the daughter of a virtuous woman; she was my Lady Feigning's daughter, therefore she came of a very honourable family, and is arrived to such a pitch of breeding, that she knows how to carry it to all, even to prince and peasant. It is true we somewhat differ in religion from those of the stricter sort, yet but in two small points: first, we never strive against wind and tide; secondly, we are always most zealous when religion goes in his silver slippers;[2] we love much to walk with him in the street, if the sun shines, and the people applaud him.

Then Christian stepped a little aside to his fellow, Hopeful, saying, "It runs in my mind that this is one By-ends of Fair-speech; and if it be he, we have as very a knave in our company as dwelleth in all these parts."

Then said Hopeful, "Ask him; methinks he should not be ashamed of his name. So Christian came up with him again, and said, Sir, you talk as if you knew something more than all the world doth; and if I take not my mark amiss, I deem I have half a guess of you: Is not your name Mr. By-ends, of Fair-speech?"

BY-ENDS: This is not my name, but indeed it is a nick-name that is given me by some that cannot abide me: and I must be content to bear it as a reproach, as other good men have borne theirs before me.

CHRISTIAN: But did you never give an occasion to men to call you by this name?

BY-ENDS: Never, never! The worst that ever I did to give them an occasion to give me this name was, that I had always the luck to jump in my judgement with the present way of the times, whatever it was, and my chance was to get thereby; but if things are thus cast upon me, let me count them a blessing; but let not the malicious load me therefore with reproach.

CHRISTIAN: I thought, indeed, that you were the man that I heard of; and to tell you what I think, I fear this name belongs to you more properly than you are willing we should think it doth.

---

[2] This term seems to suggest that he likes religion when it's in fashion, when it's *cool* to be religious, but not when it's *uncool*.

BY-ENDS: Well, if you will thus imagine, I cannot help it; you shall find me a fair company-keeper, if you will still admit me your associate.

CHRISTIAN: If you will go with us, you must go against wind and tide; the which, I perceive, is against your opinion; you must also own religion in his rags, as well as when in his silver slippers; and stand by him, too, when bound in irons, as well as when he walketh the streets with applause.

BY-ENDS: You must not impose, nor lord it over my faith; leave me to my liberty, and let me go with you.

CHRISTIAN: Not a step further, unless you will do in what I propound as we.

Then said By-ends, "I shall never desert my old principles, since they are harmless and profitable. If I may not go with you, I must do as I did before you overtook me, even go by myself, until some overtake me that will be glad of my company."

Now I saw in my dream that Christian and Hopeful forsook him, and kept their distance before him; but one of them looking back, saw three men following Mr. By-ends, and behold, as they came up with him, he made them a very low conge;[3] and they also gave him a compliment. The men's names were Mr. Hold-the-world, Mr. Money-love, and Mr. Save-all; men that Mr. By-ends had formerly been acquainted with; for in their minority they were schoolfellows, and were taught by one Mr. Gripe-man, a schoolmaster in Love-gain, which is a market town in the county of Coveting, in the north. This schoolmaster taught them the art of getting, either by violence, cozenage,[4] flattery, lying, or by putting on the guise of religion; and these four gentlemen had attained much of the art of their master, so that they could each of them have kept such a school themselves.

Well, when they had, as I said, thus saluted each other, Mr. Money-love said to Mr. By-ends, "Who are they upon the road before us?" (for Christian and Hopeful were yet within view).

BY-ENDS: They are a couple of far countrymen, that, after their mode, are going on pilgrimage.

MONEY-LOVE: Alas! Why did they not stay, that we might have had their good company? For they, and we, and you, Sir, I hope, are all going on pilgrimage.

------

3 In this context, a low *conge* seems to be *a ceremonial bow.*
4 *Cozenage* means *deception; trickery.*

BY-ENDS: We are so, indeed; but the men before us are so rigid, and love so much their own notions, and do also so lightly esteem the opinions of others, that let a man be never so godly, yet if he jumps not with them in all things, they thrust him quite out of their company.

SAVE-ALL: That is bad, but we read of some that are righteous overmuch; and such men's rigidness prevails with them to judge and condemn all but themselves. But, I pray, what, and how many, were the things wherein you differed?

BY-ENDS: Why, they, after their headstrong manner, conclude that it is duty to rush on their journey all weathers; and I am for waiting for wind and tide. They are for hazarding all for God at a clap; and I am for taking all advantages to secure my life and estate. They are for holding their notions, though all other men are against them; but I am for religion in what, and so far as the times, and my safety, will bear it. They are for religion when in rags and contempt; but I am for him when he walks in his golden slippers, in the sunshine, and with applause.

HOLD-THE-WORLD: Ay, and hold you there still, good Mr. By-ends; for, for my part, I can count him but a fool, that, having the liberty to keep what he has, shall be so unwise as to lose it. Let us be wise as serpents; it is best to make hay when the sun shines; you see how the bee lieth still all winter, and bestirs her only when she can have profit with pleasure. God sends sometimes rain, and sometimes sunshine; if they be such fools to go through the first, yet let us be content to take fair weather along with us. For my part, I like that religion best that will stand with the security of God's good blessings unto us; for who can imagine, that is ruled by his reason, since God has bestowed upon us the good things of this life, but that he would have us keep them for his sake? Abraham and Solomon grew rich in religion. And Job says, that a good man shall lay up gold as dust. But he must not be such as the men before us, if they be as you have described them.

SAVE-ALL: I think that we are all agreed in this matter, and therefore there needs no more words about it.

MONEY-LOVE: No, there needs no more words about this matter, indeed; for he that believes neither Scripture nor reason (and you see we have both on our side) neither knows his own liberty, nor seeks his own safety.

BY-ENDS: My brethren, we are, as you see, going all on pilgrimage; and, for our better diversion from things that are bad, give me leave to propound unto you this question:

Suppose a man, a minister, or a tradesman, etc., should have an advantage lie before him, to get the good blessings of this life, yet so as that he can by no means come by them except, in appearance at least, he becomes extraordinarily zealous in some points of religion that he meddled not with before, may he not use these means to attain his end, and yet be a right honest man?

MONEY-LOVE: I see the bottom of your question; and, with these gentlemen's good leave, I will endeavour to shape you an answer. And first, to speak to your question as it concerns a minister himself: Suppose a minister, a worthy man, possessed but of a very small benefice, and has in his eye a greater, more fat, and plump by far; he has also now an opportunity of getting of it, yet so as by being more studious, by preaching more frequently and zealously, and, because the temper of the people requires it, by altering of some of his principles; for my part, I see no reason but a man may do this, (provided he has a call), ay, and more a great deal besides, and yet be an honest man. For why—

1. His desire of a greater benefice[5] is lawful, (this cannot be contradicted), since it is set before him by Providence; so then, he may get it, if he can, making no question for conscience sake.

2. Besides, his desire after that benefice makes him more studious, a more zealous preacher, etc., and so makes him a better man; yea, makes him better improve his parts, which is according to the mind of God.

3. Now, as for his complying with the temper of his people, by dissenting, to serve them, some of his principles, this argueth, (1) That he is of a self-denying, temper; (2) Of a sweet and winning deportment; and so (3) more fit for the ministerial function.

4. I conclude, then, that a minister that changes a small for a great, should not, for so doing, be judged as covetous; but rather, since he has improved in his parts and industry thereby, be counted as one that pursues his call, and the opportunity put into his hands to do good.

And now to the second part of the question, which concerns the tradesman you mentioned. Suppose such a one to have but a poor employ in the world, but by becoming religious, he may mend his market, perhaps get a rich wife, or more and far better customers to his shop; for my part, I see no reason but that this may be lawfully done. For why

---

[5] A *benefice* would be a position in a church (pastor/vicar), but with benefits or income attached, such as property or income.

1. To become religious is a virtue, by what means soever a man becomes so.

2. Nor is it unlawful to get a rich wife, or more custom to my shop.

3. Besides, the man that gets these by becoming religious, gets that which is good, of them that are good, by becoming good himself; so then here is a good wife, and good customers, and good gain, and all these by becoming religious, which is good; therefore, to become religious, to get all these, is a good and profitable design.

This answer, thus made by this Mr. Money-love to Mr. By-ends's question, was highly applauded by them all; wherefore they concluded upon the whole, that it was most wholesome and advantageous. And because, as they thought, no man was able to contradict it, and because Christian and Hopeful were yet within call, they jointly agreed to assault them with the question as soon as they overtook them; and the rather because they had opposed Mr. By-ends before. So they called after them, and they stopped, and stood still till they came up to them; but they concluded, as they went, that not Mr. By-ends, but old Mr. Hold-the-world, should propound the question to them, because, as they supposed, their answer to him would be without the remainder of that heat that was kindled betwixt Mr. By-ends and them, at their parting a little before.

So they came up to each other, and after a short salutation, Mr. Hold-the-world propounded the question to Christian and his fellow, and bid them to answer it if they could.

CHRISTIAN: Then said Christian, Even a babe in religion may answer ten thousand such questions. For if it be unlawful to follow Christ for loaves, (as it is in the sixth of John), how much more abominable is it to make of him and religion a stalking-horse[6] to get and enjoy the world! Nor do we find any other than heathens, hypocrites, devils, and witches, that are of this opinion.

1. Heathens; for when Hamor and Shechem had a mind to the daughter and cattle of Jacob, and saw that there was no way for them to come at them, but by becoming circumcised, they say to their companions, If every male of us be circumcised, as they are circumcised, shall not their cattle, and their substance, and every beast of theirs, be ours? Their daughter and their cattle were that which they sought to obtain, and their

---

[6] A *stalking-horse* is a false pretext, a deceptive screen that you put up to fool people about your real intentions or goals. Essentially, he is a *pretender*.

religion the stalking-horse they made use of to come at them. Read the whole story.[7]

2. The hypocritical Pharisees were also of this religion; long prayers were their pretence, but to get widows' houses was their intent; and greater damnation was from God their judgement.[8]

3. Judas the devil was also of this religion; he was religious for the bag, that he might be possessed of what was therein; but he was lost, cast away, and the very son of perdition.[9]

4. Simon the witch was of this religion too; for he would have had the Holy Ghost, that he might have got money therewith; and his sentence from Peter's mouth was according.[10]

5. Neither will it out of my mind, but that that man that takes up religion for the world, will throw away religion for the world; for so surely as Judas resigned the world in becoming religious, so surely did he also sell religion and his Master for the same. To answer the question, therefore, affirmatively, as I perceive you have done, and to accept of, as authentic, such answer, is both heathenish, hypocritical, and devilish; and your reward will be according to your works.[11]

Then they stood staring one upon another, but had not wherewith to answer Christian. Hopeful also approved of the soundness of Christian's answer; so there was a great silence among them. Mr. By-ends and his company also staggered and kept behind, that Christian and Hopeful might outgo them.

Then said Christian to his fellow, "If these men cannot stand before the sentence of men, what will they do with the sentence of God? And if they are mute when dealt with by vessels of clay, what will they do when they shall be rebuked by the flames of a devouring fire?"

---

[7] Gen. 34:20-23.
[8] Luke 20:46-47.
[9] John 12:6; 17:12.
[10] Acts 8:19-22.
[11] 2 Cor. 5:10.

WHAT WE COVERED IN WEEK TEN

Meeting By-ends and the others

In this part of our journey, we meet a nameless man.

Actually, we learn his name, but at first, he's unwilling to tell Christian and Hopeful who he is. Instead, he dances around the topic.

When he's finally identified… confronted with his name, By-Ends says it's a nickname given by those who cannot "abide" him or can't stand to be around him, and he bears the unfortunate nickname unjustly, even so far as to say that he carries it like others of integrity who have been falsely accused. What's interesting is that he's not only entirely unashamed of his actions (of always moving with the crowd), but he also just can't seem to see that he's worthy of the name, "Mr. By-Ends".

He then, when challenged to follow Christ through good times and bad times, brings it back to a matter of personal liberty, as if following Christ only when it's immediately beneficial is a good thing and entirely Christ-worthy.

In light of Christian's recent trial, it's shocking to meet a man who is only willing to follow a form of faith which costs him nothing. Imagine that—you have just lost your friend because he stood for his faith in Jesus Christ until the end, and right after you meet someone who expects never to have to suffer or pay any price whatsoever for his faith!

He's after an easy road—a road leading to gain!

It's no surprise that Christian quickly calls By-Ends on his attitude and declares that this journey of faith is costly.

Perhaps it's a good time to be reminded of the parable of the sower and the seed.[12] One kind of seed lands on rocky soil and grows up quickly, having no root. The moment the sun comes out, it fades away. This seed is By-Ends!

---

[12] Mat. 13.

By-Ends is also somewhat like Pliable,[13] only he seems to have more success than Pliable ever did.

And with a "flexible" faith, By-Ends is content to stick with his way of doing faith *and* travel with Christian and Hopeful.

Is it any surprise that Christian will have none of this?

Isn't it interesting that By-Ends accuses Christian of being rigid and not accepting the opinions of others? When challenged, he turns to attack. Much of what he says is true, but like the words of Satan, the truth is often polluted by just enough of a lie to make it deception. I believe my gramma used to say, "Deception is carried on the wings of truth."

Notice as well that By-End's reaction is similar to the reaction of the people of Vanity Fair. Sure, they had the ability to arrest and kill, but By-Ends reacts with upset at any challenge to his way of life. Christian and Hopeful's very lives are an indictment against those who do not wish to pay the price of following Christ.

So, Christian and Hopeful leave him behind, and By-Ends is quickly joined by others. It's no surprise, actually, because a gospel of gain is a very attractive gospel, presenting itself as deeply spiritual, appearing to be driven by faith in God's goodness and power.

But in the end, these men are missing Christ. At the heart of their belief is a selfish desire for gain.

Lord, in light of the promise of eternity, any cost here in this life is so small, although I find that truth is easy to forget. Remind me of your grace and your promises of eternity as I journey towards the beautiful eternal home you've prepared for me.
Amen

---

[13] Pliable was one of the two men (along with Obstinate) at the beginning of our journey who chased after Christian from the City of Destruction to convince Christian to return home.

TALKING POINTS

1. Consider Christian's refusal to walk with By-Ends. Remember, this story is an allegory, which means *walking* does not refer to actual physical walking but is a metaphor for living the Christian life. At what point is it necessary to refuse to live your Christian life with someone who will not truly follow Christ? What does this look like?

2. Have there been times in your Christian walk when it has been harmful to keep company with others who claim to know Christ, but seek only their own benefit?

3. Consider Ephesians 20:28-25, Philippians 3:17-21, and Matthew 7:13-23. Based on what you read here, is it possible that By-Ends and his friends are wolves?[14]

---

[14] The Scriptural concept of a *wolf* is many things, but simply put, a wolf comes into the church pretending to be a true believer but comes in to devour. In a church setting, this often looks like someone who comes in and teaches a different gospel or truth than what we find in Scripture, they gather people to themselves, create their own following, and deceive people. They will invariably stand opposed to the godly shepherd (pastor) of the church on one level or another.

4. If By-Ends and his friends could continue to walk the path without guilt, holding onto a belief that so clearly goes against what Christ has taught us, what does that suggest about their spiritual state? When Jesus tells us that the Holy Spirit convicts the world of sin,[15] and the Holy Spirit is in us,[16] what does that suggest about these men?[17]

5. Consider Mr. By-End's description of Christian and Hopeful:

> ...the men before us are so rigid, and love so much their own notions, and do also so lightly esteem the opinions of others, that let a man be never so godly, yet if he jumps not with them in all things, they thrust him quite out of their company.

What does this tell you about how people will speak of you when you follow Christ?

6. Notice that Money-Love believes they have both Scripture and reason on their side of the argument. What does this tell you about those who have bought into a lie, any lie? What does this tell you about yourself? Is it possible you have bought into false beliefs about God, faith, life, and more, but you have justified your false beliefs with Scripture? If so, can you put your finger on what beliefs are affected?

---

[15] John 16:8.
[16] Eph. 1:13-14.
[17] I recognize this is a *very* leading question, but it is a truth that needs to be covered. Often we don't like to think in terms of this kind of thing, but it is important to recognize that there will be fruit in true believers. Consider Matt. 7:17-20.

7. Money-Love argues a pastor could pursue a greater position by adjusting his beliefs and that would be evidence that he is self-denying and therefore more fit for the ministerial position. Spend a few minutes thinking and discussing what might bring someone to reason this way.

8. Have there been times in your life when you, like By-Ends and his friends, have only followed Christ while it's been easy?

9. In Bunyan's words, he hopes his story *will make a traveller of thee*. How do you see yourself travelling this road to the Celestial City differently because of this week's reading? What change in heart, attitude, theology, or lifestyle do you believe God is calling you to as you seek to be the traveller he desires you be?

11. Doubting Castle

Then Christian and Hopeful outwent them again, and went till they came to a delicate plain called Ease, where they went with much content; but that plain was but narrow, so they were quickly got over it. Now at the further side of that plain was a little hill called Lucre,[1] and in that hill a silver mine, which some of them that had formerly gone that way, because of the rarity of it, had turned aside to see; but going too near the brink of the pit, the ground being deceitful under them, broke, and they were slain; some also had been maimed there, and could not, to their dying day, be their own men again.

Then I saw in my dream, that a little off the road, over against the silver mine, stood Demas (gentlemanlike) to call to passengers to come and see; who said to Christian and his fellow, "Ho! turn aside hither, and I will show you a thing."

CHRISTIAN: What thing so deserving as to turn us out of the way to see it?

DEMAS: Here is a silver mine, and some digging in it for treasure. If you will come, with a little pains you may richly provide for yourselves.

HOPEFUL: Then said Hopeful, Let us go see.

CHRISTIAN: Not I, said Christian, I have heard of this place before now; and how many have there been slain; and besides that, treasure is a snare to those that seek it; for it hindereth them in their pilgrimage.

---

[1] *Lucre* is a word for money, but especially for money gained through improper means.

Then Christian called to Demas, saying, "Is not the place dangerous? Hath it not hindered many in their pilgrimage?"[2]

DEMAS: Not very dangerous, except to those that are careless, (but withal, he blushed as he spake).

CHRISTIAN: Then said Christian to Hopeful, Let us not stir a step, but still keep on our way.

HOPEFUL: I will warrant you, when By-ends comes up, if he hath the same invitation as we, he will turn in thither to see.

CHRISTIAN: No doubt thereof, for his principles lead him that way, and a hundred to one but he dies there.

DEMAS: Then Demas called again, saying, But will you not come over and see?

CHRISTIAN: Then Christian roundly answered, saying, Demas, thou art an enemy to the right ways of the Lord of this way, and hast been already condemned for thine own turning aside, by one of His Majesty's judges;[3] and why seekest thou to bring us into the like condemnation? Besides, if we at all turn aside, our Lord and King will certainly hear thereof, and will there put us to shame, where we would stand with boldness before him.

Demas cried again, that he also was one of their fraternity; and that if they would tarry a little, he also himself would walk with them.

CHRISTIAN: Then said Christian, What is thy name? Is it not the same by the which I have called thee?

DEMAS: Yes, my name is Demas; I am the son of Abraham.

CHRISTIAN: I know you; Gehazi was your great-grandfather, and Judas your father; and you have trod in their steps.[4] It is but a devilish prank that thou usest; thy father was hanged for a traitor, and thou deservest no better reward. Assure thyself, that when we come to the King, we will do him word of this thy behaviour. Thus they went their way.

By this time By-ends and his companions were come again within sight, and they, at the first beck, went over to Demas. Now, whether they fell into the pit by looking over the brink thereof, or whether they went down to dig, or whether they were smothered in the bottom by the damps

---

[2] Hos. 14:8.
[3] 2 Tim. 4:10.
[4] 2 Kings 5:20-27; Matt. 26:14,15; 27:1-5.

that commonly arise, of these things I am not certain; but this I observed, that they never were seen again in the way. Then sang Christian:

> *By-ends and silver Demas both agree;*
> *One calls, the other runs, that he may be*
> *A sharer in his lucre; so these do*
> *Take up in this world, and no further go.*

Now I saw that, just on the other side of this plain, the pilgrims came to a place where stood an old monument, hard by the highway side, at the sight of which they were both concerned, because of the strangeness of the form thereof; for it seemed to them as if it had been a woman transformed into the shape of a pillar; here, therefore they stood looking, and looking upon it, but could not for a time tell what they should make thereof.

At last Hopeful espied written above the head thereof, a writing in an unusual hand; but he being no scholar, called to Christian (for he was learned) to see if he could pick out the meaning; so he came, and after a little laying of letters together, he found the same to be this, "Remember Lot's Wife." So, he read it to his fellow; after which they both concluded that that was the pillar of salt into which Lot's wife was turned, for her looking back with a covetous heart, when she was going from Sodom for safety.[5] Which sudden and amazing sight gave them occasion of this discourse.

CHRISTIAN: Ah, my brother! this is a seasonable sight; it came opportunely to us after the invitation which Demas gave us to come over to view the Hill Lucre; and had we gone over, as he desired us, and as thou wast inclining to do, my brother, we had, for aught I know, been made ourselves like this woman, a spectacle for those that shall come after to behold.

HOPEFUL: I am sorry that I was so foolish, and am made to wonder that I am not now as Lot's wife; for wherein was the difference betwixt her sin and mine? She only looked back; and I had a desire to go see. Let grace be adored, and let me be ashamed that ever such a thing should be in mine heart.

CHRISTIAN: Let us take notice of what we see here, for our help for time to come. This woman escaped one judgement, for she fell not by the destruction of Sodom; yet she was destroyed by another, as we see she is turned into a pillar of salt.

---

[5] Gen. 19:26.

HOPEFUL: True; and she may be to us both caution and example; caution, that we should shun her sin; or a sign of what judgement will overtake such as shall not be prevented by this caution; so Korah, Dathan, and Abiram, with the two hundred and fifty men that perished in their sin, did also become a sign or example to others to beware.[6] But above all, I muse at one thing, to wit, how Demas and his fellows can stand so confidently yonder to look for that treasure, which this woman, but for looking behind her after, (for we read not that she stepped one foot out of the way) was turned into a pillar of salt; especially since the judgement which overtook her did make her an example, within sight of where they are; for they cannot choose but see her, did they but lift up their eyes.

CHRISTIAN: It is a thing to be wondered at, and it argueth that their hearts are grown desperate in the case; and I cannot tell who to compare them to so fitly, as to them that pick pockets in the presence of the judge, or that will cut purses under the gallows. It is said of the men of Sodom, that they were sinners exceedingly, because they were sinners before the Lord, that is, in his eyesight, and notwithstanding the kindnesses that he had showed them; for the land of Sodom was now like the garden of Eden heretofore.[7] This, therefore, provoked him the more to jealousy, and made their plague as hot as the fire of the Lord out of heaven could make it. And it is most rationally to be concluded, that such, even such as these are, that shall sin in the sight, yea, and that too in despite of such examples that are set continually before them, to caution them to the contrary, must be partakers of severest judgements.

HOPEFUL: Doubtless thou hast said the truth; but what a mercy is it, that neither thou, but especially I, am not made myself this example! This ministereth occasion to us to thank God, to fear before him, and always to remember Lot's wife.

I saw, then, that they went on their way to a pleasant river; which David the king called "the river of God," but John, "the river of the water of life."[8] Now their way lay just upon the bank of the river; here, therefore, Christian and his companion walked with great delight; they drank also of the water of the river, which was pleasant, and enlivening to their weary spirits: besides, on the banks of this river, on either side, were green trees, that bore all manner of fruit; and the leaves of the trees were good for medicine; with the fruit of these trees they were also much delighted; and the leaves they eat to prevent surfeits,[9] and other diseases that are incident

---

[6] Num. 26:9, 10.
[7] Gen. 13:10, 13.
[8] Ps. 65:9; Rev. 22; Ezek. 47.
[9] *Surfeits* means *an excessive amount of something.*

to those that heat their blood by travels. On either side of the river was also a meadow, curiously beautified with lilies, and it was green all the year long. In this meadow they lay down and slept; for here they might lie down safely. When they awoke, they gathered again of the fruit of the trees, and drank again of the water of the river, and then lay down again to sleep.[10] Thus they did several days and nights. Then they sang:

> *Behold ye how these crystal streams do glide,*
> *To comfort pilgrims by the highway side;*
> *The meadows green, beside their fragrant smell,*
> *Yield dainties for them; and he that can tell*
> *What pleasant fruit, yea, leaves, these trees do yield,*
> *Will soon sell all, that he may buy this field.*

So when they were disposed to go on (for they were not, as yet, at their journey's end), they ate and drank, and departed.

Now, I beheld in my dream, that they had not journeyed far, but the river and the way for a time parted; at which they were not a little sorry; yet they durst not go out of the way. Now the way from the river was rough, and their feet tender, by reason of their travels; so the souls of the pilgrims were much discouraged because of the way.[11] Wherefore, still as they went on, they wished for better way.

Now, a little before them, there was on the left hand of the road a meadow, and a stile[12] to go over into it; and that meadow is called By-path Meadow. Then said Christian to his fellow, "If this meadow lieth along by our wayside, let us go over into it." Then he went to the stile to see, and behold, a path lay along by the way, on the other side of the fence. "It is according to my wish," said Christian. "Here is the easiest going; come, good Hopeful, and let us go over."

HOPEFUL: But how if this path should lead us out of the way?

CHRISTIAN: That is not like, said the other. Look, doth it not go along by the wayside?

So Hopeful, being persuaded by his fellow, went after him over the stile. When they were gone over, and were got into the path, they found it very easy for their feet; and withal, they, looking before them, espied a man walking as they did (and his name was Vain-confidence); so they called after him, and asked him whither that way led.

---

[10] Ps. 23:2; Isa. 14:30.
[11] Num. 21:4.
[12] A *stile* is a set of steps over a wall or fence.

He said, "To the Celestial Gate."

"Look," said Christian, "did not I tell you so? By this you may see we are right."

So they followed, and he went before them. But, behold, the night came on, and it grew very dark; so that they that were behind and lost the sight of him that went before.

He, therefore, that went before, (Vain-confidence by name), not seeing the way before him, fell into a deep pit,[13] which was on purpose there made, by the Prince of those grounds, to catch vain-glorious fools withal, and was dashed in pieces with his fall.

Now Christian and his fellow heard him fall. So, they called to know the matter, but there was none to answer, only they heard a groaning.

Then said Hopeful, "Where are we now?"

Then was his fellow silent, as mistrusting that he had led him out of the way; and now it began to rain, and thunder, and lightning in a very dreadful manner; and the water rose amain.[14]

Then Hopeful groaned in himself, saying, "Oh, that I had kept on my way!"

CHRISTIAN: Who could have thought that this path should have led us out of the way?

HOPEFUL: I was afraid on it at the very first, and therefore gave you that gentle caution. I would have spoken plainer, but that you are older than I.

CHRISTIAN: Good brother, be not offended; I am sorry I have brought thee out of the way, and that I have put thee into such imminent danger; pray, my brother, forgive me; I did not do it of an evil intent.

HOPEFUL: Be comforted, my brother, for I forgive thee; and believe, too, that this shall be for our good.

CHRISTIAN: I am glad I have with me a merciful brother; but we must not stand thus: let us try to go back again.

HOPEFUL: But, good brother, let me go before.

---

[13] Isa. 9:16.
[14] *Amain* means *quickly or forcefully.*

CHRISTIAN: No, if you please, let me go first, that if there be any danger, I may be first therein, because by my means we are both gone out of the way.

HOPEFUL: No, said Hopeful, you shall not go first; for your mind being troubled may lead you out of the way again.

Then, for their encouragement, they heard the voice of one saying, "Set thine heart toward the highway, even the way which thou wentest; turn again."[15] But by this time the waters were greatly risen, by reason of which the way of going back was very dangerous. (Then I thought that it is easier going out of the way, when we are in, than going in when we are out.) Yet they adventured to go back, but it was so dark, and the flood was so high, that in their going back they had like to have been drowned nine or ten times.

Neither could they, with all the skill they had, get again to the stile that night. Wherefore, at last, lighting under a little shelter, they sat down there until the daybreak; but, being weary, they fell asleep.

Now there was, not far from the place where they lay, a castle called Doubting Castle, the owner whereof was Giant Despair; and it was in his grounds they now were sleeping: wherefore he, getting up in the morning early, and walking up and down in his fields, caught Christian and Hopeful asleep in his grounds. Then, with a grim and surly voice, he bid them awake; and asked them whence they were, and what they did in his grounds. They told him they were pilgrims, and that they had lost their way. Then said the Giant, "You have this night trespassed on me, by trampling in and lying on my grounds, and therefore you must go along with me." So, they were forced to go, because he was stronger than they. They also had but little to say, for they knew themselves in a fault.

The Giant, therefore, drove them before him, and put them into his castle, into a very dark dungeon, nasty and stinking to the spirits of these two men.[16] Here, then, they lay from Wednesday morning till Saturday night, without one bit of bread, or drop of drink, or light, or any to ask how they did; they were, therefore, here in evil case, and were far from friends and acquaintance.

Now in this place Christian had double sorrow, because it was through his unadvised counsel that they were brought into this distress.

---

[15] Jer. 31:21.
[16] Ps. 88:18.

Now, Giant Despair had a wife, and her name was Diffidence.[17] So, when he was gone to bed, he told his wife what he had done; to wit, that he had taken a couple of prisoners and cast them into his dungeon for trespassing on his grounds. Then he asked her also what he had best to do further to them. So, she asked him what they were, whence they came, and whither they were bound; and he told her. Then she counselled him that when he arose in the morning he should beat them without any mercy.

So, when he arose, he getteth him a grievous crab-tree cudgel,[18] and goes down into the dungeon to them, and there first falls to rating[19] of them as if they were dogs, although they never gave him a word of distaste. Then he falls upon them, and beats them fearfully, in such sort that they were not able to help themselves, or to turn them upon the floor. This done, he withdraws and leaves them there to condole their misery and to mourn under their distress.

So, all that day they spent the time in nothing but sighs and bitter lamentations. The next night, she, talking with her husband about them further, and understanding they were yet alive, did advise him to counsel them to make away themselves.

So, when morning was come, he goes to them in a surly manner as before, and perceiving them to be very sore with the stripes that he had given them the day before, he told them, that since they were never like to come out of that place, their only way would be forthwith to make an end of themselves, either with knife, halter, or poison, for why, said he, should you choose life, seeing it is attended with so much bitterness? But they desired him to let them go. With that he looked ugly upon them, and, rushing to them, had doubtless made an end of them himself, but that he fell into one of his fits, (for he sometimes, in sunshiny weather, fell into

---

[17] The word *diffidence* today means a kind of shyness that comes as a result of lack of self-confidence, but when this was written it appears to have meant a lack of trust or even a lack of faith. A strange name, perhaps, for the wife of a Giant, but perhaps appropriate for the wife of despair.

[18] It was once common to use crab-tree wood for sticks and cudgels as it was strong, hard, knotty, and the bark could be quite rough. I don't think I'd like to be hit with a cudgel, but a crab-tree cudgel adds misery to an already horrible experience. A cudgel is a short stick used as a club for beating people.

[19] To *rate* them in this context means *to reprimand them or chew them out.*

fits), and lost for a time the use of his hand; wherefore he withdrew, and left them as before, to consider what to do. Then did the prisoners consult between themselves whether it was best to take his counsel or no; and thus they began to discourse:

CHRISTIAN: Brother, said Christian, what shall we do? The life that we now live is miserable. For my part I know not whether is best, to live thus, or to die out of hand. "My soul chooseth strangling rather than life," and the grave is more easy for me than this dungeon.[20] Shall we be ruled by the Giant?

HOPEFUL: Indeed, our present condition is dreadful, and death would be far more welcome to me than thus for ever to abide; but yet, let us consider, the Lord of the country to which we are going hath said, Thou shalt do no murder: no, not to another man's person; much more, then, are we forbidden to take his counsel to kill ourselves. Besides, he that kills another, can but commit murder upon his body; but for one to kill himself is to kill body and soul at once. And, moreover, my brother, thou talkest of ease in the grave; but hast thou forgotten the hell, for certain the murderers go? "For no murderer hath eternal life."[21] And let us consider, again, that all the law is not in the hand of Giant Despair. Others, so far as I can understand, have been taken by him, as well as we; and yet have escaped out of his hand. Who knows, but the God that made the world may cause that Giant Despair may die? or that, at some time or other, he may forget to lock us in? or that he may, in a short time, have another of his fits before us, and may lose the use of his limbs? and if ever that should come to pass again, for my part, I am resolved to pluck up the heart of a man, and to try my utmost to get from under his hand. I was a fool that I did not try to do it before; but, however, my brother, let us be patient, and endure a while. The time may come that may give us a happy release; but let us not be our own murderers.

With these words, Hopeful at present did moderate the mind of his brother; so, they continued together (in the dark) that day, in their sad and doleful condition.

Well, towards evening, the Giant goes down into the dungeon again, to see if his prisoners had taken his counsel; but when he came there, he found them alive; and truly, alive was all; for now, what for want of bread and water, and by reason of the wounds they received when he beat them, they could do little but breathe. But, I say, he found them alive; at which he

---

[20] Job 7:15.
[21] 1 John 3:15.

fell into a grievous rage, and told them that, seeing they had disobeyed his counsel, it should be worse with them than if they had never been born.

At this they trembled greatly, and I think that Christian fell into a swoon; but, coming a little to himself again, they renewed their discourse about the Giant's counsel; and whether yet they had best to take it or no. Now Christian again seemed to be for doing it, but Hopeful made his second reply as followeth:

HOPEFUL: My brother, said he, rememberest thou not how valiant thou hast been heretofore? Apollyon could not crush thee, nor could all that thou didst hear, or see, or feel, in the Valley of the Shadow of Death. What hardship, terror, and amazement hast thou already gone through! And art thou now nothing but fear! Thou seest that I am in the dungeon with thee, a far weaker man by nature than thou art; also, this Giant has wounded me as well as thee, and hath also cut off the bread and water from my mouth; and with thee I mourn without the light. But let us exercise a little more patience; remember how thou playedst the man at Vanity Fair, and wast neither afraid of the chain, nor cage, nor yet of bloody death. Wherefore let us (at least to avoid the shame, that becomes not a Christian to be found in) bear up with patience as well as we can.

Now, night being come again, and the Giant and his wife being in bed, she asked him concerning the prisoners, and if they had taken his counsel. To which he replied, "They are sturdy rogues, they choose rather to bear all hardship, than to make away themselves."

Then said she, "Take them into the castle-yard to-morrow, and show them the bones and skulls of those that thou hast already despatched, and make them believe, ere a week comes to an end, thou also wilt tear them in pieces, as thou hast done their fellows before them."

So, when the morning was come, the Giant goes to them again, and takes them into the castle-yard, and shows them, as his wife had bidden him. "These," said he, "were pilgrims as you are, once, and they trespassed in my grounds, as you have done; and when I thought fit, I tore them in pieces, and so, within ten days, I will do you. Go, get you down to your den again;" and with that he beat them all the way thither.

They lay, therefore, all day on Saturday in a lamentable case, as before. Now, when night was come, and when Mrs. Diffidence and her husband, the Giant, were got to bed, they began to renew their discourse of their prisoners; and withal the old Giant wondered, that he could neither by his blows nor his counsel bring them to an end.

And with that his wife replied, "I fear, said she, that they live in hope that some will come to relieve them, or that they have picklocks about them, by the means of which they hope to escape."

"And sayest thou so, my dear?" said the Giant; "I will, therefore, search them in the morning."

Well, on Saturday, about midnight, they began to pray, and continued in prayer till almost break of day.

Now a little before it was day, good Christian, as one half amazed, brake out in passionate speech: "What a fool," quoth[22] he, "am I, thus to lie in a stinking Dungeon, when I may as well walk at liberty. I have a Key in my bosom called Promise, that will, I am persuaded, open any Lock in Doubting Castle.

Then said Hopeful, "That's good news; good Brother pluck it out of thy bosom and try."

Then Christian pulled it out of his bosom, and began to try at the Dungeon door, whose bolt (as he turned the Key) gave back, and the door flew open with ease, and Christian and Hopeful both came out. Then he went to the outward door that leads into the Castle-yard, and with his Key opened that door also. After he went to the iron Gate, for that must be opened too, but that Lock went damnable hard, yet the Key did open it. Then they thrust open the Gate to make their escape with speed; but that Gate as it opened made such a creaking, that it waked Giant Despair, who hastily rising to pursue his Prisoners, felt his limbs to fail, for his Fits took him again, so that he could by no means go after them. Then they went on, and came to the King's High-way again, and so were safe, because they were out of his jurisdiction

Now, when they were over the stile, they began to contrive with themselves what they should do at that stile to prevent those that should come after from falling into the hands of Giant Despair. So, they consented to erect there a pillar, and to engrave upon the side thereof this sentence:

---

[22] *Quoth* simply means *said*. As in, "I quoth you could borroweth it, not keepeth it. Now giveth it back, you churlish bufflehead!"

OVER THIS STILE IS THE WAY TO
DOUBTING CASTLE, WHICH IS KEPT
BY GIANT DESPAIR, WHO
DESPISETH THE KING OF THE
CELESTIAL COUNTRY, AND SEEKS
TO DESTROY HIS HOLY PILGRIMS.

Many, therefore, that followed after read what was written, and escaped the danger. This done, they sang as follows:

Out of the way we went, and then we found
What 'twas to tread upon forbidden ground;
And let them that come after have a care,
Lest heedlessness makes them, as we, to fare.
Lest they for trespassing his prisoners are,
Whose castle's Doubting, and whose name's Despair.

WHAT WE COVERED IN WEEK ELEVEN

Meeting Demas
Discussion following their meeting with Demas
By-Path Meadow
Giant Despair and their escape

This section of Pilgrim's Progress can be quite difficult to work through.

First, we face Demas and his silver mine.

Second, there is a bit of a break, the time of Ease.

And third, there is the hard path, but a chance to take an alternate route, the one through the meadow.

I don't know about you, but when I read that part about the easy path beside the real path, my heart screams out, "Don't take it! Don't fall for it! Don't go there! Don't leave the path!"

And yet, that's exactly what they do.

I think this section is helpful to remind us of how easy it is to slip away from following Jesus. Especially when the easy way is so close to the real path—so near. So much like the actual way, just a little easier! How can we turn it down? Wouldn't only uptight, legalistic, fearful Christians stick to the rough, hard path in such a time? Perhaps God provided us this easier way out of his grace and mercy.

Perhaps…?

And then there is Giant Despair. And can I ask… have you ever been captured by him? Have you ever fallen into his clutches?

But first, let's step back to the beginning of this section for a moment.

Demas…

I love the interaction. Demas calls out to Christian and Hopeful, but consider their response! It is one of the more powerful statements in this book!

"What could be so interesting to see that would turn us out of our way?"

Consider this. For you, in your walk, are the things of Christ so precious and the things of the way so wonderful to you that those things off the path are dull? Are the things of your faith so glorious that those things "out there" leave you wondering, "What could possibly interest me more than what I have with Jesus?"

I think about the prodigal son. The things of the world were so attractive to him that he squandered all he had and all he was (or so he thought) on them. They attracted him so much that the good things he had at home with his father lost their shine in his eyes.

But you'll notice that Demas is not just some character in the story, but Christian recognizes him. He was a former pilgrim along the way. Paul writes to Timothy, telling him to

"Do your best to come to me soon. For Demas, in love with this present world, has deserted me and gone to Thessalonica."[23]

There are things in this world that appear to give us what we want, but they never truly satisfy.

Now, let's notice something else about Demas—and this is true of many who leave the faith to run after the world. Demas is not just content to love the world. Truthfully, loving the world will never offer lasting contentment, but sometimes it feels like it's enough… for a time. But even at this point for Demas, he wants something more. He wants to pull others off the path. Those who leave the path often seek to draw others away as well.

By the grace of God, Christian and Hopeful make it past this man, and we can hope that through God's grace we will as well.

On the other side of Demas, we find a monument to Lot's wife.[24] Isn't it interesting how much this story points back to the Old Testament, allowing it to act as a teacher to bring us to Christ.[25] John Bunyan is wise not to miss this incredibly powerful teaching!

Especially considering how much the story of Lot's wife relates back to the matter of Demas!

Lot's wife is a perfect example to us of looking back at what should be left behind. She looked back to the place of destruction, missing the hope she had ahead of her.

---

[23] 1 Tim. 4:9-10.
[24] Gen. 19:1-26.
[25] Gal. 3:24.

But when it came to Christian and Hopeful's test, when they faced the chance to look back, they held true. They endured and remained faithful, and the Lord provided a place of rest!

This is often the way after great testing, we find the Lord provides a short reprieve from the challenges we've faced. It's not always the case, but often. And we cannot forget that Vanity Fair and the Valley of the Shadow of Death were not all that far behind for Christian. A rest may be exactly what he needed.

And, of course, often after a time of rest when we have recovered, the path becomes difficult again. And though the temptation appears different, they are tempted once again to leave the path.

When they see the comfortable path, if you are like me, you might cry out "No! Don't do that!" But, as with any great story, when we don't want the character to step into danger, that's exactly what they do.

Which is interesting, because this is not just the stuff of stories. How many times have you watched someone do something dangerous and cried out, "Don't do that!" yet… they do it anyway.

But perhaps the greater matter to reflect upon is this: How many times have *we* stood before a dangerous choice, and someone else has cried out, "Don't do that!"

Yet… we did it anyway.

And when Christian sets out to leave the path, Hopeful speaks of faithfulness, only to have Christian argue his point from logic! Doesn't the path go right next to our own path? It's not likely to lead us away, is it? It's not *that* much out of the way, is it?

Is this not how all compromise happens, with the simple statement: "It's not *that* much out of the way."

It's also interesting that Hopeful, later on, points out that he thought leaving the path was a problem, but did not push too hard because Christian was older than he was. It reminds me of when Christian met Worldly Wiseman. That deceitful man stated that Christian should listen to him because of his age.

The point, of course, is not age, but something else.

And now our travellers are off the path. It is always so much easier to stray from the Lord's way than to get back on it. For sure, there is always grace—and Christ can be found anywhere at anytime. However, the way back is often difficult.

And then they meet Giant Despair who lives, along with his wife, in Doubting Castle.

On one hand, I would love to share a lot about him, but I think it's better to talk about Giant Despair with another. Let me instead give you and others some things to consider.

Lord, the path that promises temporary riches, the easy path, the longing for what lays behind often calls to me, but let me know in my heart that there truly is nothing so interesting to see that should turn me out of our way as I run towards your beautiful eternal promise!
Amen

TALKING POINTS

1. Quick reflection questions:

> a. Whose land was Christian and Hopeful on and what does that teach us?

> b. What stands out about Giant Despair's counsel to Christian and Hopeful to take their lives?

> c. What do we learn from Giant Despair's weakness?

> d. What do we learn from the fact that Christian and Hopeful cannot escape for a long time?

> e. What is the solution to despair in the story?

2. What really is the difference between the hearts of Christian and Demas?

3. What does it actually look like today to turn aside to Demas? Bunyan describes those who turn aside as falling to their death, but this is allegory. Is it possible to turn aside to Demas's mine and still be sitting in the pews at church? Singing on the worship team? On a board? An elder? A pastor?

4. Notice that Christian and Hopeful did not ultimately look down on those who turned to Demas but felt gratefulness to God for his grace to them. Why is this kind of response so important? What does it show in the heart of the one with this kind of gratefulness?

5. Why do you think the Lord provides places of rest throughout our lives? Think about that one. Do you think it's just random or intentional? If it's intentional, what does that tell us about the Provider of rest?

6. Did you notice that the area called *Ease* was very short? Isn't that often the way? While the times of rest come, they are often soon over. It is an interesting note that Bunyan uses the word "narrow" to describe this plain. Why do you think that is? What does the word "narrow" imply?

7. Christian and Hopeful did not leave the path for riches but left it for an easier walk. Riches didn't pull them, but comfort did. What tempts you?

8. Notice Hopeful says, "Oh that I had kept on my way!" not, "Oh, that we had kept on our way!" Why do you think that is? What does it tell us about the Christian walk?

9. Giant Despair's wife is named Diffidence.[26] What does that say about her? What does that say about Giant Despair?

10. What do you think the lack of food and water represents during Christian and Hopeful's time in Giant Despair's prison? Why do you think that's such a crucial part of despair in Doubting Castle?

11. Why do you think Giant Despair is an actual giant? With this in mind, how might we show compassion to others stuck in Despair's prison?

---

[26] Remember that *diffidence* represents a lack of trust or faith.

12. Isn't it interesting that Hopeful is true to his name in Giant Despair's dungeon? He lays out hope in the good times and even when facing death! How can you be more hopeful in your own walk and for others?

13. Why was Christian's key so effective?

14. Why do you think this issue of "listening to someone else" or "not challenging someone else" because of their age comes up again in this chapter as it did with Worldly Wiseman in chapter two? The issue is not age—but what is it about? What is this matter really about, and why would it come up twice in this book, just from two different angles?

15. Consider the last line of the poem we read, "Will soon sell all, that he may buy this field." Reflect on this in light of Matthew 13:44.

16. Did you notice the day of the week when Christian and Hopeful broke free from Giant Despair's dungeon? It was Sunday. Have you noticed many references throughout this book to the day of the week? No? Then perhaps this reference is significant! What might be significant about finding release on Sunday?

17. In Bunyan's words, he hopes his story *will make a traveller of thee*. How do you see yourself travelling this road to the Celestial City differently because of this week's reading? What change in heart, attitude, theology, or lifestyle do you believe God is calling you to as you seek to be the traveller he desires you be?

12. Shepherds and Wisdom

They went then till they came to the Delectable Mountains, which mountains belong to the Lord of that hill of which we have spoken before; so, they went up to the mountains, to behold the gardens and orchards, the vineyards and fountains of water; where also they drank and washed themselves, and did freely eat of the vineyards.

Now there were on the tops of these mountains, Shepherds feeding their flocks, and they stood by the highway side. The Pilgrims therefore went to them, and leaning upon their staves,[1] (as is common with weary pilgrims when they stand to talk with any by the way), they asked, "Whose Delectable Mountains are these? And whose be the sheep that feed upon them?"

Mountains delectable they now ascend,
Where Shepherds be, which to them do commend
Alluring things, and things that cautious are,
Pilgrims are steady kept by faith and fear.

SHEPHERD: These mountains are Immanuel's Land, and they are within sight of his city; and the sheep also are his, and he laid down his life for them.[2]

CHRISTIAN: Is this the way to the Celestial City?

SHEPHERD: You are just in your way.

CHRISTIAN: How far is it thither?

---

[1] A *stave* is another word for a staff.
[2] John 10:11.

SHEPHERD: Too far for any but those that shall get thither indeed.

CHRISTIAN: Is the way safe or dangerous?

SHEPHERD: Safe for those for whom it is to be safe; but the transgressors shall fall therein.[3]

CHRISTIAN: Is there, in this place, any relief for pilgrims that are weary and faint in the way?

SHEPHERD: The Lord of these mountains hath given us a charge not to be forgetful to entertain strangers, therefore the good of the place is before you.[4]

I saw also in my dream, that when the Shepherds perceived that they were wayfaring men, they also put questions to them, to which they made answer as in other places; as, "Whence came you?" and, "How got you into the way?" and, "By what means have you so persevered therein? For but few of them that begin to come hither do show their face on these mountains." But when the Shepherds heard their answers, being pleased therewith, they looked very lovingly upon them, and said, "Welcome to the Delectable Mountains."

The Shepherds, I say, whose names were Knowledge, Experience, Watchful, and Sincere, took them by the hand, and had them to their tents, and made them partake of that which was ready at present. They said, moreover, "We would that ye should stay here awhile, to be acquainted with us; and yet more to solace yourselves with the good of these Delectable Mountains."

They then told them, that they were content to stay; so, they went to their rest that night, because it was very late.

Then I saw in my dream, that in the morning the Shepherds called up to Christian and Hopeful to walk with them upon the mountains; so, they went forth with them, and walked a while, having a pleasant prospect on every side.

Then said the Shepherds one to another, "Shall we show these pilgrims some wonders?"

So, when they had concluded to do it, they had them first to the top of a hill called Error, which was very steep on the furthest side, and bid them look down to the bottom. So Christian and Hopeful looked down,

---

3 Hos. 14:9.
4 Heb. 13:1-2.

and saw at the bottom several men dashed all to pieces by a fall that they had from the top.

Then said Christian, "What meaneth this?"

The Shepherds answered, "Have you not heard of them that were made to err by hearkening to Hymeneus and Philetus as concerning the faith of the resurrection of the body?"[5]

They answered, "Yes."

Then said the Shepherds, "Those that you see lie dashed in pieces at the bottom of this mountain are they; and they have continued to this day unburied, as you see, for an example to others to take heed how they clamber too high, or how they come too near the brink of this mountain."

Then I saw that they had them to the top of another mountain, and the name of that is Caution, and bid them look afar off; which, when they did, they perceived, as they thought, several men walking up and down among the tombs that were there; and they perceived that the men were blind, because they stumbled sometimes upon the tombs, and because they could not get out from among them.

Then said Christian, "What means this?"

The Shepherds then answered, "Did you not see a little below these mountains a stile, that led into a meadow, on the left hand of this way?"

They answered, "Yes."

Then said the Shepherds, "From that stile there goes a path that leads directly to Doubting Castle, which is kept by Giant Despair, and these," pointing to them among the tombs, "came once on pilgrimage, as you do now, even till they came to that same stile; and because the right way was rough in that place, they chose to go out of it into that meadow, and there were taken by Giant Despair, and cast into Doubting Castle; where, after they had been a while kept in the dungeon, he at last did put out their eyes, and led them among those tombs, where he has left them to wander to this very day, that the saying of the wise man might be fulfilled, 'He that wandereth out of the way of understanding, shall remain in the congregation of the dead.'"[6]

Then Christian and Hopeful looked upon one another, with tears gushing out, but yet said nothing to the Shepherds.

---

[5] 2 Tim. 2:17-18.
[6] Pro. 21:16.

Then I saw in my dream, that the Shepherds had them to another place, in a bottom, where was a door in the side of a hill, and they opened the door, and bid them look in.

They looked in, therefore, and saw that within it was very dark and smoky; they also thought that they heard there a rumbling noise as of fire, and a cry of some tormented, and that they smelt the scent of brimstone.

Then said Christian, "What means this?"

The Shepherds told them, "This is a by-way to hell, a way that hypocrites go in at; namely, such as sell their birthright, with Esau; such as sell their master, with Judas; such as blaspheme the gospel, with Alexander; and that lie and dissemble, with Ananias and Sapphira his wife."[7]

Then said Hopeful to the Shepherds, "I perceive that these had on them, even every one, a show of pilgrimage, as we have now; had they not?"

SHEPHERD: Yes, and held it a long time too.

HOPEFUL: How far might they go on in pilgrimage in their day, since they notwithstanding were thus miserably cast away?[8]

SHEPHERD: Some further, and some not so far, as these mountains.

Then said the Pilgrims one to another, "We have need to cry to the Strong for strength."

SHEPHERD: Ay, and you will have need to use it, when you have it, too.

By this time the Pilgrims had a desire to go forward, and the Shepherds a desire they should; so, they walked together towards the end of the mountains.

Then said the Shepherds one to another, "Let us here show to the Pilgrims the gates of the Celestial City, if they have skill to look through our perspective glass."

The Pilgrims then lovingly accepted the motion; so, they had them to the top of a high hill, called Clear, and gave them their glass to look.

Then they essayed to look, but the remembrance of that last thing that the Shepherds had shown them, made their hands shake; by means of

____

[7] Gen. 25:29-34; Lk. 22:47-53; 1 Tim. 1:18-20; Acts 5:1-11.
[8] I find this particular sentence difficult to work through. In the *Rewalked* edition, it is phrased this way: "How far did they travel on their pilgrimage, even though they were eventually cast away?"

which impediment, they could not look steadily through the glass; yet they thought they saw something like the gate, and also some of the glory of the place.

Then they went away, and sang this song:

> *Thus, by the Shepherds, secrets are reveal'd,*
> *Which from all other men are kept conceal'd.*
> *Come to the Shepherds, then, if you would see*
> *Things deep, things hid, and that mysterious be.*

When they were about to depart, one of the Shepherds gave them a note of the way. Another of them bid them beware of the Flatterer. The third bid them take heed that they sleep not upon the Enchanted Ground. And the fourth bid them God-speed.

So, I awoke from my dream.

And I slept, and dreamed again, and saw the same two Pilgrims going down the mountains along the highway towards the city. Now, a little below these mountains, on the left hand, lieth the country of Conceit; from which country there comes into the way in which the Pilgrims walked, a little crooked lane. Here, therefore, they met with a very brisk lad, that came out of that country; and his name was Ignorance. So, Christian asked him from what parts he came, and whither he was going.

IGNORANCE: Sir, I was born in the country that lieth off there a little on the left hand, and I am going to the Celestial City.

CHRISTIAN: But how do you think to get in at the gate? for you may find some difficulty there.

IGNORANCE: As other people do, said he.

CHRISTIAN: But what have you to show at that gate, that may cause that the gate should be opened to you?

IGNORANCE: I know my Lord's will, and I have been a good liver; I pay every man his own; I pray, fast, pay tithes, and give alms, and have left my country for whither I am going.

CHRISTIAN: But thou camest not in at the wicket-gate that is at the head of this way; thou camest in hither through that same crooked lane, and therefore, I fear, however thou mayest think of thyself, when the reckoning day shall come, thou wilt have laid to thy charge that thou art a thief and a robber, instead of getting admittance into the city.

IGNORANCE: Gentlemen, ye be utter strangers to me, I know you not; be content and follow the religion of your country, and I will follow the religion of mine. I hope all will be well. And as for the gate that you talk of, all the world knows that that is a great way off of our country. I cannot think that any man in all our parts doth so much as know the way to it, nor need they matter whether they do or no, since we have, as you see, a fine, pleasant green lane, that comes down from our country, the next way into the way.

When Christian saw that the man was "wise in his own conceit," he said to Hopeful, whisperingly, "There is more hope of a fool than of him." And said, moreover, "'When he that is a fool walketh by the way, his wisdom faileth him, and he saith to every one that he is a fool.' What, shall we talk further with him, or out-go him at present, and so leave him to think of what he hath heard already, and then stop again for him afterwards, and see if by degrees we can do any good to him?"[9]

Then said Hopeful--

> *Let Ignorance a little while now muse*
> *On what is said, and let him not refuse*
> *Good counsel to embrace, lest he remain*
> *Still ignorant of what's the chiefest gain.*
> *God saith, those that no understanding have,*
> *Although he made them, them he will not save.*

HOPEFUL: He further added, It is not good, I think, to say all to him at once; let us pass him by, if you will, and talk to him anon,[10] even as he is able to bear it.

So, they both went on, and Ignorance he came after. Now when they had passed him a little way, they entered into a very dark lane, where they met a man whom seven devils had bound with seven strong cords, and were carrying of him back to the door that they saw on the side of the hill.[11]

Now good Christian began to tremble, and so did Hopeful his companion; yet as the devils led away the man, Christian looked to see if he knew him; and he thought it might be one Turn-away, that dwelt in the town of Apostasy. But he did not perfectly see his face, for he did hang his head like a thief that is found.

---

[9] Prov. 26:12; Eccl. 10:3.
[10] *Anon* means *soon*, or *shortly*.
[11] Prov. 5:22; Matt. 12:45.

But being once past, Hopeful looked after him, and espied on his back a paper with this inscription, "Wanton professor and damnable apostate."

Then said Christian to his fellow, "Now I call to remembrance, that which was told me of a thing that happened to a good man hereabout. The name of the man was Little-faith, but a good man, and he dwelt in the town of Sincere. The thing was this: At the entering in at this passage, there comes down from Broad-way Gate, a lane called Dead Man's Lane; so called because of the murders that are commonly done there; and this Little-faith going on pilgrimage, as we do now, chanced to sit down there, and slept. Now there happened, at that time, to come down the lane, from Broad-way Gate, three sturdy rogues, and their names were Faint-heart, Mistrust, and Guilt, (three brothers), and they espying Little-faith, where he was, came galloping up with speed. Now the good man was just awake from his sleep, and was getting up to go on his journey. So, they came up all to him, and with threatening language bid him stand. At this Little-faith looked as white as a clout, and had neither power to fight nor fly. Then said Faint-heart, Deliver thy purse. But he making no haste to do it (for he was loath to lose his money), Mistrust ran up to him, and thrusting his hand into his pocket, pulled out thence a bag of silver. Then he cried out, "Thieves! Thieves!" With that Guilt, with a great club that was in his hand, struck Little-faith on the head, and with that blow felled him flat to the ground, where he lay bleeding as one that would bleed to death. All this while the thieves stood by. But, at last, they hearing that some were upon the road, and fearing lest it should be one Great-grace, that dwells in the city of Good-confidence, they betook themselves to their heels, and left this good man to shift for himself. Now, after a while, Little-faith came to himself, and getting up, made shift to scrabble on his way. This was the story.

HOPEFUL: But did they take from him all that ever he had?

CHRISTIAN: No; the place where his jewels were they never ransacked, so those he kept still. But, as I was told, the good man was much afflicted for his loss, for the thieves got most of his spending-money. That which they got not (as I said) were jewels, also he had a little odd money left, but scarce enough to bring him to his journey's end;[12] nay, if I was not misinformed, he was forced to beg as he went, to keep himself alive; for his jewels he might not sell. But beg, and do what he could, he went (as we say) with many a hungry belly the most part of the rest of the way.

---

[12] 1 Peter 4:18.

HOPEFUL: But is it not a wonder they got not from him his certificate, by which he was to receive his admittance at the Celestial Gate?

CHRISTIAN: It is a wonder; but they got not that, though they missed it not through any good cunning of his; for he, being dismayed with their coming upon him, had neither power nor skill to hide anything; so it was more by good Providence than by his endeavour, that they missed of that good thing.

HOPEFUL: But it must needs be a comfort to him, that they got not his jewels from him.

CHRISTIAN: It might have been great comfort to him, had he used it as he should; but they that told me the story said, that he made but little use of it all the rest of the way, and that because of the dismay that he had in the taking away his money; indeed, he forgot it a great part of the rest of his journey; and besides, when at any time it came into his mind, and he began to be comforted therewith, then would fresh thoughts of his loss come again upon him, and those thoughts would swallow up all.[13]

HOPEFUL: Alas! poor man! This could not but be a great grief to him.

CHRISTIAN: Grief! ay, a grief indeed. Would it not have been so to any of us, had we been used as he, to be robbed, and wounded too, and that in a strange place, as he was? It is a wonder he did not die with grief, poor heart! I was told that he scattered almost all the rest of the way with nothing but doleful and bitter complaints; telling also to all that overtook him, or that he overtook in the way as he went, where he was robbed, and how; who they were that did it, and what he lost; how he was wounded, and that he hardly escaped with his life.

HOPEFUL: But it is a wonder that his necessity did not put him upon selling or pawning some of his jewels, that he might have wherewith to relieve himself in his journey.

CHRISTIAN: Thou talkest like one upon whose head is the shell to this very day; for what should he pawn them, or to whom should he sell them? In all that country where he was robbed, his jewels were not accounted of; nor did he want that relief which could from thence be administered to him. Besides, had his jewels been missing at the gate of the Celestial City, he had (and that he knew well enough) been excluded from an inheritance there; and that would have been worse to him than the appearance and villainy of ten thousand thieves.

---

[13] 1 Peter 1:9.

HOPEFUL: Why art thou so tart, my brother? Esau sold his birthright, and that for a mess of pottage,[14] and that birthright was his greatest jewel; and if he, why might not Little-faith do so too?[15]

CHRISTIAN: Esau did sell his birthright indeed, and so do many besides, and by so doing exclude themselves from the chief blessing, as also that caitiff[16] did; but you must put a difference betwixt Esau and Little-faith, and also betwixt their estates. Esau's birthright was typical, but Little-faith's jewels were not so; Esau's belly was his god, but Little-faith's belly was not so; Esau's want lay in his fleshly appetite, Little-faith's did not so. Besides, Esau could see no further than to the fulfilling of his lusts; "Behold, I am at the point to die, (said he), and what profit shall this birthright do me?"[17] But Little-faith, though it was his lot to have but a little faith, was by his little faith kept from such extravagances, and made to see and prize his jewels more than to sell them, as Esau did his birthright. You read not anywhere that Esau had faith, no, not so much as a little; therefore, no marvel if, where the flesh only bears sway, (as it will in that man where no faith is to resist), if he sells his birthright, and his soul and all, and that to the devil of hell; for it is with such, as it is with the ass, who in her occasions cannot be turned away.[18] When their minds are set upon their lusts, they will have them whatever they cost. But Little-faith was of another temper, his mind was on things divine; his livelihood was upon things that were spiritual, and from above; therefore, to what end should he that is of such a temper sell his jewels (had there been any that would have bought them) to fill his mind with empty things? Will a man give a penny to fill his belly with hay; or can you persuade the turtle-dove to live upon carrion like the crow? Though faithless ones can, for carnal lusts, pawn, or mortgage, or sell what they have, and themselves outright to boot; yet they that have faith, saving faith, though but a little of it, cannot do so. Here, therefore, my brother, is thy mistake.

HOPEFUL: I acknowledge it; but yet your severe reflection had almost made me angry.

---

[14] *Pottage* is an old word that means soup or stew, but the phrase "mess of pottage" is an idiom that refers to a ridiculously small amount. So, when it says he sold it for a *mess of pottage,* it is not only referring to the literal experience of Esau's selling of his birthright for stew, but it's pointing out how it was for a ridiculously small amount, pointing to shortsightedness. This idiom actually came from this passage of Scripture.

[15] Heb. 12:16.

[16] A *caitiff* is a *contemptible or cowardly individual.*

[17] Gen. 25:32.

[18] Jer. 2:24.

CHRISTIAN: Why, I did but compare thee to some of the birds that are of the brisker sort, who will run to and fro in untrodden paths, with the shell upon their heads;[19] but pass by that, and consider the matter under debate, and all shall be well betwixt thee and me.

HOPEFUL: But, Christian, these three fellows, I am persuaded in my heart, are but a company of cowards; would they have run else, think you, as they did, at the noise of one that was coming on the road? Why did not Little-faith pluck up a greater heart? He might, methinks, have stood one brush with them, and have yielded when there had been no remedy.

CHRISTIAN: That they are cowards, many have said, but few have found it so in the time of trial. As for a great heart, Little-faith had none; and I perceive by thee, my brother, hadst thou been the man concerned, thou art but for a brush, and then to yield.

And, verily, since this is the height of thy stomach, now they are at a distance from us, should they appear to thee as they did to him they might put thee to second thoughts.

But, consider again, they are but journeymen thieves, they serve under the king of the bottomless pit, who, if need be, will come into their aid himself, and his voice is as the roaring of a lion.[20] I myself have been engaged as this Little-faith was, and I found it a terrible thing. These three villains set upon me, and I beginning, like a Christian, to resist, they gave but a call, and in came their master. I would, as the saying is, have given my life for a penny, but that, as God would have it, I was clothed with armour of proof. Ay, and yet, though I was so harnessed, I found it hard work to quit myself like a man. No man can tell what in that combat attends us, but he that hath been in the battle himself.

HOPEFUL: Well, but they ran, you see, when they did but suppose that one Great-grace was in the way.

CHRISTIAN: True, they have often fled, both they and their master, when Great-grace hath but appeared; and no marvel; for he is the King's champion. But, I trow,[21] you will put some difference betwixt Little-faith and the King's champion. All the King's subjects are not his

---

[19] Christian's description of the bird here is that it is of the brisker sort which seems to point back to the description of Ignorance a few pages earlier. It suggested back then that Ignorance was abrupt, impatient, impetuous, and now Christian seems to accuse Hopeful of something similar.
[20] 1 Pet. 5:8.
[21] *Trow* means *think or believe.*

champions, nor can they, when tried, do such feats of war as he. Is it meet[22] to think that a little child should handle Goliath as David did? Or that there should be the strength of an ox in a wren? Some are strong, some are weak; some have great faith, some have little. This man was one of the weak, and therefore he went to the wall.[23]

HOPEFUL: I would it had been Great-grace for their sakes.

CHRISTIAN: If it had been, he might have had his hands full; for I must tell you, that though Great-grace is excellent good at his weapons, and has, and can, so long as he keeps them at sword's point, do well enough with them; yet, if they get within him, even Faint-heart, Mistrust, or the other, it shall go hard but they will throw up his heels. And when a man is down, you know, what can he do?

Whoso looks well upon Great-grace's face, shall see those scars and cuts there, that shall easily give demonstration of what I say. Yea, once I heard that he should say, (and that when he was in the combat), "We despaired even of life."[24] How did these sturdy rogues and their fellows make David groan, mourn, and roar? Yea, Heman, and Hezekiah, too, though champions in their day, were forced to bestir them, when by these assaulted; and yet, notwithstanding, they had their coats soundly brushed by them. Peter, upon a time, would go try what he could do; but though some do say of him that he is the prince of the apostles, they handled him so, that they made him at last afraid of a sorry girl.[25]

Besides, their king is at their whistle. He is never out of hearing; and if at any time they be put to the worst, he, if possible, comes in to help them; and of him it is said, "The sword of him that layeth at him cannot hold the spear, the dart, nor the habergeon;[26] he esteemeth iron as straw, and brass as rotten wood. The arrow cannot make him flee; sling stones are turned with him into stubble. Darts are counted as stubble: he laugheth at the shaking of a spear."[27] What can a man do in this case? It is true, if a man could, at every turn, have Job's horse, and had skill and courage to ride him, he might do notable things; for his neck is clothed with thunder, he will not be afraid of the grasshopper; the glory of his nostrils is terrible: he paweth in the valley, and rejoiceth in his strength, he goeth on to meet the armed men. He mocketh at fear, and is not affrighted, neither turneth he

---

[22] This form of the word *meet* means *suitable or fit*. As in, is it suitable/proper to think a little child should...?

[23] In this context, the phrase *went to the wall* seems to refer to failing.

[24] 2 Cor. 1:8.

[25] Mar. 14:66-72.

[26] A *habergeon* is *a sleeveless coat of mail or scale armour*.

[27] Job 41:26-29.

back from the sword. The quiver rattleth against him, the glittering spear, and the shield. He swalloweth the ground with fierceness and rage, neither believeth he that it is the sound of the trumpet. He saith among the trumpets, Ha, ha! and he smelleth the battle afar off, the thunder of the captains, and the shouting.[28]

But for such footmen as thee and I are, let us never desire to meet with an enemy, nor vaunt[29] as if we could do better, when we hear of others that they have been foiled. Nor be tickled at the thoughts of our own manhood; for such commonly come by the worst when tried. Witness Peter, of whom I made mention before. He would swagger, ay, he would; he would, as his vain mind prompted him to say, do better, and stand more for his Master than all men; but who so foiled, and run down by these villains, as he?

When, therefore, we hear that such robberies are done on the King's highway, two things become us to do:

1. To go out harnessed, and to be sure to take a shield with us; for it was for want of that, that he that laid so lustily at Leviathan could not make him yield; for, indeed, if that be wanting, he fears us not at all. Therefore, he that had skill hath said, "Above all, taking the shield of faith, wherewith ye shall be able to quench all the fiery darts of the wicked."[30]

2. It is good, also, that we desire of the King a convoy, yea, that he will go with us himself. This made David rejoice when in the Valley of the Shadow of Death; and Moses was rather for dying where he stood, than to go one step without his God. Oh, my brother, if he will but go along with us, what need we be afraid of ten thousands that shall set themselves against us? But, without him, the proud helpers "fall under the slain."[31]

I, for my part, have been in the fray before now; and though, through the goodness of him that is best, I am, as you see, alive, yet I cannot boast of my manhood. Glad shall I be, if I meet with no more such brunts; though I fear we are not got beyond all danger. However, since the lion and the bear have not as yet devoured me, I hope God will also deliver us from the next uncircumcised Philistine. Then sang Christian:

---

[28] Job 39:19-25.
[29] *Vaunt* means *to boast.*
[30] Eph. 6:16.
[31] Exo. 33:15; Ps. 3:5-8, 27:1-3; Isa. 10:4.

Poor Little-faith! Hast been among the thieves?
Wast robb'd? Remember this, whoso believes,
And gets more faith, shall then a victor be
Over ten thousand, else scarce over three.

WHAT WE COVERED IN WEEK TWELVE

We have reached the Delectable Mountains! "Delectable" is not a word we commonly use these days, although we use the word "delicacy," so we understand the idea.

And there, on those mountains, Christian and Hopeful meet shepherds who tell them it is Emmanuel's Land. What a beautiful name! Emmanuel means God with us, so we have entered a land of God's presence.

And to make it more wonderful, the land is within sight of Emmanuel's city! Our travellers are even surrounded by sheep who belong to the Lord of the City, those for whom He has laid down his life!

What a wonderful picture!

But what makes it more beautiful is the knowledge that we are the sheep! Our Lord, the Lord of the very city we seek, loves us so much He laid down his life for us.

But remember! We are on a journey! And what's the question you ask when you are on a journey? "Are we there yet?" Or the way Christian and Hopeful put it, "How far is it thither?"

Do you remember the answer? It was quite cryptic. It's an answer worth pondering.

But we have, yet again, come across a time of rest in Christian and Hopeful's journey. These times are important, and it is a wonderful truth that Jesus provides us with times of rest along the way, even so close to the end! Following Christ can be difficult, but our Lord gives rest when we need it.

Now, when we consider the journey, stepping back from this allegory and considering our own lives, we see an interesting truth, and it's this: some on the Christian journey face more trouble than others.

Those who walk a more difficult path rarely walk it because of some personal sin or rebellion.[32] In fact, if we look closely, we can sometimes even find that those who face great difficulty in their Christian walk can be the more faithful among us. Though we all walk the same path with the same salvation, the storms, the temptations, the resistance, and more will be *very* different for each traveller.

Even for Christian and Hopeful, their journeys have been different.

But for each of us, Christ is kind and gracious in providing times of rest—or at the very least, times of less-difficulty.

So, this means that to desire times of rest for ourselves is not wrong, and we should desire times of rest for others as we see them in need of such a thing. Perhaps that is shown in the illustration of the shepherds left at the Delectable Mountains for travellers such as Christian and Hopeful.

As we consider the paths we walk, it is impossible to know why God chooses a more difficult path for one person and an easier path for another. Consider, for instance, the difference between Joshua and Jeremiah. When it comes down to it, the Joshuas among us rarely understand the Jeremiahs.

Joshua preached for people to follow God's leading in a time of entering the land. The people were thrilled to follow; they loved Joshua, and they conquered the land. Joshua called for people to commit to the Lord, and they responded with a resounding, "YES!"

Jeremiah preached for people to follow God's leading in a time before leaving the land. The people were disgusted at the thought of following, and they despised Jeremiah. Jeremiah called for people to commit to the Lord, and they threw him in a cistern.

One called the people to conquer, the other warned the people they were about to be conquered. One called a willing people to follow the Lord

---

[32] This is a truth that most Christians would accept at face value but often prove they don't believe when trouble comes to them or to others. Note as well that this does not mean that we do not create our own trouble at times due to stubbornness or sin. This is to say that consequences for sin are often obvious, whereas when it comes to a more difficult path, we often have to make a lot of assumptions to declare the trouble we face to be a consequence of poor choices.

and had great *success*, the other called a stubborn people to follow the Lord and had what appears to be great *failure*.[33]

Yet the Lord cared for both Joshua and Jeremiah. And, for Joshua and for Jeremiah, his mercies were new every morning.[34]

I hope for you, whether you are a Joshua, a Jeremiah, or someone else, that you serve the Lord faithfully and do not allow your success or your difficulty to influence your understanding of the Lord's favour. For his favour is upon you, not because of you, but because of Jesus.

But, back to our story!

The Shepherds warn Christian and Hopeful next. I find this section quite insightful, but also quite disturbing. It's disturbing to think that we can face so many dangers and threats along the way as we try to follow Christ.

And finally, we meet Ignorance. What a name! And for Ignorance to come from the country of Conceit… wow! Insightful, yet unsurprising.

But rather than review some of this and what comes after, let's move into a time of reflection and discussion.

Lord, thank you for the times of rest, but in the times of difficulty,
remind me that your mercies are new every morning as I grow closer to
reaching Emmanuel's city!
Amen

---

[33] NOTE: I am speaking here with a certain sarcasm or tongue in cheek tone. When I speak of success, I mean success in the sense that what Joshua sought all came about with very little variation. Jeremiah, on the other hand, what he sought (repentance of the people), never came. Truthfully, Jeremiah had great success, in a manner of speaking, as he was faithful to the Lord and the Lord was faithful to him. I suspect Jeremiah's eternal reward is going to be quite impressive.

[34] Lam. 3:22-23.

TALKING POINTS

1. The Shepherd says, "Too far for any but those that shall get thither indeed." Let me rephrase that, just for the fun of it (although I know we all read archaic language quite well): "The Celestial City is too far for anyone, except those who will get there." Take a moment and discuss such an answer with one another. It's actually quite profound! So, what does it mean?

2. Consider for a moment the blind men walking among the tombs, the ones who had their eyes put out by Giant Despair at Doubting Castle. What is the difference between those blind men and Christian and Hopeful?[35]

---

[35] Be careful not to let yourself get carried away with an answer driven by concepts of success. Don't think of it in terms of, "What did Christian and Hopeful do right that allowed them to successfully get out?" Answer this question in terms of God, Jesus, and the Spirit. Answer this question in terms of relationship rather than success, personal power, morality, etc.

3. In their time with the Shepherd, Hopeful asks the following question about those who were not truly followers of Christ: "I perceive that these had on them, even every one, a show of pilgrimage, as we have now; had they not?" Perhaps this would be a good time for us to look inward to see if *our own* faith is genuine? I do not wish to cause doubt in you, but consider your heart in light of Matthew 7:21-23. Take a moment to prayerfully read through 2 Corinthians 13:1-10 and 1 Peter 1:3-9, and then talk about this with others.[36] Do not be ashamed by what's in your heart, and do not shame anyone else for what is in their hearts.

4. Although we are nearing the end of our journey, Ignorance is a key character.[37] He, unlike many others, comes back into our story repeatedly, so pay attention to him and beware of his ignorance. In life, why is it that Ignorance comes from the country of Conceit? What is the connection between the two?

5. Can Ignorance ever come from the land of Humility? Or does knowledge come from the land of Humility? What does Ignorance teach us about living in humility?

---

[36] Remember, even if you are doing this study alone, we are meant to be a part of the body of Christ. Find opportunities to discuss with others along the way.
[37] Perhaps the fact that Ignorance shows up at the end of our journey makes a profound statement.

6. Ignorance tells Christian and Hopeful that the entire world knows that the narrow Sheep Gate is far from the country of Conceit. Consider that for a moment. Why do you think that is? Is it possible to get to the Sheep Gate from the land of Conceit? Is there *any* way?

7. When Christian and Hopeful challenge Ignorance as to the genuineness of his faith, he gives a legalistic answer. What is the connection between legalism and ignorance?

8. What does the attack by Faint-heart, Mistrust, and Guilt represent?

9. Why is Little Faith malnourished for the rest of his journey? Since this is allegory, it's a spiritual malnourishment. What does it mean to be spiritually malnourished for the rest of your spiritual life?

10. If Faint-heart, Mistrust, and Guilt attack you, how might you move on after in a way that honours Christ and leaves you to walk confidently along the path as Great-grace does? What is the cost of letting go of that pain, handing your wounds up to Christ, and trusting in his grace?

11. Take note of Christian's conclusion on how we should react to hearing of others falling to faint-heartedness, mistrust, and guilt. He cautions Hopeful not to be arrogant, but to be prepared with faith, and to walk with God at our head. Why is this warning and these two responses given? Why not something else?

12. In Bunyan's words, he hopes his story *will make a traveller of thee*. How do you see yourself travelling this road to the Celestial City differently because of this week's reading? What change in heart, attitude, theology, or lifestyle do you believe God is calling you to as you seek to be the traveller he desires you be?

13. The Flatterers

So, they went on and Ignorance followed. They went then till they came at a place where they saw a way put itself into their way, and seemed withal to lie as straight as the way which they should go: and here they knew not which of the two to take, for both seemed straight before them; therefore, here they stood still to consider. And as they were thinking about the way, behold a man, black of flesh, but covered with a very light robe, came to them, and asked them why they stood there. They answered they were going to the Celestial City, but knew not which of these ways to take.

"Follow me," said the man, "it is thither that I am going."

So they followed him in the way that but now came into the road, which by degrees turned, and turned them so from the city that they desired to go to, that, in little time, their faces were turned away from it; yet they followed him. But by and by, before they were aware, he led them both within the compass of a net, in which they were both so entangled that they knew not what to do; and with that the white robe fell off the black man's back. Then they saw where they were. Wherefore, there they lay crying some time, for they could not get themselves out.

CHRISTIAN: Then said Christian to his fellow, Now do I see myself in error. Did not the Shepherds bid us beware of the flatterers? As is the saying of the wise man, so we have found it this day. A man that flattereth his neighbour, spreadeth a net for his feet.[1]

HOPEFUL: They also gave us a note of directions about the way, for our more sure finding thereof; but therein we have also forgotten to read, and have not kept ourselves from the paths of the destroyer. Here

---

[1] Prov. 29:5.

David was wiser than we; for, saith he, "Concerning the works of men, by the word of thy lips, I have kept me from the paths of the destroyer."[2]

Thus they lay bewailing themselves in the net. At last, they espied a Shining One coming towards them with a whip of small cord in his hand. When he was come to the place where they were, he asked them whence they came, and what they did there. They told him that they were poor pilgrims going to Zion, but were led out of their way by a black man, clothed in white, who bid us, said they, follow him, for he was going thither too.

Then said he with the whip, "It is Flatterer, a false apostle, that hath transformed himself into an angel of light."[3] So he rent the net, and let the men out. Then said he to them, "Follow me, that I may set you in your way again." So he led them back to the way which they had left to follow the Flatterer. Then he asked them, saying, "Where did you lie the last night?"

They said, "With the Shepherds upon the Delectable Mountains."

He asked them then if they had not of those Shepherds a note of direction for the way.

They answered, "Yes."

"But did you," said he, "when you were at a stand, pluck out and read your note?"

They answered, "No."

He asked them, "Why?"

They said, they forgot.

He asked, moreover, if the Shepherds did not bid them beware of the Flatterer?

They answered, "Yes, but we did not imagine," said they, "that this fine-spoken man had been he."[4]

Then I saw in my dream that he commanded them to lie down; which, when they did, he chastised them sore, to teach them the good way wherein they should walk; and as he chastised them he said, "As many as I love, I rebuke and chasten; be zealous, therefore, and repent."[5]

---

[2] Ps. 17:4.
[3] Prov. 29:5; Dan. 11:32; 2 Cor. 11:13, 14.
[4] Rom. 16:18.
[5] Deut. 25:2; 2 Chron. 6:26,27; Rev. 3:19.

This done, he bid them go on their way, and take good heed to the other directions of the shepherds. So they thanked him for all his kindness, and went softly along the right way, singing,

Now, after a while, they perceived, afar off, one coming softly and alone, all along the highway to meet them. Then said Christian to his fellow, "Yonder is a man with his back towards Zion, and he is coming to meet us."

HOPEFUL: I see him; let us take heed to ourselves now, lest he should prove a flatterer also.

So he drew nearer and nearer, and at last came up unto them. His name was Atheist, and he asked them whither they were going.

CHRISTIAN: We are going to Mount Zion.

Then Atheist fell into a very great laughter.

CHRISTIAN: What is the meaning of your laughter?

ATHEIST: I laugh to see what ignorant persons you are, to take upon you so tedious a journey, and you are like to have nothing but your travel for your pains.

CHRISTIAN: Why, man, do you think we shall not be received?

ATHEIST: Received! There is no such place as you dream of in all this world.

CHRISTIAN: But there is in the world to come.

ATHEIST: When I was at home in mine own country, I heard as you now affirm, and from that hearing went out to see, and have been seeking this city this twenty years; but find no more of it than I did the first day I set out.[6]

CHRISTIAN: We have both heard and believe that there is such a place to be found.

---

[6] Jer. 22:12; Eccl. 10:15.

ATHEIST: Had not I, when at home, believed, I had not come thus far to seek; but finding none, (and yet I should, had there been such a place to be found, for I have gone to seek it further than you), I am going back again, and will seek to refresh myself with the things that I then cast away, for hopes of that which, I now see, is not.

CHRISTIAN: Then said Christian to Hopeful his fellow, Is it true which this man hath said?

HOPEFUL: Take heed, he is one of the flatterers; remember what it hath cost us once already for our hearkening to such kind of fellows. What! no Mount Zion? Did we not see, from the Delectable Mountains the gate of the city? Also, are we not now to walk by faith? Let us go on, said Hopeful, lest the man with the whip overtake us again. You should have taught me that lesson, which I will round you in the ears withal: "Cease, my son, to hear the instruction that causeth to err from the words of knowledge." I say, my brother, cease to hear him, and let us "believe to the saving of the soul."[7]

CHRISTIAN: My brother, I did not put the question to thee for that I doubted of the truth of our belief myself, but to prove thee, and to fetch from thee a fruit of the honesty of thy heart. As for this man, I know that he is blinded by the god of this world. Let thee and I go on, knowing that we have belief of the truth, "and no lie is of the truth."[8]

HOPEFUL: Now do I rejoice in hope of the glory of God. So they turned away from the man; and he, laughing at them, went his way.

I saw then in my dream, that they went till they came into a certain country, whose air naturally tended to make one drowsy, if he came a stranger into it. And here Hopeful began to be very dull and heavy of sleep; wherefore he said unto Christian, I do now begin to grow so drowsy that I can scarcely hold up mine eyes, let us lie down here and take one nap.

CHRISTIAN: By no means, said the other, lest sleeping, we never awake more.

HOPEFUL: Why, my brother? Sleep is sweet to the labouring man; we may be refreshed if we take a nap.

CHRISTIAN: Do you not remember that one of the Shepherds bid us beware of the Enchanted Ground? He meant by that that we should

---

[7] 2 Cor. 5:7; Prov. 19:27; Heb. 10:39.
[8] 1 John 2:21.

beware of sleeping; "Therefore let us not sleep, as do others, but let us watch and be sober."[9]

HOPEFUL: I acknowledge myself in a fault, and had I been here alone I had by sleeping run the danger of death. I see it is true that the wise man saith, Two are better than one. Hitherto hath thy company been my mercy, and thou shalt have a good reward for thy labour.[10]

CHRISTIAN: Now then, said Christian, to prevent drowsiness in this place, let us fall into good discourse.

HOPEFUL: With all my heart, said the other.

CHRISTIAN: Where shall we begin?

HOPEFUL: Where God began with us. But do you begin, if you please.

CHRISTIAN: I will sing you first this song:

When saints do sleepy grow, let them come hither,
And hear how these two pilgrims talk together:
Yea, let them learn of them, in any wise,
Thus to keep ope[11] their drowsy slumb'ring eyes.
Saints' fellowship, if it be managed well,
Keeps them awake, and that in spite of hell.

CHRISTIAN: Then Christian began and said, I will ask you a question. How came you to think at first of so doing as you do now?

HOPEFUL: Do you mean, how came I at first to look after the good of my soul?

CHRISTIAN: Yes, that is my meaning.

HOPEFUL: I continued a great while in the delight of those things which were seen and sold at our fair; things which, I believe now, would have, had I continued in them, still drowned me in perdition and destruction.

CHRISTIAN: What things are they?

HOPEFUL: All the treasures and riches of the world. Also, I delighted much in rioting, revelling, drinking, swearing, lying, uncleanness,

---

[9] 1 Thess. 5:6.
[10] Eccl. 4:9
[11] *Ope* is an archaic version of *open* as in "Why did you leave the fridge ope?" or as a dentist might say, "Ope wide."

Sabbath-breaking, and what not, that tended to destroy the soul. But I found at last, by hearing and considering of things that are divine, which indeed I heard of you, as also of beloved Faithful that was put to death for his faith and good living in Vanity Fair, that "the end of these things is death." And that for these things' sake "cometh the wrath of God upon the children of disobedience."[12]

CHRISTIAN: And did you presently fall under the power of this conviction?

HOPEFUL: No, I was not willing presently to know the evil of sin, nor the damnation that follows upon the commission of it; but endeavoured, when my mind at first began to be shaken with the Word, to shut mine eyes against the light thereof.

CHRISTIAN: But what was the cause of your carrying of it thus to the first workings of God's blessed Spirit upon you?

HOPEFUL: The causes were, 1. I was ignorant that this was the work of God upon me. I never thought that, by awakenings for sin, God at first begins the conversion of a sinner. 2. Sin was yet very sweet to my flesh, and I was loath to leave it. 3. I could not tell how to part with mine old companions, their presence and actions were so desirable unto me. 4. The hours in which convictions were upon me were such troublesome and such heart-affrighting hours that I could not bear, no not so much as the remembrance of them, upon my heart.

CHRISTIAN: Then, as it seems, sometimes you got rid of your trouble.

HOPEFUL: Yes, verily, but it would come into my mind again, and then I should be as bad, nay, worse, than I was before.

CHRISTIAN: Why, what was it that brought your sins to mind again?

HOPEFUL: Many things; as,

1. If I did but meet a good man in the streets; or,

2. If I have heard any read in the Bible; or,

3. If mine head did begin to ache; or,

4. If I were told that some of my neighbours were sick; or,

5. If I heard the bell toll for some that were dead; or,

---

[12] Rom. 6:21-23; Eph. 5:6.

6. If I thought of dying myself; or,

7. If I heard that sudden death happened to others;

8. But especially, when I thought of myself, that I must quickly come to judgement.

CHRISTIAN: And could you at any time, with ease, get off the guilt of sin, when by any of these ways it came upon you?

HOPEFUL: No, not I, for then they got faster hold of my conscience; and then, if I did but think of going back to sin, (though my mind was turned against it), it would be double torment to me.

CHRISTIAN: And how did you do then?

HOPEFUL: I thought I must endeavour to mend my life; for else, thought I, I am sure to be damned.

CHRISTIAN: And did you endeavour to mend?

HOPEFUL: Yes; and fled from not only my sins, but sinful company too; and betook me to religious duties, as prayer, reading, weeping for sin, speaking truth to my neighbours, etc. These things did I, with many others, too much here to relate.

CHRISTIAN: And did you think yourself well then?

HOPEFUL: Yes, for a while; but at the last, my trouble came tumbling upon me again, and that over the neck of all my reformations.

CHRISTIAN: How came that about, since you were now reformed?

HOPEFUL: There were several things brought it upon me, especially such sayings as these: "All our righteousnesses are as filthy rags." "By the works of the law shall no flesh be justified." "When ye shall have done all those things, say, We are unprofitable," with many more such like. From whence I began to reason with myself thus: If ALL my righteousnesses are filthy rags; if, by the deeds of the law, NO man can be justified; and if, when we have done ALL, we are yet unprofitable, then it is but a folly to think of heaven by the law. I further thought thus: If a man runs a hundred pounds into the shopkeeper's debt, and after that shall pay for all that he shall fetch; yet, if this old debt stands still in the book uncrossed, for that the shopkeeper may sue him, and cast him into prison till he shall pay the debt.[13]

---

[13] Isa. 64:6; Gal. 2:16; Luke 17:10.

CHRISTIAN: Well, and how did you apply this to yourself?

HOPEFUL: Why; I thought thus with myself. I have, by my sins, run a great way into God's book, and that my now reforming will not pay off that score; therefore, I should think still, under all my present amendments, But how shall I be freed from that damnation that I have brought myself in danger of by my former transgressions?

CHRISTIAN: A very good application: but, pray, go on.

HOPEFUL: Another thing that hath troubled me, even since my late amendments, is, that if I look narrowly into the best of what I do now, I still see sin, new sin, mixing itself with the best of that I do; so that now I am forced to conclude, that notwithstanding my former fond conceits of myself and duties, I have committed sin enough in one duty to send me to hell, though my former life had been faultless.

CHRISTIAN: And what did you do then?

HOPEFUL: Do! I could not tell what to do, until I brake my mind to Faithful, for he and I were well acquainted. And he told me, that unless I could obtain the righteousness of a man that never had sinned, neither mine own, nor all the righteousness of the world could save me.

CHRISTIAN: And did you think he spake true?

HOPEFUL: Had he told me so when I was pleased and satisfied with mine own amendment, I had called him fool for his pains; but now, since I see mine own infirmity, and the sin that cleaves to my best performance, I have been forced to be of his opinion.

CHRISTIAN: But did you think, when at first he suggested it to you, that there was such a man to be found, of whom it might justly be said that he never committed sin?

HOPEFUL: I must confess the words at first sounded strangely, but after a little more talk and company with him, I had full conviction about it.

CHRISTIAN: And did you ask him what man this was, and how you must be justified by him?

HOPEFUL: Yes, and he told me it was the Lord Jesus, that dwelleth on the right hand of the Most High. And thus, said he, you must be justified by him, even by trusting to what he hath done by himself, in the days of his flesh, and suffered when he did hang on the tree. I asked him further, how that man's righteousness could be of that efficacy to justify another before God? And he told me he was the mighty God, and did what he did, and died the death also, not for himself, but for me; to whom his doings, and the worthiness of them, should be imputed,[14] if I believed on him.[15]

CHRISTIAN: And what did you do then?

HOPEFUL: I made my objections against my believing, for that I thought he was not willing to save me.

CHRISTIAN: And what said Faithful to you then?

HOPEFUL: He bid me go to him and see. Then I said it was presumption; but he said, No, for I was invited to come. Then he gave me a book of Jesus, his inditing,[16] to encourage me the more freely to come; and he said, concerning that book, that every jot and tittle[17] thereof stood firmer than heaven and earth. Then I asked him, What I must do when I came; and he told me, I must entreat upon my knees, with all my heart and soul, the Father to reveal him to me. Then I asked him further, how I must make my supplication to him? And he said, Go, and thou shalt find him upon a mercy-seat, where he sits all the year long, to give pardon and forgiveness to them that come. I told him that I knew not what to say when I came. And he bid me say to this effect: God be merciful to me a sinner, and make me to know and believe in Jesus Christ; for I see, that if his righteousness had not been, or I have not faith in that righteousness, I am utterly cast away. Lord, I have heard that thou art a merciful God, and hast ordained that thy Son Jesus Christ should be the Saviour of the world; and moreover, that thou art willing to bestow him upon such a poor sinner as I am, (and I am a sinner indeed); Lord, take therefore this opportunity and

---

[14] *Imputed* may be an unfamiliar word to many, although we might hear or read it now and then. It is, however, a powerful theological term that is important for Christians to know. Christ's righteousness is imputed to us. That's not so much that his righteousness is given to us as, much as his righteousness is written *on us* and *in us* as our very own—his righteousness is credited to us. This is important because we are not *just* cleaned up sinners, we actually stand before God as having the righteousness of the perfect, holy, Jesus Christ because we have *his* righteousness *imputed* upon us! Do you see that? Because Jesus's righteousness is imputed to you, you are seen by God as having Jesus's righteousness, not because of you, but because of Jesus! And that, my friends, is imputation! Isn't that worth knowing and understanding?
[15] Heb. 10; Rom. 6; Col. 1; 1 Pet. 1.
[16] *Inditing* means *writing*.
[17] This concept of *jot and tittle* is referring to tiny marks in Hebrew writing. Essentially, this is saying that nothing will pass away, not even the seemingly small and unimportant stuff.

magnify thy grace in the salvation of my soul, through thy Son Jesus Christ. Amen.[18]

CHRISTIAN: And did you do as you were bidden?

HOPEFUL: Yes; over, and over, and over.

CHRISTIAN: And did the Father reveal his Son to you?

HOPEFUL: Not at the first, nor second, nor third, nor fourth, nor fifth; no, nor at the sixth time neither.

CHRISTIAN: What did you do then?

HOPEFUL: What! why I could not tell what to do.

CHRISTIAN: Had you not thoughts of leaving off praying?

HOPEFUL: Yes; an hundred times twice told.

CHRISTIAN: And what was the reason you did not?

HOPEFUL: I believed that that was true which had been told me, to wit, that without the righteousness of this Christ, all the world could not save me; and therefore, thought I with myself, if I leave off I die, and I can but die at the throne of grace. And withal, this came into my mind, "Though it tarry, wait for it; because it will surely come, it will not tarry."[19] So I continued praying until the Father showed me his Son.

CHRISTIAN: And how was he revealed unto you?

HOPEFUL: I did not see him with my bodily eyes, but with the eyes of my understanding; and thus it was: One day I was very sad, I think sadder than at any one time in my life, and this sadness was through a fresh sight of the greatness and vileness of my sins. And as I was then looking for nothing but hell, and the everlasting damnation of my soul, suddenly, as I thought, I saw the Lord Jesus Christ look down from heaven upon me, and saying, "Believe on the Lord Jesus Christ, and thou shalt be saved."[20]

But I replied, Lord, I am a great, a very great sinner. And he answered, "My grace is sufficient for thee." Then I said, But, Lord, what is believing? And then I saw from that saying, "He that cometh to me shall never hunger, and he that believeth on me shall never thirst," that believing and coming was all one; and that he that came, that is, ran out in his heart and affections after salvation by Christ, he indeed believed in Christ. Then

---

[18] Matt. 11:28, 24:35; Ps. 95:6; Dan. 6:10; Jer. 29:12, 13; Exo. 25:22; Lev. 16:2; Num. 7:89; Heb. 4:16.
[19] Hab. 2:3.
[20] Eph. 1:18, 19; Acts 16:30, 31.

the water stood in mine eyes, and I asked further. But, Lord, may such a great sinner as I am be indeed accepted of thee, and be saved by thee? And I heard him say, "And him that cometh to me, I will in no wise cast out." Then I said, But how, Lord, must I consider of thee in my coming to thee, that my faith may be placed aright upon thee? Then he said, "Christ Jesus came into the world to save sinners." "He is the end of the law for righteousness to every one that believeth." "He died for our sins, and rose again for our justification." "He loved us, and washed us from our sins in his own blood." "He is mediator betwixt God and us." "He ever liveth to make intercession for us."[21]

From all which I gathered, that I must look for righteousness in his person, and for satisfaction for my sins by his blood; that what he did in obedience to his Father's law, and in submitting to the penalty thereof, was not for himself, but for him that will accept it for his salvation, and be thankful. And now was my heart full of joy, mine eyes full of tears, and mine affections running over with love to the name, people, and ways of Jesus Christ.

CHRISTIAN: This was a revelation of Christ to your soul indeed; but tell me particularly what effect this had upon your spirit.

HOPEFUL: It made me see that all the world, notwithstanding all the righteousness thereof, is in a state of condemnation. It made me see that God the Father, though he be just, can justly justify the coming sinner. It made me greatly ashamed of the vileness of my former life, and confounded me with the sense of mine own ignorance; for there never came thought into my heart before now that showed me so the beauty of Jesus Christ. It made me love a holy life, and long to do something for the honour and glory of the name of the Lord Jesus; yea, I thought that had I now a thousand gallons of blood in my body, I could spill it all for the sake of the Lord Jesus.

---

[21] 2 Cor.12:9; John 6:35,37; 1 Tim. 1:15; Rom. 10:4, 4:25; Rev. 1:5; 1 Tim. 2:5; Heb. 7:24, 25.

WHAT WE COVERED IN WEEK THIRTEEN

Have you ever come to a point in your life where you want to do the right thing, you want to take the right path, you want to honour God with your next steps… but… you have two paths before you? And try as you might, you simply don't know which is the right way.

Have you ever faced a fork in the road?

I expect most of us have. And it's at that point when we often hope for someone wiser than us to come along and give us some advice.

And guess what! Someone comes to help Christian and Hopeful. Unfortunately, he does not carry the kind of wisdom we hope for in a time when we are committed to walking the path laid out by Christ.

Did you notice that this man leads them on a path that turns not sharply, but by degrees? Isn't this always the way of compromise? Isn't this always how we are led astray? We always move off the path in tiny little steps. Little bit by little bit, and in the case of Christian and Hopeful, this man's efforts led them to a point where they were walking away from the Celestial City.

And Christian and Hopeful were not alarmed.

Consider this… they are led astray from the faith that they have held, yet they don't even notice! This raises a disturbing thought. Is it possible for mature Christians to be comfortably led astray? What might that look like in your life?

And when we see others around us slide away from the faith, we might think they've taken a big step away, but how many little steps led to that change? Was it really as shocking of a change for them (or for us when we do it) as it appears? Or was it the result of a series of small turns?

However, we are grateful they are not lost. When the Shining One comes to release them, he comes with a whip in his hand, but despite their drifting away, he still comes for them.

Let me share something from my heart.

This scares me.

I need mercy, for I stray far more than I would like to admit. Perhaps I stray more than most. I remember hearing a story of a pastor who stood up and said, "If you knew the kind of person I was, you'd never listen to me preach. Then again, if I knew the kind of people you are, I wouldn't be up here preaching to you!"

And as a pastor who used to preach the Word of God week after week, I know what it's like to be far from perfect, for no preacher (aside from the Good Shepherd) is perfect. We preach of love, yet our love is far from perfect. We preach of repentance, yet our repentance comes up short. We preach of grace, yet our grasp of it is weak.

And… because of my imperfections… and because of my ongoing struggle with sin… the discipline mentioned above scares me.

Isn't it good to know that God is patient, kind, gracious, and merciful? If it were not so, we would all be lost! But because of his kindness, we find more grace at every moment, even in the discipline.

But back to Christian and Hopeful! When they return to the path, they move on to meet someone else. They meet Atheist, someone very much unlike anyone they have met until this point. But when we read this section, it's almost difficult to remember that this book was written 340 years ago! We quickly find that Atheist of 340 years ago is not much different from Atheist of the 21st century. His words to Christian and Hopeful are a common script followed by those who say there is no God.[22]

But then something unexpected happens. Hopeful calls Atheist one of the flatterers. A flatterer is one who leads you where he wants you to go and spreads a net for your feet.

We're often presented with the idea that an atheist is someone who just doesn't believe in God. The world presents them as peaceful, content, and walking the road with a "live and let live" kind of attitude. Certainly, many atheists are peaceful and content in their own way, but then again, some atheists are aggressive proselytizers. While some are content to let others believe what they want, many atheists will go out of their way to tear down anyone of the Christian faith, dragging them away, and seeking to ensnare them far from the path.

---

[22] Psalm 14:1.

Which raises the question… is atheism a rejection of God, or is it an aggressive proselytizing religion, converting people to its beliefs, convictions, and values?

Oh… that's quite a thought![23]

And so, while many Atheists are not this way, Atheist in our story is demeaning, even mocking of Christian and Hopeful. It is as if he either has a drive to convince them they are fools for following Christ, or he truly looks down on them.

May God open the eyes of those who live like this man in this story.

But next, we have a peaceful conversation. Hopeful tells his story of his conversion.

I will leave the discussion of his sin to the talking points below, but let me point out that in the end, he had a vision of Christ calling him to believe in the Lord Jesus Christ for salvation!

Ponder that for a moment. Down through history, there have been many great men and women of the faith. We look up to them, admire them, and learn from them. We read biographies of them, and they inspire us!

Yet, every one of them was saved the same way. They believed in Jesus Christ for salvation.

It all comes down to that.

And the deeper we grow in our faith, and the more we learn, and the greater truths we learn about God and his Word, we all come back to this simple matter: in the end, what we find most precious is the belief that Jesus Christ saves us by grace through faith.

And this is truly where the beauty of Pilgrim's Progress is seen. Christian and Hopeful are not saved by their journey, by their effort, by their sticking to the path.

No, they are saved by faith in Jesus Christ.

And in Jesus alone!

Lord, you are my Saviour. I have no hope apart from you. But in you, I have a solid hope, a guarantee of salvation in your presence forever! And to this I hold as I march confidently forward to your eternal home!
Amen

---

[23] Certainly this would have to be evaluated on a case-by-case basis.

TALKING POINTS

1. Consider this: the entire journey has been focused on reaching one place: the Celestial City. Why is this a proper focus for a Christian who walks in the way laid out by Christ?

2. What are you focused on in your life? What are your goals? Education? Job? Money? Those may all, at times, be good things, but should they ever be a Christian's focus and goal? Do you want to root out and change your focus? Is it possible to see all these temporary things as a means to secure a greater reward in the Celestial City?[24]

3. What else are you focused on? Learning spiritual truth? Understanding one more of God's wonderful secrets? Nailing down your theology a little more? Perfecting your grasp of the Gospel and your passion for sharing it? Those are all wonderful things, but should any of those things be your ultimate goal? What would it look like to shift your perspective so all spiritual things have more to do with glorifying God and securing an eternal reward in the Celestial City than anything else?

---

[24] Matt. 6:19-21.

4. What would personal evangelism look like for a Christian focused on the Celestial City?

5. What does theology[25] look like for a Christian focused on the Celestial City?

6. What do your spiritual disciplines (Bible reading, prayer, Scripture memorization, etc.) look like for a Christian focused on the Celestial City?

7. How does a focus on the Celestial City affect your attitude towards trials and difficulties?

---

[25] Perhaps a good, simple definition of theology here might be what we believe and know about God and his ways and how we live it all out.

8. When Christian and Hopeful reach the point where the path divides, they stop and wonder about it, opening themselves up to the Flatterer. How should they have approached that divide?

9. When Christian and Hopeful are led astray, it is by minor adjustments and turns. Have you ever experienced this? What reasoning or beliefs allowed you to continue in your slide away from faithfulness?

10. It's interesting that Hopeful and Christian face the opportunity to lie down and sleep (and never wake up) in the enchanted grounds, and this happens right here near the end of their journey. Can I be bold with you? Is there a time in our lives that we tend to lie down spiritually and sleep the rest of our lives away?[26] Perhaps we say things like, "Oh, I've done my part, I'll let the younger ones step in now." In light of a life called to walk the path, what do you think is a Christ-honouring thing to do at that point in our lives?

---

[26] This is not referring to physical limitations, weaknesses, or illness which can be Christ-honouring reasons for stepping back, but a choice on the part of the believer.

11. Why is a discussion about theology a good option for Christian and Hopeful when they're threatened with sleep? What does that represent?

12. Considering Hopeful's conversion experience, can someone truly be converted/saved with no knowledge of their own sin?

13. Now, you might struggle a bit with the drawn-out process of Hopeful's conversion. It seems like he cried out for salvation, but God withheld it. First, keep in mind that this is a gospel allegory which means it's a picture that's painted to teach us something. So, why do you think Bunyan draws out this salvation experience for us, the readers?

14. In Hopeful's story of conversion, when Faithful tells him to go see Jesus, Hopeful's first reaction is that it would be pretentious to do that. Would someone as great as Jesus want to see Hopeful? But Faithful tells him he is invited to go. Take a moment and reflect on that concept, that Jesus invites wicked sinners to go see him. Wow! How does that affect your view of Jesus?

15. We learn Atheist is one of the flatterers. Why do you think that is?

16. Isn't it also interesting that Atheist hints that he used to believe as they did or at least searched for the Celestial City as they have? Why do you think atheists of today *and* Atheist of 340 years ago both often fall back on that particular argument?

17. A Caution Near the End

> Now, from around chapter twelve and on, you'll find a bit of a shift in some of the allegories. However, if you have more grey hair than the person next to you, you might not enjoy the fact that I'm pointing this out, and you might want to skip this next paragraph.[27]

> In these final sections of the book, a lot of allegories point to issues more *mature* people deal with. Yes, that's right, I'm talking about those of you who have a lot of good miles behind you. The enchanted grounds are certainly a good example of this. The young are often tempted by success, accumulation, accomplishment, lust, and more, while the non-young[28] are often tempted by ease, comfort, and *stepping back*. It is possible that anyone, of course, can fall asleep in their faith and just ride out the rest of their lives, but it is perhaps a greater challenge for those in their golden years in wealthy cultures such as western society. It is easy to figure that you've done your part, and it's time for younger people to do the work. Yet, you are still on the path, are you not? Is it possible that as energy wanes, it is not God's call for you to sit back and retire in your walk with the Lord, but rather to shift your focus?

---

[27] I'm kidding. I put the effort into writing it, the least you can do is read it. ☺
[28] Notice the great deal of effort I'm putting into avoiding calling some of you *old*.

Beware of falling asleep on the enchanted grounds, regardless of your age! This is a warning to the young *and* old, but this temptation perhaps traps more people in their later years. Heed the overt and subtle warnings in these final chapters.

18. In Bunyan's words, he hopes his story *will make a traveller of thee*. How do you see yourself travelling this road to the Celestial City differently because of this week's reading? What change in heart, attitude, theology, or lifestyle do you believe God is calling you to as you seek to be the traveller he desires you be?

14. Ignorance

I saw then in my dream that Hopeful looked back and saw Ignorance, whom they had left behind, coming after. "Look," said he to Christian, "How far yonder youngster loitereth behind."

CHRISTIAN: Ay, ay, I see him; he careth not for our company.

HOPEFUL: But I trow[1] it would not have hurt him had he kept pace with us hitherto.

CHRISTIAN: That is true; but I warrant you he thinketh otherwise.

HOPEFUL: That, I think, he doth; but, however, let us tarry for him. So they did.

Then Christian said to him, "Come away, man, why do you stay so behind?"

IGNORANCE: I take my pleasure in walking alone, even more a great deal than in company, unless I like it the better.

Then said Christian to Hopeful, (but softly), "Did I not tell you he cared not for our company? But, however," said he, "come up, and let us talk away the time in this solitary place." Then directing his speech to Ignorance, he said, "Come, how do you? How stands it between God and your soul now?"

IGNORANCE: I hope well; for I am always full of good motions, that come into my mind, to comfort me as I walk.

CHRISTIAN: What good motions? pray, tell us.

IGNORANCE: Why, I think of God and heaven.

---

[1] *Trow* means *think or believe.*

CHRISTIAN: So do the devils and damned souls.

IGNORANCE: But I think of them and desire them.

CHRISTIAN: So do many that are never like to come there. "The soul of the sluggard desireth, and hath nothing."[2]

IGNORANCE: But I think of them, and leave all for them.

CHRISTIAN: That I doubt; for leaving all is a hard matter: yea, a harder matter than many are aware of. But why, or by what, art thou persuaded that thou hast left all for God and heaven.

IGNORANCE: My heart tells me so.

CHRISTIAN: The wise man says, "He that trusts his own heart is a fool."[3]

IGNORANCE: This is spoken of an evil heart, but mine is a good one.

CHRISTIAN: But how dost thou prove that?

IGNORANCE: It comforts me in hopes of heaven.

CHRISTIAN: That may be through its deceitfulness; for a man's heart may minister comfort to him in the hopes of that thing for which he yet has no ground to hope.

IGNORANCE: But my heart and life agree together, and therefore my hope is well grounded.

CHRISTIAN: Who told thee that thy heart and life agree together?

IGNORANCE: My heart tells me so.

CHRISTIAN: Ask my fellow if I be a thief! Thy heart tells thee so! Except the Word of God beareth witness in this matter, other testimony is of no value.

IGNORANCE: But is it not a good heart that hath good thoughts? and is not that a good life that is according to God's commandments?

CHRISTIAN: Yes, that is a good heart that hath good thoughts, and that is a good life that is according to God's commandments; but it is one thing, indeed, to have these, and another thing only to think so.

---

[2] Prov. 13:4.
[3] Prov. 28:26.

IGNORANCE: Pray, what count you good thoughts, and a life according to God's commandments?

CHRISTIAN: There are good thoughts of divers kinds; some respecting ourselves, some God, some Christ, and some other things.

IGNORANCE: What be good thoughts respecting ourselves?

CHRISTIAN: Such as agree with the Word of God.

IGNORANCE: When do our thoughts of ourselves agree with the Word of God?

CHRISTIAN: When we pass the same judgement upon ourselves which the Word passes. To explain myself—the Word of God saith of persons in a natural condition, "There is none righteous, there is none that doeth good." It saith also, that "every imagination of the heart of man is only evil, and that continually." And again, "The imagination of man's heart is evil from his youth." Now then, when we think thus of ourselves, having sense thereof, then are our thoughts good ones, because according to the Word of God.[4]

IGNORANCE: I will never believe that my heart is thus bad.

CHRISTIAN: Therefore, thou never hadst one good thought concerning thyself in thy life. But let me go on. As the Word passeth a judgement upon our heart, so it passeth a judgement upon our ways; and when OUR thoughts of our hearts and ways agree with the judgement which the Word giveth of both, then are both good, because agreeing thereto.

IGNORANCE: Make out your meaning.

CHRISTIAN: Why, the Word of God saith that man's ways are crooked ways; not good, but perverse. It saith they are naturally out of the good way, that they have not known it. Now, when a man thus thinketh of his ways—I say, when he doth sensibly, and with heart-humiliation, thus think—then hath he good thoughts of his own ways, because his thoughts now agree with the judgement of the Word of God.[5]

IGNORANCE: What are good thoughts concerning God?

CHRISTIAN: Even as I have said concerning ourselves, when our thoughts of God do agree with what the Word saith of him; and that is, when we think of his being and attributes as the Word hath taught, of which I cannot now discourse at large; but to speak of him with reference to us:

---

4 Rom. 3:10-12; Gen. 6:5, 8:21.
5 Ps. 125:5; Prov. 2:15; Rom. 3.

Then we have right thoughts of God, when we think that he knows us better than we know ourselves, and can see sin in us when and where we can see none in ourselves; when we think he knows our inmost thoughts, and that our heart, with all its depths, is always open unto his eyes; also, when we think that all our righteousness stinks in his nostrils, and that, therefore, he cannot abide to see us stand before him in any confidence, even in all our best performances.

IGNORANCE: Do you think that I am such a fool as to think God can see no further than I? or, that I would come to God in the best of my performances?

CHRISTIAN: Why, how dost thou think in this matter?

IGNORANCE: Why, to be short, I think I must believe in Christ for justification.

CHRISTIAN: How! think thou must believe in Christ, when thou seest not thy need of him! Thou neither seest thy original nor actual infirmities; but hast such an opinion of thyself, and of what thou dost, as plainly renders thee to be one that did never see a necessity of Christ's personal righteousness to justify thee before God. How, then, dost thou say, I believe in Christ?

IGNORANCE: I believe well enough for all that.

CHRISTIAN: How dost thou believe?

IGNORANCE: I believe that Christ died for sinners, and that I shall be justified before God from the curse, through his gracious acceptance of my obedience to his law. Or thus, Christ makes my duties, that are religious, acceptable to his Father, by virtue of his merits; and so shall I be justified.

CHRISTIAN: Let me give an answer to this confession of thy faith:

1. Thou believest with a fantastical faith; for this faith is nowhere described in the Word.

2. Thou believest with a false faith; because it taketh justification from the personal righteousness of Christ, and applies it to thy own.

3. This faith maketh not Christ a justifier of thy person, but of thy actions; and of thy person for thy actions' sake, which is false.

4. Therefore, this faith is deceitful, even such as will leave thee under wrath, in the day of God Almighty; for true justifying faith puts the soul, as sensible of its condition by the law, upon flying for refuge unto Christ's righteousness, which righteousness of his is not an act of grace, by

which he maketh for justification, thy obedience accepted with God; but his personal obedience to the law, in doing and suffering for us what that required at our hands; this righteousness, I say, true faith accepteth; under the skirt of which, the soul being shrouded, and by it presented as spotless before God, it is accepted, and acquit from condemnation.

IGNORANCE: What! would you have us trust to what Christ, in his own person, has done without us? This conceit would loosen the reins of our lust, and tolerate us to live as we list; for what matter how we live, if we may be justified by Christ's personal righteousness from all, when we believe it?

CHRISTIAN: Ignorance is thy name, and as thy name is, so art thou; even this thy answer demonstrateth what I say. Ignorant thou art of what justifying righteousness is, and as ignorant how to secure thy soul, through the faith of it, from the heavy wrath of God. Yea, thou also art ignorant of the true effects of saving faith in this righteousness of Christ, which is, to bow and win over the heart to God in Christ, to love his name, his word, ways, and people, and not as thou ignorantly imaginest.

HOPEFUL: Ask him if ever he had Christ revealed to him from heaven.

IGNORANCE: What! you are a man for revelations! I believe that what both you, and all the rest of you, say about that matter, is but the fruit of distracted brains.

HOPEFUL: Why, man! Christ is so hid in God from the natural apprehensions of the flesh, that he cannot by any man be savingly known, unless God the Father reveals him to them.

IGNORANCE: That is your faith, but not mine; yet mine, I doubt not, is as good as yours, though I have not in my head so many whimsies as you.

CHRISTIAN: Give me leave to put in a word. You ought not so slightly to speak of this matter; for this I will boldly affirm, even as my good companion hath done, that no man can know Jesus Christ but by the revelation of the Father; yea, and faith too, by which the soul layeth hold upon Christ, if it be right, must be wrought by the exceeding greatness of his mighty power; the working of which faith, I perceive, poor Ignorance, thou art ignorant of. Be awakened, then, see thine own wretchedness, and fly to the Lord Jesus; and by his righteousness, which is the righteousness of God, for he himself is God, thou shalt be delivered from condemnation.[6]

---

[6] Matt. 11:27; 1 Cor. 12:3; Eph. 1:18, 19.

IGNORANCE: You go so fast, I cannot keep pace with you. Do you go on before; I must stay a while behind.

Then they said:

> *Well, Ignorance, wilt thou yet foolish be,*
> *To slight good counsel, ten times given thee?*
> *And if thou yet refuse it, thou shalt know,*
> *Ere long, the evil of thy doing so.*
> *Remember, man, in time, stoop, do not fear;*
> *Good counsel taken well, saves: therefore hear.*
> *But if thou yet shalt slight it, thou wilt be*
> *The loser, (Ignorance), I'll warrant thee.*

Then Christian addressed thus himself to his fellow:

CHRISTIAN: Well, come, my good Hopeful, I perceive that thou and I must walk by ourselves again.

So, I saw in my dream that they went on apace before, and Ignorance he came hobbling after. Then said Christian to his companion, "It pities me much for this poor man, it will certainly go ill with him at last."

HOPEFUL: Alas! there are abundance in our town in his condition, whole families, yea, whole streets, and that of pilgrims too; and if there be so many in our parts, how many, think you, must there be in the place where he was born?

CHRISTIAN: Indeed the Word saith, "He hath blinded their eyes, lest they should see."[7] But now we are by ourselves, what do you think of such men? Have they at no time, think you, convictions of sin, and so consequently fears that their state is dangerous?

HOPEFUL: Nay, do you answer that question yourself, for you are the elder man.

CHRISTIAN: Then I say, sometimes (as I think) they may; but they being naturally ignorant, understand not that such convictions tend to their good; and therefore they do desperately seek to stifle them, and presumptuously continue to flatter themselves in the way of their own hearts.

HOPEFUL: I do believe, as you say, that fear tends much to men's good, and to make them right, at their beginning to go on pilgrimage.

---

[7] John 12:40.

CHRISTIAN: Without all doubt it doth, if it be right; for so says the Word, "The fear of the Lord is the beginning of wisdom."[8]

HOPEFUL: How will you describe right fear?

CHRISTIAN: True or right fear is discovered by three things:

1. By its rise; it is caused by saving convictions for sin.

2. It driveth the soul to lay fast hold of Christ for salvation.

3. It begetteth and continueth in the soul a great reverence of God, his Word, and ways, keeping it tender, and making it afraid to turn from them, to the right hand or to the left, to anything that may dishonour God, break its peace, grieve the Spirit, or cause the enemy to speak reproachfully.

HOPEFUL: Well said; I believe you have said the truth. Are we now almost got past the Enchanted Ground?

CHRISTIAN: Why, art thou weary of this discourse?

HOPEFUL: No, verily, but that I would know where we are.

CHRISTIAN: We have not now above two miles further to go thereon. But let us return to our matter. Now the ignorant know not that such convictions as tend to put them in fear are for their good, and therefore they seek to stifle them.

HOPEFUL: How do they seek to stifle them?

CHRISTIAN: 1. They think that those fears are wrought by the devil, (though indeed they are wrought of God); and, thinking so, they resist them as things that directly tend to their overthrow.

2. They also think that these fears tend to the spoiling of their faith, when, alas, for them, poor men that they are, they have none at all! and therefore they harden their hearts against them.

3. They presume they ought not to fear; and, therefore, in despite of them, wax[9] presumptuously confident.

4. They see that those fears tend to take away from them their pitiful old self-holiness, and therefore they resist them with all their might.

HOPEFUL: I know something of this myself; for, before I knew myself, it was so with me.

---

[8] Prov. 1:7, 9:10; Job 28:28; Ps. 111:10.
[9] This form of the word *wax* tends to mean *to become larger or stronger*. So, this phrase would refer to their presumptuous confidence growing larger.

CHRISTIAN: Well, we will leave, at this time, our neighbour Ignorance by himself, and fall upon another profitable question.

HOPEFUL: With all my heart, but you shall still begin.

CHRISTIAN: Well then, did you not know, about ten years ago, one Temporary in your parts, who was a forward man in religion then?

HOPEFUL: Know him! yes, he dwelt in Graceless, a town about two miles off of Honesty, and he dwelt next door to one Turnback.

CHRISTIAN: Right, he dwelt under the same roof with him. Well, that man was much awakened once; I believe that then he had some sight of his sins, and of the wages that were due thereto.

HOPEFUL: I am of your mind, for, my house not being above three miles from him, he would ofttimes come to me, and that with many tears. Truly I pitied the man, and was not altogether without hope of him; but one may see, it is not every one that cries, Lord, Lord.[10]

CHRISTIAN: He told me once that he was resolved to go on pilgrimage, as we do now; but all of a sudden he grew acquainted with one Save-self, and then he became a stranger to me.

HOPEFUL: Now, since we are talking about him, let us a little inquire into the reason of the sudden backsliding of him and such others.

CHRISTIAN: It may be very profitable, but do you begin.

HOPEFUL: Well, then, there are in my judgement four reasons for it:

1. Though the consciences of such men are awakened, yet their minds are not changed; therefore, when the power of guilt weareth away, that which provoked them to be religious ceaseth, wherefore they naturally turn to their own course again, even as we see the dog that is sick of what he has eaten, so long as his sickness prevails he vomits and casts up all; not that he doth this of a free mind (if we may say a dog has a mind), but because it troubleth his stomach; but now, when his sickness is over, and so his stomach eased, his desire being not at all alienate from his vomit, he turns him about and licks up all, and so it is true which is written, "The dog is turned to his own vomit again."[11] Thus I say, being hot for heaven, by virtue only of the sense and fear of the torments of hell, as their sense of hell and the fears of damnation chills and cools, so their desires for heaven and salvation cool also. So, then it comes to pass, that when their guilt and

---

[10] Matt. 7:21.
[11] 2 Pet. 2:22.

fear is gone, their desires for heaven and happiness die, and they return to their course again.

2. Another reason is, they have slavish fears that do overmaster them; I speak now of the fears that they have of men, for "the fear of man bringeth a snare."[12] So then, though they seem to be hot for heaven, so long as the flames of hell are about their ears, yet when that terror is a little over, they betake themselves to second thoughts; namely, that it is good to be wise, and not to run (for they know not what) the hazard of losing all, or, at least, of bringing themselves into unavoidable and unnecessary troubles, and so they fall in with the world again.

3. The shame that attends religion lies also as a block in their way; they are proud and haughty; and religion in their eye is low and contemptible, therefore, when they have lost their sense of hell and wrath to come, they return again to their former course.

4. Guilt, and to meditate terror, are grievous to them. They like not to see their misery before they come into it; though perhaps the sight of it first, if they loved that sight, might make them fly whither the righteous fly and are safe. But because they do, as I hinted before, even shun the thoughts of guilt and terror, therefore, when once they are rid of their awakenings about the terrors and wrath of God, they harden their hearts gladly, and choose such ways as will harden them more and more.

CHRISTIAN: You are pretty near the business, for the bottom of all is for want of a change in their mind and will. And therefore they are but like the felon that standeth before the judge, he quakes and trembles, and seems to repent most heartily, but the bottom of all is the fear of the halter; not that he hath any detestation of the offence, as is evident, because, let but this man have his liberty, and he will be a thief, and so a rogue still, whereas, if his mind was changed, he would be otherwise.

HOPEFUL: Now I have showed you the reasons of their going back, do you show me the manner thereof.

CHRISTIAN: So I will willingly.

1. They draw off their thoughts, all that they may, from the remembrance of God, death, and judgement to come.

2. Then they cast off by degrees private duties, as closet prayer, curbing their lusts, watching, sorrow for sin, and the like.

3. Then they shun the company of lively and warm Christians.

---

[12] Prov. 29:25.

4. After that they grow cold to public duty, as hearing, reading, godly conference, and the like.

5. Then they begin to pick holes, as we say, in the coats of some of the godly; and that devilishly, that they may have a seeming colour to throw religion (for the sake of some infirmity they have espied in them) behind their backs.

6. Then they begin to adhere to, and associate themselves with, carnal, loose, and wanton men.

7. Then they give way to carnal and wanton discourses in secret; and glad are they if they can see such things in any that are counted honest, that they may the more boldly do it through their example.

8. After this they begin to play with little sins openly.

9. And then, being hardened, they show themselves as they are. Thus, being launched again into the gulf of misery, unless a miracle of grace prevent it, they everlastingly perish in their own deceivings.

WHAT WE COVERED IN WEEK FOURTEEN

Discussion with Ignorance
Discussion after Ignorance leaves

Ahh… Ignorance continues to follow Christian and Hopeful! Is it possible we are all followed by Ignorance on one level or another? Perhaps, as far as we walk on the journey, Ignorance will always remain just a few steps behind!

Ignorance, of course, is an old companion (of both theirs and ours). He has walked with Christian and Hopeful in the past—not as one giving them ignorance, but as one who himself lives in ignorance. And Ignorance is rarely aware enough to recognize his own identity.

But Christian and Hopeful recognize something important. Although Ignorance does not want their company, he would benefit from it. And such are two matters that hold true for all who live in Ignorance: Ignorance rarely enjoys the company of those who are wise, and yet Ignorance desperately needs it.

It is perhaps helpful to ask yourself two questions to see if you, like we all often do, dabble in a bit of ignorance. First, do you find those who know what they are talking about to be annoying? I don't mean people who are desperate to tell you what they think, but humble people who might know better than you on a subject? Those who are truly wise?

Second, do you avoid those who can teach you?

Sadly, those who live in ignorance can rarely hear what others have to say, imprisoning the ignorant in their own foolishness.

Ignorance, in our story, however, concedes to walk with Christian and Hopeful for a decent portion of our time in this section of the book, and we see some difficult truths.

As they speak, Ignorance insists that he will never believe that his heart is all that bad. Instead of going into this here, I have some questions for reflection on this matter at the end of this section.

But I will say this: in Jeremiah 17:9, we learn that the opposite of what Ignorance believes is true. The heart is deceitful.

Consider this… if the heart is good, how would this affect a mentoring relationship? If the heart is evil, how would this affect that same mentoring relationship?

That makes a HUGE difference. And for people like Christian and Hopeful on the way to the Celestial City, this is a big issue for them!

Ignorance then comes out with a beautiful statement declaring his faith in Christ! Sure, it may be a little off, but it's fantastic! Isn't it? At least… it appears so. But once Christian goes at the statement, we see it in a different light.

And the root problem again seems to come down to the matter of this man's ignorance. He is not only ignorant of his heart's wickedness, but he has also found a way to combine a salvation of grace and works.

How can we watch out for such deception in our own lives? Mixing grace and works is a recipe for a spiritual mess, and yet we all tend to slide in that direction.

Once Ignorance is gone, Christian and Hopeful discuss our tendency to be drawn away, calling it backsliding. Their discussion is quite interesting!

When you look closely at how each one approaches the topic, you find Hopeful speaks more about the heart attitudes and faith issues, focusing more on theoretical and theological description of the matter. Christian, however, speaks more to the actual outworking of it, the steps and the process along which people travel on their path to backsliding, focusing more on a practical approach.

But… here is the interesting connection between what these two men talk about: when it truly comes down to it, theology is strongly practical. A deep knowledge of God and his ways will always call us to live more faithfully.

Lord, please empower me to live more faithfully, never falling into ignorance of you or your ways and never sliding away from you! Protect me on this journey I am on to one day see your face and be welcomed into your eternal city!
Amen

TALKING POINTS

1. Consider Christian's bluntness with Ignorance. When do you think it is appropriate to be blunt and when is it appropriate to walk lightly around topics?[13]

2. In his bluntness, Christian says that when good thoughts agree with the Word of God, it means that we believe that in our natural state, our thoughts are evil. What do you think of that? What difference does that belief make in your life? Your faith? Your salvation? Your view of others?

3. What do you think of this idea that a heart can be evil? Or… is it good?

---

[13] If you are doing this study with others, remember that some people are naturally blunt while others are naturally timid. Try to work through and around this topic with grace rather than glorifying one personality over another, seeking to find an approach that honours Jesus over personality or preference.

4.[14] If the heart is deceitful, how will this affect:

> ...parenting?

> ...career choices?

> ...a sense of calling to full/part time Christian ministry?

> ...dating and marriage?

> ...entertainment choices?

5. Considering Jeremiah 17:9, how far can you trust your heart? How far is it deceitful? What does that mean for everyday life?

6. Considering Jeremiah 17:9 tells us that the heart is beyond all cure, what difference does Jesus make for an incurable heart?

---

[14] Do you need a trigger warning? If so, consider this it, as this is a difficult exercise!

7. Who can cure the heart? No one. Nothing. Nothing can heal the heart at all. It's absolutely impossible! Yet, we have the God in whom the impossible becomes possible.[15] Isn't Jesus wonderful? Perhaps it's helpful to stop right now and spend some time thanking Jesus for being the great healer who can heal even an incurably sick heart.

8. With all of Ignorance's ignorance, we finally come to the heart of the matter. Ignorance believes he will be saved because of his obedience to the Law. And there we have it. Now, here's the question: Do you know if you are saved? How do you know? Spend some time on this one!

9. Now, here's an enormous challenge for us. Ignorance declares that true grace and faith, a reliance upon Jesus and his work for us, leads to sinfulness. But consider Christian's response: "Yea, thou also art ignorant of the true effects of saving faith in this righteousness of Christ, which is, to bow and win over the heart to God in Christ, to love his name, his word, ways, and people, and not as thou ignorantly imaginest." What difference is made in the life of someone who has received God's true grace?

---

[15] Mat. 19:26.

10. In describing how Christ is revealed to us and how faith comes to us, Christian says (paraphrase), "No one can know Jesus unless the Father reveals him to them, and no one can have faith unless God, in his great power, gives that faith to them." What do you think of all that?

11. What are your thoughts on the three points Christian gives about proper fear of the Lord?

12. What does it mean to have a healthy fear of God? Specifically, what does it mean to have a fear of God's hatred of sin?

13. In continuing the thought of the fear of the Lord, how does proper fear of the Lord fit in with 2 Timothy 1:7?

14. When Hopeful speaks of "backsliding" or falling away from the Christian faith, he lays out a lot of reasons it would happen. Take a few moments and discuss those reasons with a few others. Do you see any common themes running through his words?

15. Consider what Christian says about how people begin to backslide or fall away from Jesus. Do you see those steps in your own life? As the steps progress, they become more visible, which means the early steps might be easily hidden from those around you. Perhaps it's helpful to re-read that section.

16. In Bunyan's words, he hopes his story *will make a traveller of thee*. How do you see yourself travelling this road to the Celestial City differently because of this week's reading? What change in heart, attitude, theology, or lifestyle do you believe God is calling you to as you seek to be the traveller he desires you be?

15. The River

Now I saw in my dream, that by this time the Pilgrims were got over the Enchanted Ground, and entering into the country of Beulah, whose air was very sweet and pleasant, the way lying directly through it, they solaced themselves there for a season. Yea, here they heard continually the singing of birds, and saw every day the flowers appear on the earth, and heard the voice of the turtle in the land. In this country the sun shineth night and day; wherefore this was beyond the Valley of the Shadow of Death, and also out of the reach of Giant Despair, neither could they from this place so much as see Doubting Castle. Here they were within sight of the city they were going to, also here met them some of the inhabitants thereof; for in this land the Shining Ones commonly walked, because it was upon the borders of heaven. In this land also, the contract between the bride and the bridegroom was renewed; yea, here, "As the bridegroom rejoiceth over the bride, so did their God rejoice over them." Here they had no want of corn and wine; for in this place they met with abundance of what they had sought for in all their pilgrimage. Here they heard voices from out of the city, loud voices, saying, "'Say ye to the daughter of Zion, Behold, thy salvation cometh! Behold, his reward is with him!' Here all the inhabitants of the country called them, 'The holy people, The redeemed of the Lord, Sought out.'"[1]

Now as they walked in this land, they had more rejoicing than in parts more remote from the kingdom to which they were bound; and drawing near to the city, they had yet a more perfect view thereof. It was builded of pearls and precious stones, also the street thereof was paved with gold; so that by reason of the natural glory of the city, and the reflection of the sunbeams upon it, Christian with desire fell sick; Hopeful also had a fit

---

[1] Isa. 62:4; Song of Sol. 2:10-12; Isa. 62:5, 8, 11, 12.

or two of the same disease. Wherefore, here they lay by it a while, crying out, because of their pangs, "If ye find my beloved, tell him that I am sick of love."[2]

But, being a little strengthened, and better able to bear their sickness, they walked on their way, and came yet nearer and nearer, where were orchards, vineyards, and gardens, and their gates opened into the highway.

Now, as they came up to these places, behold the gardener stood in the way, to whom the Pilgrims said, "Whose goodly vineyards and gardens are these?"

He answered, "They are the King's, and are planted here for his own delight, and also for the solace of pilgrims." So the gardener had them into the vineyards, and bid them refresh themselves with the dainties.[3] He also showed them there the King's walks, and the arbours where he delighted to be; and here they tarried and slept.

Now I beheld in my dream that they talked more in their sleep at this time than ever they did in all their journey; and being in a muse thereabout, the gardener said even to me, "Wherefore musest thou at the matter? It is the nature of the fruit of the grapes of these vineyards to go down so sweetly as to cause the lips of them that are asleep to speak."

So I saw that when they awoke, they addressed themselves to go up to the city; but, as I said, the reflection of the sun upon the city (for the city was pure gold) was so extremely glorious that they could not, as yet, with open face behold it, but through an instrument made for that purpose. So I saw, that as I went on, there met them two men, in raiment that shone like gold; also their faces shone as the light.[4]

These men asked the Pilgrims whence they came; and they told them. They also asked them where they had lodged, what difficulties and dangers, what comforts and pleasures they had met in the way; and they told them. Then said the men that met them, "You have but two difficulties more to meet with, and then you are in the city."

Christian then, and his companion, asked the men to go along with them; so they told them they would. "But," said they, "you must obtain it by your own faith." So I saw in my dream that they went on together, until they came in sight of the gate.

---

[2] Song of Sol. 5:8.
[3] Deut. 23:24.
[4] Rev. 21:18; 2 Cor. 3:18.

Now, I further saw, that betwixt them and the gate was a river, but there was no bridge to go over: the river was very deep. At the sight, therefore, of this river, the Pilgrims were much stunned; but the men that went in with them said, "You must go through, or you cannot come at the gate."

The Pilgrims then began to inquire if there was no other way to the gate; to which they answered, "Yes; but there hath not any, save two, to wit, Enoch and Elijah, been permitted to tread that path since the foundation of the world, nor shall, until the last trumpet shall sound."[5]

The Pilgrims then, especially Christian, began to despond in their minds, and looked this way and that, but no way could be found by them by which they might escape the river.

Then they asked the men if the waters were all of a depth. They said: "No;" yet they could not help them in that case; "for," said they, "you shall find it deeper or shallower as you believe in the King of the place."

They then addressed themselves to the water and, entering, Christian began to sink, and crying out to his good friend Hopeful, he said, "I sink in deep waters; the billows go over my head, all his waves go over me! Selah."[6]

Then said the other, "Be of good cheer, my brother, I feel the bottom, and it is good."

Then said Christian, "Ah! my friend, the sorrows of death hath compassed me about; I shall not see the land that flows with milk and honey;" and with that a great darkness and horror fell upon Christian, so that he could not see before him. Also, here he in great measure lost his senses, so that he could neither remember nor orderly talk of any of those sweet refreshments that he had met with in the way of his pilgrimage. But all the words that he spake still tended to discover that he had horror of mind, and heart fears that he should die in that river, and never obtain entrance in at the gate.

Here also, as they that stood by perceived, he was much in the troublesome thoughts of the sins that he had committed, both since and before he began to be a pilgrim. It was also observed that he was troubled with apparitions of hobgoblins and evil spirits, for ever and anon he would intimate so much by words.

---

[5] 1 Cor. 15:51-52.
[6] Psalm 42:7.

Hopeful, therefore, here had much ado to keep his brother's head above water; yea, sometimes he would be quite gone down, and then, ere a while, he would rise up again half dead. Hopeful also would endeavour to comfort him, saying, "Brother, I see the gate, and men standing by to receive us."

But Christian would answer, "It is you, it is you they wait for; you have been Hopeful ever since I knew you."

"And so have you," said he to Christian."

"Ah! brother!" said he, "surely if I was right, he would now arise to help me; but for my sins he hath brought me into the snare, and hath left me."

Then said Hopeful, "My brother, you have quite forgot the text, where it is said of the wicked, 'There are no bands in their death, but their strength is firm. They are not in trouble as other men, neither are they plagued like other men.'[7] These troubles and distresses that you go through in these waters are no sign that God hath forsaken you; but are sent to try you, whether you will call to mind that which heretofore you have received of his goodness, and live upon him in your distresses."

Then I saw in my dream, that Christian was as in a muse a while.[8] To whom also Hopeful added this word, "Be of good cheer. Jesus Christ maketh thee whole."

And with that, Christian brake out with a loud voice, "Oh, I see him again! and he tells me, 'When thou passest through the waters, I will be with thee, and through the rivers, they shall not overflow thee.'[9] Then they both took courage, and the enemy was after that as still as a stone, until they were gone over.

Christian therefore presently found ground to stand upon, and so it followed that the rest of the river was but shallow. Thus, they got over.

Now, upon the bank of the river, on the other side, they saw the two shining men again, who there waited for them; wherefore, being come out of the river, they saluted them, saying, "We are ministering spirits, sent forth to minister for those that shall be heirs of salvation." Thus they went along towards the gate.

Now you must note that the city stood upon a mighty hill, but the Pilgrims went up that hill with ease, because they had these two men to lead

---

[7] Ps. 73:4-5.
[8] This suggests that Christian became very thoughtful for a time.
[9] Isa. 43:2.

them up by the arms; also, they had left their mortal garments behind them in the river, for though they went in with them, they came out without them. They, therefore, went up here with much agility and speed, though the foundation upon which the city was framed was higher than the clouds. They therefore went up through the regions of the air, sweetly talking as they went, being comforted, because they safely got over the river, and had such glorious companions to attend them.

> *Now, now, look how the holy pilgrims ride,*
> *Clouds are their chariots, angels are their guide:*
> *Who would not here for him all hazards run,*
> *That thus provides for his when this world's done?*

The talk they had with the Shining Ones was about the glory of the place; who told them that the beauty and glory of it was inexpressible. There, said they, is the Mount Zion, the heavenly Jerusalem, the innumerable company of angels, and the spirits of just men made perfect.[10]

"You are going now," said they, "to the paradise of God, wherein you shall see the tree of life, and eat of the never-fading fruits thereof; and when you come there, you shall have white robes given you, and your walk and talk shall be every day with the King, even all the days of eternity. There you shall not see again such things as you saw when you were in the lower region upon the earth, to wit, sorrow, sickness, affliction, and death, for the former things are passed away. You are now going to Abraham, to Isaac, and Jacob, and to the prophets—men that God hath taken away from the evil to come, and that are now resting upon their beds, each one walking in his righteousness.[11]

The men then asked, "What must we do in the holy place?"

To whom it was answered, "You must there receive the comforts of all your toil, and have joy for all your sorrow; you must reap what you have sown, even the fruit of all your prayers, and tears, and sufferings for the King by the way. In that place you must wear crowns of gold and enjoy the perpetual sight and vision of the Holy One, for there you shall see him as he is. There also you shall serve him continually with praise, with shouting, and thanksgiving, whom you desired to serve in the world, though with much difficulty, because of the infirmity of your flesh. There your eyes shall be delighted with seeing, and your ears with hearing the pleasant voice of the Mighty One. There you shall enjoy your friends again that are gone thither before you; and there you shall with joy receive, even every one that

---

[10] Heb. 12:22-24.
[11] Rev. 2:7; 3:4; 21:4, 5; Isa. 57:1, 2; 65:17.

follows into the holy place after you. There also shall you be clothed with glory and majesty and put into an equipage fit to ride out with the King of Glory. When he shall come with sound of trumpet in the clouds, as upon the wings of the wind, you shall come with him; and when he shall sit upon the throne of judgement; you shall sit by him; yea, and when he shall pass sentence upon all the workers of iniquity, let them be angels or men, you also shall have a voice in that judgement, because they were his and your enemies. Also, when he shall again return to the city, you shall go too, with sound of trumpet, and be ever with him."[12]

Now while they were thus drawing towards the gate, behold a company of the heavenly host came out to meet them; to whom it was said, by the other two Shining Ones, "These are the men that have loved our Lord when they were in the world, and that have left all for his holy name; and he hath sent us to fetch them, and we have brought them thus far on their desired journey, that they may go in and look their Redeemer in the face with joy."

Then the heavenly host gave a great shout, saying, "Blessed are they which are called unto the marriage supper of the Lamb."[13]

There came out also at this time to meet them, several of the King's trumpeters, clothed in white and shining raiment, who, with melodious noises, and loud, made even the heavens to echo with their sound. These trumpeters saluted Christian and his fellow with ten thousand welcomes from the world; and this they did with shouting, and sound of trumpet.

This done, they compassed them round on every side; some went before, some behind, and some on the right hand, some on the left, (as it were to guard them through the upper regions), continually sounding as they went, with melodious noise, in notes on high: so that the very sight was, to them that could behold it, as if heaven itself was come down to meet them.

Thus, therefore, they walked on together; and as they walked, ever and anon these trumpeters, even with joyful sound, would, by mixing their music with looks and gestures, still signify to Christian and his brother, how welcome they were into their company, and with what gladness they came to meet them; and now were these two men, as it were, in heaven, before they came at it, being swallowed up with the sight of angels, and with hearing of their melodious notes. Here also they had the city itself in view, and they thought they heard all the bells therein to ring, to welcome them

---

[12] Gal. 6:7; 1 John 3:2; 1 Thes. 4:13-16; Jude 1:14; Dan. 7:9, 10; 1 Cor. 6:2, 3.
[13] Rev. 19:9.

thereto. But above all, the warm and joyful thoughts that they had about their own dwelling there, with such company, and that for ever and ever.

Oh, by what tongue or pen can their glorious joy be expressed! And thus they came up to the gate.

Now, when they were come up to the gate, there was written over it in letters of gold, "Blessed are they that do his commandments, that they may have right to the tree of life, and may enter in through the gates into the city."[14]

Then I saw in my dream that the Shining Men bid them call at the gate; the which, when they did, some looked from above over the gate, to wit, Enoch, Moses, and Elijah, to whom it was said, "These pilgrims are come from the City of Destruction, for the love that they bear to the King of this place."

And then the Pilgrims gave in unto them each man his certificate, which they had received in the beginning; those, therefore, were carried in to the King, who, when he had read them, said, "Where are the men?"

To whom it was answered, "They are standing without the gate."

The King then commanded to open the gate, "That the righteous nation," said he, "which keepeth the truth, may enter in."[15]

Now I saw in my dream that these two men went in at the gate: and lo, as they entered, they were transfigured, and they had raiment put on that shone like gold. There was also that met them with harps and crowns, and gave them to them—the harps to praise withal, and the crowns in token of honour.

Then I heard in my dream that all the bells in the city rang again for joy, and that it was said unto them, "ENTER YE INTO THE JOY OF YOUR LORD."

I also heard the men themselves, that they sang with a loud voice, saying, "BLESSING AND HONOUR, AND GLORY, AND POWER, BE UNTO HIM THAT SITTETH UPON THE THRONE, AND UNTO THE LAMB, FOR EVER AND EVER."[16]

Now, just as the gates were opened to let in the men, I looked in after them, and, behold, the City shone like the sun; the streets also were

---

14 Rev. 22:14.
15 Isa. 26:2.
16 Rev. 5:13.

paved with gold, and in them walked many men, with crowns on their heads, palms in their hands, and golden harps to sing praises withal.

There were also of them that had wings, and they answered one another without intermission, saying, "Holy, holy, holy is the Lord."[17] And after that they shut up the gates; which, when I had seen, I wished myself among them.

Now while I was gazing upon all these things, I turned my head to look back, and saw Ignorance come up to the river side; but he soon got over, and that without half that difficulty which the other two men met with. For it happened that there was then in that place, one Vain-hope, a ferryman, that with his boat helped him over; so he, as the other I saw, did ascend the hill, to come up to the gate, only he came alone; neither did any man meet him with the least encouragement. When he was come up to the gate, he looked up to the writing that was above, and then began to knock, supposing that entrance should have been quickly administered to him.

But he was asked by the men that looked over the top of the gate, "Whence came you, and what would you have?"

He answered, "I have eat and drank in the presence of the King, and he has taught in our streets."

Then they asked him for his certificate, that they might go in and show it to the King; so he fumbled in his bosom for one, and found none.

Then said they, "Have you none?"

But the man answered never a word.

So they told the King, but he would not come down to see him, but commanded the two Shining Ones that conducted Christian and Hopeful to the City, to go out and take Ignorance, and bind him hand and foot, and have him away.

Then they took him up and carried him through the air to the door that I saw in the side of the hill, and put him in there. Then I saw that there was a way to hell, even from the gates of heaven, as well as from the City of Destruction.

So, I awoke, and behold it was a dream.

---

[17] Rev. 4:8.

THE CONCLUSION

Now, Reader, I have told my dream to thee;
See if thou canst interpret it to me,
Or to thyself, or neighbour; but take heed
Of misinterpreting; for that, instead
Of doing good, will but thyself abuse:
By misinterpreting, evil ensues.
Take heed, also, that thou be not extreme,
In playing with the outside of my dream:
Nor let my figure or similitude
Put thee into a laughter or a feud.
Leave this for boys and fools; but as for thee,
Do thou the substance of my matter see.
Put by the curtains, look within my veil,
Turn up my metaphors, and do not fail,
There, if thou seekest them, such things to find,
As will be helpful to an honest mind.
What of my dross thou findest there, be bold
To throw away, but yet preserve the gold;
What if my gold be wrapped up in ore?
None throws away the apple for the core.
But if thou shalt cast all away as vain,
I know not but 'twill make me dream again.

WHAT WE COVERED IN WEEK FIFTEEN

Discussion with Ignorance
The Country of Beulah
The Crossing of the River of Death
The Celestial City

We are at the end of our journey. It's our journey through this book, but, for Christian and Hopeful, it's actually the end of every part of their journey.

And yet the beginning of something entirely new!

It is during this week's reading that our friends die. In case you missed the picture, because it's not a typical image for 21st century believers, that's what was going on in the river.

Death.

They were close to their reward, close to the One whom they love, and close to the One whom they have sought this entire time. Nearly to Jesus.

The Celestial City itself is built of pearls and precious stones, and the streets are paved with gold. The natural glory of the city and the sunbeams reflecting on it make Christian feel sick with desire. Hopeful also has a few bouts of the same sickness, leaving them in need of rest before they can move on. They even cry out because of the deep pangs of desire!

If you find my beloved, tell them I'm sick with love![18]

At that time, we meet the Gardener. He cares for the vineyard that, though it has multiple reasons for its existence, is there for Christian and Hopeful's comfort. And they find the rest they need.

Now friends, at the end… is this truly a time to be excited? When this life is about to come to an abrupt halt?

It may come as a shock for us when those whom we know and love and are at their end might be excited… about dying!

---

[18] Song of Solomon 5:8.

But perhaps death is not what they are excited about. Perhaps dying is merely the river ahead. What they are truly excited about is not the river, but the One who remains beyond the river.

We see a little of this in Paul's words in Philippians when he speaks of his desire to be with Christ, knowing that to be with Christ is better than to be here.[19]

I wonder, perhaps, if there is something that causes us to long for Christ more.

Could it be the chance to rest?

Could it be the chance to receive our reward?

Could it be the chance to finally look upon the face of Jesus Christ? To experience that relationship in a deeper way?

Could it be the chance to be with those who have gone on before us?

Could it, perhaps, be because of the path? For Christian and Hopeful, it was a path filled with difficulty and suffering. And Christ promises a life without difficulty and suffering.

Wow!

And could it be a little (or a lot) of all those things?

Whatever makes us most excited at the end, if Christ has given his gift of salvation, the result is the same.

We meet Jesus.

And isn't that what we are truly looking forward to?

So, what is it like to know you are near to seeing Jesus face to face, that he is only a matter of hours, minutes, or seconds away?

One thing we learn as we grow older is that these bodies are frail. Such a reminder gives us a greater appreciation and a greater desire for eternity.

There was a time for me when eternity and the idea of a new body and new life in Christ were more a thought or idea written on a piece of paper than anything else. Then one day, everything changed. I often jokingly say that my body betrayed me! In a way, it did. It didn't come through for me the way I thought it would—my body *failed*. Now, even this

---

[19] Phil. 1:23.

little bit of work here in this book has to be spread out over long periods of time, just so I can manage.

If you met me, my body would appear to you to be healthy and strong, but on the inside, I'm frail and ready to collapse. Day to day, my weakness reminds me that although eternity with Christ is too wonderful to behold, it is promised to me! Guaranteed! Not because I've been especially good or wonderful (if anything, the opposite is true). It's promised to me because God is good, he is gracious, and he has given me his salvation.

My suffering often reminds me of what is prepared for me. One day, I will not need constant naps to get through the day. One day, I will not have constant headaches. One day, I will not have constant struggles with my memory and focus.

One day, I will be with Christ, and the constant struggle will be replaced with constant peace in Jesus.

And for our two friends, Christian and Hopeful, they come to this final difficulty, this river. It's pointed out to us that only Enoch and Elijah took a different route. Even Jesus had to follow the path down to the river, crossing it much like we have to, although with some very real differences.

And we sure are grateful that he did!

In this part of the journey that we all must take, we see death is a fearful thing, and we even witness our courageous friend, Christian, come to a point of despair as he crosses this River, while Hopeful remains true to his name.

We see Christian wonder if he is saved, wonder if he is lost. This might shock us, but keep in mind that this is a common challenge for believers near the end. We might be tempted to shake our head and say, "How dare you lose faith at this point!" but perhaps compassion is a better approach.

If your brother or sister suffers despair or fear at the end, remember something. They may have many years of faith behind them, but physically, mentally, and emotionally, they are at the weakest they have *ever* been their entire life.

They are so physically weak, their body can no longer keep that heart pumping!

Is it any wonder at that point that Satan launches his most vicious attack?

When your brother or sister is at that point, remind them of the grace of Jesus. Remind them he is bigger and more gracious and kinder and more sure than even their struggle at the end.

He will hold them.

And if you are at the end and you despair, remember, it was never you who held Jesus, but always, **always**, *ALWAYS* Jesus who held you!

Speaking as a former pastor, I have been with fellow believers at the end. Their faith has been real and strong, but near the point of death, some face despair. I think it's something that many will go through—just like Christian in our story. And it reminds us of Satan's hatred for us on one hand, but on the other, it reminds us that Jesus holds us tightly in his hand and no one can snatch us out![20]

And in that difficult time in our story, we find Christian calls out,

"Oh, I see him again! and he tells me, "When thou passest through the waters, I will be with thee, and through the rivers, they shall not overflow thee."[21]

Once the reminder of Christ's presence takes root, our friend finds ground for his feet to stand upon.

So, when we all come to that river, remember! Remember that Jesus is with us even then!

And when Christian and Hopeful come out on the other side, they meet an angel. And, of course, the question they ask is the question we might ask. We've made it… so… what will we do there in the Celestial City?

It seems kind of funny to ask such a question at this point, but we wish to know. And we hear they will enjoy their friends again, those who have gone on before them.

Are you looking forward to being with those who have gone on before in Jesus Christ? Those you wish to spend time with again?

---

[20] John 10:28.
[21] Isa. 43:2.

I'm reminded of a verse from an old Gaither song.

And then one day I'll cross the river
And I'll fight life's final war with pain
And then as death gives way to victory
I'll see the lights of glory and I'll know He reigns[22]

Lord, you reign over all. Over life, over death, and over eternity. One day, I too will cross that river, and I know that day will be the end of the old, and the beginning of the new! And then I will spend all eternity with the Lord Jesus I love.
Come, Lord Jesus, come!
Amen

---

[22] Because He Lives lyrics © Warner/Chappell Edicoes Musicais Ltda, Gaither Music Co. Inc., Hanna Street Music, Words by Bill and Gloria Gaither.

TALKING POINTS

1. In Christian and Hopeful's final days of their journey, they experience a sickness of longing for the City of God once they are within sight of it! What do you think that means? What is Bunyan trying to point out here?

2. How do you think you can prepare for your time to cross the river? How do you think you might secure the reminders of God's grace and Jesus's presence in your heart so you might cross the river more like Hopeful?

3. What do you expect to find on the other side? What do you expect to see? Who do you expect to meet?

4. What does it mean that Christian and Hopeful can see the city and what it is made of even before their crossing?

5. Christian's reaction to the river is such a different reaction than what he felt on most of his journey. I think perhaps the only other time he wanted to find another way around (aside from when they were drawn away from the path) was when he faced Apollyon. When Hopeful and he reached the river, why do you think they lost confidence? What does this teach us in terms of compassion, care, and love towards others? What do you suspect is God's response to this kind of reaction? Take some time with this.

6. What is the difference between Ignorance's crossing and Christian's crossing?

7. I'm going to ask a question we'd all rather not be asked. Have you ever been the ferryman named Vain-Hope for someone as they crossed the river?[23]

---

[23] I'm not sure if this is an ideal question for group discussion, but perhaps it's better reflected upon personally and privately. Don't be afraid to take this matter to Jesus. He is kind and gracious.

8. In the conclusion, Bunyan states this, "Take heed, also, that thou be not extreme in playing with the outside of my dream." Certainly, this book can be ignored, but we could also take it to an extreme. Perhaps we could even see it on par with Scripture, which would be a far greater tragedy than to ignore it altogether! This book is powerful in its teaching, for sure, but how do we guard against the extremes of ignoring the truth here and in elevating this book to a higher place than is proper?

9. Remember Bunyan's hope for this story in your life? Did this book help *to make a traveller of thee?* If so, in what ways?

My friend, we are at the end of this story.
There is a sequel to this book, although it's not as popular. It was
written a few years after the first part, and it's the story of Christian's
wife, Christiana, and her own journey.[24]

I encourage you to move on to that story and see what God seeks to
teach you through it, but in the meantime, God bless you as we travel
along together, with Christian, Faithful, Hopeful, and others, all on our
way to the Celestial City.

---

[24] As of the publishing of this *Rewalked* edition, I have not yet begun a *Rewalked* edition of the second book in this series.

Answers and Extra Thoughts on Pilgrim's Progress

1. THE BEGINNING

4. In Luke 14:26, Jesus says, "If anyone comes to me and does not hate his own father and mother and wife and children and brothers and sisters, yes, even his own life, he cannot be my disciple." While we might find this a difficult passage to swallow (and it doesn't get any easier as it continues), there are two things to keep in mind. First, this is hyperbole.[1] Jesus is using an extreme statement to illustrate how extreme our love for him must be. Second, there appears to have been an ancient Jewish approach where they would give two options: one they want, one they don't, and they might essentially tell you to love the good one and hate the bad one. For example, "Simeon, it's important that you milk the cow right away, not the goat. Very important! So important, you need to love the cow milk and hate the goal milk!"

Okay, that's a strange example, but you get the point. The issue is not to feel a hatred in your heart for others, but to have such a passionate love for Jesus that all else seems like nothing. You need to be so in love with Jesus that you will turn your back on everything and everyone else in your pursuit of this salvation! In the Luke 14 passage, we then understand that we are called to set everything else in life aside for Jesus. Everything!

Considering this, we see how Christian's actions fit with this passage. He would not stop for anything or anyone in his pursuit of salvation!

---

[1] Hyperbole is an exaggerated statement that illustrates a point, a statement that's not meant to be taken literally. Consider the idiom, "I'm so hungry I could eat a horse." Well... no, your stomach is not physically large enough to do that. It's an extreme statement that declares that you are hungry.

2. THE GATE

1. Perhaps it is helpful to look at it this way. When the conviction for sin comes along with the doubts and fears, teaching and instruction will *not* solve the problem. The problem is not lack of knowledge, but lack of relationship with the One who gives the grace needed for salvation. Because of this, sixteen hundred years of good, wholesome teaching (and now coming up on two millennia) cannot solve the problem. It takes a spiritual transformation for us to rely on Christ and not give in to fear and despond.

As for this being a good thing? Why might it be a good thing? Perhaps because if we, once we feel the conviction of the Holy Spirit for our sin, find freedom from our fears in simple teaching and instruction, what need would we see for an actual genuine salvation?

Keep pushing on to the wicket gate!

3. Remember John 15:20 and 16:33. Keep in mind that if the people of his town respected Christian's choice to leave, then it places responsibility on them to consider the same option for themselves. But if they view his actions as ridiculous and worthy of mocking, then they can simply brush off the conviction.

There are many choices in life that we make and many decisions we hold to for no other reason than to avoid placing any responsibility upon ourselves.

4. Perhaps it is wise for us to understand that Carnal Policy[2] sits right next to Destruction. For us, do we have *policies* in our lives that are based solely on worldly views, fleshly desires, or unspiritual attitudes? I have often heard the phrase, "That person is so spiritually minded, they are of no earthly good." I would argue that the only way to be of lasting earthly good is to have an entirely spiritual mindset! Do we make decisions in our homes, workplaces, and churches driven by carnal policies (gathering/keeping of money, short-term benefit to ourselves, etc.) or do we make decisions in

---

[2] Carnal policies could be understood as approaches to life that are based on worldly philosophies or desires.

our homes, workplaces, and churches with a view to the gospel and a leading of the Holy Spirit?

5. This argument comes up once again later in the book. The concept here is that if someone is older, they will know and understand more than the younger person, and therefore the younger person should do what the older person wants. This is essentially a power-move. It's a way for Worldly Wiseman to tell Christian, "You should do what I tell you because I know what I'm talking about, and you are merely ignorant. Trust me and my wisdom and throw out your own discernment."

Later in the book, when this argument comes out again, the younger person brings it up and it leads him to hesitate from doing the right thing because he is younger and the one pushing for sin and rebellion is older.

In both cases, this argument pushes for people to reject Christ's path.

For us, we have to remember that there is often pressure to do what is foolish or immoral, and the pressure will often come through a statement that the one pressuring us knows more, therefore we should not question them. For a Christian, we are always to question by holding up what we are told to the measure of the Word of God,[3] not to the measure of someone supposedly wiser and more mature than us.

Additional thoughts on this chapter

The reference to Worldly Wiseman as an alien is interesting. You'll notice there are three people mentioned here and all three are defined. Mr. Worldly Wiseman is an alien; Mr. Legality is a cheat; and Mr. Legality's son, Civility, looks good, but he's a hypocrite.

These three together (alien, cheat, hypocrite) point to how this legalistic morality will lead to a life where you say one thing and do another (hypocrisy), a life that will cheat you out of what you could have (cheat), and a life where you will not be at home (alien). For Christians, we are offered the opposite of all that. We are offered the opposite of hypocrisy, which is a consistent, honest life of glorifying Christ and finding fulfilment in him. We are offered the opposite of a life where we are left cheated, which is a life where we are given all spiritual blessings.[4] And we are offered the opposite of ultimately being aliens, as any aspect of being an alien in

---

3 Acts. 17:11.
4 Eph. 1:3.

this life is temporary,[5] while what we have with Christ in eternity is our true home where we will eternally be citizens, entirely at home with Christ![6]

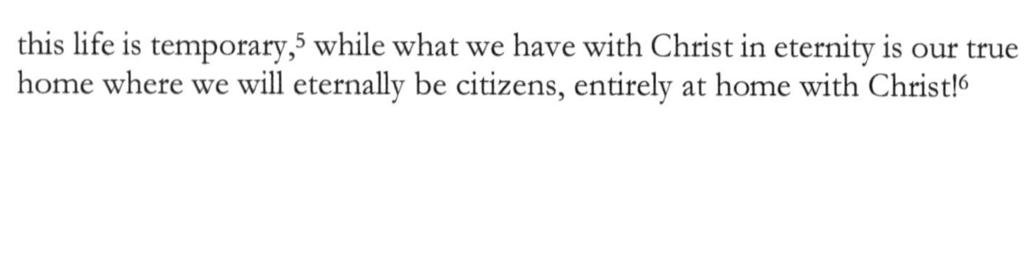

---

[5] 1 Pet. 2:11
[6] Phil. 3:20-21.

3. THE INTERPRETER

3. It is helpful to remember that Satan does not want people to be Christians. On top of that, he also absolutely hates all of us—even those in the world who think they are partners with him. He hates us all and wants an eternity of destruction for us!

7. The House of the Interpreter is best understood as the work of the Holy Spirit in our lives, leading us into all truth. He comes and helps to establish us in truth, pointing us towards Christ, warning us, guiding us. As with the rest of this book, we must remember this is allegory. As such, we cannot think that our interaction with the Holy Spirit is limited to one visit at the beginning of our journey, simply because Christian arrived at the Interpreter's house and then left. The illustration here is not to suggest that the Holy Spirit's work comes but once, but to point out how necessary he is to our journey.[7]

8. Seven short, simple explanations of the Seven Excellent Things:

> #1 The painting illustrates the godly pastor.

> #2 The dusty room illustrates the weakness and inability of law compared to the strength and ability of grace. This room is the heart of the believer, and in this room we see the difference between law and grace in one's heart!

> #3 Passion and Patience show us the difference in hearts focused on either the immediate or the eternal. This illustration is a strong parallel to the parable of the Prodigal Son.

> #4 The fires of the Pilgrim's heart that Satan tries to extinguish, yet Jesus provides the oil of grace that keeps the fire burning! Jesus continually intercedes for us[8] and strengthens us by grace.[9]

> #5 The persevering strong man who fights to enter Christ's palace! This is, of course, a picture of fighting hard to enter the kingdom of heaven and taking many wounds on the way in! Notice the

---

[7] John 16:12-15.
[8] Heb. 7:25.
[9] Heb. 13:8-9.

soldier takes up his sword and puts on his helmet. What do those two (sword and helmet) represent again?[10]

#6 The sinner in the cage who refuses the mercy of the Son of God! You'll notice that while he keeps telling us there is no hope, there is *always* hope with Jesus for anyone who seeks it. So, the real question is, what is this man missing?

#7 The final judgement! This must be kept in mind by all to keep us focused on Christ!

9. The way you answer this will be very telling of what's going on inside. If you find yourself sliding back into a general discussion of how we need to trust the Lord… you are likely avoiding the actual question. The question here is not, "should you" or even "are you like Patience or Passion," but "do you find you are a content person or a discontent person?" The difficulty with this question is the answer might indicate something deep in our hearts.

13. Ultimately, he's missing the one thing that God wants from us more than anything else: faith. The man mentions at one point that God's Word gives him no encouragement to believe. Stop and consider that for a moment. Correct me if I'm wrong, but doesn't the entirety of God's Word push for that one goal? For us to believe? Isn't *every single word* focused on that goal, that we might believe in Jesus Christ leading to salvation?

We must keep in mind at least two things from this illustration. First, this man's sin led to his captivity in that cage and his lack of trust and faith in Jesus Christ. Second, when we sin, we must remember to believe! Believe that Jesus is gracious, loving, kind, and welcoming to repentant sinners like us!

If I can give an extreme example, imagine if you declared to God that you didn't want the eternal, future inheritance he offered, and you tossed it all aside in favour of the immediate inheritance you could have in this life. Imagine you wasted everything you had and all you were on sin, engaging in that sin and revelling in it, even to the point where when all was gone and there was nothing left, you found yourself sitting in pig manure, feeding the unclean pigs, so hungry for nourishment that you longed to eat the pig's food.

---

[10] Eph. 6:10-17.

If you then came to your senses and wanted to return, would the Father welcome you back? If you returned to him, asking simply to be his servant, no longer his child, do you think he would welcome you or reject you? Do you think he would see you at a distance returning to him and stubbornly wait for you to reach his door to beg for forgiveness, or would he run like a madman to reach his child, unwilling to wait for you to take those final steps towards him? Do you think that when you told him you didn't deserve to be his child anymore that he would pay any attention to those ridiculous words?

If you're unsure, read Luke 15:11-32. It's an interesting story.

This man was locked in his cage of despair and believed he was in there awaiting punishment, but is it possible he was locked in there awaiting repentance?

14. It's important at this point to stress that this illustration is a matter of judgment, not a focus on a specific end time belief. If this is viewed as a rapture of the church, a lot of the point of this illustration is missed because our focus shifts to discussions of end times and different eschatological views, rather than what the allegory points to. We don't want to miss the point here!

Also, if you still think that this is a reference to a rapture, consider that those left behind are not set to face seven more years, but something else. While eschatology (your views of the end times) is really important, it's not the focus here. Faith, Christian living, and following Christ are the foci. Also, if you're wondering if Bunyan was a premillennialist, amillennialist, or postmillennialist, I believe he was a chiliast.

Now, doesn't that ruffle your eschatological feathers!

15. Consider the possibility that Christian is excited about living out his Christian faith, walking this path, seeking Christ, but he doesn't understand the need for a foundation. This might be a good time to reflect on the need to build a solid foundation in your Christian walk. It's very much needed! However, it might also be a time for the more mature among us to consider their responsibility to pour into younger believers.

So, we see two matters. First, young believers should take the time to learn and grow! Second, older, more mature believers should take the time to pour into young believers.

However, what we are not to learn at this point is that the goal is to hold Christian back. Not at all! If you are more mature, do not hold younger believers back from their enthusiasm! Nurture it! Encourage it! Just help them see wisdom in the midst of their enthusiasm! Pour into them, and then let their enthusiasm run free!

17. Remember that the Interpreter's House represents the Holy Spirit's work of opening our eyes to all truth. This is a time of learning and growing where the Holy Spirit can point out some necessary things for Christian to know. This doesn't mean we cannot serve Christ early in our Christian walk, it just means we need to pay attention to the Holy Spirit at all stages of the Christian journey, and when we do that at the beginning, we lay a solid foundation for our faith and we set the pattern to continue to listen to the Spirit throughout our years to come.

But if Christian leaves too early (doesn't pay attention to the Holy Spirit's leading) he would be at a serious loss, despite his enthusiasm for the path!

4. A HILL CALLED DIFFICULTY

1. The Shining Ones gave three gifts. These three gifts can be understood in the following way:

> i. The First Shining One declared, "Your sins are forgiven." This is justification by faith, a cleansing of sin.

> ii. The Second Shining One stripped him of his rags and clothed him with new clothes. New clothes illustrate a new identity and a cleansing from sin.[11]

> iii. The third Shining One set a mark on his forehead and gave him a scroll to read as he ran. The mark symbolizes being marked by the Holy Spirit,[12] and the scroll is his assurance of salvation and comfort in knowing he is saved.

2. This is a painfully difficult and complex question that has sparked much debate over the years. Let me share some thoughts on this.

It has been suggested by Spurgeon that this order of salvation is more a picture of Bunyan's own perceived experience than it is true conversion. Bunyan struggled greatly with the burden of his sin after conversion, as many of us do. It weighed him down and, although we'd like to see our burden gone at the moment of turning to Christ, we often continue to feel the weight. So, it is believed that this experience (the Wicket Gate, the House of the Interpreter, and the Cross) were based more on Bunyan's personal experience of salvation and struggle with the burden of his sin, rather than a theological order or process of salvation. In other words, this view would suggest that what we read in Pilgrim's Progress is more how Bunyan *felt* it happened in his own life, rather than how it truly happens, spiritually, when you are saved.

There's a lot of merit to that viewpoint. Salvation is something that happens through an act of God to save you, to open your eyes, to fill you and seal you with the Holy Spirit, to make you new, to cleanse you from all sin, to free you of your burden, and more! So, separating these things in the story does not line up theologically—especially separating some of these things

---

[11] Gal. 3:26.
[12] Eph. 1:13.

from the cross. However, experientially *feels* like it moves along this way. We *feel* like we're saved (the Wicket-gate), yet we *feel* like we carry the burden after salvation (until we truly see and understand the cross).

However, let me add an opinion of my own. You'll find throughout this study guide that I often remind people that this is allegory. Allegory is an imperfect process that we should be careful not to take too literally. For example, if you take the allegorical aspects of Jesus's parables literally, you'll find yourself carried away on silly stuff. Imagine hearing the Parable of the Good Samaritan and responding with, "So, what you're saying is if I don't have a donkey to put a wounded man on, I can't take him to an inn and prove myself to be a good neighbour?"

Well… that's a ridiculous conclusion to draw!

It's the same with the allegory of Pilgrim's Progress. We can't get carried away with every literal detail. For instance, Christian should not have slept at the arbour on the way up the Hill called Difficulty, but that doesn't mean sleep is bad. He sleeps later on in the story, and that's just fine. The point revolving around sleep at the arbour has something specific to do with that part of the story, with that specific part of the allegory.

I would argue that what Bunyan is doing here is pointing out three things that happen in salvation, but since this is an allegorical story that's laid out in a linear fashion (it moves along from one point to another), he has to either create a needlessly confusing Wicket Gate/Cross experience where everything happens all at once, or he needs to separate the topics and hit them one at a time.

The Wicket Gate represents the moment of salvation where Christ (Good-Will) grabs him and pulls him through, saving him from Satan's attempts to slay him. The House of Interpreter represents the Holy Spirit filling Christian and guiding him into all truth. The cross represents a release from the burden, a cleansing from sin, and a marking/sealing of Christian with the Holy Spirit. To me, those *all* sound like the salvation experience! This is what happens when we are saved.

As a fiction author, one thing I have to deal with in story is covering matters that can happen in an instant. Imagine writing a story about driving a car and your neighbour steps into the road ahead of you. In that instant, you will feel fear and shock. Your mind will also tag that person and likely attach his name to him, all in that instant. Your mind might even flash back to your last conversation with him and the fact that you haven't returned the rake he lent you. You might even, in that instant, think about how your neighbour just had knee surgery, and he can't move fast enough to get out of the way, but also, if you hit him, you're not sure he'll ever walk again.

All that can happen in an instant in real life—the brain is *FAST!* However, if you're writing that as a story… imagine trying to write that all in there and still make the story interesting! Truthfully, you can only pick one or two of those matters and quickly land on them. If you cover all of that in that scary moment, it slows down the story, complicates it, and your story becomes difficult to read. So instead, you write that his heart leapt into his chest, and he slammed on the brakes as the neighbour turned just slightly as he protectively raised his hands. The rest? You maybe cover that as you're visiting your neighbour in the hospital.

Story has to be told in a way that makes sense and flows properly so we can take it all in. You cannot info-dump everything at once.

Because of all that, I would suggest that Bunyan was laying out a singular experience of salvation, but since the book is linear and allegorical, he had Christian visit each place, one after another, to help us to focus on each of these three aspects and take it all in.

If this was a theological textbook, you can simply list and define the things that happen. But not in story. Not in allegory.

To add to the confusion of it, let me point out a fourth illustration of salvation in the allegory. When Evangelist meets up with our Pilgrim right at the beginning of the book, he points to the Wicket Gate. When our Pilgrim can't see the gate, Evangelist asks if he can see the light, and our Pilgrim does see the light. From that point on, Bunyan calls our Pilgrim by the name, "Christian". It seems Bunyan was suggesting that this opening of the eyes of the heart to see the light of salvation might actually have been the experience of salvation, although Christian was entirely ignorant at that point of everything to do with the faith. Then again, aren't we all when we come to know Christ?

So, we have the following experiences:

> a. We see an opening of the eyes through the gospel to see the way of salvation.

> b. We see a perseverance to reach the Wicket-gate and enter through to the new path.

> c. We see a visit to the Interpreter's house and experience the Holy Spirit leading us into all truth.

> d. We see an approach to the cross leading to a release of the burden, a new identity, cleansing, and more!

All these are pictures of the salvation experience, on one level or another, and I would suggest that Bunyan was drawing out the salvation experience so we could see what happens. It's simple in a theological textbook to lay out all the wonderful things God does in and through us at the moment of salvation, but to write a story, you need to walk people along step by step.

However, if I could make an adjustment to Bunyan's story, it might have been better to place the cross as the place to run to, rather than the Wicket Gate, but... I have to admit, the illustration of the gate is beautiful and the picture of Christ pulling Christian through to a new life is perhaps quite helpful for us. So... I'm not going to suggest I could do it better.

I'd encourage you to reflect on all this. This might seem very academic, and in a way, perhaps it is. But it's also deeply relational. It brings us to this matter of how Christ saves us. And is there anything more beautiful to reflect on that the work and life and person of Jesus Christ?

Thoughts?

4. In this section, Presumption illustrates a man who believes he is safe and secure despite the lack of proof for his belief. You'll notice he simply tells Christian to go away because he is just fine where he is. How does he know he's safe? He just *knows* it. It is important for us as Christians to search out and understand. We are wise and noble when we seek out answers rather than just assume.[13]

6. Connecting Formalist and Hypocrisy with the town of Vain-glory is a fascinating concept! We can often play the games of formality and hypocrisy in our churches and in our lives, and what do these games give us? Vain-glory! Let me translate that for you: formalism and hypocrisy gives you worthless glory! That's what they give. Living as Formalist and Hypocrisy give us a glory that is entirely worthless!

7. Formalist and Hypocrisy came from a place called Vain-glory (worthless glory) and believed they were heading to a place called Mount Zion, where they expected to receive more glory. We often fall into thinking that our eternal rest is all about fulfilling our cravings (for our own glory), rather than as a place where God dwells in his goodness and for his glory. We think of eternity as a place to do what we want, have everything we want, experience all we want.

---

[13] Acts 17:11.

Do we recognize that when we think of eternity as a place to satisfy our desires, we have made eternity about us? Is eternity not about Jesus? While it is certainly true that it is a place where we will receive our reward, when you read the description of eternity in Scripture, we quickly find that it's more about God and his glory than us and our glory.[14] Do we see eternity as a place where we get everything we want and crave, rather than a place where Christ is praised? Ultimately, for us, while there certainly is reward, the greatest gift and reward we receive in eternity comes down to that we get to spend eternity with Jesus! That's the true blessing of eternity!

10. As a pastor, I sometimes met with people in my church who spoke of their Christian life but had no concept of actual salvation. They simply lived their lives as Christians and were often very good at the whole "church thing". Sadly, this is all too common in our churches. I suspect as the church has fallen out of favour with society in recent years, this has become less common, but it is still there. Perhaps it is helpful to remember that salvation is a work of God in our hearts. As such, their inability to see beyond just a formal, hypocritical Christianity—of acting it out and pretending—is an indication that the Holy Spirit has not opened their eyes. It is an indication that they climbed the wall rather than entered through the wicket gate.

12. Often in this book it's helpful to be reminded that we are dealing with allegory. This allegory gives us a picture of the spiritual life. It's not designed to be entirely consistent all the way through, since each section is pointing to specific spiritual truths. For instance, it is wrong here for Christian to fall asleep, but there are plenty of places throughout the book where it was proper for him to sleep. The book is not inconsistent, it is teaching us something. This was a picture of a place where Christ provided a chance for Christian to rest for a moment before continuing the journey, but the goal was not rest, but getting up that hill! To fall asleep was to set aside the task God had for Christian and satisfy the flesh, the self, rather than live obediently for Christ. In other places, the Lord of the Way provided places

---

[14] This is not to suggest that there is no glory for us in eternity. We often like to swing the pendulum to one extreme or the other. We, as Westerners, often swing the pendulum of glory in eternity to the extreme where it's all about us, and if someone questions that we want to swing it to the other extreme by saying, "Are you suggesting that there is no glory for us in eternity?" The other extreme is not good either. Perhaps a proper understanding would be to see eternity as a place where God is glorified first and foremost, and the glory we receive is that which comes as a result of his grace and kindness to us.

specifically to rest and sleep, and in those places, the right thing to do is sleep.[15]

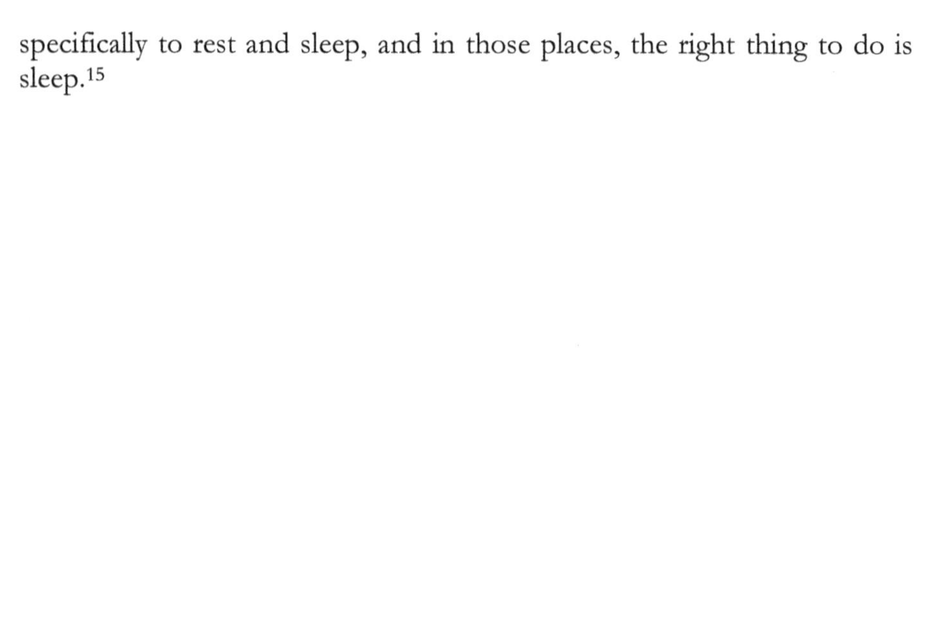

---

[15] Consider 1 Thess. 5:4-11.

5. THE HOUSE BEAUTIFUL

2. Remember this book is allegory. This is not a matter of, "Wait, sometimes we all mess up. Sometimes we all act in fear. That doesn't mean we're not saved!" Once again, remember, this is allegory, so Bunyan is trying to point out something. I would suggest that Fearful and Timorous are illustrating for us either the truth that fear can absolutely cripple our ability to walk the path (running in the opposite direction) or that they were simply not believers, therefore they would not ultimately continue along the path.[16] Either way, the point here is that we need to trust the Lord of the Way.

4. The House Beautiful, or Palace Beautiful, is understood to be a picture of the church in whose company Christian finds comfort, care, direction, encouragement, and more! Although he only stays for a short while, this is not a picture of the church only being necessary for short periods of time or only for young believers. On the contrary! Remember, this book is allegory, so it's landing on certain points to teach and instruct and reveal!

Christian's time at the House Beautiful points out deep teaching of beautiful truths about living for Christ, a dinner where they remember the Lord (the Lord's Table), a time of learning and growing in what the Lord has done, and an equipping of the saint with the armour of God.

Altogether, you see how this is a beautiful, yet necessary, place for Christian to stop and be established in his faith. As the House Beautiful is a stationary location, it does not travel with him, but the point of this allegory is not to encourage a solo existence apart from the Body of Christ. The ongoing interaction with others along the way, companions such as Faithful and Hopeful in the days ahead, are examples of how this ministry continues as Christian travels.

6. Consider this possibility. Discretion wishes to be careful about decisions made, paths travelled, words spoken. Discretion in a church is beautiful as it leads to a safe, protected place. We act carefully not to hurt one another, but also not to head in directions that do not honour Christ or promote love and growth of the body.

---

[16] Matt. 24:13.

Now, when Christian requests to enter the House Beautiful, consider what part Discretion and the others play. It is wise for churches to be careful about membership. Sure, the doors are open to one and all, all those who desire to hear the gospel proclaimed, but when it comes to someone settling in as a genuine part of the Body of Christ, do we not show more discretion, seeking those who truly believe in Jesus to be a part of our church family? You'll notice when Christian seeks to enter the house, he's met by not only the porter named Watchful, but Discretion, Prudence, Piety, and Charity. They examine Christian, in a manner of speaking, to see if he is a true Pilgrim!

Perhaps Discretion's tears come from the joy she feels as a saint comes forward, looking to step into what is helpful for him and for the rest of the church.

11. Since the coat represents his cleaning of sin, that he is clean and righteous and stands as a new person before God, then we understand that when we truly know who Jesus has made us, we can live confidently, standing against the temptation of sin!

His scroll represents the assurance of salvation. As such, when we stop and consider that we are truly saved, that we truly belong to Jesus, it gives us confidence and conviction that we don't have to live the old life anymore, since Christ has empowered us to live for him!

A focus on the Celestial City gives perspective! This life is short. This entire life is short! So make the most of it! Live for Christ!

13. Often we think very independently as believers. We often think that it's all just a personal faith, and we just hang out with other Christians because it's fun or because we're supposed to. But the reality is, we not only have a personal faith in Christ, but we are saved and made a *part* of this beautiful thing called the Church! This… *House Beautiful!*

And the Church, when it is healthy, functions for us as a place of equipping. The Body of Christ is to function together to build us up to a place of maturity.[17] When we consider this, is it any wonder that Christian is equipped to stand strong (the armour of God) in the Church (the House Beautiful)?

---

[17] Eph. 4:11-13.

6. THE VALLEYS

5. It's important to remember with Satan that he is the father of lies.[18] Everything he says is a lie! However, there's an old saying, "Deception is carried on the wings of truth." Satan lives that one out quite well. For example, if you look at his words in Genesis 3 where he deceives Eve, much of what he says is true, but because he mixes in lies, it all becomes a deception!

So in this case, when Satan accuses us, the followers of Christ, of our sin, he's likely accurately detailing our sin. However, it's all a lie! While the sins actually happened, what he's saying is that we are sinners, but the truth is, we have been forgiven and declared righteous. So, we may have sinned, but Christ's atoning work on the cross covered it, and now we are truly clean! So, any accusation of us as sinners in that regard is false!

6. When working through this issue, there are two helpful points to remember. First, how do we defeat Satan?

We remember that Jesus already defeated Satan, and Jesus will continue to defeat Satan until the end. When we feel alone in this moment, we are not. Christ is with us. So, how do we stand? There are many helpful answers to this, such as holding onto Scripture, trusting the Lord's work in our lives and his power to radically transform us, prayer, and more. However, as we learn in Eph. 6:10-17, we are called to stand firm.

Do you hear that? When all is done, take your stand… and stand strong!

7. Notice that Apollyon's declaration of impending victory comes immediately after Christian loses his sword. What does the sword represent?[19]

10. Here are some opinions of mine on the allegory. I would say there are a couple reasons Apollyon doesn't call Christian by name. First, to call Christian by name suggests relationship/connection. I don't think that kind

---

[18] John 8:44.
[19] Eph. 6:17.

of relationship is typical of Satan. He doesn't care about us. The second reason is I think to call our Pilgrim by his name puts Apollyon in an awkward spot. If he calls Christian by his name, "Christian", then he's declaring our main character belongs to Jesus Christ.[20] Of course, if he goes in the other direction and calls our Pilgrim by his old name, Graceless, then I think Apollyon knows he'll lose any chance of pulling Christian back!

11. We often confuse humility with insecurity, and that causes us to back away from it, but humility is a calling on every believer's heart! It is important for many reasons, but let us focus in on an unusual, but theological, one. If you consider much of what God calls us to, we find he calls us to live and act in a way that imitates his own heart. We are called to love one another, then we find out that God is love![21] We are called to be kind and show mercy, then we find God is a kind and merciful God![22] There is much in Scripture that calls us to follow the character of God. What about humility? Yes, we are called to humble ourselves, but would God have cause to humble himself? Doesn't that seem like an odd path for the God of the universe? Nope! Jesus Christ humbled himself far more than we have to! Jesus is the God of humility, and he desires humility from us![23]

So why does God call us to humility? Because it honours the heart of the humble God!

The Identity of Apollyon

Apollyon's name means *destroyer.* He is understood to be the angel of the bottomless pit, as mentioned in Revelation 9:11, and he is the king over the devouring locusts in that same chapter. Apollyon also represents in Pilgrim's Progress the spiritual forces of evil and worldly influence on a Christian's heart.

So, when we consider Rev. 9:11, we see Apollyon as some kind of chief demon, of sorts. The challenge, however, is in Pilgrim's Progress, Apollyon bears many similarities to Satan himself.

---

[20] Think of the word *Christian* as *Follower of Christ* or perhaps even *Little Christ.*
[21] John 13:34; 1 John 4:8.
[22] Eph. 4:32; Jam. 2:13; Psa. 148:8-9.
[23] Jam. 4:10; Phil. 2:4-11.

Apollyon tempts Christian to return to his old life, just as Satan is the tempter.[24]

Apollyon accuses Christian of sin and failure, just as Satan is the accuser of the brethren.[25]

Apollyon is the Prince over Christian's former life, much like Satan is the ruler of the old life.[26]

Apollyon fights with flaming darts, just as the evil one does.[27]

Apollyon's name seems to be a reference, on some level, to the Greek god Apollos. Both names (Apollyon and Apollos) carry with them the meaning *to destroy*. Apollos was considered among the Greek gods to be the most beautiful of gods, which is interesting as Satan is described "the signet of perfection, full of wisdom and perfect in beauty."[28] The Greek god Apollos would also easily fit into the category, in Scripture, of demon, as we see Paul calls all pagan sacrifice as a sacrifice to demons.[29]

So, although Apollyon is understood to be a demon who serves Satan, even one of his prince demons, Apollyon ends up functioning as a representative of Satan in the story. He enters our story as a picture of Satan's influence on our lives.

In the end, the best way to understand Apollyon is the evil worldly forces that seek to bring us under subjection to their sinful ways, tempting us to return, and revealing to us not only the pressure and influence of Satan himself but also his deep hatred for us and desire to destroy.

Pope and Pagan

These two characters are difficult to address, as their meaning isn't entirely obvious, despite the clarity of their names.

I remember reading a Catholic perspective discussing this section of Pilgrim's Progress. The writer suggested that Pope and Pagan were two extremes, one representing formal religion, the other representing a lack of formality, perhaps even a religious "free-for-all". He suggested then that

---

24 Matt. 4:1-11.
25 Rev. 12:10.
26 John 8:39-47. NOTE: This passage refers to Satan as the Pharisee's father, but the theme in that passage is obedience (under Satan's command) in addition to the familial connection.
27 Eph. 6:16. The evil one here is generally considered to be Satan.
28 Ez. 28:12.
29 1: Cor. 10:20.

Protestantism was considered the balance between the two (Catholic, formalistic religion and pagan, chaotic religion). He believed this was a Protestant perspective, which I would suggest might be a bit misleading as this would focus, perhaps, only on forms of religion, not to mention that it would completely ignore the flow and content of this part of Bunyan's allegory.

Now, from the standpoint of forms (such as actions, style of worship, religious rules), Paganism certainly includes more free-for-all type activities than Catholicism (which maintains a great deal of structure in most areas of faith and practice). However, Bunyan's allegory continually comes back to grace and faith. In light of seeing things in terms of following Christ on his path and the threats that seek to pull us away from trusting Jesus, the Lord of the Way, I think it's better to understand Pope and Pagan in light of *threat* to the Christian walk, rather than extremes of style and form. This is especially meaningful considering the countless bodies around the mouth of the cave.

Perhaps it's better to understand Pagan as representing the persecuting pagan religions of the past, those that led to great persecutions and deaths (threat) among Christians. The early church experienced a great deal of persecution from pagan leaders, and there are ten such persecutions which stand out, starting with Nero's persecution (A.D. 64) and ending with the Diocletian persecution (A.D. 303-311).

Paganism was responsible for the death of many, many Christians over the years. A threat indeed!

Now, to understand Bunyan's character named Pope, we have to remember that as the church developed and grew, great compromises entered the church's practice. By the time of the Protestant Reformation (A.D. 1517), the Catholic Church had grown corrupt in many areas involving abusive clergy, greed, and indulgences (specifically, payments collected in exchange for absolving from sin and purgatory). These kinds of things led to the great Reformation, but they weren't the only problem within the Catholic Church.

Even before the Reformation, the Catholic Church, led by the Pope, called for the death of many who challenged their beliefs or pushed for a greater adherence to Scripture. Jan Hus would be a good example of this (martyred in A.D. 1415). After the reformation, the Catholic Church aggressively pursued Protestant believers, leading to the Roman Inquisition (starting A.D. 1542). It is difficult to know how many Protestants died because of

Roman Catholic persecution as estimates are all over the place,[30] but it is reasonable to assume that at least tens of thousands died.

So, when we approach these two characters from the perspective of threat to faithful pilgrims, what we understand is that Bunyan was pointing out two religious threats to a grace-based Christianity. First, Paganism killed many believers but had since died out.[31] Second, Bunyan was pointing out that while the Pope still remained, his power to kill, at least in England at the time, had lessened greatly, and as a result, he was far less of a mortal threat to Protestant Christianity.

To add yet another thought to this section of Pope and Pagan, perhaps it's helpful to consider the flow of this chapter as well. Remember that after our friends at the House Beautiful equipped Christian for battle, he faced Apollyon in the Valley of Humility, then entered and endured the Valley of the Shadow of Death. He stood strong through these challenges, by the grace of God, and then the next thing he faces are threats from the institutions entrenched in this world.

It is helpful, perhaps, to remember as we walk the path that those who stand firm (the battle with Apollyon) can expect continued persecution.[32]

---

[30] Estimates come in anywhere from thirty thousand to fifty million, although the latter number appears to be unsubstantiated.

[31] In current times, paganism is experiencing a bit of a revival in some western nations.

[32] Thanks to Rev. Matthew Richards for pointing out this interesting connection.

7. A FAITHFUL COMPANION

2. This is absolutely a good thing! We should be motivated by others to grow in our spiritual lives and passion for Christ! Remember the allegory. Walking the path is living the Christian life. To run and make significant progress along the path at this point in our story is a picture of growing in your faith. Just because Christian fell to pride doesn't mean we shouldn't be motivated by one another to grow!

4. Keep in mind that the Christian life was never, ever, ever meant to be lived alone. We are part of the body of Christ, and the members of the body have been placed within the body to build one another up. Without a healthy Christ-honouring Christian community, we will never grow the way we were meant to.[33]

11. One thing you read in Scripture is that sexual sin is related very closely to idolatry. Could this be an illustration for us to keep our faith and worship pure? As in not adding in worship of other things into our lives?

In addition to this, Jesus defines sexual sin as not only physical but also an emotional/mental experience.[34] So, could this be pointing out that Faithful had struggled with his thought life during that time of his journey? Or… continues to?

12. As we grow in our faith and maturity and not only learn to cast aside sin but also find how much we fall to it, we begin to see sin as a violent intrusion on the life that Christ has called us to, the life that we want. Temptation is an assault on who we are and what Christ has made us. But the good news is, Christ will always, always, always be victorious!

13. It is considered that the following three experiences are connected: the spring at the bottom of the hill, the old man (Adam the First), and Moses. Now, it's easy to tie the second two together in the story, but the spring is

---

[33] Heb. 10:25; Eph. 4:11-13.
[34] Matt. 5:27-30.

interesting. If you look back to the time when Christian came to the bottom of the hill, he drank from the spring, a moment of refreshment on his journey. Faithful, however, did not. Barry E. Horner argues that because Faithful did not drink from such a strategically placed spring, "he becomes inclined toward the carnal proposal of Old Man Adam the first..."[35]

So, on the climb, Adam the First comes along and offers Faithful the world. This is the very thing that Adam chose instead of God. He chose sin and fleshly desires over a perfect relationship with his Creator! Faithful, of course, was right to see that this would lead to his slavery, and then we find that when he tries to leave, the old man reviles him, threatens to send someone after him, and pinches his flesh so hard it felt like the man had ripped off a piece of Faithful's flesh!

Now, Adam's threat was to send someone after Faithful who would make his life horrible, and shortly after Adam leaves, someone comes running after Faithful who is unable to show mercy. This is important as we realize that seeking the temporary world only leads to sin and merciless judgement under the law.

16. This is an important question. People love the extremes, and Christians are no exception to this. Christians love to dive completely into the Law, or they love to toss it out completely. The Law functions as a teacher to bring us to Christ, therefore we should love the Law, not as a form of salvation, but as something that God uses to point out his glory and the wonders of his gracious salvation!

It is understood that John Bunyan came to know Christ under the conviction of the law. He felt convicted of the sin of breaking the Sabbath! Consider that! We might want to declare, "No! You're not under the law because Jesus has freed us from the Law! Don't feel bad about that!" But... Bunyan didn't have Jesus! So, he had no one to free him from that Law!

God used that conviction of Sabbath breaking to draw Bunyan to Christ! Isn't that amazing? I think we should shout out, "Wow! Isn't the Law a wonderful gift because it points out that we have no chance of fulfilling it and therefore no hope apart from Jesus Christ?" When we truly understand that, we rush to the cross, drop to our knees, and trust the Lord as the weight of the Law and our sin and our heavy burden fall away and roll into the empty tomb!

---

[35] Themes and Issues of the Pilgrim's Progress, Great Christian Books, 2001, Barry E. Horner, p. 113.

17. No, the point here is not that only some need the church. Not at all.[36] Remember, this is allegory, and this is story. I would suggest that the point here is that Faithful (who is faithful to the Lord as his name suggests) is focused on following Christ and would not stop for anything. Remember when we meet him? He won't even stop on the path long enough for Christian to catch up! We also have to remember that he just endured terrible temptation and consequences for his failing, which helps us to make sense of his determination now. The point here is not to suggest that church is unimportant. In fact, I would suggest that the point here has nothing to do with the church. The point here has to do with emphasizing Faithful's focus and determination.

22. I would suggest that the best way to get out of discontentment in your life is to focus on two things. First, focus on the love of God towards you personally. He loves you, and his heart towards you is filled with love! Second, focus on the goodness of God towards you. Continually remind yourself that despite the circumstances, ultimately, whether experienced here on earth or in eternity, God has promised good for you, and he will bring it about!

---

[36] Heb. 10:25.

8. A TALKATIVE COMPANION

3. We live in a time when social media is driven along by people who cry out against things of which they do not approve, all the while doing little to nothing about it themselves. If you are on social media, you will likely repeatedly read someone say, "Someone needs to do something about this!" Yet few, if any, do anything about it themselves.

This mindset enters the church as well.[37] How do we combat this? Perhaps it's by stepping up ourselves and ensuring that we, ourselves, are not all talk. Take responsibility and grow! Live out your faith! Let it affect every area of your life!

5. The other obvious angle of this issue is what approach to take to church membership in terms of Talkatives (people who are all talk but have no genuine conversion). This is where discernment in church membership is extremely important for a healthy church.

---

[37] Questions like, "Why isn't the pastor doing this?" or "When are we going to reach out to...?" are often examples of this. As a pastor, I often ran into situations where someone was upset that the church or the pastor was not taking care of a problem that they could have addressed easily on their own.

9. VANITY FAIR

4. I would suggest that an attitude of humility would help with this issue. As we see the sin of others, it will often turn us away, but a humble heart recognizes that we are all in need of God's grace and mercy. There's the old saying, "Except by the grace of God, there go I." It's true. If it wasn't for God's grace, where would any of us be? So let us always remember to show grace to others who have fallen to sin.

On the other hand, let us always remember as well that our goal isn't just to recognize sin, but to flee from it. So, in our own lives, when we see we struggle with sin, always seek God's grace to be free of that sin.

7. Don't underestimate the effect of this *dirt* on the lives of those who are smeared with dirt. Sometimes you will be the one smeared with dirt, slandered and spoken against, and other times it will be those around you. Keep in mind the need to love and support others when their reputation is smeared.

11. Here's a little hint… if you come up with an answer that doesn't upset the *sellers* of Vanity Fair, you might not be landing on the issue!

There are many things in life that anger those around us if we, as pilgrims progressing along the path, do not take part in them. Growing up, I found if I did not participate in certain activities, it upset people. These days, if you do not take part in certain activities, you can be mocked, while avoiding other activities will enrage the *people of Vanity Fair.*

In every age, there will be areas a Christian avoids so as not to dishonour Christ, and this avoidance will anger the sellers at the allegorical market of life. When it comes to how our speech will upset the sellers, consider the difference between a life spent glorifying yourself and the things of this world with your words, or a life spent giving glory to God with your words. You will find the sellers at Vanity Fair will not accept the idea of giving God the glory for much of anything.

12. Consider the items sold at the market as items purchased to satisfy needs or wants. So, spiritually speaking, the items sold at Vanity Fair are things

that the world offers to satisfy our desires rather than finding our satisfaction in Christ.

Just like the list in the book, this can be anything from money to a comfortable lifestyle to marriage to friendship to fun to… whatever. Whatever is offered or pursued in your life that is meant to satisfy you, rather than Christ.

13. A man in the fair asked, "What will ye buy?" to which our Pilgrims answered, "We buy the truth."

This, of course, was the turning point in the interaction at Vanity Fair. We face the assumption on the part of the sellers that Christian and Faithful were going to buy something.

"How could they do anything other than buy from us? This is what everyone does! They partake of the things this fair offers!"

It is often a terrible offense in the eyes of those who wish to corrupt a Christian walking the path when we do not do what they demand, when we do not buy what they are selling. But perhaps the greater offense to the sellers is for Christian and Faithful to declare that they would only buy the truth! That is to suggest that everything offered for sale is a lie and to call the sellers on their inability to provide something so obviously good.

14. Consider Romans 8:18 regarding this question. Consider as well how long your life is here compared to eternity? Is there value in seeing this life as temporary compared to your life with Christ as eternal?

15. In Christian and Faithful's journey, this is the first real, all-out, clear-as-day experience with persecution (previous experiences weren't as bad or as obvious). You'll notice that when they defended themselves, the examiners simply didn't believe them but insisted that they were insane or intentionally trying to disrupt. This can be the way persecution goes. A believer acts in kindness, grace, patience and more, yet ends up accused of many things. I think for believers, we sometimes think that persecution will involve a threat to our lives or safety based on whether we will deny Christ,[38] but persecution is rarely so simple and clear cut.

––––––––––––––––––––––––––––––––

[38] As in, "Deny Jesus or you will die!"

The focus of the attack was on what the people of Vanity Fair felt was important. They didn't really care if Christian and Faithful believed in Jesus, they just could not tolerate a rejection of the ways and customs of the Fair.

This is often the way. The goal of the attack against Christian and Faithful was to tear them down, not to focus on truth. Truth was irrelevant. What was important to the court was winning, allowing them their opportunity to punish Faithful for his rejection of their ways.

17. Consider this question regarding Christian and Faithful's imprisonment. The arrest, the questioning, the imprisonment, and the accusation that our pilgrims were responsible for the brawl… is that fair? The answer is obvious. No, it's not. It's not fair at all. However, this is often how persecution goes. Do not think that persecution will adhere to the truth. Remember that Jesus *is* the truth (John 14:6), while Satan *is* the father of lies (John 8:44). We shouldn't be surprised when false accusations are raised against us or against others as persecution arises.

However, it is difficult to separate truth from lies, even in these difficult circumstances. The better focus, rather than try to figure it all out, is to trust the Lord that he is at work in the lives of persecuted people, and trust God's grace despite accusations.

And most importantly, pray for those you know and love who are under persecution!

Final thoughts on this section:

In the end, it is good to read the encouragement that not only does Faithful continue to live with Christ, but Hopeful is now following the Lord of the Way. And even more than that, there are many others who will soon follow because of what happened. There is an old saying by a one of the early Latin Church Fathers, "The blood of the martyrs is the seed of the church."[39] If you spend time reading church history, especially the times of intense persecution, it does not take long to see that this is true. When people suffer for Christ, it sends a clear message of the beauty of the gospel and attracts many to the cross.

And that, my friends, is what we are declaring. That this message of Jesus Christ calling us to himself is a beautiful, beautiful thing.

---

[39] Tertullian, Apologetics, 197 A.D.

1 & 2. What does this actually look like in real life? Does it mean you refuse to even speak with someone? Or does this mean something deeper? We have a strong aversion to pushing people away—as if there is no situation in which this would be proper—but is it possible that walking the Christian life with By-Ends is dangerous? Or immoral? Would 2 John 10-11 apply here?

Now, the 2 John passage would apply specifically to someone who is teaching a different gospel, and the meaning of the passage seems to be a matter of supporting them in their work, but how do we wrestle through this kind of challenging topic? At what point is it dangerous to walk hand-in-hand with someone who is a corrupting influence on you in your Christian faith?

5. Read the statement from By-Ends again. If you have heard someone describe another believer in such a way, knowing nothing of the actual person, what would your opinion be of the person described? You would likely see them as arrogant and legalistic.

Now, if you *are* the one By-Ends is describing, can you live with a description such as that following you around? How best should you respond?

Understand that this is one circumstance, one specific situation, but there are many times when By-Ends or others will speak ill of those who follow Christ. It is important for Christians to be careful not to listen too quickly to accusations. We should always be discerning when we hear our brothers and sisters criticized.

7. Money-love's arguments for why a minister is honourable for pursuing gain are actually quite solid. In fact, his reasoning is good (at least from a non-Christian perspective). However, it ignores a couple things. First, it ignores proper faith and the belief that truth belongs to God. Truth is not ours to adjust and change according to our whims. Second, it assumes that

God would never desire poverty for anyone.[40] Consider how God has chosen the poor of this world to be rich in faith.[41] Is it possible he wants some of us to be poor here, but wealthy beyond imagination in eternity?

Ultimately, I would suggest that Money-love does not truly believe that God sits on the throne.

So, this raises a question for us. Do we truly believe that God sits on the throne? Do we understand how sovereign he is? Or do our decisions and choices reveal a deeply held belief that God is not sovereign?

8. This question isn't intended to attack, but to reflect. If we can identify times in the past when we have sought only ease and comfort, perhaps we can avoid falling into this in the future. Spend some time reflecting on this matter and seeking the Lord's forgiveness. He is gracious, and he will joyfully welcome our repentant hearts.

---

[40] Perhaps we should ask the question directly. Might God desire poverty for someone? More specifically, might God desire poverty for you?
[41] James 2:5.

11. DOUBTING CASTLE

1. Quick discussion questions:

a. They were on Giant Despair's land. Don't miss that! They were not on the path. They were on the land belonging to Despair. This does not, of course, mean that anytime we feel despair, doubt, or depression that we have sinned, but it should act as a caution for us. We need to be careful not to travel through Giant Despair's land—even for a minute! Our thought lives must be protected as despair imprisons us. At the same time, understand that Giant Despair ruled *Doubting* Castle. Doubts certainly lead to despair. The way to combat doubts is not to travel to the castle, but to combat doubts with the truth of God's word and promises!

b. Giant Despair counsels Christian and Hopeful to take their own lives. Amid despair, this is often an option that our despair lays before us, and in those moments, it can easily appear as the most reasonable option. Be wary of Giant Despair's counsel!

c. His fits come on him on sunny days! Remember this is allegory, so the point is not sunny weather. The point is despair cannot thrive on good days. It thrives on the dark days when everything looks dim and disappointing.

d. Despair often grips our lives when we live within the clutches of doubts. This can last days, weeks, months, and even years! It is crucial not to step in this direction, but rather to seek the truth the Lord of the Way has given us! And perhaps this is a helpful reminder for us to be patient and gracious to our brothers and sisters who are lost in despair.

e. The name of the key is CRUCIAL! It's crucial for you when you are caught in the clutches of Giant Despair, and it is crucial for others in despair! If you are caught in despair, grab hold of the promises of God and do not let go! This is, of course, a matter of faith. We find freedom when we wrap our hearts around the promises of God, trusting God in faith that his word is true!

2. The difference is in their love (or lack thereof) of the world. Demas loved the world.[42] As we consider Christian and Hopeful, we see that Hopeful, being the younger of the two (not necessarily in age, but in terms of his

---

[42] 2 Tim. 4:10.

spiritual maturity) might have a little of the love of the world left. Perhaps that is why he considered leaving the path for the riches offered by Demas.

3. Let me encourage you here not to see an opportunity to look around and judge the hearts of others, but to take the time to reflect on your own heart. Are you in love with this present world?

7. When we come to the narrow plain of ease, the word narrow suggests that the area is not just small, but that it's wider than it is long. In other words, they could have stayed in the plain called ease for potentially a long time—they would only need to turn to the right or the left and leave the path. Even amid the gift of rest offered by the Lord of the Way, the temptations to leave the path are relentless for Christian and Hopeful!

8. This is an important truth that we need to grab hold of! Sometimes we need to walk alone. Sometimes those around us will leave the path. They will reason it out, they will sound mature, wise, good, holy, pure, and any number of things that sound Christ honouring. Yet, even with their reasons, they are leaving the path for comfort, wealth, fame, etc. And in those times, we, as men and women of faith, are called to walk alone. That is, my friends, a very difficult truth, but it is truth nonetheless.

10. An impressively well-suited marriage. It is interesting to note that a castle to live in and a strong spouse doesn't feed Diffidence's faith, but rather leaves her in an untrusting state. The things in which we find comfort in this life will not feed our faith!

It is also interesting that a Giant named Despair does not instil trust in his spouse. We have to remember that Despair is joined in matrimony to a lack of trust and faith!

If you wish to fight despair in your life, be a man or woman of faith! Hence, the way out of the dungeon is to use the key named Promise (have faith in God's promises)!

11. If we think of food and water in terms of nourishment, then we understand that our despair is only made worse by a lack of spiritual food and nourishment. Amid Giant Despair's clutches, feed yourself with the

nourishing food of the Word of God and the nourishing food of the community of believers.

12. Giants are big. Very big. With this in mind, we need to remember to show compassion to those held in Giant Despair's prison. Despair is strong enough to hold us, so instead of responding with judgement, perhaps we can respond with compassion and truth to those held in his prison.

16. Release on Sunday carries with it several pictures for us. First, Sunday is the day of resurrection! Christ broke free of the tomb on that day. Second, Sunday is the day when Christians have traditionally met to worship since the time of the Apostles. In our story, we read that on the day when Christians receive clear teaching from the Word of God, when we worship together, when we fellowship, break bread together, when we act and live together as the Body of Christ, that's when we find freedom from despair!

Choosing Iniquity

Job 36:21 says, "Take care; do not turn to iniquity, for this you have chosen rather than affliction." Iniquity is best understood as evil or sinful behaviour. In our section here, Christian and Hopeful came to a time of affliction, a difficult part of the path, and do we notice what they do? They choose iniquity (leaving the path) over affliction.

And for us, when we choose iniquity over affliction in our own lives, is not despair and depression often the result? Consider Esau's choice in Genesis 25:29-34. You have a man struggling with the affliction of hunger, and he sells his birthright to save himself from such affliction! He chose evil, short-sighted behaviour to save himself from some temporary affliction. In Hebrews, Esau is described as sexually immoral and unholy because he sold his birthright for a single meal. "For you know that when he desired to inherit the blessing, he was rejected, for he found no chance to repent, though he sought it with tears."[43]

Perhaps it's helpful for believers to recognize that we can easily despise our birthright because of the affliction we face in the moment. When we do this, we can quickly choose iniquity (sinful behaviour) to avoid that affliction.

---

[43] Heb. 12:15-17.

What of Christ's gifts are we willing to give up simply to have a little relief? A bit of stew? Something to ease our feet from the affliction of a difficult part of the path?

The Two Pillars

In this section of the book, did you notice that there are two pillars, and both are placed upon the path to warn pilgrims? The first one is the pillar of salt, Lot's wife, there to warn pilgrims not to leave the path for wealth. The second is the pillar erected by Christian and Hopeful. It is placed there as a warning to pilgrims not to leave the path for ease as leaving leads to Giant Despair and Doubting Castle.

12. SHEPHERDS AND WISDOM

1. This is a profound statement! What we're reading reminds us that the Celestial City, eternity with Christ, is entirely out of reach. It is impossibly far. Not a soul can ever, ever, ever reach it. Unless…

Unless Christ has saved us and provided the way through the cross! So, the way to the Celestial City is too far for anyone, except for those who will get there (those whom Christ has saved).

2. The interesting difference is that God was gracious with Christian and Hopeful. Sometimes we approach this kind of thing from an angry perspective, looking at the *fairness* of the matter and say, "It's not fair that those people suffered." But that's not the right perspective. What happened to those men is the same as what should have happened to Christian and Hopeful, but God was gracious to our pilgrims. Everyone deserves to suffer for their sin, but God is often gracious! What this means for us, then, is that when we do not receive the proper condemnation for our sin, we are receiving mercy from the Lord. Such a thing should not lead us to arrogance, but to humility. It brings us to a point where we kneel before a loving Saviour and confess, "Except for the grace of God, there go I."

4. We often equate humility with ignorance and pride with knowledge. For example, "Wow, you're really good at that!" And here's our humble reply, "Oh, no… I'm not really good at it. I just try my best." Wait? Are you good at whatever this is? Probably, but we think a response like that sounds humble. If we deny our strengths or live in ignorance of them, we think that suggests humility. But does it? Isn't that just denying what's true? In other words, we think humility travels hand in hand with ignorance.

Truthfully, a humble person is fully aware and has their eyes wide open. They see their strengths and weaknesses and are aware of them, but their strengths do not lead them to arrogance. Arrogant (or conceited) people tend to be entirely ignorant. They strongly believe they are great and wonderful, have it all figured out, regardless of the facts. This is perhaps part of why they so easily fall. Their conceit produces ignorance.

It makes perfect sense that Ignorance comes from the land of Conceit, since ignorance walks the path hand in hand with arrogance and conceit!

6. Remember that this is allegory. Distance in this story is not the same as distance in real life! The truth is, the Sheep Gate is within reach of us all, isn't it? So why is it so far from the country of Conceit?

Perhaps because salvation only comes to the humble!

When we are saved by Christ, we come to a point where admit that we have no power in and of ourselves to save ourselves. Salvation can only come through an act of the Almighty God to rescue us! As long as we are filled with conceit, we think we can be good enough, that we might manage to be our own saviours. Only the humble, repentant sinner can recognize their need for Christ's saving work.

7. If we can define legalism here as using works and effort to earn your salvation, to appease God with your effort, then we find that this is ultimately the religion of humanity down through the ages. If you look at most of what we see in religion, apart from the grace offered in the Christian faith, everything appears to be an attempt to make yourself right, make yourself righteous, make yourself good enough. Everything from ancient idolatry and paganism to contemporary attitudes within cancel culture has all been about seeking an affirmation of righteousness or a declaration that someone is good!

Ignorance of the depth of our sinfulness and the failure of our efforts to cleanse us of that wickedness imprisons us in a lifestyle of effort, trying to legalistically fulfil a requirement to be good enough. It is only in the truth revealed to us in the gospel through the Holy Spirit that we find salvation by grace through faith, not of works!

8. The attack points to a Little-Faith's fall to sin. As you read through the context of this, it's not suggested that Little-faith's experience is unusual, but his reaction is.

9. Little-faith's loss points to that which we lose when we fall to sin (Faint-heart, Mistrust, and Guilt). He is then left unable, as a man who has little faith, to move past it. His faith is not great enough to fully trust in God's grace. This leaves him to struggle. His jewels represent the reward in eternity, something of little value in this life, but his wallet/purse/silver is

something that should be possible to increase here.[44] He should have trusted the Lord's grace to provide for him along the way.

10. If you're struggling with understanding why Little-Faith struggled so much after the attack by Faint-heart, Mistrust, and Guilt, consider two things: first, what Little-faith was lacking, and second, what Great-grace had in abundance.

Great-grace trusted in God's grace to him. This means that when he sinned, he trusted the Lord to cover his sin—completely! Little-faith, however, was lacking in faith. He had some, but not very much. As such, he struggled to believe (have faith) that the grace could be applied fully to him.

Thoughts about Great-grace

Great-grace, in contrast to Little-faith, is someone who, although he is scarred and has struggled in his battles, is someone who fully uses the grace offered to him to stand strong for the Lord of the way. Pay attention to the fact that Great-grace is scarred! What does that tell us? It tells us he has suffered defeat just like Little-faith. Great-grace, however, has managed to move forward, trusting in the grace of the Lord!

On this note, we might be tempted to see Great-grace as a picture of Christ. While in a manner of speaking, this is a good understanding of this man, it is because this man is living faithfully before Christ, not because he is Christ, that we are seeing Christ in him. There is also a reference to Great-grace as the Apostle Paul. However, that's not to suggest that Great-grace *is* Paul, but that Paul *was* a man of *great grace*. Great-grace can be any of us, anyone who trusts in God's grace!

---

[44] Remember, this is allegory, so his wallet does not represent financial benefit in this life.

13. THE FLATTERERS

1. We often shy away from an eternal perspective, a perspective intent on the Celestial City. We see it as an extreme, and we love arguing against extremes. In fact, you'll find people today often argue for one thing simply by condemning the other extreme.

But God actually calls us to a heavenly perspective. Our focus above should affect everything in our lives, so much so that we are called to consider ourselves dead to the old life.[45]

But what if an eternal perspective is not a bad thing? What if our focus is meant to be on the Celestial City, on our eternal reward? What if God wants us to live a life that glorifies him here, passionately loving the chance to honour Christ, enjoying his blessings, all the while keeping our sights on eternity? Could that be what Christ means when he tells us not to lay up treasures here, but to lay up treasures in heaven?[46] Perhaps the healthy place is to understand that Christ can be best glorified this side of glory if our heavenly focus influences our lives here and now!

2. This concept of using all these things in life to secure a greater reward may seem like an odd concept, but consider this: what if God gave you money for the purpose of using it for his glory so you could gain greater rewards in heaven? Christ tells us to build up treasures in heaven where moth and rust do not destroy rather than here on earth where moth and rust do destroy.[47] Perhaps, then, the things of this earth are given for the purpose of his glory and result in eternal reward for us. Giving to the poor results in greater rewards in heaven. Using your money to support missions results in greater rewards in heaven. Giving here means *getting* there. So, in other words, you are able to *exchange* the temporary money you have here on earth for eternal *money* that never fades. It's an exchange, in a manner of speaking!

Could we not do this in all areas of life? Just as God gives you money for his glory, perhaps your education or lack of education is given for that reason? Perhaps your home, your time, your energy, your mind, your

---

45 Col. 3:1-3.
46 Matt. 6:19-21.
47 Matt. 6:19-21.

everything is given for God's glory, and you can use it all to secure greater reward in heaven!

Now, consider that none of what you've just read is radical in any way. This is simply how we are called to view everything in life! Consider again Matt. 6:19-21. But, even though this is common Scriptural teaching, it does not mean we all easily hold to it. It is an ongoing struggle for all of us to keep our sights set on the Celestial City and storing up treasures there!

8. Remember the shepherds? They warned them of the flatterer, but they were also given a note of the way. That note was what they needed at that moment! For us, this is a reminder that when you face a question of direction in life, pull out your Bible and seek the Lord's "note"!

11. I have to admit, if this was a real-life situation, a theological discussion might be the last thing you should do when you're falling asleep. I can't help but think a deep discussion when you're extremely tired and on the verge of sleep will only hasten the inevitable.

However, this is not a real life, but allegory. I would suggest the theological discussion is a way for them to focus, grow, mature, and take responsibility for their lives, faith, and commitment! So, in light of the temptation to lie down and ride out the rest of their lives, to stop moving and to call a halt on their journey towards the Celestial City, an allegorical discussion of theology is perhaps exactly what they need! They needed to remind themselves of the beauty of following Christ and the wonder of God's saving grace!

When we are tempted to simply stop, perhaps encouraging one another in our mutual love for Jesus is exactly what we need to do!

12. When Hopeful shares about his conversion, he shares he had never imagined that the work of God in his life would start by God awakening him to his sin. Now, that's a bit of a shocking concept because even in the church, we often shy away from talking about sin. We want to focus on the love of Christ—and that's certainly good and wise! But do we lose something by avoiding the discussion of sin?

13. This can be a challenging one, but perhaps it is helpful for us yet again to be reminded that even Hopeful's testimony is allegory. So, we have to

ask what is being taught here? Remember the fifth Excellent Thing in the Interpreter's House? Here's the brief description of that experience:

> [The Fifth Excellent Thing is] …the persevering strong man who fights to enter Christ's palace! This is, of course, a picture of fighting hard to enter the kingdom of heaven and taking many wounds on the way in!

Remember that we are called to push on, to fight, to sacrifice all for Christ.[48] Salvation is worth everything we have! Perhaps it's helpful to understand Hopeful's struggle in light of a man desperate to find the saving grace of Jesus, and this illustration should remind us of the value of the prize!

15. Atheist, amidst his rejection of the true God, represents our declaration that *we* are gods. It's a statement that we stand all on our own and are sufficient for ourselves. This is flattery to the extreme. Remember as well that the flatterers come to spread a net for the feet of those they seek to ensnare. If you re-read the section with Atheist, you will see very quickly that he is not sharing his opinion. Instead, he is trying to convince them of his belief. He puts pressure on them! He wishes to pull them into the same trap he's fallen into!

He is a flatterer!

16. This is a big one as it functions as a way to belittle someone's belief. It's a way for Atheist to declare with no actual evidence or argument that the other person is immature in their beliefs and simply too inexperienced or too unwise to know what Atheist knows through solid experience. This is a heavy dose of manipulation carried through with an overwhelming level of confidence.

---

[48] Luke 14:25-33.

14. IGNORANCE

2. Such a view drives us to our knees before God. When even our thoughts cannot be counted on to glorify God, then we cannot buy into the philosophy of "follow your heart" and we have to trust God that God's ways are right, true, and best. When we understand how corrupt even our thinking is without Christ, it brings us to a point where we have to trust God to transform our hearts.

3. Now, when Ignorance tells Christian that he will never believe his heart is "that bad," what does that tell you about Ignorance? Consider his name, as well. What does his statement tell us in light of his name? What do we learn from the fact that this view of a heart's goodness and the freedom to follow one's heart comes from a man named Ignorance? What difference does it make in your life, your direction, your choices, if the heart is good?

6. It's important to understand that Jesus does the impossible. Jesus is the only one who can cure an incurable heart! That doesn't mean that when you're saved, you should start following your heart, but rather that in salvation, Jesus starts to transform your incurable heart. One day, we will have truly pure hearts as we live with Jesus forever!

14. The big theme comes down to what is temporary. He suggests that a man who is about to backslide holds his faith in Christ until whatever drove him there fades in his mind and heart. Christian sums that up well after Hopeful finishes.

15. THE RIVER

1. It is often the case for believers with a strong, mature faith that they long for what Christ has promised as they near the end. When we get close to receiving the reward and meeting Jesus, the longing can overtake us. While for those who remain behind, it can feel like rejection, considering faith and love for Christ, it's not a bad thing.

This is a blessing of growing older. As the years pass, we begin to look more to our hope of eternity with Jesus!

3. Eternity with Christ, the Celestial City, is many things for us as believers. It is rest from all our journeys. It is reward given by a God who is passionate about generosity. It is a coming together with those who have gone on before us. But I think what eternity is ultimately about, and this we sometimes overlook, is Jesus! It's about spending eternity with Jesus. It's about our God living among us! It's about existing for all eternity in a close relationship with him! It is when we see him face to face and then we will be like him, for we will see him as he is.[49]

4. Remember, this book is allegory! This is a picture of the end of their life. It doesn't mean that when we are older, we will see heaven from our chair in a nursing home. What it means is when we get that close to the end, that close to seeing Christ and receiving our reward, we can sometimes almost see it in the sense that it is on our minds and in our hearts—a lot! At the end of this life, the view of eternity is so much clearer. When we are young, the view of eternity feels distant, unreal, and sometimes even unimportant. This is allegory, so while our eyes do not physically see eternity, our sights are definitely on it near the end!

6. It's easy to say, "Oh, Ignorance found an easy way to get across the river," but it's far more than that! Why is it possible for Ignorance to cross that river that way and for Christian and Hopeful not to?

Why? Because they cannot tolerate vain hope! They have held onto the belief that it is all Jesus's work on the cross that has led to their salvation.

---

[49] 1 John 3:2.

That leaves them at the end with nothing else to hang onto! Ignorance can hold on to his works, his lifestyle, his attitudes… his ignorance. But Christian and Hopeful are left relying on nothing more than faith in the One who tells them he will open the gates of eternity to them!

And as they have placed their hope in Christ, they have placed their hope in the only thing that is sure!

A Call to Compassion

Death is the enemy. We must remember that. It can be terrifying, despite what hope we have in Christ. To cross that River is not something we should ever take lightly, nor should we ever expect others to just "be bold" and move forward without a care for the cost. I think we have to keep in mind that when a man or woman comes to the point of death, their bodies are at the weakest point they will ever be at. Think about it. Your body is at a point where it is so weak, it can no longer continue living! Perhaps when we are weakest, that's when Satan launches his most vicious attacks!

Yet, with Christ, there is always good news! And the good news is, as weak as we are, God is strong.[50] And in our weakness, God is gracious. Always gracious. Always patient. Always kind. Always holy, loving, powerful, caring, immutable, and entirely sovereign! And just as God is gracious and strong to us in our weaknesses, when those around us face weakness, we should be strong and gracious to them! To those who are at the end of this life as they deal with their fears and concerns and more, we have an opportunity to love and care for them.

The end of a person's journey along the path laid down by the Lord of the Way is a time to show compassion to those we love, even if they struggle.

---

[50] Isa. 4:28-31; 2 Cor. 12:8-9; Eph. 3:16-19; Phil. 4:6-7, 13.

Pilgrim's Progress
Rewalked with Study
Guide and Helps

Pilgrim's Progress
Original Edition with
Study Guide and Helps

Pilgrim's Progress
Rewalked

Pilgrim's Progress Online

About the Author

Shawn P. Robinson has a passion for teaching God's Word and seeing people grow in their faith and has had the privilege of serving in Christian ministry as an Associate Pastor, Lead Pastor, and as a Church Planter.

In 2017, a viral infection in his brain pulled him from pastoral ministry, changing the course of his life from a focus on ministry to trying to recover. Eventually, Shawn's health forced him to step down from ministry. Amid the illness, Shawn began to write a children's book for his sons and from that grew a passion for writing fiction, which has proved to be an exciting blessing from God during a time when he can no longer serve in vocational ministry.

As Shawn continued to write fiction, learning to trust the Lord in this new direction of life, he quickly found joy both in sharing stories and in sharing gospel allegories.

In time, the Lord laid it on Shawn's heart to create a modern-day rewrite of Pilgrim's Progress which would not only remain faithful to the original but also be presented in a more contemporary narrative format, hopefully opening up the story to a new generation. With this, Shawn set out to provide study guides with deep and challenging questions based on a study he offered to his church years before.

Shawn has a Bachelor of Arts in Christian Studies from Briercrest Bible College in Saskatchewan and a Masters of Divinity from Carey Theological College in British Columbia. Shawn is ordained with the Fellowship of Evangelical Baptist Churches in Ontario, Canada. Shawn and his wife and two sons live in Southwestern Ontario.

CHECK OUT THESE BOOKS BY
Shawn P. B. Robinson

Adult Fiction (Sci-fi & Fantasy)

The Ridge Series (3 books)
ADA: An Anthology of Short Stories

YA Fiction (Fantasy, Sci-fi, Dystopian)

The Sevordine Chronicles (5 Books)
Greks (2 Books)—Coming Soon
The Modder's Run (2 Books)—Coming Soon

Books for Younger Readers

Annalynn the Canadian Spy Series (6 Books)
Jerry the Squirrel (4 Books)
Arestana Series (3 Books)
Activity Books (2 Books)

Pilgrim's Progress

Pilgrim's Progress *Rewalked*
Pilgrim's Progress *Rewalked* with Study Guide
Pilgrim's Progress Annotated Original with Study Guide

www.shawnpbrobinson.com/books